STRIKE ZONE

STRIKE ZONE

BY JIM BOUTON

AND ELIOT ASINOF

VIKING

VIKING
Published by the Penguin Group
Penguin Books USA Inc., 375 Hudson Street, New York, New York 10014, U.S.A.
Penguin Books Ltd, 27 Wrights Lane, London W8 5TZ, England
Penguin Books Australia Ltd, Ringwood, Victoria, Australia
Penguin Books Canada Ltd, 10 Alcorn Avenue, Toronto, Ontario, Canada M4V 3B2
Penguin Books (N.Z.) Ltd, 182–190 Wairau Road, Auckland 10, New Zealand

Penguin Books Ltd, Registered Offices: Harmondsworth, Middlesex, England

First published in 1994 by Viking Penguin, a division of Penguin Books USA Inc.

1   3   5   7   9   10   8   6   4   2

PUBLISHER'S NOTE: This is a work of fiction. Names, characters, places, and
incidents either are the product of the authors' imagination or are used fictitiously.

Grateful acknowledgment is made for permission to reprint excerpts
from the following copyrighted works:
"Caribbean Queen (No More Love on the Run)" by Keith Diamond and Billy Ocean.
Copyright © 1984 Willesden Music Inc./Keith Diamond Music Inc. (controlled by
Willesden Music Inc.)/Aqua Music Inc./Zomba Music Publishers Ltd. (controlled
by Zomba Enterprises Inc.). Reprinted by permission of CPP/Belwin, Inc.,
Miami, Florida. International copyright secured. All rights reserved.
"I Saw a Stranger with Your Hair" by John Gorka. Reprinted with permission.
"Our Day Will Come" by Bob Hilliard and Mort Garson. © Copyright 1962 by
Better Half Music and MCA Music. Copyright renewed. © Copyright 1962 MCA
Music Publishing, a division of MCA Inc. and Bourne Co. Copyright renewed.
Used by permission of Better Half Music and MCA Music. All rights
reserved. International copyright secured.

LIBRARY OF CONGRESS CATALOGING IN PUBLICATION DATA
Bouton, Jim.
Strike zone: a novel / by Jim Bouton and Eliot Asinof.
p.   cm.
ISBN 0-670-85214-7
1. Baseball players—United States—Fiction.   2. Baseball umpires—
United States—Fiction.   I. Asinof, Eliot.   II. Title.
PS3552.O8366S75   1994
813'.54—dc20   93-49818

Printed in the United States of America
Set in Times Roman

For Paula

        J.B.

For my son, Martin

        E.A.

Fable has it that Satan challenged Saint Peter to a baseball game.

Saint Peter laughed. "Are you kidding? I've got Babe Ruth, Ty Cobb, Christy Mathewson, and a host of all-time greats. Who have you got?"

Satan snickered. "The umpires."

ACKNOWLEDGMENTS

The first person I want to thank is Al Silverman, editor-in-chief of Viking, not just for editing this book, but for getting me started as a writer twenty-seven years ago. Al was the editor of *Sport* magazine in 1967 when the Yankees sent me down to Syracuse, and he paid me $500 to write an article called "Returning to the Minors."

I thank my children, Michael, David, and Laurie Bouton, and Hollis and Lee Kurman for their love and valuable suggestions. I am indebted to special friends, Marty Goldensohn, Don Dewey, Dr. Craig Hersh, Michael Schacht, and Katri Stanley for their expert assistance, and Bill Murphy and Don Segal for encouraging me to write over the years. I also want to thank the Chicago Cubs, especially Rick Wilkins and Willie Wilson, for their warm welcome last summer at Wrigley Field.

And most important, I thank my wife, Paula Kurman, my Magic Lady, and the best editor I ever had, on or off the laptop.

J.B.

STRIKE ZONE

SATURDAY

6:20 PM

My name is Sam Ward and I'm a major league baseball player. I'd like to say I'm a star pitcher for the Chicago Cubs, but actually I'm only a "Scrubeenie." That's what they call the guys who've just come up from the minor leagues. It's even lower on the food chain than "extra man" or "benchwarmer."

Getting called up to the big leagues is usually pretty exciting. Unless you happen to be thirty-two years old, and then it's more sad than anything. Nobody wants to set a record for being the oldest rookie in baseball.

That's one reason my family is not throwing a party in my honor. The other reason is, I don't have much of a family since my wife left me last year. I can't blame Julie. It's not much fun living out of a station wagon. Especially one that's plastered with bumper stickers from twenty-eight states. And two foreign countries.

My mom thinks I'm a baseball bum, my dad says I'm irresponsible. And who's to say they're wrong? I dropped out of college to pursue a dream and now I'm ten years behind everybody else my age. The problem is I've been so close all these years. I'm like a poker player who's got so many chips in the pot he can't fold.

Sometimes I doubt myself, too. This is not good. One thing you don't want to do is stand on a pitcher's mound with doubts in your mind. Unless you're in a hurry to take a shower. If you want to get big league hitters out, you've got to believe you're better than they are. That's not easy. It's hard to believe you're somebody when you're nobody. So I walk around trying to believe in myself.

Right now I'm trying to believe in myself on an elevator at the Westin Hotel in downtown Chicago. It's the night before the last game of the year, Chicago Cubs versus the Philadelphia Phillies, the deciding game to see who gets into the National League Playoffs. And I have a good seat for the game. I'll be in the dugout counting pitches with a little clicker. If the sun comes out, maybe I'll catch a few rays between innings.

I step off the elevator. The lobby is crowded with autograph seekers. This peculiar breed of fan, which hunts in packs, is attracted to the hotel by half a dozen Chicago Cubs players whose stay here is communicated to other members of the species by a system as yet unknown to science. The biological imperative of *Celebritum vicarius* is to get autographs on as many items as possible before the player says, "How many more of these things do you have?" Or "Fuck off."

About twenty kids wearing Cubs hats and jackets are comparing notes and plotting strategy near the bell captain's desk. A smaller group of older men with armloads of scrapbooks and baseball cards are working the entrance to the coffee shop. Strategically positioned in the center of the lobby, waving a camera, is a large bleached blond lady in a Cubs uniform shirt with Ryne Sandberg's name and number on the back.

One of the kids spots me, but he's not sure who I am. He searches frantically through his baseball cards, trying in vain to match the face. I guess I look like a ballplayer; 6'1", tan, in good shape. Some people say I resemble the actor Woody Harrelson.

After a brief conference the kids come over to check me out.

"Are you anybody?" asks the leader of the group.

"My name is Sam Ward," I say. "I'm a pitcher."

"Are you any *good*?" he asks, looking me over like he was inspecting cattle.

"I won sixteen games last year."

"Wow!" says a chunky little kid with braces. "How come we never heard of you?"

"Well," I say, "I won all sixteen in Des Moines."

"Who is it, Jason?" hollers one of the men standing across the lobby.

"It's only Sam Ward, Dad."

"Well, get his autograph anyway," says the father. "You never know."

Now I get my picture taken with the blond lady, which requires standing with my arm around her for five minutes while a bellman tries to figure out how to work the camera.

"Thank you very much, whoever you are," says the lady. "And could you do me one more favor? Could you please get Ryne to sign the picture for me?"

As my mind considers all the possible responses to this request, the assistant manager comes walking over.

"Mr. Ward," he says. "The Cubs are trying to reach you. Manager Vern Bateman wants you to call him right away."

Bateman? What does this mean? As I look at the pink message slip, I get a weak feeling in my chest. Am I getting released? Before the last day of the season? The sonovabitches!

But then I relax. And smile to myself. It's the old "let's get the rookie" trick. The way it works, a veteran player leaves a message for the rookie to call the manager, and it's either a massage parlor or the Lincoln Park Zoo. That's if you're lucky. If you're not lucky, you get the manager entertaining a lady friend. And if you want to spend a few years playing ball in Bison Turd, North Dakota, in the Barren Plains League, you go up and knock on the manager's hotel room door without calling first from the lobby.

Has to be a joke. They can't possibly release me now. We've got pitchers dropping like flies. They need all the arms they can get. Hell, I don't even know whether it's "we" or "they." I've only been up here three weeks and I haven't even pitched one inning yet!

Remember last year when the Cubs traded Danny Jackson to the Pirates for Steve Buechele and a "player to be named later"? I was the player named later. A minor league throw-in. In lieu of a bag of balls. I'm only up here now as insurance, in case something happens. Like if an asteroid lands in our bullpen and wipes out the pitching staff.

During the last month of the season, teams are allowed to call up minor leaguers to evaluate and use as limited role players. Since these Scrubeenies need to get paid, and take up space in the locker room, most teams only call up a few. Then they try to find something useful for them to do, like pinch-run or man the autograph booth.

My job is to pitch batting practice. And make juice. It's not easy to eat healthy when you're traveling around the country, so I always carry a juicer with me and keep it in my locker. On my way to the ballpark I pick up fresh vegetables like beets, carrots, spinach, or whatever looks good. Then I mix my own concoctions for whoever might be in the mood for something besides beer or soda. Usually one or two guys. A lot of players come by, though, to help name the new drink. "No 'panther piss' for me, thank you," someone will say. "That's a beautiful color, Ward. When my dog makes that color, I take him to the vet."

I head for the telephones just off the lobby. I know it's a put-on, but I'd better call anyway. Since they just called me up, it makes absolutely no sense to release me. Unless they need my locker to store extra bats.

That's it! They're releasing me *precisely* because it makes no sense. They want to cut me one last time in some creative new way. This'll be the topper. Better than all those times I found out in the newspapers, better than when the kid who polishes the spikes in the clubhouse told me, possibly even more imaginative than when I got the ax from a toll collector on the Florida Turnpike.

Baseball has changed for everybody except minor league players. We're still just pieces of meat. Columbus needs a pitcher for three weeks? Send Ward. Never mind that he just arrived in Albuquerque from Buffalo. In ten years of professional baseball with thirteen different organizations, I've been released, sold, traded, optioned, loaned, farmed out, or waived to, by, or from: the Appleton Foxes, El Paso Diablos, Chattanooga Lookouts, Buffalo Bisons, Albuquerque Dukes, Columbus Clippers, Birmingham Barons, Edmonton Trappers, Richmond Braves, Calgary Cannons, Maine Guides, Monterey Sultans, Portland Beavers (twice), Tabasco Cattlemen, Poza Rica Oilers, Oklahoma City '89ers, and Des Moines Cubs. Our apartment in Oak Park, Illinois, is filled with boxes and piles of different-color spikes and sweatshirts. After a while, Julie didn't ask where, she only asked, "What color sleeves?"

And this is my seventh "cup of coffee"—that's a few days in the big leagues. The joke is, that's all you have time for. My combined major league record with the Twins, Angels, Yankees, Braves, Red Sox, Mariners, and Cubs is 0 wins and 1 loss in 27⅓ innings, all in relief. I've had so many cups of coffee my teammates call me Juan Valdez. And I don't even drink coffee.

Right now I'm looking at a piece of paper that says: "Vern Bateman. Hyatt Regency. 565-1234 (Room 1018). Urgent!" Sure. That's how you know it's bullshit. Can't be a release. It's one of the guys. I dial the number.

"Bateman here."

It's him! I recognize the voice: a two-pack-a-day baritone wheeze. He doesn't say what it's about, just get over to the Hyatt as quick as I can. He sounded sort of friendly, like hangmen probably did when they kibitzed with the hangee.

I go outside for a cab. The night air hits me and I feel a chill all over my body. Meanwhile, I'm boiling hot inside and I feel like the biggest jerk in the world. Julie was right. I should have quit this game a long time ago.

It's a short cab ride and now I'm debating whether to leave the cabby a buck or a buck and a half tip. When I'm not feeling good, I worry about money. I hate this.

Maybe I shouldn't even go. The hell with them. Don't give them the satisfaction. Better yet, I should quit before they get a chance to release me. Good idea. But not before I say a few thousand well-chosen words.

Bateman's on the tenth floor. Probably can't afford to stay in a penthouse suite like the ballplayers.

I'm rehearsing my speech on the elevator. "I've got the best career record of any pitcher on the whole damned team—124 wins, only 71 losses. And I could have won all those games in the big leagues, too, if anybody ever gave me a shot. But the only thing you guys know is fastball, fastball, fastball. You don't like slow stuff because you don't understand it. Anything you don't understand scares the hell out of you."

My problem is the label. The tag. The rap that follows me around from team to team like a bad smell: "Doesn't have big league stuff." Ten years ago some coach with a radar gun clocked my fastball at only 80 miles per hour and that was it—you don't have a major league fastball, you can't be a major league pitcher. The logic is perfect. They say you'll never make it, then they prove themselves right by not giving you a chance.

5

I used to throw "heat" before I hurt my arm. Heat is what we call a 90-mile-an-hour fastball. "Serious heat" is 95-plus. I could "bring it," as they say. My pitching strategy was fairly simple: I'd throw the ball as hard as I could. If I got in a jam, I'd rear back and throw a little harder.

I was a hot prospect, a flame-throwing right-hander on my way to the big leagues, the "Bigs," the "Show," the "Magic Kingdom." And then I got lost one night in Denver, Colorado.

Temperature at game time was 40 degrees according to the general manager, who was expecting a big crowd on "Earmuff Night." All I know is that the puddle under our water fountain in the visitors' bullpen was frozen solid. In the middle of my warm-up before our game that night against the Denver Bears, I popped a good fastball and felt an electric shock go all the way down my arm. A fierce buzzing jolt, as if I had stuck my arm in a transformer. I tried tossing a few more after that, but my arm was dead. I had to tell our manager to get somebody else.

Over the years I'd had dozens of sore arms, inflamed tendons, stiff shoulders, bad backs, strained forearms, blisters, the works. And for all kinds of reasons, too: not enough time to get loose, too many pitches in a game, too many days in a row. I'm not complaining. You make your living throwing a baseball, something's gonna hurt. You just have to pitch through it. Besides, if you sit around, you get splinters. Or a ticket home.

But this was different. I'd never felt pain like this before in my life. My arm was on fire. And so was my career.

I tried to hide it from everybody, including Julie. But she knew right away something was wrong. She always does.

When I came back from the road trip, she said, "You didn't pitch the other night. How come?"

"Nothing major," I said, shrugging.

Julie looked at my face.

"Maybe you'd better tell me, Sam," she said.

I didn't want to alarm her. So I eased into it.

"I think I hurt my arm a little bit."

"That means you hurt it a lot, Sam," she said quietly. "Because you never have a sore arm, even when it's killing you."

I hate it when she translates what I say.

"Okay, you're right," I said, my voice cracking. "I'm going on the disabled list tomorrow."

Julie put her arms around me and squeezed tight.

"Oh, Sam," she said, her big green eyes filling up. "I feel so bad for you."

This was a real kick in the ass. Just when I was about to make it, too. We'd been talking about how much fun it would be to start going first class, visit places like New York, L.A., San Francisco, invite friends to the games, *pay off all our bills!* Julie's mom had been telling neighbors it was about to happen. My dad was already acting like a big shot at the club. And then it was over. On one pitch. I went from a prospect to a suspect.

"I'll go through rehab and all the rest," I said, in an unaccustomed fit of candor. "But I think it's pretty serious."

Julie knew what that meant.

"Well," she said brightly. "At least we can still make love."

Julie always came up with good ideas in rough situations.

At the end of the season, they operated on my shoulder. And the following spring I was throwing again. But it wasn't the same. My fastball was gone. When it didn't come back, everybody thought I was going to quit. They all wanted me to. How could we continue living on a baseball salary of $14,500 without any hope? I couldn't argue with them.

But I couldn't quit, either. I refused to believe my career was over. Instead, I became a junkball pitcher. A little of this, a little of that, change speeds, knuckler, move the ball around in the strike zone.

The elevator stops at 10. Bateman's suite is down the hall. My body is shaking and my knees are wobbly. This is it. I'm through with baseball.

And I just figured out why they're cutting me tonight. If the Cubs win the division championship tomorrow, they'll save on the postgame celebration. One less bottle of champagne!

I knock on the door, and I can hardly breathe.

The door opens and it's ... Bobby Rapp? Rapp is the third base coach. He's one of these explosive little drill instructor types you never want to get into a fight with at a bar.

"Come on in, Ward," he grunts, with his closed-mouth smile.

Rapp sticks out his hand and I find myself shaking it. What the hell is this? All the coaches are here. And so is Bateman. The place is a mess. They've got styrofoam cups, whiskey bottles, cigars, and cigarette butts all over the room. Looks like they've been locked in here for a week.

"Can we get you a glass of carrot juice?" asks Bateman.

The coaches laugh.

Bateman is a former catcher with a thick neck, medium-fat body, and fingers that look like the Mafia didn't want him to play the piano anymore. His face is round and bumpy, with sad eyes, and tiny purple veins straining to burst from a walnut-pitted nose. Bateman could have been created by a sculptor throwing handfuls of clay from three feet away.

Just when I'm about ready to launch into my speech, Bateman invites me to sit down.

"How you feeling, son?" he asks.

How am I feeling? What is this, a doctor's appointment?

"He should be in pretty good shape," says Rapp, whose voice sounds like metal scraping against concrete. "He's been pitching lots of batting practice."

Batting practice? That's a joke. All I do is throw my weak fastball down the middle so the hitters can smash it out of the ballpark. They won't let me use the knuckleball or my other junk because it throws off their timing.

"What we're getting at, son, is this," says Bateman. "How do you think you'd go against the Phillies?"

"Me?"

What the hell is he talking about? The Phillies! That's tomorrow. Am I going to be in the bullpen?

"I could go three or four innings," I say as confidently as I can with no vocal cords, "if you need a long man."

A long man is the first guy out of the bullpen if the game gets out of hand early. A live body to put on the mound for a few innings while you save the good guys. The job goes to low man on the totem pole. A pitching staff hierarchy is like this: five or six starters, two or three closers, and a couple of long men, also known as "mop-up." Whoever's hurt, struggling, and/or on the shit list are the long men.

"Son," says Bateman, looking very tired, "I need you to start tomorrow."

Start? Holy shit! Is this happening? I can't believe what I'm hearing. How the hell can I be pitching tomorrow? What happened to Foster? What about Rodnickey? They must have just died. I nod my head like it makes perfect sense.

"I'm not going to bullshit you," says Bateman, examining a wrinkled piece of paper. "We got a very tired pitching staff, as you already know, plus the injuries. Now, tonight I find out we got a case of flu that's worse than the blue bonic plague. And a *personal disease* of some kind."

Bateman rolls his eyes.

"Your off-speed stuff could tie them in knots," says hitting coach Bill Robinson.

"You got more experience than the younger guys," says Rapp.

The coaches are staring at me like I'm about to tell the sheriff where the gold is buried. Except for the pitching coach, Brad Gilson, who looks at the ceiling.

"Go as long as you can," says Bateman. "Give us five innings, then we'll get you the hell out of there. I don't know *who* we'll bring in after that. Maybe *I'll* pitch the last four."

I get to my feet in slow motion. The coaches are a blur of jogging outfits. The room is tilting to the left. My stomach just jumped off the building. But I'm cool.

"I think I can handle it," I say. "I faced some of those guys in the minors and I got them out down there."

The word *think* is important here. Saying I *know* I can beat them is too cocky and indicates fear. Besides, I need to come at this from the underdog angle. It's amazing what goes through your mind in a split second.

"Good," says Bateman. "And to throw them off track a little, we're going to keep this secret until just before game time. Let 'em wonder who we're using."

I'm already on my way out the door. I figure I've got about sixteen hours to get my head screwed on straight.

"And one more thing, son," says Bateman, taking a very deep breath. "Try not to get hit by a bus."

SATURDAY

6:35 PM

Open your hotel room door, the first thing you see is that little red blinker on your telephone. It says, hey, I've got a message for you, pal; somebody is waiting to give you the bad news. When you get to be sixty, you couldn't care less. I sit on the bed, take off my shoes to wriggle my toes. I've been on these old feet for over six hours working a double-header at Wrigley Field where the Cubs just took both ends. This is the way the season ought to end. Crucial ball games. Good for baseball, for the fans. Tomorrow's game decides who gets into the National League Playoffs with yours truly, Ernie Kolacka, working behind the plate in his last game.

My last game. Three litle words that stick in my throat. I can't even speak them; it's like I'm at a mortuary picking out the marble slab for my own grave. After thirty-eight years in the blue suit, this is it.

You're six-oh, you gotta go. That's the official National League policy. They put you to pasture because they don't want coronary attacks in the middle of August doubleheaders. Even heavy breathing scares the baseball

10

establishment. There've been a few unkind words written that I've slowed down, that I didn't get into position fast enough to see if the left fielder made the catch or trapped that sinking line drive. Maybe so. The mind says go, the legs say no. And maybe, like Cal Greber, National League director of umpires, told me, I'm missing calls behind the plate I never missed before.

But as I sum it up, I'm still as good as they come. I'm the same 165 pounds I've always been. I keep in shape. I play a lot of golf on the road and I don't ride around in the carts. I go to workout rooms and punish the StairMaster. Except for an occasional cigar, I don't smoke. When I drink I'm a moderate low-bottom. After the tensions of a ball game, umpires need to party a bit even more than the players.

I'm not a complicated guy. Things have to be straight and simple. I like this. I hate that. If something gets too much for me, I lop it off. When I have a passion for something, I live for it and nothing gets in the way. I love what I do. I'm a good umpire, as good as they come, they say. How many people have anything like that going for them? You don't have to give me a trophy or write a book about me. Like me or don't like me, my life has never been a popularity contest. If you're an umpire, that's all there is because you're alone out there in blue. It's all jeers, never cheers.

My last game. It's not the World Series, it's not even the playoffs. Umpires get to work those prize games on a regular rotation basis. In the dozen years I've been in the majors, I've had my fair share. But the dozen years should've been twenty-four and maybe more. Too many years in too many minor leagues. I feel like an innocent man who'd served time in prison. You can't help being pissed off at lost years. It's a wound that never heals; it's always there stirring in your gut for all the damage it heaped on your life, on your marriage, even on the way you see yourself. You think, Jesus, how everything would've been different with Enid and the twins, how I would've been a whole other household figure if I wasn't a bum in the boondocks.

Wriggle your toes, forget your woes. If you keep on wriggling, you can live forever.

The trouble is, some people don't retire so easily. It doesn't matter that there's a $55,000 annual pension after twelve years in the majors. They could double it, I would still rather be in a blue suit than on a rocking chair.

So okay, blinker, what've you got for me? Is the president of the United States greeting me from the White House? Or is it the legendary Bill Klem, one of the game's greatest old umpires, on a special hookup from the Pearly Gates? Most likely it's my wife wanting to know when I'll be home so she'll be sure not to be there.

"Please call Roger Abercorn at once. 555-5000. Room 1521."

Hey, Roger! Still among the living. The sound of his name always sparks me like he was put on earth to make people happy. I never know when he's going to turn up, which makes it even more of a treat. He's a marketing V.P. for Maynard's, one of those discount department store chains. His job takes him here, there, and everywhere. When I became a National League umpire, he thought that was the greatest thing that ever happened. He became a top-of-the-line baseball fan. He'd bring clients to the game, show me off. I didn't mind, hell, I loved the guy, and not just because once, in what I think of as another life, he rescued me from the jaws of death itself.

"Hey, Rog, you fat-assed pile of rancid bullshit!" A routine term of endearment, if you please. I always expect worse in return.

"Ernie, damnit, I've been waiting!"

It's his voice, all right, but he sounds like a savage dog protecting a bone.

"Look, I just got in," I say.

"Meet me out front in fifteen minutes!" he snaps.

"What?" This is too fast for me. "What's going on?"

"Fifteen minutes!" He hangs up on me.

It's got to be a gag. He's setting me up for a typical Abercorn switch. I've known him for forty years, always thought of him as the first baby in history to come out of the cooker actually laughing. Just to look at him, beaming with rosy red cheeks, twinkly eyes. The voice on the phone that crackled with pain had to be a put-on.

Wrong. All I need is one quick look. His brown eyes are glazed like they're oozing fear. His mouth is pinched, grim lines cut deep into a scowl. His heavy body sits low in the car seat. Picture Harpo Marx made up to play the Hunchback of Notre Dame. He looks like he's been through hell and barely made it back.

I can't even say hello. He nods, working his face muscles into what he hopes is a smile. Whatever he tries to say gets stuck in his throat. We drive off the instant I get in.

This is no gag. There's not going to be any gag.

The large rented Caddie is like a rolling house, everything in it but a toilet—including a six-pack of Beck's for my benefit. I indulge as he drives in silence. When he parks, his right hand is tapping the wheel while his knee goes bobbing up and down to its own mad rhythm. Even in profile, the Abercorn charm is dead, his mouth twitching like he's going out of control.

I sip beer and wait.

"I'm in trouble, Ernie," he begins. "Jesus!"

I can tell you, those simple words are the worst I ever heard. It's like the pope telling the College of Cardinals that he's just turned atheist. Roger tries for a deep breath but can't make it.

"I need your help," he mumbles.

My help? All kinds of things race through my head. Is he sick? Is he really sick? Hell, I'm no doctor. I don't even know any doctors. Is it money? Is it his family? In all the years I've known him, he always came on like he had the world by the gonads.

"Hey, anything, anytime, anywhere," I say.

Before he can get it going, he sucks in air. Even then, what comes out is a mumble.

"The game tomorrow ..."

Another deep breath, much more twitching around the mouth.

"The Phillies, Ernie. The Phillies gotta win."

They do? I've no idea what he's getting at.

"You're behind the plate tomorrow," he goes on.

I'm slow. Because I'm tired? I let the Beck's glide down my gullet as his words suddenly begin to mess up my head.

"Balls and strikes," he goes on. "Balls and strikes. Nobody can control the game better than the man behind the plate."

This time I can't look at him; I try to get more beer down, but I gag. I've never heard words that sounded anything like what he's just said. I've heard all kinds of bullshit, chickenshit, birdshit, but I've never heard this. What the fuck am I supposed to say?

"What! What?"

"Ernie, I've got serious problems. I've made some bad mistakes. Dumb, dumb mistakes."

I don't know what to say.

"I'm into them for a bundle." He says the word *bundle* like it could mean a trillion.

"Them?" I ask. "Who is them?"

"Businessmen. You know. With connections." He whispers the word like there are big ears all around us. "I had to borrow ..."

Borrow. It's a word that always scares me.

"Okay, how much do you need?" I don't know what I can scrape together, but whatever's there is his.

He shakes his head, raises his eyes to the roof of the car.

"Ernie, I'm talking *big bucks*!"

He spills it out. He'd gotten hooked on gambling. First the nags. I knew that; he'd taken me to the track a few times, win or lose fifty bucks, no big deal. But after a while, the numbers got bigger. Then he hit the poker tables. High-stakes poker, win or lose five grand, maybe more. Before he knew it, he was visiting Vegas, or Atlantic City when he was east. Crap tables, blackjack, even roulette. He started to lose heavily. He borrowed, recouped, and the eternal cycle was on. Stakes got higher and higher. He mortgaged his home, he borrowed on his insurance. His wife had money, he had to lie to her about what he needed it for. He invested in a risky development deal that was supposed to make him rich overnight and erase those gambling debts.

"What the hell!" I feel numb. This is Roger Abercorn, Mr. Hardworking Middle-Management All-American family man.

"I got greedy, Ernie ..." His confession is so full of shame it makes me wince. "That's when you get suckered. You try to climb out from under, but you dig in deeper. That's what they like. That's when they can do what they want with you."

He swallows, but he wanted to spit.

"It's all down the tube, Ernie. When it starts going bad, it's an avalanche."

"Jesus ..." I mumble.

"Ernie, look. This is their idea. They're giving me this chance. Believe me, they're smart. You can't believe these guys." Words come rushing out like he's got to tell everything. "They can find angles in a circle. What they do, they punch Roger Abercorn in a computer, out comes the Silver Star. War Hero. They make some calls, punch some more computers, and up pops Ernie Kolacka, the National League umpire. Believe me, they knew we were friends. They knew all about us. One more call gets them up-to-date with the big news, all the pieces packaged for the big game tomorrow."

"But it just happened a couple of hours ago!" I say.

"Yeah, that's the way they work. They *anticipate*!"

"So they sent you here, in case?"

He nods.

"From where, Rog? Where are they?"

"Vegas," he mumbles.

The name makes me shudder.

"The Cubs'll go with Foster, that right?" Suddenly he's talking about the pitching staff. I don't know who they're going with. I couldn't care less.

"The Cubs are favored, 7–5," he goes on. "How do you figure that?"

Odds? I don't give a shit about odds. But I tell him the obvious.

"Big bats. They put numbers on the scoreboard. They've got momentum." Then, suddenly, I can't stand this anymore. "Roger, *what the fuck are we talking about?*"

His thoughts sail into the air like he has it all figured out.

"It's workable, Ernie. All you've got to do is stop the Cubs' hitters."

For maybe ten seconds the silence is dreadful. *I've* got to stop them? The negatives are oozing out of me. It's worse than that. It's pain. I've been pinned to the leather car seats taking vicious body blows. This is like asking a kid to kill his mother.

"Roger . . ."

I can feel him getting ready to explode.

"Goddamnit!" Out it comes. "We're talking about one fucking ball game. What's the difference who wins, who loses? What am I asking you to do, kill someone? The players will still be millionaires; the baseball world won't be changed one hair. Nobody'll know anything. It's just one goddamn game that went the way it might go anyway!"

"That's not the point, Roger—"

"The point! What point are you talking about? What are you worried about? What do you owe them, all the bastards who've made your life so miserable? How many times have you bellyached how they screwed you because you were honest? Am I right? Because you were a real umpire and not some asshole who played it safe. Am I right? Jesus, if there ever was a guy who should hate their guts! What do you owe them, Ernie? The name of the game is money. How much and who gets it. That's what they're about. They wrap it in 'The Star-Spangled Banner,' the National Pastime, the great American game. Are they kidding? Baseball is a stinking greedy business run by millionaire pirates looking for kicks. They eat up honest guys like you. They've been chewing on your ass for over half your life. Ernie, Ernie, it's all bullshit. You, of all people. You taught me that! You're loyal to a pile of bullshit!"

He can't sit still. He pulls out a cigar. Usually he clips off the end; this time he bites it off like it's chewing tobacco. I used to think he handled a smoke like he was caressing a woman. Not this time. This time he goes at it with fury.

"I'm right," he says again. "Admit it, Ernie, I'm right and you know it."

I don't want to argue. I'm too choked up to argue. I never once argued with this guy. I'm not good at it, not like him. He makes his living talking to people. Me, I make my living, any sonovabitch argues with me, I throw him out of the game.

"What if it can't be done, Rog?" The words sound feeble, pathetic. "I mean, even if I wanted to?" It's not me talking. I never say *what if?* I never even think *what if?* "Jesus, Roger, this is my last game in a blue suit!"

When he hears that, he pounces on it like it's just what he wants to hear.

"Hey, then it's perfect!" he cries out.

"What? What's perfect? What are you talking about?"

"You'll be gone, Ernie. You'll be out of it."

"No! No, Roger. I can't do it!"

"Ernie, listen to me. Listen to me good." His voice is pitched like his words are coming out of a grave.

"I don't want to hear, Roger!" I cry out.

"Ernie ... if you don't do this ... oh, God! ... if you don't do this, I could end up—" He swallows the thought, shaking his head like the unspoken part is too horrible to think of.

"For crissakes!" I can't stand this kind of shit. I pinch the bridge of my nose to keep my head from flying off. All of a sudden he's got me drowning in a pool of guilt. All because of Korea. Forty-odd years ago, everything began in Korea. Korea, the shithole of my life. Because of Korea, I'm sitting here in this Caddie.

Korea. Look at it on a map; it dangles into the Pacific like a fat gnarled dick. Forty years ago, thousands died there. What was I doing there? I was a ballplayer and suddenly I was a fucking soldier. I was supposed to be in Fort Lauderdale at spring training with the New York Yankees. You could scream yourself nuts at the way history jerks you around. Can you beat a switch like that? I'd spent my nineteen years on earth trying to get to the biggies, there was no other place I wanted to be, I was the hottest young shortstop to come out of Hempstead, Long Island, but suddenly they drop me off in Korea. Suddenly I was just another dogface in GIs. We were in Inchon, an infantry unit bogged down in a sea of mud. Came that stinking day, three of us on patrol got ambushed. Blam! Blam! Blam! We took enemy bullets, the other two guys got their heads blown off. Me, I took one in the right shoulder, another in my right side. I went down screaming. All I could think of was the hole in my throwing arm. Take my right arm, you take my life away from me. I started yelling at them. "Kill me! Kill me, you fucks! Kill me!" I yelled until I couldn't yell anymore, and I settled under a rock, bleeding to death.

Then Roger, my buddy from my platoon, came crawling with a first-aid kit. He gave me a shot of morphine and a line of cool bullshit right out of a Hollywood war movie.

"Kolacka, the hot news is, Marilyn Monroe is coming to entertain the boys and the lieutenant wants you to be her special escort." Meanwhile, he was cutting away the bloody O.D.'s, stuffing sulfa pads into the wounds.

"Fuck you, Abercorn. Fuck the lieutenant. And fuck Marilyn Monroe."

"Yeah, but if you had to pick one?"

"I just wanna die."

"Be thankful you still got your dong."

"I'll swap. My dong for my right arm."

I couldn't keep this jabber going. I was cracking up. "Oh, Jesus, oh, God, oh, goddamn sonovabitch . . ."

"Hey, easy, Ernie, easy. I'll tell you something, what they can do now is terrific. They can make you a new arm, an amazing contraption with batteries and steel springs and a super-rubber stretch gizmo attached. With the new arm you'll have a gun from deep shortstop that'll be awesome . . ."

I began to fade. I wanted to die. He put his arms around me, held me, hollered in my ear.

"*You gotta live, Ernie!* Say it: 'I'm gonna live!' "

"Go fuck yourself, asshole," I mumbled.

"That's more like it."

That was all I could remember.

Later, I'd learn how he wanted to wait until dark to bring me in, but he worried I might not hold out that long. So he risked it and took a bullet of his own, tearing flesh in his ass as he dragged me in. How he'd made it back to the lines had been a miracle. All the years I'd known him, he never said anything about it.

Now this. I sit there in that Cadillac like a drowning man with my life flashing through my head. I mean, I can smell myself bleeding to death under that rock. I can smell my fear as my body was turning rotten. I can hear Roger yelling at me to fight for myself. He saved my life, all right. He wasn't told to do it. No one sent him out to risk his ass. It didn't matter if I didn't care whether I lived or died. He gave me my life back. *He saved my life!*

I grab another Beck's. It's a goddamn joke. Life is a fucking joke. How else can you figure it? The man who once saved my life comes back to take it away from me. Life means one thing one day and something else on another. No matter how tough you think you are, at my age the limits start shrinking. My head sinks into my hands, fingers press temples. I don't believe any of this. I can't believe it.

"There's no time, Ernie." He is on me with a fresh burst of energy. "To them, that's the beauty part of the whole thing. Wham, bam, thank you, ma'am. It's almost five PM in Vegas. They're waiting to hear . . ." His hand is tapping the car phone. I can see him struggling to keep cool.

"Well, it'll have to wait," I say. "I mean, hey, it's my life you're asking for."

Suddenly this really breaks him. "*Your* life? Where is it *your* life? Nothing is going to happen to you! It's *my* life! Good God, Ernie! They'll mess me up! They'll go after Louise and the kids! Don't you get it? Don't you see?"

Now he is all over me.

"I don't believe this. Damn you, Ernie, all these years, I could say to myself what I did for you was worth it. I didn't have to talk about it; it was the best of me. I risked my life for a friend. God, I had pride!" Tears are streaming down his cheeks. He punches my thigh with his fat fist. "You owe me! Ernie, *you owe me!* What kind of man are you? You do this thing for me because *you owe it to me!*"

He spits the words like he is condemning me to eternal damnation. I mean, they are like the last blows of the ax. I've never suffered such scorn from him.

I know. I have to do this thing. I say the words to myself: He saved my life. *He saved my life.* What else could matter? Even if it destroys me. I owe him. The only thing that matters is that I owe him.

So I say it. "Okay, Roger." Once I say it, I've got to mean it. "Okay, I'll do it."

He stares at me, wanting to be sure he heard it right.

"You'll do it." He lets out a deep breath.

I nod. But even as I do, I'm figuring the possibilities.

"Look, you gotta realize, it's no sure thing. Anything can happen in nine innings. Bloop hits. Bad throws. Passed balls. How can anyone control everything that happens out there? I mean, there's just so much an umpire can do."

He's ready for me. His head can adjust like turning off one faucet, turn on the other.

"They know that," his voice suddenly calm. "These guys deal in numbers all the time. If you make the calls, it's as if they'll be playing with marked cards. They understand the odds. Gamblers live by the odds. Any gambler would settle for that."

"Okay, then."

"You scared me." He grins. "But I knew you wouldn't let me down."

I nod and he sighs like he was just reprieved from the gallows. I am the one who has to try to do this thing. Me? Do this? My mind starts crawling around like a snake about to chew its own asshole. After all the years of calling them strictly as I see them, suddenly I'm supposed to call them as I don't? After thousands of games when I never once cared who won or lost, suddenly I'm supposed to care about nothing else? It'll be like telling a brain surgeon to scrub his hands in shit. Can I get my right hand to punch out Strike when my eyes see Ball? How many times will I have to do that?

How many times before somebody tags me as a crook? I mean, won't they see what I'm doing? The TV? Won't they smell the shit on my hands?

I'll do it, Rog, I said to him.

I'll risk my ass to save yours.

I said yes because I owed him, and now I'm in worse trouble than he is. Jesus!

SATURDAY

7:30 PM

It's a beautiful night in the city of Chicago. And my heart is singing a happy tune. As I wait for a cab back to the Westin Hotel, I try out a few scenarios. Hi, my name is Sam Ward, Starting Pitcher for the Chicago Cubs. Hello, my name is Sam Ward. Yep, I'm the guy that's pitching tomorrow. Fine, thank you.

The doorman waves at a line of taxis and I'm happy to give him the buck. Hell, I can't be standing out there in the street hailing my own taxicab. I could get hit by a bus.

A taxi pulls up and I jump inside. And what is this? The cab is like a living room! Color TV, audiocassettes, stereo sound system, magazines, newspapers, box of tissues, restaurant guide, car phone, snacks. A disc-jockey voice booms out of the speakers.

"Welcome to the city of Chicago," says the cabby as he pulls out into traffic. He's a black guy with Spike Lee eyes and a gap-toothed smile. He's wearing a red baseball cap and talking into a handheld microphone. A sign says his name is "Yogi," if you can believe that.

"Welcome aboard," says Yogi, checking my reaction in his rearview mirror. "Sit back and relax; you are riding with the best cab in the city of Chicago. Nobody has a show like this, nobody has a cab like this. Coming up next, Caribbean Queen."

The stereo pumps Billy Ocean into the backseat.

"... she walked by me in painted-on jeans ..."

The song reminds me of Julie. She's got a great pair of legs. But I don't want to think about her now. Because then I start missing her and I feel like shit. And you can't hit the outside corner with a good curve when you feel like shit.

The speakers are booming.

"... in the blink of an eye I knew her number and her name ..."

I can't help myself, I think about her. It seems like I've always thought about her. Ever since fifth grade. We were childhood sweethearts, only Julie didn't know it. I'd ask to carry her books home from school and she'd say no thanks. I'd run ahead and wait for her to walk by, and that's what she'd do; walk right by. Julie was beautiful even back then, with those big green eyes, hair the color of root beer, and nice soft lips. They *looked* soft, anyway. The problem was, she was too advanced for me. And too tall. Julie was only interested in older guys, like seventh-graders.

But I dreamed about her anyway. I even had sexual fantasies about Julie based on the charcoal sketches the bums drew on the walls of the viaduct by the railroad tracks. At age ten, I wasn't sure what all the parts were, but it was exciting trying to figure it out.

I'd also imagine myself performing various heroic acts that would make Julie realize how terrific I really was. Until that day in sixth grade. We were in Mrs. Stanley's class together at Ben Franklin Elementary in Elgin, Illinois. There were forty kids in the class, too many even for Mrs. Stanley, so they split it up. One morning the principal came in and started reading off names to go across the hall with a new teacher, Mr. Dabby. First name on the list was Julie Wheeler. As the principal read more names, it became obvious that only the top kids were going with Mr. Dabby. It was a cruel test to see who would be chosen. I waited to hear my name.

Suddenly the principal stopped reading. Only *fifteen* kids had made the cut! The rest of us were staying behind. Then all hell broke loose. I'll never forget the feeling of shame, sitting there in a torrent of flying erasers and whistling spitballs, watching the better kids march out of the room. Julie was really out of reach then.

The cab pulls in front of the Westin. Yogi picks up the hand mike. "That's it for now, you've heard the sound, we'll see you around, in Yogi's fine, fine cab."

I let Yogi keep the change from a ten and I take one of his business cards. What a ride! Now all I need is some dinner and a good night's sleep. I walk into the lobby of the hotel.

And guilt rears its ugly head.

Sitting there is a young lady named Susan somebody. I'm drawing a blank on her last name. I just met her recently, and I completely forgot I'd made plans to see her tonight. I do that sometimes. I get so focused on one thing, I forget about everything else. It's like I'm in another world. Whenever this happened at home, Julie would try to get my attention. "Earth to Sam," she'd say. "Earth to Sam."

Susan whatever-her-last-name-is is about 5'6" and cheerleader pretty, with light brown hair. I know very little else about her except that she has a great attitude. I walk over and sit down. And who should happen to wander by at this particular moment? Two of my fellow Scrubeenies, Mike Owens and Rawley Alexander. They smile, and nod, and wink, and give me a thumbs-up sign. Real subtle.

I'm not really in the mood to make love tonight, even though it's been awhile. On the other hand, it doesn't have to be a marathon. I just need to be polite. Not like an old teammate I knew who suffered from premature ejaculation. As soon as he'd climax, he'd holler like some radio announcer after a game-winning home run, "*There* goes your ball game!"

It hasn't been easy getting back into circulation after Julie left. Every once in a while I'll make a date just to have company, or check to see if my parts are still working. Right now the only part working is my mind, and it says I've got a ball game to pitch tomorrow.

But I can't just send her home. I suggest we talk in the coffee shop. I need to explain why we can't go upstairs. If I say I'm pitching tomorrow, she might tell a sportswriter. Hell, she might *be* a sportswriter for one of the tabloids. So what do I say? My grandmother just died? I'm married? I've got this rash? I decide to take a chance on the truth.

"Sorry," I say. "We can't make love tonight. I'm pitching tomorrow. But don't tell anybody."

"How fun," she says, without missing a beat. "Can you get me a ticket to the game?"

To be honest, I expected a touch more disappointment in her voice. But I'm happy to be done with the matter. I promise to leave a ticket at the Reservation Window. After we finish our tea, I walk her through the lobby, give her a courtesy kiss goodbye, and put her in a taxi.

"And don't forget to leave the ticket," she says.

As the cab pulls away, it occurs to me I have until tomorrow to remember her last name. I walk back inside the lobby and who do I bump into? Owens and Alexander again. This is a real pair. Mike Owens is a stocky, 5'10" wisecracking catcher from Bloomfield, New Jersey, whose main goal in life is to get a mustache to grow in properly. Rawley Alexander is a skinny, 6'3" pitcher from Parkersburg, West Virginia, with huge ears which he claims allow him to pick up ESPN off the satellite. A bucket and a mop. They're smiling and looking at their watches.

"That boy just set a new league record," announces Alexander in his mountain twang. "Nine minutes!"

"She must be exhausted," says Owens sarcastically.

My mind is straining for a comeback. They can't wait to hear what it is. I say the only thing I can think of.

"She went to get reinforcements."

"Surrre," says Owens. But they laugh, giving me credit for the line.

Owens himself is not exactly Mr. Sensitive when it comes to women. Alexander likes to tell about the time Owens had this girl up in his room and they're getting undressed and Owens asks her if she minds if he turns on the radio. "Of course not," says the girl. "I like having the radio on when I make love." And Owens says, "Great, there's a ball game I want to listen to."

They ask what I'm doing about dinner. I invite them to grab a bite with me at Gutowsky's Tex/Mex Health Food Café. They say thanks but they're not that hungry, and what's more, they hope never to be that hungry as long as they live. Owens and Alexander like the kind of restaurants where they have pictures of food on the menu.

It's a ten-block walk to Gutowsky's, but I can use the fresh air. And I need to sort out my feelings. Listen to me, for crissakes, I sound like Julie. I never used to talk like this. Julie would ask me what I was feeling and I'd be stuck for an answer.

Now I go through a whole different routine. I try to figure out what's bothering me. Was it something somebody said, the tone in my father's voice, an old memory, money? Julie taught me that just by naming it, I could actually feel better.

Right now it feels like nostalgia. After grade school, Julie went to a different high school and I didn't see her again until we were in college. We were sophomores at Southern Illinois University. She was on her way back from tennis practice and stopped to watch a ball game I was pitching. She was as beautiful as ever. Her hair was still the color of root beer, only now it cascaded to her shoulders and bounced when she walked. And she had those incredible eyes. Eyes so clear and honest that you knew she'd never tell you anything that wasn't true. Julie was sexy in a quiet sort of way, with a reserved, thoughtful manner that made me wonder what it might be like to see her lose control.

Of course, I recognized her immediately, but I didn't say anything.

"Ben Franklin Elementary?" she asked, with a shy smile.

"Hello, Julie," I said, not wanting to go off the deep end.

"I thought it was you," she said, the sun glancing off her hair. "You really got tall."

"And handsome, too," I said. And we both laughed.

We hadn't bumped into each other before this because I was in the business school and Julie was taking liberal arts. Also she spent a lot of time at the library.

Julie said she liked watching me pitch. I said I liked watching her breathe. Within a week I was carrying her books. And her lips turned out to be as soft as they looked.

I arrive at Gutowsky's and sit at a table made from a wagon wheel embedded in Lucite. The house special is Free-Range Medallions of Pork with Organic Grains. I take a shot at the Vegetarian Gaucho's Pie.

My best memory of Julie is the weekend we found Madame Fifi. We were staying at this old inn up in Wisconsin. Lots of lovemaking and antiquing on rubbery legs. At a craft show we saw this two-foot-high handmade stuffed doll. The "doll" was a fiftyish dance-hall girl with fishnet stockings, a feather boa, and a black lace top with "anatomically correct" pink cloth nipples peeking out. She was an absolute riot. So we had to buy her even though she cost $150. And we named her Madame Fifi.

We perched Madame Fifi on a bookcase next to an antique gin bottle, her stockinged legs dangling in front of the books. It looked like she had just consumed the gin and was waiting for a proposal of some kind. Not necessarily decent. But as Julie said, "That doesn't make her a bad person." One of my nicknames for Julie when she's feeling amorous is Madame Fifi.

Now I've got tears in my eyes. Goddamnit, why did she have to leave? I told her I only needed one more season. Okay, I told her that a few other times, too. But this is an expansion year. The two new teams mean twenty more pitching jobs. I'm right on the edge of that. The proof is, I'm *here!*

The anger ignites a spicy eruption from the Gaucho's Pie in the pit of my stomach. I signal for the check. I buy some papaya tablets to counter the heartburn, and head for the door.

The temperature has dropped down into the 40s. I break into a trot. Something else doesn't feel right. Maybe I can run it off. Was it something somebody said?

Bateman! A terrible thought explodes in my brain. I know why Bateman wants my pitching to be a secret. They're planning to switch at the last minute. I'm just a *backup.* I'm only pitching if they can't find anybody else!

Now I'm sprinting to the hotel. Sweat is popping out on my back. What do I expect to find? My replacement! This happened to me once in Portland. I walked into the lobby and the new pitcher told me the general manager wanted to see me. The guy not only takes my job, he gives me the bad news. A river of cold sweat runs down my spine.

I'm out of breath as I burst into the lobby. I look around for somebody who might be a ballplayer. The place is practically empty. Suddenly I hear a grating sound behind me.

"You better get your sleep, Ward."

It's Bobby Rapp. He's standing behind a potted plant, waiting to catch somebody coming in late. It's not midnight yet, so I'm okay. Does the warning about sleep mean I'm still pitching tomorrow? Not necessarily. Maybe he's waiting to see if my replacement arrives. Maybe I'm going nuts.

I stop at the front desk for messages. There's a call from my brother, Marty. Probably wants tickets to the game. Or he's just trying out a new telephone gadget. Marty's into technology. He's never without his pocket phone, Walkman, beeper, calculator, Fuzzbuster, and compass watch. He loves to have somebody ask a question, like what's the weather going to be or what time is it in Bombay, so he can punch a few buttons and come up with the answer. I tell Marty one of these days he's going to walk by a construction site and set off the dynamite.

His best routine was when he would drop by the apartment to visit. Julie is one of these people who never goes to somebody's house without calling first and she expects the same courtesy in return. So Marty, who's not so formal, would accommodate her. The telephone would ring and it would be Marty, who lives twenty minutes away, asking if it was okay to come over. I'd check with Julie, she'd say sure, and before I'd hang up, the doorbell would ring. Guess who?

Marty's a year younger than me and we've always been close even though we're very different. He's taller, with dark curly hair and glasses. He was the student and I was the jock. He got good grades and I got grass stains. We'd play ball and I'd break the window. He's got a good job with a computer company. He's not separated from his wife. The family joke is that Mom likes Marty best. And I have to admit, Marty *is* more likable.

I get to the room and dial his number.

"Hi," I say. "What's up?"

"Can you leave me two for tomorrow?" asks Marty. "I'll pay for them."

"Hey, I told you before, these are free tickets," I say. "Everybody gets four. This is the big leagues!"

"By the way, I'm taking your daughter," says Marty.

Beth is our nine-year-old soon-to-be-beauty. She's got her mother's green eyes and my dirty-blond hair. Beth and I are each other's biggest fans. She's into swimming, soccer, ballet, and karate, among other things. She's a good little competitor, too. Last year she asked me to pledge $5 a lap for a charity swim after assuring me she'd never done more than five. Julie finally had to pull her out of the pool on the seventeenth lap!

"Big game tomorrow, huh?" says Marty. "Everybody's talking about it. Who's pitching for you guys?"

"Uhhhh, well," I say. "You'll never guess."

"Foster?" he says.

27

"Guess again," I say, smiling into the phone.

"Elvis," says Marty. "He just got called up. I don't know. Who the hell *is* pitching?"

"Me."

There's a long silence.

"Uh-huh," says Marty.

"No, I'm serious," I say. "I'm in there."

Another long silence.

"Well, you sonovabitch!" he says finally. "That's fabulous. You sure it's not a joke? Just kidding."

"They could switch at the last minute," I say. "But whatever they do, don't tell anybody, okay? Especially Mom and Dad. I've got my reasons."

"Sure," says Marty. "I understand."

I turn on the radio by the bed to set the alarm, and classical music comes on. But I'm in no mood for Relentless Melancholy Number 23, from Hockmocker's Wistful Series in B Minor, conducted by Neville Wembley of the Moline Symphony Orchestra, soon to be followed by ten minutes of additional details including the exact time and place Hockmocker first conceived the idea for this particular tune, so I change the station to rock & roll and set the alarm for 7:00 AM.

Then, just in case I set it wrong or the electricity goes out, I call the hotel operator and leave a wake-up call for 7:05. I'd rather wake up to music than a jangling phone. I always think it's the middle of the night when it rings.

With a 7:00 AM wake-up, I'll be showered and dressed by 8:00, done with breakfast by 9:00, and cab it to the stadium by 9:30, four and a half hours before game time. I like to take my time on a day I'm pitching. Or *might* be pitching.

But I can't think about the game now because then I'll just get too psyched up, or pissed off, or both. And I can't think about Julie or Beth because then I start missing them and feeling like shit. And if I think about sex, I'll never get to sleep. So what am I going to think about?

The wall.

A stone wall.

A freestanding stone wall.

No cement. The stones locked in place by nothing more than a snugness of fit; the glue of carefully crafted juxtaposition.

A giant jigsaw puzzle.

A three-dimensional mind bender without a picture on the box.

Twenty-one tons of stone, all shapes and sizes. Big awkward fifty-pound stones, L-shaped forty-pounders, thirty-pound flat stones, and 5,000 battered, broken, concave, convex, curved, oblong, oval, round, square, and wedge-shaped stones. Stones shaped like birds, turtles, animals, and fish. Formed by pressure, heat, eruption, and explosion. Chipped, cracked, crazed, fissured, pitted, pockmarked, scored, smooth, stained, streaked, stratified, and variegated stones in a million shades of red, brown, gray, and purple, in a hundred moss- and lichen-coated combinations.

I'm trying to remember what it felt like clawing through a pile of dusty stones on a winter morning and suddenly spotting the perfect shape to fill a yawning gap along the wall.

I'm remembering a nice reddish-brown rock in particular, early on, that I tried to place at least a dozen times, but I could never make it work. After a while I got tired of picking it up just because it looked good and I tossed it in a pile. Months later, with an awkward space to fill, I came upon this beauty in the weeds and it made a perfect fit.

A feeling of satisfaction and completion washes over me ...

SATURDAY

8:10 PM

After Roger leaves me off at the hotel, I see two guys in my crew waiting for me in the lobby. Dinner. I have no more desire to eat than run a marathon.

Lew Sirotta spots me first. "Hey, old-timer, where've you been?" He's ten years younger than me and hates getting old. So he rubs it in every chance he can. I go back a lot of years with this guy and none of them are what you'd call pleasant. He rises to greet me. He's built like a fire hydrant with ear flaps. When he walks, the first thing you think of is a penguin.

"Where?" I answer him. "A whorehouse on Division Street, that's where. Had to get my eyes cleaned."

I say this with a straight face. Tell him the truth and he'll think you're lying. He's such a born liar, even his ears tell lies.

"At your age?" Sure. He can't resist it.

"Hortense was asking for you, Lew," I go on. "She says she loves to fuck a duck."

Big John Koenig cracks up. The Mountain, we call him. He's thirty-nine, an ex–pro-football lineman, 6'5", around 265 pounds of smiles. They say he came up from the pile once too often without his helmet on. What he lacks in brains, at least he's lovable. Call him a second-rate umpire—he's too happy just being there—but he's not a "homer" like Sirotta, always calling them for the home club. There's not a dishonest bone in Mountain's body.

Missing is Roy Luger. The Gun, we call him. Every four-man crew seems to have a kid in it. He's in love with the world, especially the women in it, and being a big league umpire is not without perks. If there are a thousand groupies for the ballplayers, there are always a few left over for the men in blue.

"So where's the Gun?" I ask, just to be sociable.

"Shooting the old spermatozoa," Sirotta says. "Where else?"

Mountain laughs. "Time for a libation, on me." He likes that word. He'll even offer to buy the drinks just to use it. I'm not itching for company, but I've got to act normal. A few minutes of bullshit Sirotta-style isn't going to kill me. He'll ask the bartender for a "bot of Shurbon" like he asks the waitress for a "coff of cuppee." He thinks that's a riot. If someone laughs, he'll give you the kicker—"Yeah, that shickles the tit out of me"—and he'll give you the elbow in the rib to make sure you get it. It goes with his exaggerated talent for sucking. Lew Sirotta as crew chief is like Mickey Mouse as commissioner of baseball.

"Did you hear Bateman in the second game?" Sirotta always has something ready, especially with one foot on the bar rail. "Like they say, Bateman comes at umpires only on days ending with the letter *Y*. Well, Bateman comes at me, hollering in my face, but it's about a dent in his fender. Would you believe this? He's not protesting a call, he's yelling about some guy bumping his car in the lot, made a dent that big, spreading his arms like I'd just missed a call by that much!" Sirotta always laughs hardest at his own jokes.

I laugh, too. It goes with feeling like a spy in enemy territory. I'm thinking if I fuck up today, I hang tomorrow. I don't even want to think about what I've got to do when I'm in blue.

Mountain gets into the act. "That Bateman, he said to me once: 'Mountain, you're the second-best umpire in the National League. The other twenty-three are tied for first!' "

People look over at us, a trio of laughing soulmates. Me, I can hear my heartbeat hammering inside my skull. I pinch the bridge of my nose again to ease the pain.

"You got problems, old boy?" Sirotta puts in.

I let him have his little baiting practice. He had always been a master baiter.

I shoot for a show of cool. "They're turning out the lights, Lew."

"They should throw you a party, Ernie." Mountain puts a friendly paw on my shoulder. "Give you a gold watch or something."

Or maybe a pair of silver handcuffs. What do they do with crooked umpires anyway? Bring back the guillotine? After over a hundred years of major league baseball, no umpire has ever been tagged with a fixed game. Umpires may be blind bums who call them for the hometown fans, but they're never out-and-out crooked. Maybe we ought to dress in white suits.

Sirotta drinks up, says something about dinner at the Palm. Mountain says sure.

"My stomach just sent me a message," I beg off. "It says, 'Call your wife.' "

Sirotta shakes his head. "If my stomach said that, I'd pump it."

Mountain lays a ten on the bar for the beers. "Well, that's how Ernie stays thin."

"I'm lean because I'm mean," I snarl through my best game face. "A hundred and sixty-five pounds of hard-assed nastiness."

They leave me to suffer alone. And I'm not going to call Enid. I'm going to pace my room like a bear in a zoo cage until I collapse on the bed thinking I'm not going to sleep a fucking wink tonight. A part of me suspects maybe I won't ever sleep again. It's my last time in a blue suit after maybe 5,000 games in a dozen leagues from Canada to the Dominican Republic, in shitville dumps to glittering new domes. Now this.

Maybe I *should* call my wife. Maybe I should tell her the big bad news. Maybe I should open up to her, let her into my fears and confusions. When I tell her it's Roger, maybe she'll see the craziness. I mean, Jesus, doesn't that cry out for a phone call? Maybe she'll even fly out to Chicago to be with me. Maybe it will help us come together for whatever is left of our lives. Maybe what Roger has put me up to doing will lend a purpose to it all. Maybe if I tell it to her right, she'll catch the guts of what I'm going through and she'll take my hand like she did at my mother's funeral.

I dial my home number. When you've got one foot in the grave, a few more toes won't make all that much of a difference.

"You sound dreadful," she says for openers. All I said was "Hello," but she can tell my blood pressure.

"Well, I went to this big party last night at the Playboy Club and there were three luscious blondes who went to work on me nude in the hot tub. I tell you, Enid—"

"Sure, sure," she cuts me off. "I hope you got that on videotape."

"Come to think of it, yeah . . ."

"Ernie, if it showed you had an erection, I wouldn't recognize you."

I laughed; we had a dozen versions of that joke. After forty years of a tired marriage, there's more than one factor that dictates to a dick. Besides, I'm a man about to wrestle with a two-ton polar bear and I called to tell her the truth. I'm thinking, sure, why not, let it out to see where and how it settles. This is your wife, Ernie. The old partner of a lifetime for better or for worse. She has a right to know. She sure as shit knows everything else. Even the thing with Trisha. I'd had one too many dreams about Trisha where I'd fly to Hawaii and ring her doorbell, and there she'd greet me with open arms. What the hell, I can dream with the best of them.

"Roger showed up," I say. Think about one thing, talk about another. It's the sad song of our marriage the way it becomes easy to do that.

"What'd he want, tickets for the big game?"

"I got him seats in the Goodyear blimp."

Here I am, facing the biggest fucking thing that could possibly happen to me, but when it gets to the moment of truth, I can no more share it with my wife than pack my balls in a sack of ice cubes.

"I'm going to Boston, Ernie," she says.

She's going to visit our daughter Amy, married to car salesman Carl Overton, who once insisted that I buy a new car from him. So I did. I traded in a perfectly fine Buick for what turned out to be a lemon of an Olds. The inevitable happened: both Carl and Amy got angry with me. I guess I didn't thank them enough. I guess it was bound to turn out that way. I never was enough of a father to bring out the best of a daughter's feelings. As for the twin, Joe, proud owner of Joe's Car Wash, Richmond, Virginia, he used to brag about how he made more money on a paper route than I made in salary, and he was only *nine*! The big joke was when I was umpiring in Richmond, he came to the game with a flock of his friends in JOE'S CAR WASH T-shirts hollering, "Kill the umpire!" They had it on TV. "It was good for business," he said. If I *did* get killed out there, he'd probably raise his prices.

"Send my love," I say to Enid. It's like sending love to an anthill.

"So don't expect me when you get home," she says.

After tomorrow's game, I might not want to go home. I might want to jump off the Sears Tower, to see if I can fly. Or maybe Trisha will be waiting for me outside the stadium, having come all the way from Hawaii to melt in my arms. You bet.

"I hope you have a nice last game," says Enid.

The way she said it, it was like telling a general to have a nice war.

"Enid, when I call the last man out, I'll be thanking you for what it took to make it all happen."

"Well, I can guess how tough this must be for you."

"Yeah. I can hear the fat lady warming up her pipes."

"It'll be a happy song, Ernie," she says, and hangs up.

Sure. I'll be smiling all the way to my funeral.

When I hang up, too much is running through my head. My skin prickles little beads under my collar. I feel like I'm dangling in midair. I need to get off this bed, out of this hotel room. Jesus, there've been too many hotel rooms. I'm not famous for being a barfly, but on this occasion, to the bar I fly.

Some drunks are mean, some lovable, some plain stupid. I always thought all drunks are pathetic, and now I prove it. After a double scotch on the rocks, I begin to feel mean. It's like I've got to get into trouble. So I start picking on people at the bar. Then a big guy and his woman edge up to the bar beside me. They're laughing at God knows what, so I don't like either of them. I block his way with my shoulder. "Sorry, sir," he says. The "sir" gets me. I don't want his respect, I want his contempt. I want him to mess with me, and fast, so I can get this over with. All he has to do is look at me sideways and I'll cuss him out. With his woman right there, he'll have to do something. He'll have to knock me on my ass. But this guy, he apologizes. I mean, I can't even pick a fight. Because I'm too old? Sure, I'm the oldest guy in the place. I don't attack, I drink. Immediately, it becomes the zinger that puts me over the edge. I can't even hold steady on the stool. Suddenly I hear a howl of laughter around me and I look up at the TV and there's a replay of Sirotta going belly-to-belly with Bateman with that bullshit he spoke about, only now they've got it in slow motion. The laughter is too much. Big fucking joke. The fucking TV and the fucking clowns. Beside me, the Sir-Sayer is roaring with laughter. He says something about it being the best part of the game. I say, "Sure, if you're an asshole." He doesn't bat an eye. He ignores me. I don't know what hits me, I'm too shit-faced to know, but suddenly I'm laughing, too. Every bone in my body wants to pick a fight, but everyone is laughing tonight. When I turn back to the bartender for another beer, I'm out of control. For the first time in my life, my body can't keep control. I see the bartender wobbling, the bottles of booze lined up behind him lose shape, the whole room is moving, all sounds are weird, and down I go like a clown slipping on a banana peel.

What's left of the night can only get worse. Later, in my bed, the room whirls around me. My stomach rebels. I go to the bathroom to toss my cookies. You could wipe the floor with what's left of me. Tell me I'm going to croak, I'd tell you I hope so.

SUNDAY

7:00 AM

I hear singing.

"... our day will come, and we'll have everything ..."

Music is coming from the radio.

A tremendous wave of anxiety hits me. I just remember what's happening today. Or *might* be happening. I feel uneasy. Like a bullfighter with a pulled hamstring.

I pick up the phone and tell the hotel operator that Ruby and the Romantics already woke me up, and please cancel my 7:05 wake-up call.

"... we'll share the joy, falling in love can bring ..."

It occurs to me that another type of music would be more conducive. I thumb the little plastic wheel that passes for a dial on the side of the radio to see what else is on. Some idiot is screaming about stereos. The Anonymous Strings are playing "light" music. A guy with a dramatic voice is talking about God, which he pronounces "Gaud." Sounds more important that way. A classical station is playing music to accompany a battle at sea involving very big boats.

I stop turning for a second. There's that song!

"... by the way, how is my heart? ..."

It's by John Gorka. And it always makes me think of you know who. But it's not the kind of music that wins ball games. I should be listening to that boat music, or gunfighter ballads.

I'm still on edge. And my fingers feel cold and numb. This shoots another dose of anxiety into me. Cold fingertips are smooth and you can't grip anything. Like a baseball, for example. In cold hands a baseball feels like a croquet ball, hard and heavy with a glazed, unforgiving surface. Like it would sail out of your hand if you tried to throw it.

I get up to go to the bathroom. I've got a hard-on. Julie would always say, "Is that for me or do you have to pee?" Some mornings I'd say, "Both."

Maybe I'll feel better if I spend a few minutes thinking about Julie and get it out of the way. I was thinking that even though she left me last year because of baseball, among other things, she'd be happy for me now. She really would. She's a good person. Okay, that's it.

I splash hot water on my face and blast a big pile of shaving cream into my left hand. Did you ever notice that even though, let's say, you're right-handed, there are some things you always do with your left hand? Like apply shaving cream, for example? Or jerk off?

Maybe I'm feeling frustrated because I haven't made love in such a long time. If Julie were here, she'd take matters into her own hands. Or mouth. Boy, I could use her warm body right now.

I'm not going to take a leisurely shower this morning because I don't want the hot water to tire me out. Besides, I never take a long shower in a hotel. The drains never work and after a few minutes you're standing in three inches of water. It's not widely known, but these drains are specially made by the American Dysfunctional Drain Company, designed exclusively for hotels to cut down on water consumption.

My fingers still feel cold and smooth. If I committed a crime right now, I wouldn't leave any fingerprints. Cold fingers and jangled nerves. It's not a good combination.

The shower hits my body with another wake-up call. Someone had set the Adjustable Ultra Massage shower head to drill. Now I try to lather up with the miniature bar of translucent soap they put in that basket along with the little shampoo and skin cream samples I save for Beth, and the clear

37

plastic shower cap that Julie would use to cover leftovers in the refrigerator.

I use two towels to dry off, and slap some St. John's Bay Rum aftershave lotion on my face. Julie used to say I could just rub it on, but men like to hear that slapping sound. I told her I was afraid to try it without the slaps.

No deodorant. When I'm pitching I want my body to breathe, without Aluminum Zirconium Tetrachlorohydrex Gly blocking my pores. The same goes for when I *might* be pitching. The people I'm planning to spend the afternoon with won't notice anyway.

Whoa! There's that Tilt-A-Whirl feeling that starts in my gut and spreads all the way up to my shoulder blades. My body is registering Ball Game Today. *Big* ball game!

But that doesn't bother me. I actually look forward to that feeling. I'll use it to my advantage. Guts is not the absence of fear, it's the creative use of it. If I can ever get rid of this other, unsettled thing that's riding along in the Tilt-A-Whirl. What the hell do I do about that?

It's 7:45. I put on fresh jeans, a long-sleeved black cotton turtleneck, and a gray wool sport coat. Casual but cool. I call the number on Yogi's business card and tell his dispatcher to have Yogi pick me up in front of the hotel at 9:15.

I take the elevator down to the lobby, run the autograph-seeker gauntlet, and head for the coffee shop. Even though there are plenty of tables, I wait in line. The hostess, a very important lady with a clipboard, is busy writing and crossing off names on a list and looking irritated. I ask if I can sit at one of the empty tables. The lady gets a look on her face that suggests I've just made an obscene remark.

I finally get seated. A waitress comes by with a coffeepot and asks if I want some. I tell her no, thanks, but I'm ready to order. She says okay and now I can't get her attention again. She's perfected the "no-look pass" which enables her to walk right by your table without being bothered by annoying comments like "I'm starving to death."

Too bad Marty's not here. One time when he couldn't catch a waiter's eye, he called the restaurant on his portable phone and asked the guy who answered to please bring him a glass of water. The guy says, "Where are you calling from?" Marty says, "Table twelve."

He's good at getting tables, too. One night we were outside a restaurant with our wives, looking at the menu in the window, and Marty calls to make a reservation. A lady says, "Sorry, we're all filled up." So Marty, who's looking in the window, says, "What about that table to your right, next to the plant?" She gave it to us, too. Probably afraid not to.

I eventually order banana pancakes with butter-flavored sugar goop. Of course, they don't have real maple syrup. I also order glasses of orange juice and grapefruit juice, plus an extra glass to mix them together.

I wish I knew if I was really pitching today. They're certainly not going to call me this morning as a courtesy. "Sam, we wanted to let you know you're not pitching, in case you wanted to order the sausage and gravy over biscuits. Heh, heh, heh."

If I *am* pitching, I'll know as soon as I walk into the locker room. A new baseball will be sitting in my shoe. That's an old tradition. A coach always puts a new ball into one of the spiked shoes of the starting pitcher. It's always a thrill, even when I know I'm pitching, to walk into the locker room and see that new white ball nestled in a freshly polished shoe on the floor of my locker. Like an Easter egg in a basket of grass. If I'm not pitching, the baseball will be in somebody else's shoe.

Three bites into the pancakes, a guy at the next table lights up a cigarette. I hate cigarette smoke. So I do what I always do in this situation. I tell the guy, very nicely, that I'm an asthmatic and ask if he would mind not smoking. It's not true, of course, but it usually works. I figure if a smoker is willing to risk my health, I can risk telling a lie. Fortunately, he puts the cigarette out. I'm in no mood for an argument about his right to make me breathe smoke. I was fully prepared to promise this guy that if he wouldn't pollute my air, I wouldn't piss in his drinking water.

Boy, am I tight. I can't even enjoy the idea that I may be pitching today in the biggest game of my life. I should be having a great time with the whole thing.

It's 8:45. I come back up to the room to brush my teeth again. I look in the mirror at my agitated face.

And then I get a crazy idea. I can't even believe I'm thinking about it, but it feels right. I've got plenty of time. The cab doesn't come for another half hour. The only question is, will it relax me *too* much?

It will certainly be a career first. Maybe even set a major league record. In a few minutes I'll become the first pitcher in baseball history to masturbate just before a game that decides who wins the National League East Division Championship. As far as I know, anyway.

Masturbation. Sounds more scientific than jerking off. But I'm not going to use the Mystery Lady routine that an old teammate designed. He painted red fingernail polish on the fingers of one hand and then stood by the edge of a mirror so all he could see was this hand with red fingernails stroking his cock. Good thing he didn't have hairy hands.

This will be like a medicinal fuck that you have once in a while to make yourself feel better. Only you don't have to talk anybody into it. All I have to do is think about what I've been trying not to think about ever since last night.

Julie, wearing nothing but a short slip, sitting back in a big chair, a glass of wine in her right hand, a strap off her left shoulder exposing a breast, her legs apart, one of them dangling over the arm of the chair, inviting me in. And now we're at a party and we go upstairs to the room where the coats are thrown across a bed and Julie's not wearing underwear and we start fucking and someone comes into the room and we don't bother to stop. And now I'm lying on a beach and Julie's on top of me, rocking back and forth, licking her lips and moaning as she starts to come and . . .

There goes your ball game!

SUNDAY

7:40 AM

I'm behind the plate and it's hot, one of those killer afternoons when you go into your crouch and your underwear crawls up your crack like a rusty knife. It's the end of the ninth of a seesaw tie ball game full of vicious rhubarbs. I can hardly breathe, my voice rasps, the juices are sapped out of me. My one thought is to get this game over, but I sense it will never end. On the mound, the pitcher checks the runners, moves out of his stretch, kicks, throws, and suddenly *two* balls come flying out of his hand. *Two* fucking balls! One is high and wide, way out of the catcher's reach, and the other is down the slot, the batter swings, pops it high to the infield. What kind of shit is this? Which one counts? I hear 50,000 people roaring, both managers come storming out of the dugouts, faces red with rage as if this were my fucking fault. I can feel tobacco juice spraying my face; I put up my hands to block them, but they keep crowding me, shoving me, spitting at me. "You're horseshit, Kolacka! You're horseshit!" and they sound just like Enid! When I hear her voice, I go apeshit. I go at them with fists flailing

41

with a greater fury than I've ever known, but I can't hit anyone, they are all Enid-ghosts. I'm so mad I can't even see. Sounds explode in my head, but I can't hear them. I've gone bonkers.

Then, gasping for air, I wake up. It takes seconds before I realize it's a nightmare. I turn on the light and finally make out what bed I'm in. Some gruesome nights never end, the dues you pay for your fucked-up life.

"You sound dreadful," Enid had said.

Soon enough *dreadful* is going to seem like a happy word compared with what's going to go down with me.

I'm not one to put the blame on Enid. If Roger saved my life, it was Enid who kept me going. It was all there in that San Francisco Army Hospital six weeks after I came back from Korea. My right shoulder was useless and so was the rest of me. I was a nineteen-year-old hunk of rotting flesh. On the ward, my best buddy was a cripple named Jess, even more bitter than me. They called us "two clouds without a silver lining." We'd sit for hours throwing shit at each other to see who had it worse.

"I had a dream," he'd say. "I was in the jungle, tigers in front of me, a river full of crocodiles to one side, a 200-foot gorge on the other."

"And behind you?"

"A truly beautiful naked woman."

"Ah!" I pictured a happy ending. "So?"

"I jumped into the gorge."

"What! Why?"

"It's a dream, dumbhead."

He had it worse, all right. He slit his wrists with a kitchen knife. He left a note: "Life without hope is a bird without wings." I kept pretending I would grow a pair.

Came then the visiting war hero, Roger Abercorn, a sweeping grin across his round face. He was coming through San Francisco after a month of rehab in Hawaii; he was maybe ten pounds heavier than when I saw him last. The Army had given him the Silver Star for the gallant rescue above and beyond the call. Oh, he deserved it, all right. But from where I sat in that wheelchair, I had been the prewar up-and-comer with legit dreams of glory, and he, some kind of a nerd shipping clerk pushing cartons on a freight deck. When you're hurting, everything makes you hurt more.

"You look like shit, Ernie," he offered.

Call that an understatement. I didn't say anything.

"You look like you're taking a course in how to pity yourself."

"I got an A," I said. "First A I ever got."

"Ernie, there's more to life than being a ballplayer."

"Write that on my cast. That way I won't forget it."

That "more-to-life" bullshit was going to be my cross to bear. Even my father said it when I called him. He was a carpenter who loved what he did.

"You'll be happy to know I got a job," Roger went on. The colonel regimental commander was an executive in the Maynard's chain. He was taking the war hero into the firm.

"Congrats. With the Silver Star on your chest and the bullet hole in your ass, you should do great. You could even prove that there's more to life than being a shipping clerk."

He hated that. When the nurse came by with the regular afternoon medication, he tried to wave her off.

"Nurse, your patient doesn't want the medicine. All he wants is sympathy. He wants the whole world to feel sorry for him. He wants to bury his head in a barrel of garbage."

The nurse was Enid, and it was the first time I'd seen her smile.

"Interesting therapy," she said.

"You know what sympathy is, Ernie? It's in the dictionary between shit and syphilis." Then, to Enid: "Pardon me, Nurse."

"Interesting thought," she said.

"Can you heal a man with his head up his anus?"

Again she smiled. "I don't recall anything about that in nurses' training."

"Fuck you, Roger." I scowled. "It's my head. It goes where I want it to go."

He sighed, then sank to his knees directly in front of her. "Give me a cyanide pill, Nurse. Or a bottle of arsenic. Or a Colt .45 with a silver bullet. Please, Nurse, I can't stand it anymore!"

She laughed, a sudden uncontrollable outburst that was so surprisingly childlike I couldn't help laughing in spite of myself.

And so did Roger. He got up, bowed with one arm across his belt like an actor taking a curtain call. Then he came to me, put a hand on my good shoulder.

"Hey, Ernie," he said. "Something good'll happen. You'll see."

It was pitiful. I wanted to cry, but I laughed with him. For the first time, though, I wanted it to happen. If only for the moment, I wanted it.

"Roger, you know what they say in Buckingham Palace? 'Go take carnal knowledge of yourself!' "

When he left, I was still the same fucking cripple. Like they say, you can't make a silk purse out of a paper asshole. Everything hurt worse than before.

"Your friend is a man of action," Enid said.

"He thinks he's too good to be true sometimes."

"And you, soldier? You are perhaps the opposite?"

She was staring at me for maybe five seconds and our eyes met for the first time. Was she trying to figure out what was going on inside of me?

That was the day I became aware of Enid Wynant. She was nothing much to look at, I guess some were better than others, but I wasn't in a mood to care. Like the rest of her, her face was lean, she had dark hair packed in a bun under the nurse's cap, dark eyes—the opposite of Roger. She looked better in profile than head-on. She knew that, I guess, because she would often turn her head to the left and look at you sort of sideways. I think maybe I noticed her because she seldom smiled. Too many nurses think they've got to play Miss Sunshine and flash their pearly whites every time they stick a needle in you. Miss Wynant held back, and when she smiled, you knew it was for real.

She was slightly on the tall side. She spoke softly, just loud enough to be heard—and never more than she had to. No dumb jokes to pretend at cheering you up. She couldn't stand the thought of being a phony. Sometimes I would tease her just to see her reaction, if any.

"You know what? You've got a neat derriere," I said, repeating something I'd heard on a TV show.

"Is that a compliment, soldier?"

"A woman without a neat derriere is like a peacock without feathers."

"I'll try to remember that."

"Call me Ernie, Miss Wynant. *Ex*-soldier, *ex*-ballplayer."

"Ernie," she said. "I'll try to remember that, too."

A few days later, she went behind the wheelchair to examine the shoulder where I couldn't see her, but she was there, all right. She pulled back the robe collar, then took some Vaseline, and her hand went to neck flesh, gently laying it on. Fingers were moving slowly across my back like they were probing for some sign of life. The right hand joined the left with more grease, more warmth, more probing. She went from neck to shoulder and down the left side. Her hand moved under the robe and lingered like it couldn't decide which way to go. She began to hum softly in rhythm with the movement of her hands. Her voice was sweet as sugar. I mean, I wasn't expecting anything like it. I hadn't heard a girl sing in so long, it gave me goose bumps. Suddenly I got the feeling that this was more than her being a nurse. It was so satisfying, I didn't move, lest I jar the pleasures of flesh tingling around the touch of her fingers. My heartbeat seemed so loud, it embarrassed me. Could she hear it? As her right hand rubbed soft circles on my neck, her left went gently down my good side, pressing flesh up and down, up and down. She was making magic. Even her voice rose in pitch as it melded with my reactions. And sonovabitch, for the first time since I could remember, slowly, gradually, unfuckingbelievably, I got a hard-on.

I sighed. I could feel the blood pouring into my cock; my whole body was leaping to life. I didn't look down, but shut my eyes to all existence. There was happiness pounding inside my ribs that brought on tears.

She knew, all right. The hands that had worked the magic kept moving across my chest. I felt her breathing close to my ear, I smelled her lemon-scented soap. Her face came close to mine, her hair brushed my cheek, and finally, wanting this to happen more than even being alive, I felt her left hand come down to my stomach and close around my hard-on. I will swear that I'd never experienced such sexual pleasure as I did at that instant.

Enid came from Wausau, Wisconsin, where her father worked for an insurance company. In Wausau, a high school girl either got married or became a secretary. As she told it, the boy she went with joined the Marines, then just disappeared from her life. It chewed a hole in what little confidence she had. She had to get out of Wausau. She went down to Chicago and took up nursing.

In San Francisco the doctors liked her quiet competence and said nice things about her, but no one asked for her phone number. She wasn't the vivacious type with flashy sex appeal.

If the healthy Marine got away, the wounded soldier stayed captive. She made me feel special. There was never so much as a suggestion that she used stroking therapy on other patients. As for love? What was love? She was too smart to utter such a threatening word. But I couldn't help myself. I began to tumble in head over heels.

And in what magical places, one more secret than the next. Our first sex was in the linen room on a pile of GI blankets. Dark, quiet, she stroked my legs till my cock was throbbing. When we went at it, she manipulated her lubricated parts until I so wanted to scream, she had to cover my mouth for silence. Another time, in the laundry to the rhythmic hum of washing machines. Once, on the floor of the pantry under shelves of large cans of applesauce. I didn't care where. The more it had to be secret, the better I liked it. My hands hungered for the feel of smooth satiny skin around her buttocks, the inside of her firm full thighs. When you looked at Enid in nurse's garb, she seemed so slender you wouldn't know how lush her breasts really were, how soft the feel of her shoulders. And always, there was the sound of her sexy voice. The sex stuff was fantastic, but the voice gave it extra meaning. I loved the sound of her. She could heal me with words. When she gave me medications, or massage, it was always with those healing sounds, and I would shut my eyes, the better to hear my heartbeat.

Forty years later, you think of moments like that and you can see how fucked up everything became. That my life should've turned on an erection is truly pathetic. If Enid had hands of magic, the way I was, what else did she need? I mean, I was so whacked out I thought she was an angel sent down from heaven to give me another chance at life. Put it another way, I couldn't throw a baseball, but I could fuck. Even better, because of that, I could feel something inside me that started to sprout wings.

I must say, I was healing. I'd look in the mirror often enough to see how it filled out my face. My blue eyes lost the bleary look. My mouth seemed quick with a smile. I shampooed my brown hair and combed it a half-dozen times a day. I even used aftershave lotion. When my father would call, he said I sounded so cheerful, it worried him, like maybe I was in such deep shit I was putting on an act to hide it.

All the while, she had me working therapy on my shoulder, a lot of stretching exercises to build up atrophied tissue. If I couldn't throw a baseball, eight months after Korea I started to play Ping-Pong. Enid loved Ping-Pong; you could see her eyes sparkling in the middle of a point.

One evening—it was my twentieth birthday, April 27—she had me over for a home-cooked dinner and my first taste of champagne. Her present was a large book of American poems.

"You love baseball, I love poetry," she said. She'd never told me that. And on the birthday card, she'd written a poem:

I have entered your life as you have mine,
The wounds of the past are curing.
We've made a miracle as heady as wine,
May the magic be sweeting and enduring.

So tidings of love on this day of your birth,
From Enid the Crab to Ernie the Taurus.
We'll make this the happiest day on earth,
May both of our Sun Signs adore us.

"*Hey!*" I mean, it really rocked me. In all my wildest fantasies, I never thought I'd ever be here. I mean, I'd been snatched from doom and gloom by this angel with a poem. I got misty-eyed looking at her. I kissed her. Not one of those sexy-hungry kisses, but soft and sweet. It moved from her lips to her cheek, it touched her eyes, then her hair, and my hand found hers and fingers locked. I was twenty years old and my girl wrote me a poem, and I'd discovered a new way to kiss someone you love, all in one day.

Then she read me "The Raven" by Edgar Allan Poe. She made it sound so great, it knocked me on my ass. And when we went to the sack, the sex ended with glorious sounds that, for the first time, didn't have to be stifled.

A few weeks later came the real surprise. We were alone in the rec room at the hospital playing Ping-Pong. Lots of laughs at this shot or that. We were a pair of ex-brooders who'd forgotten how to brood. She was so excited, she suddenly popped the message in the middle of a volley.

"You know what?" Ping!

"Can't say that I do." Pong!

"I'm pregnant." Ping!

I didn't return the pong, staring to see if she was serious. Her face was so lit up, she looked beautiful. Me, I must've looked the opposite. The word caught me in the throat; hot flashes zapped me. Suddenly everything became different. I was being attacked by a horde of bees. She was beaming, I was steaming. I was thinking, hey, she was a nurse. Aren't they supposed to know about that sort of thing? But the way she said it, it was like it was the most wonderful thing that could've happened. I mean, it made me ashamed of being shocked. What was I supposed to say? How could she be so fucking happy if I was so scared?

A part of me wanted to run. Where? Where could I run? I was still a soldier. It would be like desertion, for crissakes. Another part said I should level with her, tell her I didn't want a baby, I wasn't ready for a baby or marriage. I was a twenty-year-old with a limp arm and a stiff dick, but I was anything but an adult.

Say this for me, I didn't ask, "Are you sure?" I didn't go smart-ass. I said: "Well, it sure makes you look beautiful."

"I feel beautiful." She smiled, waiting for the follow-up from me. There wasn't any. I was too scared to say anything.

After that she never so much as mentioned the word *marriage*. She didn't even bring up the pregnancy. She even pretended that nothing had changed with us, that everything was fine and dandy. You bet. It was like believing that I could suddenly throw bullets from deep shortstop, that the next guy in the door would be from the Yankees with a fat contract in his attaché case, and that Enid was so happy for me she would rush to get an abortion.

Then, gradually, she changed. I could see the new sad look in her eye that nothing was coming out the way it was supposed to. One day, there was another nurse on the floor, the happy-happy type who drove me up the wall. Enid had been shifted to another ward. I saw her hardly at all, even after work hours. She was avoiding me, and that scared me even more than the baby. Suddenly I was alone again. I needed her. Without her, I was a washed-out rag. I was less than a month from discharge, and then what? What would I do with myself? What would she do without me? I mean, it shook me up.

One Sunday afternoon, I went to her apartment and waited on the steps for her to come home. She plumped down next to me, not the least surprised to see me there. For a while, neither of us spoke.

"How's the shoulder?" she asked.

"How's your belly?"

"You doing your exercises?"

"Where you been, Enid?"

"You look pale, Ernie."

I couldn't handle the moment. I didn't even know why I was there. Something had to give. I caved in. I couldn't help myself.

"We should get married," I mumbled.

She reached for my hand and brought it to her lips. She was smiling as tears ran down her cheek. I kissed the salty wetness. "I love you, Ernie," she said.

"Hey, I love you, too."

I'd said it without knowing if it was the truth. The words just dripped out of me. What did I have to go home to? If there was more to life than being a ballplayer, what else did I have but her?

Forty years later, though, you get spooked by the memories. All the should've-beens and might've-beens, they're like dried birdshit on your windshield. You can wipe them off, but there's always more coming, you see the world through blotches of birdshit. All these years, I never had a clean, clear view.

Now I'm doubly spooked by the sound of church bells. What is this day but a knife in my gut? It's like I'm about to commit mass murder. On a Sunday, no less. This is the day I've got to befoul the cathedral. I've got to pour blood on the sacraments, I've got to commit suicide of the soul. When I was a kid who did something wrong, my mother would threaten me: "God will punish you!" I didn't know whether to believe that or not. One day, I lied to my father about where I'd been. He hated lying as much as he hated stealing. That Sunday, I sat in church and got sick. When he stood to sing a hymn, I mouthed the words, but not a sound came out. I was afraid that God was taking away my voice, that I'd never be able to talk again. It wasn't God, it was me running scared. When I admitted the lie, my father nodded. That was all, just a nod, but it was enough to take away the fears.

Now the bells are slapping me around like hot spikes burning the word *fix* in my brain. *Fix* the old ball game, Ernie. Need a *fix*, Ernie? A shot of heroin, maybe it'll *fix* you up. Get hit by bricks, take your licks, join the pricks. Man, are you in a *fix*!

I finally push my body out of bed and take a hot shower. I soap up three or four times like I have to clean away all the shit in my life. Then I switch to cold. Let it come like ice, I'm into punishing myself. I slap myself hard.

Maybe I should've brought a whip with me. I don't step out until I'm shuddering. Then, reaching for a towel, my right elbow cracks against the shower door, right on the funny bone. For seconds, I'm paralyzed by pain. I can't dry off. I stand there, shuddering worse than ever. This is God punishing me. *"Fuck!"* I cry out.

It's one goddamn sonovabitching way to begin a day like this.

How am I going to get myself out of this room?

SUNDAY

9:15 AM

"Good morning, on a great day in the city of Chicago," croons Yogi as I climb into his cab.

"Wrigley Field," I say in a very mellow voice.

"Wrigley Field!" announces Yogi into his microphone. "Home of the hopeful Cubs. And here to help out the home team, we've got the Sunday Morning Gospel Hour coming your way from the Friendship Baptist Church on the South Side of Chicago."

The radio comes on in the middle of a sermon.

"... He can sa-a-a-ave you today, until your *hands* look new! He can sa-a-a-ve you today, until your *feet* look new! He can sa-a-a-ve you today, until your ..."

I strain to hear about the remaining body parts as we go under a bridge. I also wonder what He might have thought about my pregame ritual at the hotel, if anything.

I never would have done it as a fastball pitcher. But I don't need to be strong for nine innings today, I need to be sharp for five. Besides, it's what my body wanted and I pay attention to what it has to say. I'll be doing that all afternoon. It's the only chance I have. To get that feeling that tells me which pitch to throw, and when, and how to throw it. Talk to me.

It's something I had to learn after I hurt my arm. *Ruined* my arm is more like it. The doctors called it a labral tear of the glenohumeral joint. In English, that's torn cartilage in the shoulder. "You ever pop a chicken bone out of its socket?" explained the surgeon. "That white rubbery material in the joint is what you tore." In my case the tear was so violent that a portion of bone ripped off the joint. It's called an avulsion. To rhyme with revulsion. So they did what's known as a Bankart procedure, which involves reattaching the bone and the cartilage to the joint.

I remember lying on my back, getting wheeled down the hall into the operating room, watching the ceiling lights flash by, looking up into strange faces, people wearing masks telling me to relax. Then, about three hours later, I was in the recovery room, with tubes coming out of me and Julie holding my hand. And kissing my forehead.

"I love you, Sam," she said, with an incredibly sweet smile and a very furrowed brow. "I can't stand to see you in pain."

"The only pain will be if I can't throw a ball anymore," I said, before dozing off from the medication.

For three weeks I walked around with my arm in a sling. Then light movement for a month, followed by a year of pain in a forest of machines down at the gym; pushing, pulling, lifting, stretching. Then I'd come home and hang from the doorjambs, push against walls, lift books, with Julie timing the workouts, counting the repetitions. And by April I was ready. Not to pitch, but to throw a ball with some velocity to see how it felt.

It was a beautiful spring day. The ground was still soft from the winter snow, but the grass was green and forsythia buds were peeking out. A small crowd had gathered to witness the big event. Julie made lunch, the folks brought the video camera, and Marty got the catcher's glove out of the basement. Beth, a year old at the time, was watching from her portable playpen on the lawn.

I picked up the baseball and moved to the far end of the yard, rotating my arm above my head as I walked. Marty positioned himself about thirty feet away and pounded his fist into the pocket of his glove.

"Not too hard, now," said Dad, adjusting his viewfinder.

With the camera rolling, I lobbed one across the yard. The ball made a soft poof as it landed in the pocket.

"How did that feel?" asked Marty.

"I can't tell until I cut loose," I said anxiously.

I continued lobbing the ball, with Marty moving farther and farther back as my arm loosened up. After ten minutes of soft toss, a short break, and more tossing, it was time to find out.

"Here we go," I announced.

I held the ball in my hand, calculating just how much I wanted to put behind it. I was loose enough. I'd worked out all winter long. I couldn't keep babying the damn thing. I looked across the yard at Marty, sixty feet away, bending forward in a modified catcher's squat.

"Hummbabe, waddyasaaay, heynnnnnaw," hollered Marty, making fun of baseball chatter.

Dad pointed the camera.

Mom crossed her fingers.

"Be careful, Sam!" said Julie.

I reared back just a little bit ... not too much ... and let it go.

The pain was instantaneous.

"Aaagh," I yelled, as it left my hand. "Shit!"

And what began as a picnic to celebrate my recovery became a wake for my dearly beloved fastball.

"Can I ask why you were pitching in 40-degree weather?" the doctor had said.

"Earmuffs," I replied. "Six thousand earmuffs on Earmuff Night."

Wrigley Field, home of the hopeful Cubs, comes into view. The sight rolls my stomach over.

"Take me around to the players' entrance, please," I say, checking Yogi's reaction in his rearview mirror.

"Well now, what have we here?" says Yogi. "Would you be one of the baseball players?"

"I'm Sam Ward," I say. "With the Cubs."

"Sam Ward!" yells Yogi, with polite enthusiasm. "I've heard of you. What position do you play?"

"I'm a pitcher," I say, with a touch of pride. "In fact, I might be pitching today. But don't tell anybody."

"Wait a minute," says Yogi, "isn't this the game that decides who gets into the playoffs?"

"You got it," I say. "If I win, I'll give you a call and you can take me back to the hotel. If I lose, I'll probably walk back. Or over to the river."

Yogi laughs. "I hear you," he says.

The cab pulls to a stop on Waveland Avenue, just beyond the left-field wall. Some early-bird autograph seekers are milling around, sniffing the cool morning air for ballplayers.

"Tell you what," says Yogi. "I'll listen to the game on my radio, and if you win, I'll be out here waiting for you. Reason I have to wait is because otherwise you can't get a cab. There's too many people."

I thank Yogi and hand him a ten.

"I'll be listening," says Yogi as he drives away.

A gust of wind blows my hair. My heart thumps in anticipation. Here we go, boys and girls! This could be it. Put up or shut up. All or nothing. Do or die. The whole enchilada. It's a good thing that jangled feeling is gone. Now I'm free to deal with the pure terror of it all.

Wrigley Field looms above me. But it doesn't loom very high because the stadium is pretty small. Which is why it's called "the friendly confines." It's also known as "America's most beautiful stadium." That's on the inside. The outside is another matter. The green-and-white exterior walls are not so much walls as a system of facings and support columns for the two decks of stands and exit ramps, all of which are partially visible through a latticework of wire fencing which wraps the stadium and appears to hold it all together. The total effect is of a giant chicken coop.

The autograph seekers have spotted me.

"Who is it?" somebody asks.

"One of the rookies."

"Nah, he's too old."

"It's that *old* rookie, what's his name?"

"Ward, I think."

"Mr. Ward," they call in unison. "Can we have your autograph?"

I sign yearbooks, scorecards, balls, gloves, hats, T-shirts, and baseball bats. And I smile to myself at how excited they'd be if they knew they were getting the autograph of today's possible starting pitcher.

I enter a back door to the stadium and make a left to the locker room. I

smell popcorn, cooking oil, and wet cement. I see people talking and I wave.
I hear my footsteps echoing off the walls. I sense vendors opening boxes,
pouring liquids, and wiping counters in preparation for the invading hordes
scheduled to arrive in about an hour and a half.

Wait a minute. Where am I? What the hell is this? This is the goddamned
visitors' locker room! I should've made a right back there. I've made a right
turn every other day since I've been here.

Earth to Sam!

I retrace my steps, walking right past the very same people I just passed
in the other direction. Maybe they'll think I'm a plainclothes security guard
checking things out.

I finally arrive at a blue door with red letters stenciled on the front. It
says CHICAGO CUBS LOCKER ROOM—PLAYERS ONLY! This appears to be the
place.

The security guard gives me a nod. I push through the door. I'm engulfed
by the smell of wood bats, leather gloves, analgesic, and the hot air from
giant clothes dryers. Also, the smell of freshly polished spikes. My eyes
quickly dart to a pair of shoes across the room.

Happy Easter!

SUNDAY

9:20 AM

I'm no better off in the coffee shop than I was in my room. I can feel doom sneaking up on me. I order medium-boiled eggs, a bran muffin, coffee, but I seriously doubt I can eat anything. I wait, fidgeting like a kid in the principal's office. At the adjacent table, someone left parts of the Sunday *Trib*. I'd rather read the fucking comics than think of what I have to do today. Then my eye settles on the horoscope at the top of the page. It means nothing to me, but I could no more pass it by than an ice-cream truck on a summer afternoon. I go at Taurus, the bull. That's me, born April 27. But the words come at me like banderillas.

"This is not the time to accept unconventional offers. Abjure all risky ventures. Find a safe harbor to weather the stormy seas."

Abjure. I never heard the word, but I know what it means. Fuck off, that's what it means. It's all bullshit. Why am I even playing games with it? Who believes this shit anyway? What's it got to do with anything real? But it gets me. Somehow that paper was sitting there at the next table, someone had left only that section, it was open to that page. I mean, maybe this was a message that was meant to be. Like the church bells. Can you fuck around with that? Can you? I look at the eggs and can't eat them. The muffin is sawdust in my mouth. The waitress comes by. "Is everything all right?" I can't even fake a smile.

All I know is, I've got to get back to my room. I've got to call Roger. We've got to have another talk.

But when I do, I get the bad news.

"Sorry, sir. Mr. Abercorn has checked out."

Sure. Any questions from me draw a blank. Any speculations sink me deeper into the pits.

I go to the window. Sometimes when I look out a window, I get an idea. This time there's a knock on the door. Three quick raps, then right off, three more.

"Yeah!" I call out, thinking it's got to be Roger. Right?

Wrong.

It's a tall thin man with thick jelly-jar glasses, in a dark worsted suit, white shirt, and striped regimental tie. His face is all bones and sharp edges. His thick black hair is all over his head. He's carrying an umbrella and an old-fashioned briefcase. There's a beefy guy with a barrel chest and no neck who looks like a professional wrestler who had one too many falls. The skinny one works cheek muscles into a semblance of a smile that would terrify Dracula on the best day he ever had.

"Mr. Kolacka . . ."

His throaty sounds make my name seem like it belongs to someone else.

"I'm busy," I say. I think he might be a used-Bible salesman.

"Mr. Abercorn suggested I visit you."

Roger? This man is from Roger?

With a polite nod, he walks in. "Cy," he says to the goon, "would you be so good as to wait in the hall?" Nonchalantly, he sits in the club chair by the door, the briefcase resting on bony knees. The light catches his glasses, so I can't see his eyes. He is staring at me. I know that.

"They call me the Professor, Mr. Kolacka."

Not a salesman, I think; more like an undertaker.

He takes his time. Is he sizing me up?

"Mr. Kolacka, I'd appreciate knowing . . . Is there a cause for concern over Mr. Abercorn's request? A doubt in your mind that perhaps this is not a proper thing for you to do?"

Well, how about that for openers? I'm stunned. It's like he can see inside my head.

"Okay, I don't like it," I say. "I don't like it at all!"

He nods. "To tamper with the outcome of a baseball game; that offends you?"

"In my whole life, I never made a dishonest call."

"You remain loyal to the game even though you've been abused and exploited? Held in the minor leagues for over half your career?"

He's a man who knows how to push the right buttons. What can I do but play it straight?

"I love the game, yes. I don't give a damn about the rest of it."

He smiles, nods again. It's like I've said what he wanted me to say.

"In other words, Mr. Kolacka, you would not betray baseball even though its mentors have repeatedly betrayed you."

It's my turn to nod. "That's right."

"But you're also loyal to the man who saved your life."

Not a question, this time. This time, he was attacking.

"I owe him. There's no question, I owe him."

He nods, having convinced himself of my purity. "There are certain traditions in our business, Mr. Kolacka. To preserve our way of life, they must never be violated. When one incurs a debt ..." He raises a hand from the briefcase, palm up.

I get the message. No welshing on debts permitted.

"You see, Mr. Kolacka, when you agreed to do this, the wheels began to turn. Last night, over two million dollars were wagered on the Phillies. More even as we speak ..."

I'm thinking, well, tough shit, Professor. If I say no dice, they can switch those bets if they have to. They can do anything in Vegas, can't they?

Again, he can read my mind.

"*The fix is in,* Mr. Kolacka!"

I don't know what to say. I don't know what to think. There's a new menacing feel to his words that shuts me up.

At this, he rises from the chair, crosses to the bed, pushes aside the bedclothes with his umbrella to level the surface for his briefcase.

"Since this is our business, Mr. Kolacka, I'm here to put this on a business basis."

He unbuckles the old strap and draws apart the leather lids. Then he reaches in with both hands and withdraws thick bundles of cash. I have to gasp. I've never seen so much money. I've never dreamed of seeing so much money. It's so much money I can even smell it. I'll never forget that smell.

"That's $100,000, Mr. Kolacka. Down payment for your professional services." He lets that sink in, then adds his dessert. "At your successful completion, there'll be another $100,000. Shall we say, right here, tonight at seven?"

I'm too dazzled to respond. I can't even swallow the junk forming in my throat. I've got a mixed bag of reactions too confusing to make sense of. I stare at the money. How could I not stare? I mean, you see a gorgeous nude walking down the beach, even if you love your wife, you look. You look! Then there's the goddamn meaning of it. Down payment on professional services? Business deal? Jesus, what bullshit, it's a fucking bribe!

"Look ... I don't know," I say.

He eyeballs me as he buckles up the empty briefcase. I get the feeling this amuses him.

"Mr. Kolacka, you're forcing me to add a threat."

"What?"

"You're committed. There's no turning back. You are fixing this game for the Cubs to lose!" Then he pulls himself up to his full lean height. "Or else, Mr. Kolacka ..."

Or else what? I don't ask. I don't want to know. His smile betrays secret knowledge. I don't want to know that either.

"Believe me," he goes on, "I don't like to deal in such matters."

Sure. I nod but start to seethe because he pushed the wrong button. I've got my own threat to throw back at him.

"I'll tell you something, Professor. You don't understand what's involved here. This ain't like rolling fixed dice. Blam, seven. Blam, eleven. This ain't even a jockey holding back a horse down the stretch. And maybe, just maybe, I can't do it. You want to know something? It scares the hell out of me. It scares me even to think of it. Like I told Roger, there's eighteen men out there, any one of them can fuck it all up and there's not a thing I can do about it. It don't matter how much money you put on that bed or how much bullshit you theaten me with. *Because I can't guarantee a fucking thing!*"

He regards me patiently with one of those are-you-finished? looks. Then he shakes his head, side to side, side to side, his mouth curling in disgust.

"Just do it, Mr. Kolacka! Just do it!"

He jostles the piles of money with his umbrella, then menacingly jabs me in the ribs.

"Have a good day, Mr. K.," his voice mocking the idiocy of those words, even to the way he ends with a rhyme.

Then he leaves me. I watch him tuck the umbrella under his left arm to free his right hand to open the door. I think, he's so skinny he could slide under the door. And there is Cy the goon, waiting for him. The Professor with the big words and smooth talk and uncanny ability to make your head spin. Smart, like Roger said, they're smart. You have to be impressed by the way they put this thing together, the way they get it all locked up, you're in it even though you don't want to be, you can't get out, so maybe it's not so terrible, you're getting all this cash with the threats, they're so slick you can't tell the difference, it's all one well-packed ball of wax.

So what am I supposed to do? I do it, or else. I do it or maybe Roger spends the rest of his life without his gonads. I do it, and suddenly I'm rich. For the first time in my life I'm getting big bucks for respecting "tradition." I'm being paid for being "loyal."

What choice do I have?

Dial 911?

I reach down to the bedload of cash to get the feel of it. It's enough to raise my head to the mirror on the dresser to suffer the sight of my stupid grin.

I go to the closet for my travel bag, start stuffing the money in. To make room, I remove four dirty shirts. For the next $100,000 I'll throw away a pair of gabardine pants with too many miles on them. That, too, makes me grin. Then I consider taking the bag with me to the ballpark. I always do. I go to the airport right after the game, don't I? But this is different. I've got that 7:00 PM date with a bonanza. And six will get you five the Professor will be in the lobby right now to see that there's no bag in sight. He'll have his pal with him. Not so lean and twice as mean.

I zip it shut, add the lock at the end. I never used that lock. I don't even have a key. But I lock it. I'll put the next wad of money in another compartment. When you're a crook, you've got to think in a whole other way.

Have a good day, Mr. K.

Sure. We're all friends here in the greatest corruption of the National Pastime since the 1919 Black Sox Scandal.

"Say it ain't so, Ernie."

It is now so certain I can read it no other way. Taurus can shove his stars up his ass, for there will be no abjuring of unconventional offers, no safe harbors to weather the storm. Old Ernie Kolacka is going to count his money, not to be sure it's all there, mind you, but to get the right and proper feel of it. I'm thinking, this joke is getting bigger all the time. I mean, this is my last game in blue, a whole lifetime in one long, hard-nosed career that ends with a sellout. And for the first time in my marriage, my wife would approve. She'd take a dry bath in all those C notes. I can picture her tossing them in the air like feathers after a pillow fight. All the years I was an honest ump, the best I could be, she thought I was a fool. Well, she's wrong. Look how wrong she is. She never would've dreamed there'd be a payoff for being my kind of umpire. See, Enid? I've worked hard, dedicated to being the best, suffering all the abuses for a pittance in pay, then they actually hand me a pot of gold! So ha ha ha ha. This is going to be *my* reward, Enid. All mine.

And the best part is, no one will ever know.

You have to wonder, what is life? What's it all about, anyway? How can it be that, because you're an honest man, you end up getting paid a bundle to be a crook? What's behind it all? My father once told me: "Never ask. Just live it, that's all." He lived it and got caught with his hand in the till.

I can tell you, pal: if there's an easy way to figure it, I sure as hell haven't found it.

THE CLUBHOUSE

9:30 AM

I'm biting the inside of my cheek to keep from smiling at the sight of that egg nestled there in my shoe. If the coaches see me smiling, they'll think I'm nervous. Or not serious. They like to see players wearing a "game face," which can be anything from a scowl to a zombie trance. A smile does not count as a game face. Unless your eyes are crossed at the same time.

It's three and a half hours before game time. When the family was together, I'd come as late as possible so I could spend more time at home. Now I come in early to get my mind off personal things. The locker room is my sanctuary, the mound my isolation booth.

I've always enjoyed being in a major league clubhouse. Located beneath the stands, it's a cavernous, often windowless place, like the underground forts that Marty and I used to build when we were kids. A subterranean realm of subdued lighting and wall-to-wall carpeting with pile so thick it muffles the sound, conveying the feeling of stepping into a showroom for very expensive furniture. It's the ultimate club for members only. A hideout for big kids where the milk-carton seats have been replaced with stained-oak lockers wide enough to sit in and read a book; lockers with shelves and cubbyholes and built-in storage chests, not for cap pistols and peashooters, but for the highest-quality wood bats and leather gloves that money can buy. Fantasy toy chests in a magic castle.

This is the best time to be in the locker room, before the players come in and mess it up. It looks like a barracks for commanding officers. Forty freshly cleaned white uniforms hang in military formation from the same hooks in their respective lockers. Lined up on the floor of each locker are three pairs of freshly polished blue spikes, toes pointing out. And sitting neatly on forty stools are forty little stacks of mail. Perfect symmetry. Not counting the shoe with a ball in it.

Like a soldier who deflects fear by preparing his gear, I get dressed for the day. White cotton sanitary socks, thigh-length undershorts, three-button sweatshirt with navy blue sleeves, and the jockstrap with a pocket that holds the plastic protective cup. The cup calls to mind that old taunt directed at struggling pitchers: "Get the married men off the infield."

Properly attired in baseball underwear, the unofficial uniform of the locker room, I can now do a crossword puzzle, play cards, watch TV in the players' lounge, have a cup of coffee if I drank coffee, listen to music, sign the six dozen new baseballs that sit out on the table every day, or, as we Scrubeenies like to say, "read the letter from my fan."

I wander into the trainer's room to see what's going on. It has a nice trainer's room smell. Coffee, liniment, clean towels, tape, and essence of medicine cabinet. It's a cozy kind of place. Players sitting or lying around with various body parts baking in heat packs, dipped in the whirlpool, or clamped into a diathermy machine.

Someone is hollering in the hallway at the far end of the room.

"... no fucking business pitching *him* today!"

Him is me! A bolt of anxiety slams me in the chest.

"Who's that?" I ask, trying to look unconcerned, my mind laboring to place the voice.

"Don't pay any attention to him," says hitting coach Bill Robinson. Robby's one of the best coaches in baseball. He'd be a manager if he were white. "That's just Foster. He thinks *he* should be pitching today even though he has a badly bruised earned run average."

Foster's won a lot of games over the years, but he's been getting "lit up" recently and they've lost confidence in him. And I'm sure he's not the only one who thinks he should be pitching instead of me. We've probably got *outfielders* who think they should be pitching today.

"Let me know if you want a massage today, Sam," says trainer Gary Tuthill, a muscular little guy with glasses.

"No, thanks," I say. "I couldn't stand the excitement."

"He doesn't need a trainer, he needs a shrink," says Owens, who is wearing a T-shirt that says SCRUBEENIES LOCAL 69. "His inner child needs a spanking."

"He doesn't throw hard enough to need an arm rub," says Buddy Ray Hatchet sarcastically, through a mouthful of chewing tobacco. A few of the guys laugh.

Hatchet, with his bullet-shaped head, and a crew cut and sideburns, is picking his toenails and throwing them toward a spittoon. The nails ping as they bounce off the metal. Jesus, I hope they don't let *him* catch today. Hatchet caught me this summer in Des Moines. He handles the knuckleball pretty well for a Scrubeenie, but he's not one of my favorite people. And I'm not one of his. We're exact opposites. He's in favor of guns, tobacco, heavy metal rock, and capital punishment. And I'm against all four, except for capital punishment in the case of Hatchet.

Hatchet will never forgive me for screwing up a deal with his agent, Frank Toniolo. Last year Toniolo wanted to add seven players to his stable from the Cubs farm team in Des Moines, with help from Hatchet. If any of the players made it to the big leagues, Toniolo would get 10 percent of their salary and Hatchet would get a piece of that. But I said it was a conflict of interest for an agent to represent more than one player at the same position—which pitcher does he push, for example? I also guessed out loud that Hatchet was not exactly a disinterested party. Hatchet argued that he *was* interested and I should keep my fuckin' mouth shut. Hatchet's idea of retaliation these days is to spit tobacco juice in my direction and give me the finger.

I grab an emery board for my fingernails and head back to my locker. Foster's voice is still in my head.

" 'tsup?" says Jerome Davis, a chess fanatic who's setting up a chess-board in front of my locker. I taught Jerome how to play last year at Des Moines when he was a twenty-year-old rookie shortstop. I needed a partner, so I told Jerome that 92 percent of all big leaguers played chess and it would help him to fit in if he learned the game. Of course, nobody else plays chess, which explains why Jerome has been camped out in front of my locker every day since I got called up.

"Choose," says Jerome, extending two black fists.

I slap Jerome's left one, which contains a white pawn.

"Looks like I get the good guys again." I laugh.

I notice a phone message in my locker. Marty wants me to leave an extra ticket, if possible, and call him back only if I can't.

"What are you waiting for?" I ask.

"White goes first, big guy," says Jerome, chuckling to himself. "This is going to be easy."

I move a pawn as a large shadow falls across the board.

"Hey, you two," says veteran outfielder Leon Banks in a super-friendly tone of voice. "Leon needs tickets today. Got everybody coming, agents, lawyers, women, lots of women. Whaddya say?"

"I need two for friends and I promised my other two to Sandberg," says Jerome.

"Sandberg?" whines Banks, squinting his eyes in disbelief. "You got tickets, baby, you gotta save 'em for the brothers. You 'stand what I'm sayin'?"

"All that money you got," says Jerome, studying the board, "you should be *buying* seats."

Jerome is referring to Banks's $28.5-million contract, which he happily signed a few years ago, but which no longer meets the needs and desires of Leon and his entourage.

"What about you, Ward?" asks Banks, who is looking at Jerome like he was vermin.

"Sorry," I say, "I need mine for family and friends."

"Listen to these rookies," says Banks, moping back to his locker, his arms flailing wildly in the air. "Haven't even been here long enough to *make* friends. I'll be remembering this. Shiiiit, man."

Between chess moves, I work on my fingernails with the emery board. Your nails have to be just the right length to throw a knuckleball. Too long and they bend when you press your fingertips into the ball. Too short and your fingertips roll. One time I filed jagged edges into my fingernails, like teeth in a saw, to see if the little points would dig into the leather. But they kept breaking off. And they weren't too popular in bed, either.

The locker room is filling up. The guys are a little more wired than usual, anticipating the one game that means everything. The murmur of voices is punctuated by loud cackles of nervous laughter. And complaints! The sanis have holes, it's too fuckin' hot, a bat is too light, the coffee's too weak, and who's got the *mother*fuckin' toilet paper!

Definitely sounds like the guys are ready.

Jerome moves a knight as another shadow appears. This time it's the pitching coach.

"What the hell is this?" asks Brad Gilson. These are the first words he's spoken to me since I was called up, if you don't count "Get your ass over here" and "Eight more laps."

"I thought a game of chess might relax me."

"You don't want to be too fuckin' relaxed out there," says Gilson. "Those Phillies aren't going to relax."

Jerome rolls his eyes up into his head and carefully places the board on a shelf inside my locker.

"We'll finish this later," says Jerome. "And don't be messing with the board. I got every piece memorized."

Gilson sits on Jerome's vacated stool.

"We got the boss coming down today," says Gilson. "And I know he don't want his pitchers playing any goddamn board games."

The boss is William Mulcahy, Jr. I don't know much about Mulcahy except that he likes to bring his friends down into the clubhouse to examine the specimens.

"Everybody knows they got a good-hitting ball club," says Gilson. "But I got a little piece of advice for you."

He leans in close and lowers his voice.

"They got some black guys and some Latins that don't like that ball up in here." Gilson points to his throat.

I've heard this a lot in baseball. Gilson likes pitchers to use fear as a weapon because that's the kind of pitcher he was. Gilson's about 6'3", a square-jawed, lumberjack-looking guy with a vein in his neck that swells up whenever he's angry. He was famous for knocking guys down, then striking them out.

"Even your 80-mile-an-hour fastball can hurt somebody," says Gilson. "The problem with some of you guys today, you don't have the guts to come inside."

"Come inside" is code for intimidation. I could never pitch that way. One time I accidentally broke a guy's wrist with an inside fastball and I ran up to see if he was okay. This was considered stupid on my part because I missed a chance to "send a message."

Using fear is bullshit.

"To me, guts would be meeting the hitters in the parking lot after the game," I say, "and let them throw balls under *your* chin."

Gilson's eyes flash. The vein throbs.

"Well," he says. "You just better do the fucking job out there." And he gets up and walks away,

Now I feel sick. What the hell did I just do? Why did I have to confront him like that? Why didn't I just say okay, and then not do it? Maybe my dad is right. I don't know when to keep my mouth shut. Now I'm wondering if Gilson will go tell Bateman I don't have what it takes to pitch in a big game. I pop a couple of papaya tablets.

But I can't be thinking about this. I have to pitch my game. And I don't want them to be afraid. Just the opposite. I want them cocky and free-swinging. Let them get *themselves* out. Besides, what if I hit somebody and he doesn't go down? It could be embarrassing. Especially if he doesn't even rub it.

I just remember that I have to leave tickets, so I go over to the pass list and leave three for Marty and one for Susan somebody. I still can't think of her last name, so I just scribble a name, like a doctor writing a prescription, figuring they'll give it to anyone named Susan who asks for a ticket left by Sam Ward.

Now I get dressed to go out for batting practice. I pull on my white pinstriped Chicago Cubs uniform shirt. The tag in the collar has somebody else's name crossed out, but it's a big league shirt and it feels good. I lean back on my stool and put both legs into my uniform pants at the same time. I always put my uniform pants on like this. It makes a liar out of anyone who says "He puts his pants on one leg at a time just like everybody else."

I stick my feet into practically new spikes. I grab my hat, walk over to the mirror, and check myself out. I smile, and cock my hat at just the right angle. I sure *look* like I have a good fastball.

My spikes crunch on the cement floor of the tunnel that leads to the field. The tunnel is lit every ten feet or so by lightbulbs glowing behind banged-up wire-mesh covers that are encrusted with repeated coatings of blue enamel paint. A few bulbs are missing where the wire mesh has been smashed flat against the cement wall, victims of a swung bat, a slammed glove, or a thrown catcher's mask. Or a fist.

The sharp crack of wood on a new leather ball gets my blood pumping as I enter the dugout. Leon Banks is in the batting cage launching shots into the bleachers. Rawley Alexander is pitching batting practice.

Here comes Bateman, a stuffed sausage in double knits, smoothing non-existent hair as he puts on his hat. I haven't seen him since last night at the hotel. He looks like he's been up all night.

"How you feeling today, son?" he asks, staring at a piece of paper as he walks. Then, before I can say anything, he says, "Fine, fine. That's fine." And he keeps walking.

I decide to loosen up with a few sprints along the outfield wall. I can't stand to sit around and do nothing before a game, like a lot of pitchers. As I walk between sprints to catch my breath, I check out the wall. I'm always checking out walls now. Even brick walls like this look good, although I figure they cheated by using cement. I'd never put ivy on my wall, though. It would hide the beauty of the stones.

My running has attracted Gilson's attention. He's standing in the outfield with Foster and some of the veteran pitchers. They look at me and shake their heads. They probably think I should be sitting in my locker, resting. Or eating rusty nails. It looks like they're laughing.

An old feeling comes up from the depths of my soul. A feeling I get from time to time. That maybe I really *am* weird. Why can't I be like other people? Why do I have to play chess, for example? Is it really more fun than poker or am I just trying to be different? Why keep a juicer in the locker room? What's wrong with beer and soda? And there are other things, too. Like the petitions I've signed, and an incident once in a clubhouse with President Nixon, of all people.

But here's the irony. Baseball people think I'm strange because I'm not like them, and my family thinks I'm strange for being like baseball people. I can't win.

Except I *have* won at a very high level. Just not in the big leagues. The problem is, anywhere but the big leagues is nowhere.

"Hey, Ward," hollers Bobby Rapp, "you gonna hit?"

Holy shit! I'm supposed to be taking batting practice. I'm so used to hitting early with the Scrubeenies, I almost forgot. I run across the field, wondering if Gilson is still watching.

Mark Grace, Rick Wilkins, and Leon Banks are standing around the batting cage watching Willie Wilson spray line drives all over the joint. They're laughing and having some kind of hitting contest.

"Watch me now," says Wilson, waving his bat back and forth over the plate. "I'm going deepish right here. Y'all better be careful."

"Swing hard, just in case you hit it," cracks Wilkins.

Wilson lines a cannon shot to center field.

"Damn," he says to himself. "Don't *hit* it so hard!"

Now Banks jumps in, cocking his bat high over his head. He drills the first pitch down the left-field line.

"That's a *damn* shame," says Banks, admiring his hit. "Hurt your back trying to follow that motherfucker."

Banks hits another rope. Jeez, these guys can hit! You don't realize the power of a big league hitter until you get up close. That ball *jumps* off the bat. This is not a good thing for pitchers to be watching just before a game.

Wilkins, who'll be catching me today, walks over. At 6'2", 215 pounds, he looks more like the linebacker he was at Furman University. Wilkins has an open, friendly face that makes him appear much younger than his twenty-six years. A kid's face, really. Like an enormous Little Leaguer. And he has this sly grin, like he knows something you don't.

"Gonna get you a bunch of runs today," he says, planting a seed of optimism he hopes will bear fruit in a few hours. "Give you something to work with out there."

"If I get more than fifteen," I say, "I should be okay."

"Hell, don't worry about these sonsabitches," says Wilkins, laughing. "They're not *that* fuckin' good."

"Just don't be throwing no fastballs to Matthews," says Banks, aiming down the barrel of his bat like it was a rifle. "He will definitely waste that motherfucker."

Mark Matthews is the Phillies' big home run hitter. He's one of these guys who likes to stand at home plate and gaze at the majesty of his blast for a few minutes before trotting ever so slowly around the bases. He's got 49 and would like to finish the season with 50. Personally, I think 49 is plenty.

"He *will* hit the fastball," says Grace, joining in.

"Don't worry," I say to Wilkins. "I don't throw any fastballs. It'll be mostly knuckleballs. You caught many knucklers?"

"Is that the one that jumps all around?" asks Wilkins, having a little fun. "Hell, yeah," he says. "I've caught plenty of them. No problem."

Wilkins jumps in the cage and belts the first pitch off the wall in right. Hey, these guys are gonna score some runs. Their optimism cancels out Gilson. My mind considers all the possibilities, up to and including a 15-to-0 no-hitter.

I slide a weighted donut over a bat handle and take a few practice swings. I'm not a great hitter, but I can do what pitchers are supposed to do. I can bunt, and ground to the right side, moving a runner to third. And I love the bunt and slash: square away like you're going to bunt, and when the fielders charge, take a short swing and drive it past them. Any grounder is likely to be a hit because the fielders are out of position. But I'm not going to practice the bunt and slash today. A coach for the Phillies is sitting over there in the dugout right now watching every move we make.

I lay down eight good bunts, take a few swings, and head for the dugout. It's 12:15. An hour and forty-five minutes to go. And counting. I sit on the bench and grab a towel.

And here comes trouble. With a chaw of tobacco in its mouth.

"You know who should be catching today, don't you?" says Buddy Ray Hatchet, jamming his fingers into his mouth and pulling out a large slimy brown wad.

Not you, I think to myself.

"Nobody knows you better than me," says Hatchet. "I been catching your shit all summer."

Hatchet throws the disgusting wad against the blue cement wall, the dark brown juice splattering on the water cooler.

"You gotta tell Bateman I should catch," says Hatchet, stuffing a fresh chaw into his face. "They'll do it if you say something."

"That's ridiculous," I say. "Wilkins is the best catcher in the league. He knows the charts on all these guys, he's a great hitter, and he's caught plenty of knuckleballs."

Hatchet shifts the wad from one cheek to the other.

"Oh, yeah?" he says, unleashing a brown stream onto my spikes. "If he caught so many knucklers, how come he has to borrow my glove?"

Then he gives me his trademark finger and walks away.

Umpire's Locker Room

10:45 AM

They build palaces for kings to dignify royalty, but they make umpires dress in dingy holes, which tells you something else. For more
years than I care to remember, I dressed in dank rat-ridden shithouses that
insult the nose and rot the flesh. But I can tell you, pal, no matter what, I
always walked on the field looking like a prince. Black shoes shined, pants
pressed to a sharp crease, clean shirt right out from under the iron. In my
kit were all the tools to make it so. Once, needing a shave after a long car
ride, I had to collect water from a rain puddle. Other times, there was no
locker room at all, and I'd shave and dress in the car. If you had to scrounge
to look right, so much the better for satisfying your pride.

At Wrigley Field, an umpire can dress in relative splendor. There's carpeting, comfortable chairs, pleasant lighting, plenty of space. The facilities
are excellent. It's still hours before game time and I'm alone. On this day,
I need the solace of the locker room. I'm hoping it will swallow up the
fucking echo from the skinny sonovabitch in the dark suit and jelly-jar
glasses:

"Have a nice day, Mr. K.," he'd said. Have a nice day or you'll never have another.

It's like Al Capone telling the doctor "Cure my syphilis or you die!" and in those days, there was no penicillin. And now, where is the umpire's manual on *How to Fix a Ball Game Without Getting Caught*?

You'd think, after forty years in blue, I'd have all those answers. You'd think, what's the big deal? You'd think, with that sack full of money and the promise of doubling it, I'd be a bundle of smiles.

Okay, okay, I tell myself I can handle this. I won't get caught. The perfect crime is when no one even knows there's been a crime. In my head, I begin to write the manual:

1. Balls and strikes. On average, there are 288 pitches in a nine-inning game. Breaking balls stretch the size of the plate. I've got to stretch it for the Phillies' pitcher and squeeze it for the Cubs'. I've got to pick my spots. Whenever possible, work the first pitch to my needs. Balls on Phillies' hitters, strikes on the Cubs'. Be extra cautious on full count, that's the call that brings Bateman out screaming.

2. Should I throw out Bateman? Throw out a hot hitter? Not if I can help it. It's counterproductive. It's dangerous. It could be a move that tips my hand. I've got to do everything I can to avoid suspicion. But I *could* throw out the Phillies' skipper!

3. Balks: Jesus H. Christ, be careful with balks. Use only if necessary. Still, it may be the best weapon I've got in a tight situation.

4. The rules of baseball: I'm umpire-in-chief, the last word on any controversy over what happens on the field, on the bases, in the stands. In a rundown, did a runner go out of the base path to avoid being tagged? Did he interfere with a throw? Did a runner leave too soon on a tag up? Did a fielder illegally block a runner or vice versa?

5. Close plays at the plate, especially on collisions: there's always a cloud of dust to make it a tough call. Be prepared to make the call the way I need to make it. I can make or break a game on a collision play. Remember, it's not what you see, it's the way you think!

6. Spectator interference: Rule 3.16. "Spectator interference occurs when a spectator reaches out of the stands, or goes on the playing field, and touches a live ball." These are Cubs fans. God knows, they're crazy enough to try anything. "If spectator interference clearly prevents a fielder from catching a fly ball, the umpire shall declare the batter out."

Okay, be alert, think. *Anticipate!*

Finally, I assemble my gear. The man behind the plate goes at this the way a knight puts on his armor. Metal cup to cover my vitals. Long underwear to absorb sweat to keep the blue suit from showing any. Knee-high woolen socks to protect my legs from the rubbing of heavy-duty plastic shin guards. My shoes are black steel-plated square-toed oxfords with dull-tipped spikes; the long steel tongue extends from the toes to the laces, then up the ankles to the shin guards. The chest protector fits snugly under the jacket. So will heavy-duty plastic shoulder pads and straps. Then there's the blue cap that fits tight on my head because it's not supposed to come off, whatever I do with the mask. In my jacket, there's the balls, strikes, outs indicator on which I register every pitch, every out. Calling first base yesterday, only the cap was the same.

Then I think, what if the Cubs start beating the hell out of the ball? What if the Phillies blow a few routine plays in the field? It could happen; I can't control everything. If it's a one-run game, I'll be in control. If not, the important thing is to hold that line if possible, not to quit on it, try to pull it back a little at a time. Like they say, it ain't over till you hear the fat lady sing.

I'm given five dozen new shining white baseballs, still in tissues. They have to be rubbed up before the game. Here in the umpire's room is a three-pound coffee can with special mud collected from the Delaware River basin with just the right texture to take the sheen off the surface of the cowhide. You dip two fingers in the can, smear it on, then rub with both hands. This time I stop at the first feel of the ball. My hand tightens on the surface, fingers find the seams like they were made for each other. With a baseball in hand, a power surges through me. It's a mystical reaction. No matter that I can't throw hard, I imagine that I can. In my head I can throw it through the wall of a house. There's no ball like it. It's a perfect missile. The 108 hand-stitched seams make the difference, turning S-like around the surface in a wonderful symmetry, raised just enough to give the fingers a proper grasp for the throw, it doesn't matter how they grab it. I close my eyes to feed this caress with my memories. I'm not a sentimental type, but today I can't resist it. When you're sixty, whoever you are, you have memories; you're a fool if you live them, but you're nothing if you throw them all away.

Me, I started life with a baseball in my hand. When I was a kid, nothing else mattered. I remember my father most because he was the first one to see the way I handled myself. I had quick feet and sure hands. It was like I was born to wear an infielder's glove. When I was eighteen, I signed with the New York Yankees for a $7,500 bonus. I might've gotten more from Philadelphia, but I cared less about the money; my dream had me playing for the Yankees. In 1951, my first year as a pro, I hit .362 in the rookie league in Florida. Next winter, they asked me to come to spring training at Fort Lauderdale for a good hard look-see, but I never got there. There was no look-see and I never played baseball again.

I've been an umpire all my adult life. I think now I'd most likely have become one even if I'd made it as a player so I could stay in the game. Some umpires played ball, most didn't. Those who didn't, say it doesn't matter. Baseball writers say the same thing. I say, bullshit. They teach the trade at umpire's school, but anyone is eligible. I say, every man applying should've at least played in high school; he shouldn't be accepted without a coach's recommendation. No matter how good the training, the standards would be a lot higher if the trainees had played the game. Sure, you might lose some good umpires along the way, but you'd eliminate some of the sucks like Sirotta.

Put it this way: in my first pro season umpiring in the Class D Florida State League, I was calling them at first base. With two out, a rookie slapped a frozen rope to left center and rounded first, hustling to make it to second. But the big first baseman made the kid run around him; he didn't move out of the way. It didn't matter if it was unintentional, he obstructed the runner. I saw it because that had happened to me more than once when I played. It's against the rules. The base paths belong to the runner. Rule 7.06. But umpires never call it unless there's contact.

The kid was thrown out at second, but my call nullified the play. A few innings later, the first baseman confessed he'd been doing it deliberately, and he always got away with it. "Were you a ballplayer?" he asked me.

A moment like that, I never forgot it. The satisfaction is knowing what has to be done, then doing it right no matter what. Umpiring is a religion. The blue suit is like the turned-around collar and you're always dealing with sinners. Baseball is the only game where managers can come out on the field to humiliate you. It's the only game where the fans believe in their right to abuse you. One old ballplayer put it this way: "My favorite umpire is a dead one." Umpires like to say that good umpires are born, not made. If so, they're born biting the obstetrician's finger.

Thirty-eight years, it was never a picnic, but then, I never liked picnics. I'd rather ward off a spray of tobacco juice than a horde of ants. Thirty-eight years, I never wanted to be anywhere else.

Except today. Maybe 5,000 times before games, wherever I was, I felt my blood stirring, from beat-up bandboxes to spick-and-span superdomes, it was always the same thrill. Today, it's upside down. I've got a whole new fear crawling all over me. Suddenly it's not the right-or-wrong business or even the possibility of failing that scares me. Suddenly I'm hit by a fear of getting caught.

It could happen. A couple of days from now, someone might hear a rumor out of Vegas. Someone who lost a bundle. The game tapes could be reviewed, all those fucking camera angles, Jesus, I'll bet they save them all. They could compare the way I called this game with past games to analyze my strike zone. If it's Foster on the mound for the Cubs, he'd be the first to sense the bad calls against him. Or Wilkins, the catcher. If I make it too tough on Cubs hitters, if they get a couple of veterans to review the tapes, pitch by pitch, wouldn't that help put the mark on me?

Okay, okay, I've got to have just the right feel. Everybody knows umpires have good days and bad days—just like ballplayers, just like managers, just like maybe God Himself. I can rely on that. I can cover my ass with it, call a few bad ones against the Phillies, too. Umpires aren't perfect. One umpire in the crooked 1919 World Series, Billy Evans, said he must be a big dope because "that series looked all right to me."

I hear the door open and there is Lew Sirotta staring at me, shaking his head with mock disgust.

"Terrible," he moans.

"I've seen worse," Mountain sighs.

I get it, it's their act for the day. Okay, I look like shit. They know about my binge last night, so they're having their little joke.

"He won't be able to see." Sirotta is talking behind my front. "He'll invent a whole new strike zone. Ankles to eyeballs. The pitchers will kiss him on the way to the dugout."

"It'll be the fastest game in history!"

Sirotta tosses me a book of matches. "They'll hold your eyes open, Ernie," he says.

More jokes. I pocket the matches. You never know when you might want to set Sirotta's clothes on fire. I go back to rubbing baseballs when Roy Luger marches in, singing as usual:

"Take me out to the brawl game,
Put my ass on the line,
Eyeball the corners on every pitch,
Whatever I call I'm a sonovabitch!
So it's hoot hoot hoot at the umpires,
If they survive it's a shame,
For it's one-two-three calls you're dead
At the old ball game."

Then he comes over to greet me. After all, we haven't seen each other since yesterday afternoon.

"Have a nice day, Ernie," he says with a twinkle in his eye.

What the hell is that supposed to mean?

Pregame Meeting

12:40 PM

After batting practice we come back into the clubhouse. There's a big commotion across the room. I see people with tape recorders, notepads, and TV cameras. It looks like a press conference for the Persian Gulf War. But I don't see any generals.

Someone points in my direction. Suddenly the cameras swing around, bright lights glare, and the cameramen start walking toward me in a crouch. As I get closer, they crouch backward. The group, like some giant organism, is talking all at once.

"Sam, Sam, over here, Sam. We need a few words, Sam."

A path opens as I arrive at my locker. It's a motley crew with one thing in common: blue press passes in plastic holders pinned to their clothes. The jostling crowd blocks nearby lockers. I'm worried about what my teammates are thinking.

"Hey, fuck, man," grouses Leon Banks. "Somebody get these mother-fuckers the fuck out of here." The group pays no attention.

"Jerry Holtzman with the *Tribune,*" says a dapper-looking guy in a sport coat and tie. "A win today gives the Cubs a shot at their first league championship since 1945 and their first world championship in 85 years. Does this add to the pressure?"

"Now that you mention it," I say.

Some guy wearing a helmet of blond hair snaps his fingers and a TV cameraman shines a light on him.

"Are you aware," says the guy in the blond helmet, "of the controversy among your teammates over your selection?"

"I know the vote was close with a few abstentions," I say.

A few reporters smile.

"Apparently," says another guy, "the Cubs tried to trade for Doug Drabek, but the Mets claimed him on waivers."

"Tough break for Doug," I say.

Everybody laughs.

While I'm talking, the TV cameraman shoots the nameplate above the locker next to mine ... then he pans over to my name written with Magic Marker on a piece of adhesive tape.

"Mr. Ward," says a kid who looks like he's still in high school. "How much money did you make this year? And how does it feel to pitch against players making $3 million?"

"I keep my salary private to avoid embarrassment," I say. "And I don't care what anybody else makes."

"Do you think today's ballplayers are overpaid?" asks a young lady in a purple pantsuit.

"They make less money than a lot of corporate executives," I say. "And they didn't lay anybody off."

More smiles.

"Didn't you sign a gay rights petition a few years back in Oklahoma City?" asks a guy with a tape recorder. "What was that all about?"

"Simple fairness," I say.

This was an antidiscrimination statement I signed that got printed in the local newspaper. I remember that the general manager said he wouldn't let it affect his opinion of me. Then he gave me a single room on road trips.

"How will your belief in God strengthen you today?" asks some fellow with a tremendously earnest smile.

"Uh ..." I say, stalling for another question. "To tell you the truth, uh ... I'm not that sure about, uh ..." A newspaper headline pops into my mind: CUBS PITCHER TO GOD: TAKE A HIKE.

"Did you do anything special to relax for this game?" asks the purple pantsuit. Another headline comes to mind: ROOKIE JERKS OFF BEFORE BIG GAME.

"Sam," says Blond Helmet, snapping his fingers to turn on the light. "What are you thinking right now?"

Right now I'm thinking I have to fart, but if I do, it'll be on the six o'clock news. Highlights at eleven.

"I'm trying to stay focused on the game," I say.

Suddenly I hear a loud banging noise like someone is pounding a baseball bat on a table.

"Meeting, gentlemen," growls Bobby Rapp in his best Marine sergeant voice. "Everybody out. That means you!"

Put me down as a member of the Bobby Rapp fan club.

The players are all sitting in front of their lockers waiting for the team meeting. A few reporters try to ask "just one more question," but the bat continues banging on the table, and it's all over. The group gathers up its paraphernalia and heads for the door, filing past the players like lepers through a marketplace.

"Did you see that pecker-checker in the purple pantsuit?" says one of the guys.

"All right, listen up!" says Rapp, introducing manager Vern Bateman with a wave of his fungo bat.

Bateman puts one foot up on a bench at a table in the middle of the room. He has a piece of paper in one hand and he scratches the top of his mottled head with the bill of his cap in the other. He looks extremely tired.

"Let's talk about the signs," says Bateman, his eyes closing at some horrible thought.

"Now, goddamnit," he says, "everybody's getting our signs except us. They pitched out three times yesterday and caught two guys stealing. They would have caught three, but *our guy* missed the sign! *That* confused the hell out of them."

The players are trying to keep from smiling. Some of them look down at the floor. I get the feeling that most of the guys really like Bateman, even though they imitate the way he stands and picks his nose with his thumb during a game.

"So we're going with new signs today, boys," he says hopefully. "And we're going to make it real simple so nobody forgets."

Bateman nods toward Bobby Rapp, who steps forward and takes a feet-apart, hands-on-hips, third-base-coach's stance.

"First sign, hit and run, is the *hat*," says Bateman. "Anywhere on the hat."

Rapp reaches up with his right hand and grips the bill of his hat. Then he alternates, reaching up with his left hand to touch the back of his hat.

"*Hat, hit* and run," says Bateman. "*H huuuh.* Go by the sound."

"Bunt is the *belt*," says Bateman, pleased at the beauty of his system. "*Belt, bunt. Buuu* sound."

Rapp hitches up his pants by tugging at his belt.

A few players try to stifle grins. Most, however, nod to each other at the sheer brilliance of it all.

"Hey, Vern," interrupts first baseman Mark Grace. "Let me guess. The take sign. *Testicles?*"

Everybody laughs.

"No sense having a take sign," says Bateman. "All you guys do is swing, anyway. Some of you got *contracts* saying you don't have to take. So just use your fuckin' heads up there."

Everybody looks over at Leon Banks, who feigns indifference.

"The last sign is the *steal*," says Bateman. "*Skin* on skin. Anywhere skin touches skin. *Skin, steal. Sssss.*"

Bobby Rapp touches his right forearm with his left hand, then his right cheek with his right index finger.

"Anywhere on the body," says Bateman. "If Rapp pulls out his pecker, you better be running."

"But Vern," says third baseman Steve Buechele, "if Rapp pulls out his pecker, nobody's gonna *see* it."

This gets a big laugh from everybody, including Bateman and the coaches. Even Rapp is laughing. And you can see him straining for a comeback, but he can't locate one.

"Got it?" says Bateman. "*Hat;* hit and run. *Belt;* bunt. *Skin;* steal. As always, it'll be the first sign after the indicator, which will be either hand across the letters. We may change the indicator during the game. Just check before you go up there. Any questions?"

"On that steal sign," says Leon Banks, "what if Rapp claps his hands?"

The players enjoy this question immensely. They all lean forward on their stools to hear the answer. Bateman takes off his hat, puts his hands on his hips, and smiles at Banks.

"Well," says Bateman, in a perfect imitation of Oliver Hardy, "when you clap your hands, does your skin touch?"

Banks pauses to consider the question.

"Not if I'm wearing batting gloves," he says.

The room explodes in laughter. Bateman shakes his head and smiles.

"And one more thing, boys," says Bateman above the noise. "Looks like we got Kolacka behind the plate today. You all know him. Low-ball umpire. Don't give him any bullshit."

Kolacka? I remember that name from somewhere. Spring training, maybe? I get a strange feeling in my stomach.

"Give 'em hell, boys," hollers Bateman. "We come this far; let's go all the way."

Hands clap, half a dozen stereos begin blasting, fists pound into gloves, water starts running in a sink, and somebody hollers, "Let's kick ass today!"

It's 1:10. Fifty minutes until game time. And here comes Jerome. He's cranking a fist in the air, one of his many gestures, which include a double-clutch forearm handshake that I have yet to master. He's smiling and pointing at something in my locker.

"Got plenty of time," he says.

Jerome wants to finish our chess game, in which he's considerably ahead. He senses a quick kill. Talk about mean.

"No way, Jerome," I say. "I have to warm up pretty soon. Let's forget this game and call it a draw."

"Your mama, too," says Jerome.

Suddenly the room gets quiet. William Mulcahy, Jr., has just walked in the door. Bateman comes back out of his office tucking in his shirt and zipping up his fly. Players straggle back from the trainer's room, toilets, and the players' lounge.

Mulcahy's about 6'2", with brown hair combed in a neat little wave above his well-tanned forehead. He's wearing green slacks with a shirt and tie under a blue nylon Cubs warm-up jacket. He picks up a bat and grips the handle like he's checking the weight.

"As you know, gentlemen, this is not my first time in a clubhouse," says Mulcahy, adjusting his crotch. "I know what it's all about because I ran track in college. I, too, have worn the jockstrap."

The players smile and shake their heads. Bateman looks over at the coaches and winks.

"And I know what it takes to be a winner," says Mulcahy, gesturing with the bat. "You gotta go after it! Just having a good year is not enough. I promised our fans a winner and I'm paying you fellows a lot of money to deliver on that promise."

The players are not smiling anymore.

"It's nut-cracking time, boys," says Mulcahy. "We're gonna find out who's got 'em and who doesn't. And we got Stan pitching his first game today and we'll learn a few things about him, too."

Some of the players smile and shake their heads. Jerome slaps my leg with the back of his hand. "*Do it,* Stan!" he says.

"You can laugh if you want to," says Mulcahy. "But you each have a responsibility to conduct yourselves as professionals. And by the way, whoever wrote 'Best Fucking Wishes' on that autographed ball for my wife should be man enough to admit it."

The players grin and point accusing fingers at each other. Bateman looks at his watch.

"In closing, gentlemen," says William Mulcahy, Jr., "I just want to remind you that when you're making the kind of money you're making . . . you gotta produce. That's the bottom line. Now go get 'em!"

Mulcahy raises the bat in the air triumphantly and strides out of the clubhouse.

As soon as the door closes, the players start laughing and hollering.

"Hey, Vern," shouts Mark Grace. "Stop that guy. He just stole one of our bats."

Bateman holds up his hand and tries to say something as Rapp bangs on the table again with his fungo bat.

"Listen up!" hollers Rapp, trying to quiet everyone down.

Bateman moves to the center of the room. And he doesn't look too happy.

"What you just heard," says Bateman, speaking very slowly, "is a bunch of horseshit! ... it's an insult to your intelligence and your character ... you're not here to keep an owner's promise ... you're here to try and win a ball game for each other ... for your own pride ... and whatever personal reasons you might have ... and I'm proud of every one of you ... that's it."

The players cheer and clap their hands.

But I'm still thinking about Kolacka. Was it during the off-season? At a luncheon of some kind?

Sports awards dinner!

Uh-oh.

Umpire's Locker Room

1:35 PM

I have only three more new baseballs to rub up. I grab one of them with my right hand while my left digs into the bottom of the can for that Delaware mud. There'll be just enough. Everything is coming to an end.

It's getting late, but I take my time about it; I don't want it to end. I'd like it if someone put another new box on the table. I want the can filled with a fresh batch of mud. I want to rub baseballs forever.

Now there's only one left peeking out of the clean white tissue. It's just another baseball, but my eyes fasten on it like it's extra special. I've got to really see it so I can remember every stitch, every letter of the official National League logo, the way the light bounces off the shiny cowhide. All the balls are in the big bag but this one. One more and it's turn out the lights, the party's over.

All of a sudden, there's a hand on it. I look up to see Lew Sirotta.

"I'll take that, Ernie." He's smiling. "If you don't mind, I want to save it."

Sure, a compliment. He wants to save the last ball of my last game. Maybe he thinks it'll be worth something. He's always looking for an angle. He's got eyes dedicated to finding angles.

I want to protest. Maybe I want that baseball for myself. But he's got it, all right, and he's the crew chief. If he can steal a dozen, he sure as hell can take one. He steals baseballs the way a cook steals beef. Sometimes he'll walk out with his bag so loaded he can barely lift it. He thinks it's his right. It's the way he lives. Everything about him makes me think of a scumbag. Watch him suck up to the big league stars at the home ballparks. When they steal second, he's so eager to call them safe he can barely keep his arms from spreading until the throw gets there. Then he'll punch out a journeyman with such flair, his penguin body will leap six inches off the ground.

Above all, he was a scab.

We were at spring training in Florida, 1979. Sirotta and I were Triple A umpires. I was ten years older with twenty-four years' minor league experience, years past when I should've gotten the big league call. The major league umpires were organizing under Richie Phillips the way the ballplayers did under Marvin Miller. Sick of lousy pay (average salary $17,500) and feeble pension plans, no vacations, no redress from the league officials who owned their contracts. On March 30, a week before opening day, all fifty went out on strike.

It was something, all right. The season was about to begin. The big leagues started to recruit college umpires, local minor league umpires, whatever retired umpires they could find. Above all, they needed experienced working professionals who could call a game properly and knew how to control it. AAA umpires were the best alternatives. I was on the top of the wanted list of replacement umpires.

So here was my chance. The National League offered me a contract at $22,500, more money than most strikers had made the previous year. I was guaranteed a job for the full season, even if and when the strike was settled. They even promised me a continuing major league contract in coming years.

"At last, at last!" Enid cried out. I never saw her so happy. She even arranged a surprise party for me to celebrate the promotion. My kids were there with their families, the usual spring in Fort Lauderdale.

Surprise! Surprise!

But I'd turned it down.

She didn't understand. She tried to, but it didn't happen.

"I won't scab, Enid."

"What's that supposed to mean?" She wanted it all laid out for her. I explained as best I could. Because big league umpires got screwed, they were striking for a better deal. If they win, sooner or later minor league umpires would benefit, too. But if I scab, I'd be making it rougher to win the strike. I'd be helping the league officials to maintain their greed. I'd be working for the same sonovabitches who'd fucked me over for years.

"But now they're bringing you up!" she argued. "Now they're doing what you've always wanted them to!"

Sure, that was the irony part. They chose me because I was the best they could turn to. They'd kept me in the minors as a lesson to any umpire who thought he could defy them. They fuck you, then they suck you. Always they think they can't lose.

"Enid, I'm sorry. No matter how much I want this to happen, I can't do it this way."

"What's it going to get you? What?"

"I don't know. In the end, something."

"The end? What's the end? What are you, a young kid with a future? Ernie, you're forty-three years old!"

How to answer that? She was forty-three, too. All these years, she'd suffered in her way because of what I was. She had waited for the big league offers just as much as I had. She could have laid *that* on me with a vengeance, but she didn't. She could have spelled it out how I cared only about myself, I had to do things my way, I hadn't even discussed this offer with her, had I?

I knew why I hadn't, and that's what hurt the most. It was because I *knew* what she'd say. That's what chopped me up the most. It set us apart on a principle that went beyond the paycheck and the status and all the other goodies. For maybe the first time in my life I was part of something bigger than I was, something that mattered to the way things were. I mean, I would rather eat more years of minor league shit than scab for what I wanted to be. With Enid, I guess what I wanted was that she'd share that with me. Maybe I even hoped she would be proud of me for it.

Sitting at the party was my twenty-three-year-old son, Joe, his pink-faced kids on his lap, my grandchildren. Jesus, I hardly knew them.

"I'll tell you something, Dad: you sure can turn a surprise party into a downer."

"You got something to say about it, Joe? Like what do you think? What?" I really wanted to know.

"It's about family values, Dad. You don't understand about family values. You never did."

When he was a kid, I wasn't around to play ball with him. I never knew what to say to him. I'd come home, I'd feel like a fish out of water. The kids used to call me "Semi-Dad." when they grew up, the way I spent my life, they thought I was a "Semi-Jerk."

Hit a crisis like this, all the pigeons come home to roost. Before you can turn around, you're covered with pigeon shit.

"What do I think, Dad? You blew it, that's what I think."

His wife, Nicole, came from the kitchen with cookies for the kids. She was all smiles. She was always all smiles. In a week or so, they'd go back to Richmond, Virginia, to his car wash.

As for the strike, I went the whole way. I started calling other AAA umpires advising them not to scab—including Sirotta, since he, too, had been offered a scab contract. "If you accept, you'll be hurting the best thing umpires ever tried to accomplish!"

"If I don't do it, they'll get someone else," he replied.

God, how I hated *that* argument. Of all the excuses made by man, it was among the sleaziest.

"Not so, Lew," I said. "They want only you. They've been waiting for the strike so they'll have an opening, just so they can hire you." Sarcasm worked like a thumb in his eye.

"Fuck you, Kolacka. You're an asshole who loves to make trouble."

"Make sure you tell them that when you sign up."

"Believe me, they know it."

He was right about that, anyway. Letters I wrote to minor league umpires found their way to major league officials. They knew about my phone calls. Every time I contacted an umpire, somebody immediately warned him off. Ernie Kolacka, Troublemaker.

When the dust settled, they got fifty replacements from all over. Nine from AAA leagues—including Lew Sirotta. The joke had it that he wanted to debate the matter with his conscience, but he didn't know where to find it. He told everyone he did it for the wife and kids.

Like they say, you win some and you lose some, and some get rained out.

I don't have to look to know that Sirotta is grinning at me.

"Hey, Ernie, you hear who's pitching for the Cubs?"

"Yeah, Elvis is back," I say. "He's spent the last dozen years in the Nether Leagues working on his moves."

"A rookie," he says. "A junkster named Sam Ward."

That lifts my head, all right.

"I know him," says Mountain. "Throws more shit than a racehorse."

Yeah, I know him, too. Maybe a half-dozen years ago, where was it? Fort Lauderdale, spring training? I was speaking at some luncheon on what it was like to be a big league umpire. And then he got up and shit all over me for what I said.

I know Ward, all right. *He's* pitching today? I can hardly keep from laughing.

"Hey, Ernie!" Mountain is grinning as he tosses me a protective cap.

"Shit, I'm covered!" I call back.

"With this guy pitching, I'd cover my asshole, too."

Too many jokes, too many threats, too many doubts. All of a sudden, I feel a queasiness coming on. It's time to put on my protective gear. Shin guards, chest protector, toe-plated shoes—then the blue pants and jacket to cover it all. I'm thinking, the last words he said to me this morning were "Have a good day, Mr. K." The four corniest words in American lingo. When you've got the shiv up a guy's crack, you can say anything you want. What the hell, he paid for the right to say it—plus all the threats that went with it, for that's the heart of the Golden Rule: when you've got the gold, you make the rule.

And when you take the gold, you better live by it.

They say about an umpire, when he starts calling them in the big leagues, he's got to be perfect ... and then he has to get better every year.

Now it's my last game, and for the life of me, I've got to be even better than that.

Amen, pal.

THE WARM-UP

1:35 PM

Rick Wilkins is sitting next to me in front of my locker. We've just gone over the hitters and now he's talking about the umpire.

"So Kolacka's working behind the plate," says Wilkins, who enjoys telling a good story. "And Barry Bonds takes a half chop, but Kolacka says 'no swing' and calls it ball one. I say, 'Ernie, he went too far, that's a strike.' So we go back and forth and I ask Kolacka to check it with the first-base ump, Art Williams, who's black. Williams signals no swing, and Kolacka laughs. 'Well,' he says, 'now you have it in black and white.'

"It's one of the few times I ever heard the guy laugh," says Wilkins. "Usually he's pretty serious, especially when he's behind the plate. They're all a little tense when they're working the dish."

The knot in my stomach just got tighter. I was hoping to hear that Kolacka's a fun guy with a great sense of humor.

And a short memory.

It happened at a sports dinner during the off-season about five years ago.

The Sportsman's Club in Aurora, Illinois. With an umpire and a local minor league pitcher sharing the dais, it was not exactly your social event of the year. But for Julie and me it was a free dinner and a good excuse to get a baby-sitter and have a night out.

It was your typical sports awards dinner. The Sportsman's Club is a non-descript cinder-block building with a forty-foot bar, pinball machines, and a moose head hanging on the wall. Head-table guests featured a high school football star, a wrestling coach, an ex-boxer, the mayor, a master of ceremonies, and a priest. There's always a priest. Plus the aforementioned representatives from the world of professional baseball.

The MC's job at a sports dinner is to be as insulting as possible without causing the priest to get too embarrassed. This requires frequent apologies to the priest, which are always accepted with a good-hearted laugh. The dirtier the joke, the funnier it has to be.

After the roast beef dinner, with the rubber ziti appetizer and the melted ice-cream parfait, the MC introduced the mayor. "They're making a movie about the mayor's greatest sexual exploits," said the MC. "It's called *Home Alone*." This got a big laugh from the audience and registered a 4.5 on the priest's chuckle meter. The MC then took a shot at the Chicago Cubs. "People are losing a lot of weight on the new Cubs Diet Plan," said the MC. "You only eat when they win."

Then it was time for Kolacka, "the best umpire money can buy." Of course, the crowd roared. But Kolacka didn't even smile, as I remember it. Instead, he got up to the podium and took his revenge by putting everybody to sleep. The best part was the ending, as Kolacka explained the three things an umpire must never do: (1) Never park your car in a space marked umpire. (2) Never wear glasses in public. (3) Never call a balk. This received a fair amount of applause, but it was hard to tell if it was in appreciation for the joke or an exit cue.

Finally it was my turn.

"This next fellow may be familiar," said the MC, "even though you've never heard of him. His specialty is getting cut two days after they take the team picture."

Julie winced and the audience laughed. With people getting up to go to the bathroom, scraping chairs, and looking at their watches, I needed something funny to grab their attention.

"Well," I said, smiling over at Kolacka. "Now we know there's a *fourth* thing umpires must never do. Never pick up a microphone."

This got a big laugh from everybody. Except for Kolacka, who just smiled a little and nodded his head.

Julie said it wasn't too smart of me to make fun of an umpire. But what the hell, I figured we were all getting roasted, what's one more joke?

"You never know," she said.

I tell the story to Wilkins to see what he thinks.

"Will it matter that I made that joke?" I ask him. "You think Kolacka will hold it against me?"

"Nah," says Wilkins, waving his hand. "Nothing to worry about. This is the best umpire in the league. I guarantee, if you make the pitches, you'll get the calls. Besides, he's heard worse than that over the years. Hell, he's an umpire!"

Of course. What the hell am I worried about? This guy's a major league umpire. It's the most important game of the year. He's going to be bearing down just like everybody else. My heartbeat returns to normal. I can breathe again.

"And I'll tell you another thing," says Wilkins. "That sonovabitch knows the rules. I remember a couple years ago, he was behind the plate and had to cover third when one of his crew was out sick. With a runner on first, the hitter singles to right and Kolacka runs down to third base, where he knows the runner from first will be sliding in. As Kolacka runs, an extra baseball pops out of the ball bag on his hip. Now the runner and the throw from right field arrive together in a cloud of dust, and the ball bounces away. 'Safe,' hollers Kolacka, and the runner gets up and heads for home. The third baseman sees the ball that fell out of Kolacka's bag, picks it up, and throws home, beating the runner by ten feet. 'Safe,' hollers Kolacka again because he knows it's the wrong ball. As the catcher starts to argue, he sees the *hitter* going to second base, so he fires the ball there and when the hitter gets tagged, the second-base ump calls him 'out' because he *doesn't* know it's the wrong ball. Now both managers are steaming onto the field."

"So what happened?" I ask.

"So Kolacka quotes the rule about extra balls coming onto the field. Word for word. By *heart*! Didn't even need the book."

Wilkins looks at the clock. It's 1:40.

"Time to go to work," he says, cracking his knuckles and slapping the back of his hand into the pocket of the big glove.

I feel that sweet ache in my lungs. It's warm-up time in the old corral. I reach for my glove and stick a nail file in my jacket pocket. I take the game ball out of my shoe. I put on my hat, and head for the door.

A dozen pairs of spikes clatter on the cement as we go through the tunnel. A few guys are still repeating lines from Mulcahy's speech. "I, too, have worn the jockstrap" is a big favorite.

My stomach is dangling at the top of the Ferris wheel, but that's where I want it. You need a certain amount of anxiety to fuel a good peformance. An actor without jitters will be flat. A lion tamer without fear is called lefty.

I jog to our bullpen down the left-field line. Gilson is waiting with his arms folded across his chest. Wilkins sets up behind home plate. I feel a charge as I rotate the ball in my hand, testing my different grips for each pitch. Middle and index fingers spread apart for the sinker, middle finger pressing against a seam for the curve, ball choked back in the palm of my hand for the change, the tips of four fingers digging in for the knuckler. Got to have the knuckler today. That's the pitch I start warming up with.

To throw a knuckleball, you need the fingertips of a safecracker and the mind of a Zen Buddhist. The idea is to throw a ball *without any spin* so that it jumps around in the air on its way to the plate, sixty feet six inches away, and passes through a strike zone approximately seventeen inches square. This is akin to throwing a butterfly with hiccups into your neighbor's mailbox across the street.

It's the same principle that caused the old musket balls to lose accuracy after about twenty feet. In colonial days they were killing more bystanders than combatants. This led to the invention of rifling, the spiral grooves inside gun barrels that cause bullets to spin like footballs. The consistent airflow around a spinning bullet keeps it on line with the target.

Everybody hates the knuckleball except the knuckleball pitcher. Coaches can't teach it, catchers can't catch it, and hitters can't hit it. And most pitchers can't throw it. The Zen part is that you can't *try*. You have to get out of the way and let it happen.

Right now a cold sweat is shooting across my shoulder blades. *The knuckleball is not happening!*

"Looks like it's not breaking," says Gilson.

Mr. Confidence.

"Sometimes I have nothing in the bullpen," I say, lungs sucking thin air. "Then it comes to me during the game."

Gilson picks up the phone to the dugout. He's telling Bateman to start getting Foster ready, just in case. Fuck him.

I put the towel around my neck, drape the jacket over my shoulder, and head for the dugout. Hundreds of fans are leaning over the low wall that runs next to the bullpen, waving scorecards, hollering encouragement, begging for autographs. Amid the shouts, I hear the sweetest sound known to man.

"Hi, Daddy!"

Beth and Marty are jammed in against the wall. What a nice surprise to see them down here! I make a quick detour to say hello.

Beth is a knockout, with her blond hair pulled back in a French braid, emphasizing her big green eyes, her mother's eyes. And instead of her usual jeans and sweater, she's featuring a navy blue dress, like she was going to a party. And she's *smiling,* like old times. She must be pretty excited about me pitching today. I hope she's not expecting too much.

"Are you nervous?" asks Beth. As always, getting right to the heart of the matter.

"I've only thrown up twice," I say.

"Oh, Daddy," says Beth. "You're kidding. Aren't you?"

And then she laughs.

"You want me to call Dial-A-Prayer?" asks Marty, who's wearing a heavily pocketed vest to accommodate his communications appliances.

Now I'm laughing, too.

Suddenly Marty's upper left pocket starts ringing. He pulls out his cellular phone.

"All lines are busy," he says like a recording. "Please stay on the line for our next available operator." Then he hangs up the phone.

"Everybody's calling to tell me to turn on the television set," he says. "Must be something happening."

"Good luck, Daddy," says Beth. Then she gives me a Cracker Jack–flavored kiss through a thicket of ballpoint pens.

As I break into a trot, a voice booms out of the sky. "And pitching for Chicago, number 65, Sam Ward."

The crowd buzzes on my name. A collective murmur of the word *"Who?"* And why did they have to announce my number, for crissakes? Sixty-five is embarrassing. It sounds like a left guard.

Wilkins comes up alongside of me.

"Just pitch your regular game," he says. "Remember, you got a good umpire back there. You don't have to thread the needle."

I grab a seat in the dugout. Bill Robinson comes over and pats me on the leg. Jerome gives me a thumbs-up, A-okay, and rolling-fist, but fakes the double-clutch in favor of a medium high five. The other players sneak glances, then look away. They just want to make sure I'm breathing.

The starters are poised on the dugout steps, bouncing nervously up and down on their toes, pounding their gloves, grabbing their crotches.

"Let's get it *on!*" yells Leon Banks.

And here comes Owens, like he wants to say something. He leans over and whispers into my ear.

"Fuck these guys," he says. "Win one for the Scrubeenies."

Suddenly the organ breaks into the Cubs fight song. My teammates charge onto the field. I stand up. I wipe my face with the towel, toss my jacket on the bench, and point myself toward the mound. My stomach is in a free fall. I walk as if I'm in a dream. The crowd is standing and roaring. I wonder if this is what it was like when the Lions played the Christians at the Colosseum.

THE NATIONAL ANTHEM

1:55 PM

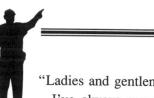

"Ladies and gentlemen. Please rise for the National Anthem."

I've always sung "The Star-Spangled Banner." I love the fact that no games begin without it. When I was eight, my father took me to Yankee Stadium. My first big league ball game. I remember "The Star-Spangled Banner" most because of the way my father sang it. He stood tall with his hat over his heart, and though everybody was singing, it was easy to hear his strong deep voice. I never felt so close to him as I did at that moment.

But today I can't sing. I move my lips in case the TV camera spots me, but nothing is coming out. My voice is locked up tight.

At the end of the anthem, the crowd can't wait. Like they say, the last two words are *"Play ball!"* This time, the yelling doesn't stop. The crowd is pennant hungry, demanding to be fed. And they're going to keep on yelling. I can take the bite as long as they don't start feeding on me. I want none of that bullshit today. Bateman will be perched on the top step of the Cubs' dugout ready to launch his beer-bellied body at me like he had a rocket sizzling up his ass. He'll do whatever he can to get the crowd on me, stamping his feet, doing his fat-assed dance. What he doesn't know is that I'm not going to bust him, not today. Everything is different today.

A few minutes ago when we all met at home plate to exchange batting orders and cover the ground rules, he was cool, all right.

"All I ask of you, Ernie," he said, "is establish your strike zone early and call every pitch the way my boys want them called!"

Phillies manager Jim Fregosi laughed. "You got any problems, Ernie, any problems at all, you just come to me."

I laughed at nothing. I said, "I just hope both of you guys are still around to see who wins."

But Bateman had to have the last word.

"Ernie, I'm gonna miss you."

Fucking Bateman. He thought he was seducing me. In the first game I confronted him, maybe five years ago, I was calling them at third. There was one out, man on first, full count on a left-handed hitter. The runner went on the pitch, the batter checked his swing, the plate ump called: "Ball four!" as the catcher threw the runner out at second—then immediately asked for an appeal on the checked swing. I called, "Strike!" So the batter was out on strikes, and the runner was out at second. Instead of runners on first and second and one out, the inning was over.

Out came Bateman, his big red snout leading the way. He was livid, his fists together in front of him like he was holding a bat imitating the perfect checked swing, see? No breaking of the wrist, see? I came back with the official rule 9.02(c), see? The checked-swing call is a ball-and-strike ruling, and any manager protesting such a call can be ejected from the premises. When Bateman persisted, in front of all the spectators and ballplayers and TV cameras and maybe God Himself, my bullet-ruined right arm swept majestically across my body, fist punching sky.

"You're gone!"

To the reporters, Bateman blamed the loss on "Bad calls!"

No one asked for my opinion.

Some days you tame the tiger, some days the tiger has you for lunch.

I'm not going to miss *you*, Bateman.

Now I'm alone at home plate. Except for the three others in my crew, there's no one on the field. Sirotta is at third, Mountain at second, Luger at first. I'm here, but I don't want to be. For the first time since I began to wear the blue suit, I'd like to disappear. I can't get lower than this.

Look at the U.S. flag, Ernie. Look at it fluttering in the breeze. You couldn't even sing the anthem, could you? There are so many fucked-up notions spinning around in your head, you can't see the beauty of the soft green grass, the clean brown dirt of the base paths, the bright white lines to the foul poles. You're a mess, no doubt about that. Not since you dangled on the brink of suicide have you been such a mess.

There's a stabbing pain at such memories. Like Enid said, "You have the look of darkness." Jesus, I was no Sunny Jim, that was for sure. In those early years of the marriage, I was forever in the pits. She was three months pregnant when I took her back to Hempstead, Long Island, figuring I'd have a better chance at everything in the town where I grew up. Right from the start, though, life was shit-for-the-bird. First off, it turned out that she was carrying twins. Having one kid was scary enough, but the prospect of a double terrified me. Then she had a difficult pregnancy, too many days when she was too sick to get out of bed. I went to get a job as baseball coach at my high school, but they wanted a geometry teacher who also knew the infield fly rule. I ended up clerking at a sporting goods store for $50 a week and commissions. The twins weren't even born when I knew I wasn't going to be a winner.

Then there they were, one of each. Amy and Joe, with Enid taking such a beating in delivery that it seemed like the end of the world. But we loved each other. At least, that's what we kept telling each other. But what's that supposed to mean? I mean, we were kids a year out of our teens. Maybe if we had a pile of money we could've made it work. Maybe we could have had some laughs. But there was barely enough to get by, and the nightly siege of nonstop squalling was too much.

Poor Enid. She wasn't well enough to come up smiling. She didn't complain, but it was there in her eyes, that *Help me* look. Or maybe it was *Do something!* What could I do? Business went bad and they laid me off. In that first year, I could feel the roof caving in and the squalling kids would bring it all down. It was like they were hollering at me for being a fuck-up. The truth was, there was no way it was going to get any better.

Then my mother got sick. Cancer. After a while, my father quit work as a carpenter to take care of her. The best job I could find was driving trucks part-time for the highway department. I tried to sell vacuum cleaners door to door. One day I heard something that knocked me off my pins: my father didn't quit because of Mom, he was caught ripping off the contractor he worked for. I couldn't believe this.

"Jesus, Pop, what *is* this?"

"He's a crook, I'm a crook, that's the building trades, kiddo."

"But this is *you,* Pop. I mean, I thought—"

"Butt out, Ernie. You'll end up with your own head in the gutter."

He turned away. He was never one for a lot of words. He just let it sit there like a pile of ratshit in the kitchen corner. He was quitting on himself.

You start going down, you get trapped in the fall. It becomes unstoppable. I couldn't take the nights at home any more than the nickel-and-dime bullshit of the day. Try to find a way to make any sense of it, the mind rattles with the stupidity of everything. My mother died; she just didn't want to keep on fighting. It rocked me. Everything about my life seemed hopeless. I couldn't even pretend.

Never did anyone feel like so big a bag of shit as Ernie Kolacka after eighteen months of marriage. I couldn't sell vacuum cleaners any more than I could teach geometry. What scared me was the way you needed money to have hope, and you needed hope to get money. After a while, it got too painful. Tomorrow had to be worse, the day after, on and on. How could it get better? How?

So I was the bird without wings. How long can you suffer that kind of shit? I was tired. Man, I was so fucking tired I could barely draw breath. I could no more fly than I could laugh. Everything hurt but nothing mattered. It was like a big grubby hand had me by the throat. I mean, I didn't care if I lived or died.

Then, one Saturday morning in May, the sun came out after days of rain. It was warm and bright, the grass was a lush spring green, trees popping new leaves. Everything smelled like perfume. God, I never saw it so beautiful! Then I saw teenage kids with spikes draped over their shoulders, gloves in hand. One kid had a black bat on his shoulder. That was me, by God. That was *me*! My knees buckled. That's when I knew what I had to do. I was sure of it. Slit my wrists with a razor? Take pills? Jump off a building?

I decided I would do it in my car. Carbon monoxide by way of a vacuum cleaner hose from the exhaust pipe into the car under the floorboard.

I filled the tank with gas, adjusted the idle to be sure it wouldn't cut off on me. I bought a quart of bourbon and hid it under the seat. That night, I would park near the beach, attach the hose, start the engine, roll up the windows tight, nurse the bottle of booze until—*bingo!*

That afternoon, I passed the ballfield, the field I had practically grown up on. There was a game going on. Guys I knew in their fire department team uniforms, part of the Greater Hempstead League. I used to play with a lot of them. I couldn't help but picture myself at short, glove down, body set as the pitcher released. I could feel that instant of anticipation at contact. Hit it to me! You can't get it by me! You're all mine! I was so good, so fucking good, my legs had springs, my glove was a basket, my arm was a rifle.

I got out of the car, leaned against the hood. Immediately, the guys on the field called out to me:

"Hey, it's Ernie!"

"Coach third for us, Ernie!"

No, thanks, I just wanted to die. I could tell you, pal, there was no way I could ever be near a ball game. Not with what I was going through. It was like watching the girl you loved fucking another guy. I didn't think anything like this could get to me anymore, but it did. It sure did.

Then it happened. I didn't see it, but I heard it. A foul tip slashed by the catcher's mitt and caught the umpire under the mask just below the Adam's apple. It sounded like someone had dropped a melon on concrete, and the poor guy went down like he was dead. He was through for the day, all right. The ballplayers stood around, not knowing what to do next. Came, then, Ernie Kolacka. I moved into the action, driven by a force of nature. I couldn't stop myself. I picked up the mask and cried out, "Okay, let's play ball." My voice rang out like a command. I went behind the plate with no protection except that mask, but for a man about to die, what difference did it make?

I got behind the catcher in a crouch, my chin just over his shoulder in a position I'd never known. The first pitch cut the inside of the plate and I turned my body, jabbing my right hand hard as I called out, "Steeeerike!" Suddenly I felt so alive, it was magical. I called balls and strikes like I'd been doing it all my life. I hustled down the baseline behind the runner to make calls at first. I was all over the field, working the whole game by myself. I even ran into the outfield on sinking line drives. The ballplayers got the message: this was not just a crummy sandlot game, it was *baseball* and it had to be played right. And when it was over, everyone came to thank me.

They took me for beers that tasted like they were brewed in heaven. The talk sent me soaring, baseball talk that rang with all the right stuff. They loved the game. Some were just out of high school, some were in their forties. They all wanted to play forever. But it was old George Bennett, a catcher who'd been up with the Phillies for a cup of coffee, who hit it on the button:

"You were terrific, Ernie. No question, you'd make one hell of an umpire!"

A line like that, you could say that it saved my life.

Suddenly I'm jarred by a deafening roar, and here come the Cubs out of the dugout like Hollywood Marines coming over the top. The crowd greets them like they're going to save the fucking world.

At the plate, catcher Rick Wilkins greets me with his usual grin.

"Howdy, Ernie, how's the missus?"

He's never met Enid. He never asks this of any other umpire. Just me. Once, I was calling them at second, he slid in with a double. As he brushed off the dust, he asked me: "How's the missus?"

"She's dying to meet you," I said.

This guy is big. He should be playing first base, where he wouldn't block my view. Get behind Wilkins, it's like trying to see a canoe around a battleship. He's quick, too. I've got to be quicker, especially when a man is stealing and Wilkins's big body rises in front of me before I can see the pitch. He's played enough ball to give him control of crucial games. He sees everything. He knows my strike zone. He talks a lot. I'm thinking, with Wilkins and this junkster on the mound, playing *fix* is like trying to fuck a shark.

On the mound, Ward actually seems at home throwing his dink pitches like he was having a backyard catch with his grandmother. What's he doing out there? It's like they found a janitor in the hospital basement and brought him up to do brain surgery on the President. How can he win a big league game no matter how I call them? I ought to be jumping for joy that it's Ward on the mound. And since I'm going to royally fuck whoever it is, you'd think I'd be salivating like a dog at a steak bone. You'd think it would make my day.

I glare at him through the mask. Let him wonder. Maybe he can feel my eyes on him. He's poised, all right, I'll give him that. It's like he doesn't even care. I'm the one with butterflies. He is cool. In comes the warm-up throw, it dips and turns, turns and dips. It bounces in the dirt. Wilkins doesn't block it and it goes back to the screen.

"Oops!" he says, then opens his mitt for another ball.

"That mitt big enough?" I ask.

"Don't worry. He can't break a pane of glass."

He's smiling and I get the message: he wants to let the Phillies think that Ward has so much stuff, Wilkins can't even catch it.

He throws to second, ending the warm-up. The ball circles the infield as I step in front of the plate, ass to the pitcher, and dust it off. Suddenly I break into a sweat. My head starts spinning with a wave of dizziness. My stomach is churning and I'm woozy enough to worry.

Under my mask I mumble, "Okay, fruitcake, throw your best pitch, then back up third!" It's time for the two magical words, but my jaw is locked. I've got to struggle to let them out, the words I've loved more than any other—until now.

"Play ball!"

GAME TIME

2:00 PM

"Play ball!" hollers Kolacka.

And the crowd roars.

I'm just the right amount of scared. Blood pumping, stomach churning, lungs working to get into a rhythm. This is my art, my craft, the moment I live for. Nothing else matters once I zero in; not family, friends, money, or world peace. I'll be concentrating enough to miss an explosion.

The sky is overcast. Temperature is 62. Wind blowing out is good for the knuckleball; the resistance makes it jump around more. Bad for long flies. However, I have no plans at the moment to give up long flies.

Over in the on-deck circle, Phillies' center fielder Lenny Dykstra, the best leadoff hitter in the league, is twitching and stretching with a weighted bat. Dykstra has a compact, muscular body that moves in spasms, like an action figure in a video game.

I turn around to check my fielders. Mark Grace just off the grass at first. Ryne Sandberg slapping the pocket of his glove at second. Jerome Davis smoothing dirt with his left foot at short. Steve Buechele leaning in at third. Leon Banks medium depth in left. Willie Wilson shading to pull in center. Sammy Sosa the same in right.

Wilkins squats behind the plate. Dykstra mashes his helmet down onto his head with the heel of his right hand and maneuvers himself into the batter's box. He cranks his body left and right, waggling his bat in my direction. The crowd gets quiet, anticipating. I look in for the sign. Knuckleball. I nod. Might as well go with my best. We *have* liftoff.

I wind up . . . and the first pitch is . . . belted . . . toward deep right center . . . goddamn! A rocket . . . a personal assault on my body. The sound of it makes me feel faint. The ball caroms off the wall . . . so hard it bounces all the way back to the infield. The outfielders never even *touched* it! Sandberg, turning for the relay, actually fields the ball behind second base. His quick throw to third base holds Dykstra at second with a double. Holy Christ!

The bombs bursting in air.

I never saw a ball hit that hard in my entire life. It's a "Fuck you, Sam Ward" shot. I try to clear my head. I'm looking out at the spot on the wall where the ball smashed through the ivy before ricocheting back to the infield. Boy, that was quick. One pitch, man on second, nobody out. It only took six seconds! The crowd is gasping, asking itself what the hell happened. Me, too.

The Phillies are laughing and howling in their dugout. "Welcome to the big leagues!" somebody hollers. My stomach belches acid up into my throat. My lungs ache.

It takes tremendous effort, but I force the fear out of my mind with the next hitter. This is also part of my business. Damage control. The last pitch is history. Only one thing matters right now: the *next* pitch.

Second baseman Mariano Duncan, who's currently massaging the ball at a .321 clip, steps into the batter's box. I look for the sign. Wilkins calls for the curve, but I shake him off. I want the knuckler again. It's my best pitch and I've got to get it working. Plus, I don't want the Phillies to think I'm afraid to throw it. And *I* don't want to think it, either.

I go into my stretch. I check the runner at second. I kick and throw. And it's . . . blasted . . . *shit!* A long fly ball . . . deep left field . . . *Stay in here, you sonovabitch!* Banks going back . . . back . . . back . . . he waits . . . he jumps! And *makes* the catch at the base of the wall. *Hallefuckinglujah!* After the catch, Banks guns a bullet to third, holding Dykstra at second base.

Relief and nausea sweep my body with conflicting messages. I've got one out, I'm getting killed. Meanwhile, fifty thousand fans almost fell off a cliff. The decibel level rises and falls in alternating waves of agony and ecstasy. They don't know whether to shit or eat popcorn.

I refuse to look over in the dugout, the first sign of a pitcher in trouble. In moments like this my outward demeanor, in contrast to the train wreck inside, is one of total control. Hey, I always give up a few bombs. Makes the game more exciting that way.

Man on second, one out, and here's Phillies' first baseman John Kruk. He may look like a beer league guy, but that's not what the scouting report says. Wilkins calls for the knuckler. I check the runner. I wind up and let it go. And it's ... ball one. Good thing, too, because it didn't break very much. Try to stay positive. Wilkins, looking to build my confidence, calls for the knuckler again. And this one *does* break, but it breaks wide and now it's ball two. At least it's breaking. Two balls and no strikes. Now what? Do I throw a sinker here to try and get a strike? Or go with my best pitch? And how good *is* my so-called best pitch, anyway?

I step off the mound to get my breath. Can I count on the knuckler? What about that rocket off the wall? And the bomb that almost went out? Why didn't those knuckleballs jump around? Or did they jump and get hit anyway? Suddenly I feel tired. And very alone.

This is bullshit. I can't be thinking like this. I need to show some guts here. Kick myself in the ass, reach back for a little extra. Fuck it. I'm as good as they are. I'll stay with the knuckleball. I get the sign. I kick and throw. The ball feels good as it leaves my hand. The knuckler ... jukes and jives its way to the plate. Unfortunately, it jukes out of the strike zone.

Ball three.

The crowd groans, like what the hell is this? What's going on out there? Who *is* this guy? But there is no booing. Not yet, anyway. Cub fans are pretty patient. Why not? What choice do they have?

What choice do *I* have? I need a strike here. I hear a ball slamming into a catcher's mitt in the bullpen as I look in for the sign. This is my last hitter if I don't get him out. Wilkins calls for the sinker and I don't blame him. I'm remembering a great sinker I once threw with the bases loaded in Mexico City to win a game. *That's* the one I want. I kick and throw. Kruk swings ... and drills a screaming line drive ... toward third ... Buechele dives to his left ... he's *got it!* ... Dykstra, on his way to third, does a

U-turn . . . Buechele comes to his knees, throwing hard and straight to second base . . . Dykstra slides . . . but not in time, and he's out at second for a double play!

And our flag was still there.

The place goes nuts. The crowd is on its feet, laughing and slapping itself on the back, congratulating itself on its good fortune, trying to figure out how two rockets and one bomb equals no runs.

Me, I'm numb. I can't believe the inning is over. Just like that. Did it really happen? *Not one good pitch!* I walk, in shock, toward the dugout. There seems to be no other place to go.

As I reach the foul line, Jerome comes up from behind and claps me on the back.

"Way to go," he says, without any sarcasm, like I'm supposed to think I just had a good inning. Jerome is from a different dimension.

Gilson, unfortunately, is in the here and now, waving a towel as he stomps around in the dugout.

"Kiss my ass if I know what the *fuck* we're doing," he shouts, loud enough for everybody to hear.

The flinch originates in my stomach and reverberates up to my chest; a spasm of doubt and apprehension. It's not a new feeling.

Meanwhile, my teammates are whooping and hollering. Buechele is being pounded on the back as he tries to get to the water cooler.

"Way to go, Boo!" shouts Mark Grace.

"Somebody get me a batting helmet," cracks Leon Banks, referring to the velocity of certain batted balls.

The topic of conversation centers on Dykstra's cannon shot off the wall that started the game. Terms like howitzer, rocket, bullet, decapitate, whiplash, and snapped my motherfucking neck off are bandied about. I can even tell the Spanish-speaking guys are talking about it just by their gestures. Lots of big eyes, and pointing, and jerking their arms. And laughing. The whole team is laughing, partly because it didn't cause any damage, except maybe to the ivy in right field. And my psyche.

Players are comparing it to other blasts they remember: line drives that shook light towers, smashed seats, cleared roofs, sent people to the hospital. Willie Wilson recalls an old video of Frank Howard's line drive into the speakers at Yankee Stadium off Whitey Ford. Ryne Sandberg remembers Darryl Strawberry's moonbeam off the roof in Montreal which made the announcers wonder if it was actually a home run because it came crashing back down onto the field so fast.

"I've seen balls ricochet like that before," says Sammy Sosa, wrenching his head from right to left. "In jai alai."

Some of the lines are pretty funny. Mark Grace says I'll probably get a bill for the ivy. Even my fellow Scrubeenies are getting into the act.

"Well," says Rawley Alexander, casting an elongated Mickey Mouse shadow on the dugout wall, "you made the highlights tape."

I'm laughing on the outside, but inside my stomach is ripping a new exit. I'm worried about the knuckleball. I can't afford to throw any more bad ones. Not even one more. It's not the kind of pitch where you can sprinkle in a dud once in a while. It's too damn slow. A knuckleball that doesn't break is like a fluorescent deer on opening day of the hunting season. With a bull's-eye up its ass.

What the hell is happening? I don't have *anything*! And I can't get it over the plate either. Before, I was just nervous. Now I'm scared. Maybe there's too much pressure. Maybe the scouts were right. Maybe I don't belong up here in the first place.

I've got to get rid of this feeling. I take a seat at the far end of the dugout so I can be alone.

And I think about the wall.

It wasn't necessary that it be a stone wall. Or even that it be a wall. The rotted wood fence that separated my family's lake property from our neighbor's half acre could have laid in the weeds another fifty years, for all anyone cared. Except I had an idea. In exchange for a strip of the neighbor's land, I'd build a stone wall along the new border. The extra land would help center our cabin on a misshapen lot. But more important, it would save an old tree earmarked for firewood. A tree that happened to contain a tree house built by Marty and me when we were kids. The tree house would be preserved as a historic landmark. The wall would last forever.

And it would solve a few other problems.

This was right after Julie and I had separated last fall. I remember working late one night in the rain with a flashlight. My concentration was such that I didn't even realize it was raining until a local cop came by and asked what I was doing. I told him I was building a wall. "On a Saturday night?" he said.

A Saturday night without Julie was like all other nights. Long.

So I lost myself in the work. Hard and heavy and exacting work. Visually measuring an open space along the wall, memorizing the cavity with my fingers, scanning a mound of stones for a telltale shape, spotting a likely candidate, digging through jagged edges with gloved hands, wresting it loose from the pile, staggering back with the prize, and shoving it into place with a satisfying clack, like the closing of a meat-locker door.

Of course, the stones didn't always fit. The unwieldy blocks smashed my fingers, and the unrelenting weight punished every muscle in my body. And it was every day and most nights. Progress on the "stone monster" was barely measurable. I'd give myself pep talks to keep going. "If this were easy," I'd say, sweat stinging my eyes, mud caked on my chest, "everybody would be doing it."

That's what I tell myself now, as I sit here on the bench. And Foster is throwing in the bullpen. And the pitching coach is plotting my departure. And the manager is staring at a wrinkled piece of paper.

Our leadoff man, Willie Wilson, yanks a bat from the bat rack and stares out at the Phillies' pitcher, Tommy Greene.

"I'm gonna get on top of some shit right here," he says.

My teammates are back into the game. I'm into my life. Am I still pitching? Christ, I've come all this way and I'm still only a phone call away from the turnpike.

I'm watching Bateman to see what he's going to do. He whispers something to Gilson, who picks up the phone. He's calling the bullpen! I'm either dead or alive here.

"Tell him to sit down," says Gilson.

I'm *alive*!

	1	2	3	4	5	6	7	8	9		R	H	E
PHILLIES	0										0	1	0
CUBS											0	0	0

I raise my mask to spit. Buechele, you can take the rest of the day off. I had the ball game in my pocket, but the sonovabitch snatched it. It was like finding diamonds, then losing them for a hole in your pocket.

"This is not the time to accept unconventional offers. Abjure all risky ventures. . . ." That horoscope keeps following me around like a drunk grubbing for another handout.

Phillies catcher Darren Daulton comes to the plate with his mask on top of his head, his mouth fierce with anger. "Bubba," they call him. A veteran team leader. "Lucky bastards!" he snarls. I never mess with him. He begins to warm up Tommy Greene, swearing the dreaded *L*-word with every throw back to the mound. "Lucky sonsovbitches!" He is so mad, he throws furiously back to the mound. Greene refuses to handle it, and it rolls to center field like a lost rabbit. Catchers are likely to be hotheads. It goes with the mask and mitt and thousands of bounces to the cup. But this guy always knows what he's doing.

Today I want peace. Today's game has to be beyond luck. Nobody gets lucky but what I say so.

Meanwhile, my stomach is bubbling. When I go to dust off the plate, I suddenly cut loose with a fart. This one, Jesus, maybe they can hear it in the center-field bleachers.

Daulton can't resist having a go at it.

"That should be good for extra bases," he says.

"And fuck you, too, Bubba," I growl.

I can't help myself for the fart any more than I can help myself for the memory. When I was a kid, my father used to whack my ass when I did it, even the silent ones.

"But I can't help it, Pop!"

"You'd better learn how," he said. Then he tossed in the real threat: "It's bad luck." He scared me into keeping a tight asshole.

When I was in umpire's school, I was dusting the plate, just like now. My ass was facing the instructor, a minor league umpire named Larson, and I happened to let one blast. Others bust out laughing like a bunch of kids in a classroom. But not Larson. He turned red-faced, eyes popping like I'd committed the original sin.

"Damn you, Kolacka, anyone who can't keep a tight asshole will never work in organized baseball! Do that again and you're out of here!"

The trouble was, guys like Larson, when they get on your ass, they never leave off. The day before, he saw me helping my roommate adjust his chest protector, and he came at me like I was taking his job away. A couple of days later, I was behind the plate calling a practice game when I slapped a new ball in the catcher's mitt. "*Throw* it to the fucking pitcher, Kolacka. It looks good when an umpire throws the ball." I explained why I couldn't throw it. "Shit, what else can't you do? This ain't a school for cripples!" Like a jerk, I named two major league umpires who would put the ball in the catcher's mitt. Again, that's what you don't do. Not to Larson, anyway. Not where they judge you on "Attitude." There were over 100 candidates, and only a dozen would be recommended for jobs in the rookie leagues. If Larson didn't like your "Attitude," you went back to calling little leagues.

I can tell you, pal, there was a whole lot of bullshit in umpire's school. Start with the candidates, all sizes and shapes, most of them from the cold north looking for a few weeks in the Florida sun. How many times did we have to line up on a foul line: on command, we'd run three steps, lean over with hands on knees, fling the fist across the body like we were punching a ghost in the gonads, and holler *"Out!"* like somebody just bit you on the dick. We'd spend days learning how to take off the mask without losing our hats. God forbid, an umpire lets his hat fall to the ground. With your left hand you take off your mask as you dip your right shoulder, stick the mask under your arm as you swing away from your body, all in one move. Big deal, all right. Practice, practice, practice, always in front of a mirror. Mirrors weren't invented for good-looking women, they were invented for umpire's school. You actually got graded for how many times out of ten your hat stayed on your head.

Then there was the time I dusted off the plate with my ass facing the stands. Bad news. An umpire *never* does that; too insulting to the paying customers. The umpire's ass must always face the pitcher—another way of saying that it's okay to insult the pitcher. Another time, we're working on how to confront a pissed-off manager who comes ripping at you to protest a call. "No!" Larson blasted me. "Don't stand with your arms folded across your chest. That shows *weakness!*" And he mock-imitated my stance like I was a cowering dog. Instead, he stuck his hands in his back pockets, thrust his chin out like he was daring you to hit him. "Get the picture?" Laying a splatter of tobacco juice on my face to make sure I did.

I almost spit back at him. I was so sick of this bullshit, I wanted to quit. I had four more weeks to go, but I couldn't handle four more minutes. Maybe I could become a professional umpire just by being one. Maybe this was just a crazy dream that couldn't pay off anyway. Maybe Enid was right. Back in the dorm, I stood in front of the mirror, hands in back pockets, chin protruding, only this time I didn't see me, I saw fucking Larson. Suddenly, with one shot of my fist, I smashed the image. Blood and glass all over the place. They could sew up my hand, but at least the mirror was dead.

That night I dreamed I was in front of another mirror, and this time it wasn't me I saw, and it wasn't Larson, it was *Roger*. He was in the blue suit, one hand in his back pocket, chin out, and one finger jabbing at me. "What kind of horseshit are you? *Quit? Are you thinking quit?*" He was in such a rage, I couldn't get out of his face. "You're an umpire! This is you! This is what you were put on earth to do! *So do it!*"

Roger's ghost had it right. You want something badly enough, you go for it. When you get those wheels spinning, it's amazing how much shit you can take. After six weeks, they graduated me in the top ten. I was sent to the Georgia-Florida rookie league for $250 a month. I was on my way, goddamnit.

And for all the thousands of times I've dusted the plate, I never farted again. Until today.

You could make a big thing out of that. What the hell, this is no ordinary day. It's a day when my sphincter might serve as incriminating evidence. A slip of the lip. I could even picture Daulton testifying before an investigating commission. "Mr. Daulton, was there anything in Kolacka's calls that led you to suspect he was fixing the game?" "No, sir." "Nothing at all?" "Well, sir, come to think of it, he, well, he never did this before: *he farted!*" They could check the records. Thirty-eight years as professional umpire, and this was the first time! How the hell could I explain it?

When I left umpire's school for that first year in the rookie league, I was pure. I was blessed with virtue and armed with courage. I went into battle with the glorious flag up my ass. This was where the managers were mostly ex–big leaguers twice my age, all of them hungry to eat me alive. I was living in the belly of the beast, fair game for their spitting rages. Everybody had the same dream. Everybody would do anything he had to do to get back to the big league cities.

If they lost, it was always the umpire's fault. Always. But especially at home parks, where managers worked the crowds to intimidate the umpires. Joining this orgy were announcers and reporters. Even the kid-rookies learned how to squawk if the crowd was with them. Nobody took the umpire's side, nobody except maybe another umpire. The way to get out of trouble was not to get into it. The way it was, the perfectly called ball game was not necessarily a lot of perfect calls, it was a game without controversy, a game in which nobody knew the man in blue, in which the ump was a stump, in which he was there in the air but who's to care. To make it happen, you'd have to call every play with one eye in your face and one in your asshole. The "home field advantage," they call it, but you'd never hear an umpire admit it.

Let me tell you, pal, I worked at it. I learned the power of concentration. I would steel myself on every call. My mind was an instant camera, everything recorded through my lens eye, always in perfect focus at exactly the right angle. Nothing must ever compromise the way I saw it. Umpiring was a religious experience. We were missionaries in the fields of the Lord. We should forgive the vain and spiteful managers, sinners who know not what they do, but we should throw them out of the temple if they dare to defy our godliness.

Then I learned how the high priests worked the catechism. In the Georgia-Florida League, I was behind the plate in Moultrie, Georgia, on a steamy night when an eighteen-year-old kid named Jimmy Reed, fresh out of the local high school, was pitching a perfect game. He was small, no more than 150 pounds soaking wet. Unlike the typical big league prospect, he couldn't throw 90 miles per hour, he didn't strike out half the side. But he was masterful. Every pitch had a different velocity. His sneaky fastball seemed to pick up speed as it reached the plate. His breaking ball dipped like it fell off a table. He consistently hit corners like the plate had no center. All along, he was making batters hit what he wanted them to hit. Some innings he threw no more than seven or eight pitches. It was the most beautiful thing I'd ever seen.

Then we moved into the ninth inning, and since it was 1–0 ball game, the tension was double-thick. The crowd, maybe 900 strong, sounded like half a million. Everyone was pulling for him. When he got the first batter on a one-hopper, the "Go, Jimmy! Go, Jimmy!" sounded like thunder. Next came the visiting slugger, a real threat from the left side of the plate. With the count at 1–0, he rifled a shot down the right-field line that veered foul at the last instant. Reed worked carefully, and the count went to 3-2, then he got the hitter to pop up behind the plate. The catcher settled under it, but I could see he was in trouble, his feet weren't set, and the ball popped out of his mitt like it had a mind of its own. As the 900 fans gasped in horror, the catcher stared at the ball and cursed himself. Here the air became thick with a new kind of tension, the calm before a giant tornado. Everyone sensed something terrible was about to happen. The kid stepped off the mound, rubbing the ball as if he could erase any touch of evil from its hide. I could see he was tired. He would have to be tired. With full count, this would be the pitch that decided it all. It was a gutsy tantalizing off-speed breaking ball that started outside the line and spun in slowly. The batter was totally fooled. He began his stride much too soon, then checked his swing like someone had suddenly tied a rope around his arms. The pitch started to

113

break into the strike zone but never made it. I followed it all the way, but it never made it. A part of me wanted to call it a strike, but my eyes refused. My left fist swung across my body toward first base.

"Take your base!" I cried out.

First, a moment of stunned silence, then I heard escalating sounds of fury that came down to a rhythmic chant: *"Kill him! Kill the ump! Kill him!"* On the mound, the kid remained poised as the catcher came out to talk to him. So did the manager. With one out and the tying run on base, he was still working on a no-hit shutout, but everyone knew that the big event was over. Suddenly the next hitter blooped a double down the line, driving in the tying run. A moment later, a clean single to center drove in the lead run. In a matter of seconds, the wheels had come off. No perfect game, no no-hitter, no shutout. Not even a win, as it turned out. And when the game ended a half inning later, they came to get the Devil. Dozens spilled over onto the field, jeering, screeching abuse as they surrounded me. Someone jumped me from behind and I spun around in a fury—nobody touches an umpire, ever!—and I caught him in the face with my elbow. The ballplayers came to save me from the worst of it, taking me into the locker room, where I stayed until it was safe to leave. Safe? My car was a wreck, windshield smashed, tires slashed. The police took me to my motel, where I needed no advice to get out of town fast. For $45 I had a taxi drive me to a motel in Valdosta. But when he left me off, I took no chances and moved to another, where I registered under the first name I could think of: Roger Abercorn. I was smart. Hours later, that same taxi was back with a load of scumbags looking for blood. You'd think I had raped the pastor's twelve-year-old daughter.

A week later, I was in the Georgia-Florida League office to review my report of the game, especially since it itemized a request for $450 damages and expenses incurred in the course of duty. The president, a local banker named A. B. Woodson, tried to conceal the worst of his displeasure. On his desk, there were clips from Moultrie newspapers.

"It says here: 'Kolacka is one of these umpires who likes to play God, but he ended up playing the Devil.' " He looked over his glasses, expecting a comment. When I had none to offer, he read a quote from the catcher: " 'It caught the corner. The pitch was a strike!' " Again, he stared at me. "Seems to me, Kolacka, you might have given that pitch to him."

I said the only thing I could possibly say. "The ball was outside the plate, Mr. Woodson."

He shook his head. "It never ever crossed your mind to call it a strike, did it? You never saw the larger picture. You saw the tree, Kolacka, but you missed the forest."

"It was outside," I repeated. "That's what I saw."

He pushed the papers from him in anger, then rearranged them. He wasn't going to let this chance go by, that much was clear.

"I'm gonna set y'all straight on this, Kolacka. You made a goddamn dumb call. It could've been a strike, now, couldn't it? You didn't have to ruin that perfect game. A strike woulda made history for young Reed. We need that for our boys. We need that especially over in Moultrie. The entire league, in fact. Heroes are the ballplayers, Kolacka, not some goddamn umpire. Heroes are what bring people to the ballparks to pay your salary. They don't give a hoot in hell about umpires. Look what happened, Kolacka, you turned that magnificent game into hell. You ruined that kid. You fouled up the lives of all those good folks. I even got a complaint here against you: *You broke a boy's nose!*"

He paused again, waiting for me to say something. I refused. I could've told him how my elbow felt fine, but I clammed up.

"You still think you made the right call? That's really what I'd like to know."

I saw it clearly enough. President A. B. Woodson was the forest and I was the tree. If I admitted I'd done wrong, maybe he wouldn't piss on my roots.

"The pitch was outside, Mr. Woodson."

In the end, I got half my $450 and all of the bum rap. What hurt the most was when I found myself on the official umpire's shit list as well. I was tagged with using "bad judgment."

If you want to survive, pal, you've got to know the *real* difference between a ball and a strike.

Daulton is still cursing as Greene takes his last warm-up throws. I get down in my crouch for a front-seat view of what I'm going to be looking at. This guy throws like an SST compared with Ward's Piper Cub. And from the other side of the rubber, it's a whole different view with a different rhythm.

In front of me, there's a different catcher with different body movements. Above all, this time I'm the pitcher's umpire. This time I've got to put the hitters in trouble. I've got to be careful. It's a lot easier to get away with a bad call against a pitcher than against a hitter. Pitchers are less likely to squawk, especially a rookie like Ward. Call a bum strike against a pro like Sandberg and you'll hear it from somebody.

I look up into the TV booth for the signal to start play. The director checks his monitor. When the commercials end, he takes a white towel off his shoulder. An unwritten law says, if an umpire allows a single pitch to be thrown while a commercial is still on, he gets thirty days on bread and water. Do it twice in one game, it's a capital crime.

"Batter up!" I call.

Don't get careless, I tell myself. There's a direct connection between the asshole and the brain. Let the brain run the game, Ernie. Work!

The big trouble is that these Cubbies can hit. I told that to Roger first off. They've got hot bats. The balls they hit have eyes, not like the Phillies in the top half. These guys drive baseballs into the gaps, then run for fun.

Cubs leadoff man, Willie Wilson, looks like he can't wait to take his cuts. His back foot digs in his spikes, he bounces up and down like a puma ready to pounce. He's got that anticipating grin like it's just a question of which pitch he's going to rattle off which wall. I go into my crouch, I watch and I wait, ready to call them so the real umpire in me won't think that anything was wrong. No one should think anything is wrong. Even you prick bastards in Vegas, suffer, I'm going to do this the way I have to do it.

With 2 and 1, Greene catches the corner, and Wilson takes. I like the pitch. "Strike!" I call.

It doesn't bother Wilson, but it sets off Bateman. "Bear down, goddamnit!" the first squeak from the dugout steps.

Wilson rips the next pitch to left field and the crowd erupts like it's going for extra bases, but Incaviglia pulls it in without moving but three quick steps.

I think, hey, twenty-six more of these and I'm home free.

Jerome Davis makes me work by making Greene work. The first pitch stings the inside corner and I call a defiant "Strike!" Davis stares at the imaginary line, questioning the call, or maybe he's just checking his position in the box. Greene then throws a snapper, it can be called either way, but

I'm careful, I give it to Davis. The count goes to 2 and 2, then Davis grounds out sharply, short to first.

Ryne Sandberg steps in, jumps all over the first pitch, and drives it to deep right center field. My heart is pumping as the crowd explodes, for it looks like it might go out. Between my teeth I'm begging, no ... no, until Lenny Dykstra gloves it against the wall, maybe 400 feet away.

So the first inning ends with two goose eggs.

I'm not winning, but I'm not losing.

	1	2	3	4	5	6	7	8	9	R	H	E
PHILLIES	0									0	1	0
CUBS	0									0	0	0

Bateman is standing next to the bat rack with his left hand stuffed into the front of his pants. Like Napoleon with jock itch.

"All right," he says confidently. "Keep swinging. We'll get 'em."

Ryne Sandberg has just flied out to end the first inning and my teammates are running onto the field. Am I ready to join them? I honestly don't know. Depends on the knuckler.

"Don't be afraid to pop that thing," Wilkins had said between innings. "I'll handle it."

If it gets past the hitter first.

Not having your best pitch in the big leagues is like being wounded in the jungle. Sooner or later something bigger and faster is going to drag you down and rip out your throat. There's no place to hide on a pitcher's mound. I feel like a lion tamer without a whip. And the lions have seen the scouting report.

This is the most scared I've ever been. I know it's not life and death, but

I don't want to humiliate myself. I want to be respectable. I don't even have to win, to tell you the truth. I just want to know one thing. I'd like to know that I could have pitched in the major leagues if they had given me a chance. That I'm not crazy. That's all.

How long will Bateman go with me? He doesn't have anybody warming up right now because he doesn't want to undermine whatever confidence I might have left. But if that first batter gets on, you can bet somebody's going to be throwing.

I take my time walking to the mound. I need to get myself together.

And not just together. I need to get pumped.

My metal spikes bite into the freshly mowed grass as I walk. Now a single crunch as I step into the brown clay base path. Now back to grass. Beyond the infield dirt cutouts, the ones that look like giant paw prints from the window of an airplane, a carpet of bright green sweeps across the field to meet the dirt warning track, a ribbon of brown just below the darker green ivy clinging to the imperceptibly curved brick wall.

I get a flash thought of a rainy Saturday morning. It's about a year ago. I'm standing in the office of the Pasvalco Stone Company. A wire-haired guy with the name EMIL stitched on the pocket of his khaki shirt is explaining the problem.

"To build a freestanding wall," says Emil, "you have to build two walls at the same time, because you have two sides. Then you throw the broken stones in the middle."

Emil takes some scrap paper and draws a cross-section of a wall.

"The other thing is," says Emil, "the mountain fieldstone is hard to work with because it's all different shapes and sizes. You ever worked with stone before?"

"No," I say. "But I'd like to give it a try."

"For a sixty-foot wall, four feet high and two feet wide," says Emil, scribbling numbers, "you'll need fourteen pallets. Each pallet holds a ton and a half of stones."

"How long will something like this take?" I ask.

Emil smiles. "How long you got?"

The memory gets my juices flowing as I take the mound. And I will *take* the mound. I belong out here, damnit. This is my place, my enclave, my headquarters. I've spent a good piece of my life standing on a mound. I've begged to be out here and I've fought to stay out here. Over the years I've been through it all—from king shit to whale shit. The top of a mountain or a bottomless pit. Nobody ever had more fun on a pile of dirt.

The challenge is the thing; a hundred and twenty-five pitches, a hundred and twenty-five separate confrontations. Immediate feedback. A bad pitch is a line drive. No waiting for the quarterly report. The pitcher is credited with wins or losses because *he* is responsible. The pitcher is the point man, bounty hunter, navigator, matador, platoon guide, lightning rod, and burnt offering. Right here in public. When you are on the mound, you are definitely not dead. And sometimes you can actually laugh out loud. But don't get too cocky.

I duck my head as Wilkins fires my last toss down to second base. Mark Matthews, the Phillies' big home run hitter, is digging a toehold in the batter's box. I'm remembering what Leon Banks and Mark Grace had said about not throwing fastballs to Matthews. They've got to be kidding. You could time my fastball with a sundial. I can't puff a lip, as they say.

I look in for the sign. Knuckleball. I press my fingers into the leather. I kick and throw. And the first pitch ... flutters across ... for strike one! *Finally.* A pitch that isn't blasted somewhere. The crowd roars at the achievement, like proud parents at a dance recital. Even Kolacka makes a big deal out of the call, bellowing and stabbing the air with his right hand, like he's excited for me. Boy, he's got a loud voice for a little guy.

Another knuckler is wide and a sinker is pulled foul down the left-field line. One ball and two strikes. A pitcher's pitch. If the ball is close, the batter might swing to protect against a called third strike. Perfect spot for a hellacious knuckleball. Wilkins is thinking the same thing. Here we go. I kick and throw. The ball ... perfectly still ... floats in ... so slow you can count the stitches ... Matthews ... eyes getting big ... jumps at the pitch like a bass after a june bug ... he takes an enormous swing ... the ball hits a bump in the air ... the bat whistles underneath ... and it's a pop-up! A tremendous pop-up to the infield. If that sonovabitch ever comes down, Matthews is going to be out.

It does. And he is.

Yesss!

My first legitimate out today with big league stuff. But don't get too cocky. Got to stay focused.

Dave Hollins, the Phillies' third baseman, steps in. A switch hitter, Hollins will bat from the left side against me. Wilkins calls for the knuckler. I kick and throw. Hollins swings ... and pounds it into the dirt toward first. A nice little sixteen-bouncer. Mark Grace moves in, scoops it up, and steps on the bag for out number two.

Okay!

Here's catcher Darren Daulton. A knuckler misses outside. A sinker is low. A curve is fouled back. A second knuckler is swung on and missed and the count is even at two balls and two strikes. Now Wilkins calls for the sinker, but I shake him off. I want the knuckler. To send a message. I kick and throw. The ball breaks right ... now left ... now right again ... weaving in and out of imaginary traffic on its way to the plate. Daulton swings ... and misses by a foot. But so does Wilkins, who chases the ball down after it bounces off his shin guard. Luckily it doesn't roll too far and Wilkins throws to first for the out. And the message is: that first inning is ancient history.

I walk to the dugout breathing cool mountain air. Fans are hollering my name, but I decline to look up. I don't want eye contact to break my concentration. I need to stay in a world of my own making, my place on the bench, my own thoughts.

I sit by myself at the end of the dugout. I take off my hat and drape a towel over my head to soak up the perspiration. I stare out at the field, like Lawrence of Arabia scanning the horizon for clouds of dust. My teammates move by me like I'm not even here.

I go back to last September. I'm at the cabin by the lake near Galena, Illinois, in the northwest corner of the state. It's a beautiful lake, cool and quiet in the fall. Which explains why it was a pretty exciting event when the stones arrived one morning, in three separate truckloads. All fourteen pallets' worth.

"Whatcha gonna build, Sam?" asked the old guy who lives across the road. "A castle? Heh, heh, heh."

"A wall?" scoffed another neighbor. "Like the one in China? You'll be working on that until the year 2008."

That's what I wanted. I'd need at least that much time to recuperate after Julie left. A "trial separation," she called it. It was a trial, all right. I couldn't sleep. I couldn't eat. I couldn't think.

All I could do was feel sorry for myself. I even volunteered to move out so Julie and Beth could stay in the apartment. "Don't worry about me," I said sarcastically, "I'll live out of my car." I was a pretty good martyr. But the car got too uncomfortable, so I switched to my parents' summer cabin. I was the type of martyr that liked indoor plumbing.

"Sam, you don't understand," said Julie. "It feels like Beth and I are being dragged along on this crusade of yours."

"But you like to travel," I said. And I repeated my standard joke. "Think of all the wonderful places we've been: Rome, Paris, Cairo." Julie knew the punch line: Rome, Georgia; Paris, Indiana; and Cairo, Illinois. But she wasn't laughing anymore.

"When are you going to get serious, Sam?" she challenged. "That was fine when Beth was younger, but she's in school now. You've got to start being a father to Beth, not her big brother."

Julie loved traveling in the beginning. Just the three of us, cruising along in "Emerald City," our green Ford station wagon, counting barns and cemeteries and outhouses. We didn't miss a cave, waterfall, alligator farm, or scenic overlook. Not to mention all the souvenir and gift shops that Beth insisted we patronize. "Well, I guess so" on the authentic Indian moccasins and Day-Glo lipstick; "okay, but just one" giant dinosaur egg; "not now" on the red spangled cowboy boots; "no, thanks" on the Hansel & Gretel Motor Lodge; and "you know better than to even ask" about firecrackers, pecan logs, Dalmatian puppies, and minnows. Minnows?

"But they're sooooooo cute."

When I wasn't rolling along in the station wagon with Julie and Beth, I was gobbling up the miles in a bus or plane with nineteen ballplayers, two coaches, one manager, and a trainer. And sometimes the trainer's dog, who got off the bus and peed on the side of the road like everybody else.

We even had our own big-kid travel games. In Mexico we counted burros. One side of the bus against the other, losers bought the *cerveza.* One point for a burro, five points for a *burro umberega,* meaning with a hard-on. If the exact condition was in dispute, partial points were often awarded.

Mexico was an adventure. Those people really love their baseball. And if the baseball got boring, the fans made up their own game. Somebody would set fire to a balled-up newspaper and toss it in the air. The ball of fire would land on someone, who would just laugh and throw it into the next group of fans. It was quite a spectacle, especially at night. Beth called it "the flaming wave."

In a land of primarily black hair and brown eyes, we were curiosities. People would stare at us in a market or on a bus. And the neighborhood kids would always ask Beth to play with them, which she happily did even though her Spanish, in the beginning, was limited to *"Amigo"* and *"Dónde está el baño?"*

I was sort of a big shot in Mexico, particularly in Poza Rica, where I pitched Los Drilleros to the league championship. Kids would recognize my picture from the newspapers and follow me in the street. "Knocklebowl!" they'd shout, waving their hands all around. "Knocklebowl!"

That was the fun part. The bad part was getting jerked around at the whim of some owner or general manager. Professional baseball is not exactly famous for its employee relations. Julie hated the lack of consideration, which ranged from unthinking to insulting. Finally, it was utter lack of respect that pushed her over the edge.

This was after my great spring with the Yankees, year before last. My knuckler was dancing, I was hitting the corners, getting people out, and they had no choice but to give me a big league contract. After all those years, I had made the New York Yankees. They said I could even leave training camp a day early to drive my family up to New York.

If that wasn't the happiest day of our lives, it was right up there. We pulled out of Fort Lauderdale, singing all the way, "Big league baseball here we come. / Who cares where we started from?" And Beth's personal favorite, "I want to wake up in the city that never sleeps."

As we exited the Turnpike near Fort Pierce to pick up 95 North, a big beefy guy in dark aviator glasses got out of his little tollbooth and walked in front of our car.

"Are you Sam Ward, the baseball player?" he asked.

"Yes," I said, smiling proudly. "I'm with the New York Yankees. How did you recognize me?"

"I didn't," he said. "We have instructions to look for a green station wagon with Illinois plates and a bicycle on top. I got a message for you."

The toll guy handed me a piece of paper. It said: "Return to Fort Lauderdale. Call Hal Ramey." Hal Ramey was in charge of minor league operations for the Yankees.

Return to Fort Lauderdale?

The dirty, no-good sonovabitches! Back to the minors. Again! I refused to believe it.

"Who gave you this message?" I asked bitterly.

The guy behind me honked his horn.

"We got a call from the state police," said the toll guy.

The guy behind me honked again.

"So what?" I shouted. "That doesn't mean anything. Maybe it's a joke. Maybe it's—"

I couldn't think of any other possibilities.

Now the whole line of cars was honking.

"You'll have to pull off to the side and let these other cars through," said the toll guy.

"I'll go when I'm good and ready," I said defiantly.

"Sam," said Julie. "Please!"

So, with everybody honking and my hands shaking on the steering wheel, I pulled over to a rest area near some telephones.

"Bullshit!" I hollered at the dashboard. "Bullshit!"

I got out of the car and slammed the door. I had to walk around, get moving, do something so I wouldn't explode any more than I already had. I knew I was scaring Beth and I had to get myself under control. I paced back and forth for a while, but that didn't do any good, so I sat down on a bench and tried to figure out what to do next.

"Sweetheart," said Julie softly as she sat down next to me. "I've got a good idea. Let's go home."

"We're not going home," I said.

"The car's packed," said Julie. "We've got all our stuff. Let's just—"

"We're *not* going home," I said, louder.

"Come on, Sam," she said. "I'll start driving. If we leave now, we can be home by tomorrow night."

"We're *not going home*!" I shouted.

"Well," said Julie, with a new edge in her voice, "*I'm* not going back to Fort Lauderdale."

"Let's get in the car," I said, feeling in my pockets for the keys.

Julie made no move to get up from the bench. I tried to remember what I had done with the keys.

"Where the hell are my keys?" I said.

There was a long silence.

"I've got them," said Julie. "You're in no shape to drive."

"Bullshit!" I screamed again.

I was angry. I was frustrated. I didn't know what to do. I just knew I had to get the hell out of there. I looked over at the car, trying to remember where I had put the hide-a-key. Under the bumper? Behind the license plate? My eyes drifted up to the bicycle on top of the luggage rack. Beth's bicycle.

I walked over to the car. I undid the straps on the luggage rack. I lifted the bike down. It was a pretty good-sized twelve-speed bike, with hand brakes and a brown wicker basket. So what if it was pink?

I got on the bike, wobbled around until I got my balance, and started pedaling. It was the strangest thing. While I was doing it, part of me knew it was crazy. But another part of me, the bully part, took over. I couldn't make myself stop. And then it was too late to turn back.

"Where's Daddy going with my bike?" Beth asked.

"I'm not sure, honey," said Julie, trying to keep her voice steady. "I think he's going south."

And those were the last words I heard until the car pulled up alongside me about ten minutes later. The rest of the trip back to Fort Lauderdale was very quiet. Except for Beth's next question.

"Where are we going now, Daddy?" she asked.

There was a long silence. "That's a very good question," said Julie, sounding curiously distant. "I'd like to know the answer myself."

Where was I going? Why was I risking so much for that one-in-a-million chance to be a major league baseball player?

It was a question I asked myself while I worked on the wall.

After the stones were delivered, I bought some tools: work gloves, hammer, shovel, long wooden stakes, measuring tape, twine. I drove two stakes into the ground sixty feet, six inches apart, the distance between the mound and home plate. Why not? As an arbitrary span, it's as good as any. Opposite these stakes, exactly two feet away, I drove the other two stakes and connected all four with twine, stretched tight a few inches off the ground. This long, skinny rectangle, running along the property line, would be the perimeter of my wall.

Next, I used the shovel to dig a three-inch-deep trough within the borders of the twine. Emil had told me to lay the base stones a few inches below ground level to prevent heaving. Now it was time to lay the first stone. Unfortunately, the one that looked like it would make a good corner happened to be at the bottom of a pallet, so I had to spend three hours unloading. *Now* I was ready to lay the first stone. Or rather, roll it end over end into position because it was too damn heavy to lift. I wondered if Emil meant *me* when he was talking about heaving.

That first stone sure looked beautiful sitting there on the corner. It looked so nice I even took a picture of it. Now I needed to find a stone for the other corner, but it had to be a certain size and shape to fit between the first stone and the twine border. Of course, the perfect stone just happened to be at the bottom of another pallet. Where else?

By the end of that first day I had learned a few things. What I learned was that I needed a few more pieces of equipment as follows: heavy-duty reinforced work gloves, weight lifter's belt, steel-toed boots. And the next morning I discovered even more. Namely, that my body could hurt as much as my heart, that fourteen hours may be a little too much on the first day, and that you shouldn't lie down until after you've taken a shower if you don't want to wake up filthy dirty the next morning on the couch.

"Hey, whaddya say," hollers Leon Banks, pressing a black, sticky pine-tar rag against the handle of his bat. "Let's jump on this long-neck, flat-ass, no-account motherfucker."

My sentiments exactly.

	1	2	3	4	5	6	7	8	9		R	H	E
PHILLIES	0	0									0	1	0
CUBS	0										0	0	0

So, I'm still not winning. I'm a long way from winning. seven and a half innings to go. I feel like a guy in jail putting daily X's on a calendar though he doesn't even know when his time is up. I mean, this is definitely not where I want to be.

I look at Leon Danks as he moves to the plate. He's the Cubs' multi-million-dollar hot-shit left-handed cleanup hitter. He comes up swinging four bats. Not even Babe Ruth swung four bats. He's got two in each hand, over and under like he's a giant baton twirler. No weighted donut for this baby. You can bet the TV camera is on him. He tosses away three bats, then plays with his Velcro straps, zip/slap, zip/slap, then slides his hand up and down the barrel like he's stroking his dick.

Finally he steps in.

Greene's first pitch is a breaking ball, maybe wide, maybe not.

Question: When is a ball not a ball?

Answer: When the umpire says it's a strike.

"Streeerike!" I yell, my right fist zapping air.

The big bastard grins.

Green curves him again, this time in the dirt. The count goes to 2 and 2 and then Greene's curve hangs. Banks lashes it to right field for a single.

I don't like the leadoff man getting on. I don't like the hanging curve that made it so. Things like that, they upset my stomach. They build up the cotton in my mouth.

Mark Grace fouls off the first two pitches, takes a waste pitch in the dirt. On the 1-2 pitch, I bang him out on a fastball close enough to the inside edge.

The first pitch to Wilkins is high for ball one. The second is on the corner, and the big catcher hits a checked-swing blooper down the right-field line that falls in for a double. Banks cruises into third clapping his hands as the crowd tells me everything I need to know.

With runners on second and third and one out, I've got to eliminate Buechele. He has that eager look in his eye like this is going to be his great big day. Me, I'd give 10 percent of what's in my travel bag if someone would tell Greene to throw breaking balls; it helps me make the plate as wide as it needs to be. But no, he loves the heater. Rear back and throw that heater. So it happens. Exactly what I was afraid would happen. I can even feel it coming. Buechele swings and the heater leaves his bat hotter than when it arrived. The ball rifles through the infield, creating instantaneous crowd reactions, horror sounds of triumph piling waves on top of each other as two Cubs runners cross the plate in front of me.

Two solid minutes of rising thunder rubs salt on the bad-news wound. I tell myself, easy does it, easy does it. Nothing has happened but what you knew was likely to happen. You can't have it all your way. Give a little this inning, take it back the next. Isn't that the way it has to be?

The mind says *go,* but the heart says *no.* There's a worm crawling in the apple.

Like my mother used to say, "God is punishing you!"

There's a conference on the mound, the usual gang. Maybe I ought to go out there and tell Greene, hey, get smart, throw curves. Or maybe I could tell Daulton what pitches to call. Or maybe I should faint dead away.

Sammy Sosa comes to the plate like he's another great slugger. He fouls off the first pitch, then I give him a doubtful breaking ball. With 2 and 2, he tops a dribbler for the force at second, but it's too slow for a double play.

Two outs, and here comes Ward. He steps in like he doesn't hear the applause. Tip your hat, fruitcake, because you'll never hear that sound again. I'm happy for you, Ward: if it hadn't been for the two RBIs, if there were more men on base and less than two out, your ass would be gone for a pinch hitter. And I'm happy for me. I'd rather have his knuckleball than Foster's heater. The next time around the batting order, the Phillies will eat him up.

He takes two strikes down the slot, then swings at a pitch that misses by a foot, and the inning finally is over.

The Phillies run in and the Cubs run out, but the two runs are bullets in my gut. The roaring 50,000 around me makes it worse. I can't help thinking: you shouldn't have let go with that fart.

The ball boy comes over to refill my bag. As he hands me a half dozen, he asks, "Is this really your last game, Ernie?"

"Yeah, 'fraid so."

"Well, they all say you're the best," he says.

As he hustles off, the man in the stands ruins the moment with a second opinion.

"Kolacka, you're a bum!"

There's one in every crowd. You can't wear a blue suit without hearing that fucking word. Enid once said, "Baseball is a a game where there's always someone sitting behind you calling your husband a bum."

Enid could be witty enough. But not often enough. Once, maybe a thousand years ago, I called home to say hello and Enid, poor Enid, couldn't help but give me the bad news: the baby twins were running 103°, throwing up their guts. The Olds wouldn't start, we needed a new car. The toilet was fucked up, it wouldn't stop flushing. Blah blah blah. Me, I'd be lying in a cruddy motel room, the cheapest I could find. It stunk like rotten eggs, there were eighty-nine cockroaches as big as my fist, I'd been *dining* on carrots and celery to send home every dime of my $350-a-month paycheck. It'd be too hot to do anything but wait for the night game where I'd bust my ass to be the best but, no matter, some scumbag would be there to call me a bum.

Sure, I'd wonder what I was doing. Why was I doing it? I mean, there were times when I didn't know who the fuck I was. I was sorry for Enid, I was guilty about being away all the time. When I got home, I was such a stranger, sometimes it took three weeks before my kids would sit on my lap. Maybe, like Enid really wanted, I ought to quit, even if it meant driving a truck for the Hempstead Highway Department.

So what made me stick it out? Like I said, pal, I loved it. No matter how bad it got for me, I never stopped loving it. Baseball was my life.

Like the ball boy had said: "You're the best!" What does *he* know? I don't want to hear that today. Today I'm someone else. Today I picture that kid leaving the ballpark with *his* baseball cap turned around, peak to the rear, like everything has to be the opposite of what it's supposed to be. Ballplayers can't wait to fill the dugout up with caps turned backward. It's the style wherever you go. You've got to look like a zombie. Even the uniforms are wacko. Preseason, equipment managers get them measured with micrometers for the exact size of their buttocks so the ballplayers can look like ballet dancers in leotards. What kind of bullshit is that? The big change in baseball is not dome stadiums or Astroturf or designated hitters or even the new gloves that are bigger than toilet bowls. It's *spandex*. I heard of a million-dollar free agent who so loved the look of his ass he hired his own tailor to make his uniform. It was in his contract that the club had to pay for it. The club loved the idea for the mileage they got from the public relations. As one wag put it: "You want to explain the new popularity of the national pastime? It's *tight pants*." Don't they know how many hit-by-pitches they lose with skin-tight uniforms? If a pitched ball merely brushes cloth, the batter gets his base. A loose-fitting shirt might be worth a dozen runs a year. On a hot day, a hitter would even feel better swinging a bat. Instead of pants down to the shoes, set them back at the calves and they'd shrink the strike zone. Show me a leadoff man in an old-fashioned baggy uniform and I'll show you somebody who can give a pitcher serious trouble.

I know, I've been around too long. I see players with 10-pound travel kits full of perfumes and cosmetics and blow-dryers. I see 225-pound sluggers in Velcro batting gloves swinging featherweight bats that break even on bunts. They can't hit their weights, but they get more money in one season than Willie Mays made in his lifetime. I see born-again heroes who brag about how they found God, but they can't find the cutoff man. I see young big bonus babies with 90-mile-an-hour fastballs who've been so pampered since high school they couldn't make a flight reservation, much less wipe their own asses. They say ballplayers are better than ever, but I see big stars go 0 for 4 enough times to go 0 for September. They say the game is better than ever, but I say fuck those three-hour 1–0 games and exploding scoreboards and endless rock music. An umpire can figure he's lucky if some asshole dressed like a fucking chicken doesn't sneak up and piss on his leg.

Sometimes I feel like I'm a hundred years old.

Sure as shit, I'd feel a whole lot younger if I was two runs ahead.

		1	2	3	4	5	6	7	8	9		R	H	E
PHILLIES		0	0									0	1	0
CUBS		0	2									2	3	0

I walk out to the mound leading 2–zip, but it means nothing to me. I pretend the game is tied. I don't want to be affected by the score. Some pitchers are better when they're winning, which is another way of saying they're not so good when they're losing. Me, I pitch the same no matter what the score is. Ten runs up or ten runs down, I'm a machine. That's what I tell myself. In case I fall behind.

With some guys you can tell the score by their body language. The slump of the shoulders, the barely perceptible drop of the head, the first hint of resignation that the matador looks for in a bull. When the head gets low enough, it's time to place the sword between the shoulder blades.

Meanwhile, Phillies' left fielder Pete Incaviglia is stepping into the batter's box. My first pitch is a curve that breaks over the outside corner for strike one. A knuckler misses inside for ball one. A sinker looks pretty good, but it's ball two. A change-up is almost in there, but it's *ball three*. Damn, I'm just missing. And a pretty good knuckler is wide for ball four.

Shit! I *hate* walking the leadoff man. Especially the number seven hitter. But I'm standing tall.

And here's shortstop Kevin Stocker. How about a nice one-hopper back to me for a double play? Wilkins gives me the sign. I kick and throw. And it's ... a swinging strike knuckler that jumps so sharply it bounces off Wilkins's glove. That's the good news. The bad news is that Incaviglia steals second base without even drawing a throw. That's one of the problems with the knuckleball. Stolen bases. Another problem is managers and pitching coaches who hate easy steals on knuckleballs, especially after a walk. It looks like a gift. Or two gifts. They'd much rather see a guy hit a double in the first place. Doubles they understand. You figure it out.

Man on second, nobody out. A knuckleball dives in the dirt for ball one. A sinker just misses low for ball two, and ... I hear a glove popping in our bullpen. What the hell's going on? I've got good stuff out here! Pisses me off. But I can't let it get to me. I kick and throw. Stocker ... swings and misses for strike two. Sonovabitches. A knuckleball is wide for ball three. Full count on Kevin Stocker. Wilkins calls for the knuckler. I check the runner. I kick and throw. And a corkscrew beauty ... just ... barely misses the outside corner for ball four. Whoa! That one looked pretty good.

Men on first and second, nobody out and the pitcher, Tommy Greene, gets ready to hit.

And here comes the pitching coach.

Shit! This can't be good. Gilson's not going to take me out, because Bateman always does that himself. Gilson just wants to give Foster a little more time to get loose. They'll let me pitch to Greene and *then* I'm gone.

The heartbreaking thing is that I'm throwing the ball well right now. Walks are part of the deal with the knuckleball. Hell, if it's breaking, nobody's going to hit it. They *can't* take me out. I'm just getting started!

Kolacka calls time out and the infielders converge on the mound to see what Gilson has to say.

Goddamn!

"Awright, bunt situation," says Gilson, who doesn't even look at me. "Get the easy out at first. Play it safe."

Everybody nods. It's a routine play. Grace and Buechele will charge in from first and third to field the bunt, Sandberg will come over from second base to take the throw at first, and Jerome will drift toward third.

Gilson heads back to the dugout, waving his hat at the bullpen to ask if Foster is ready yet. The answering wave doesn't come, which means Foster needs a few more pitches. And a few more pitches means, after the bunt, I'm out of here. That's it. I'm through. Forever.

"Jerome!" I stop him as the other infielders return to their positions. I've got to *do* something.

"Hey, how about I throw to you for the force at third?" I say, a crazy man trying to sound sane.

This is a big long shot because Jerome has to race from his shortstop position, beat the lead runner to third base, *and* take the throw from me at the same time. If it fails, you've got bases loaded and nobody out. I've done it a few times before, but only as a called play. I've never seen it done when the coach specifically says to play it safe and get the out at first. And it's not only my ass at stake, it's Jerome's. I see the doubt all over his handsome young face. He can easily shake me off with a sensible "No way, José" and I'm doomed.

"Sheeeit," he says with an evil grin. "I'm a streak of motherfucking lightning. Let's do it."

He actually *likes* the idea.

Yeah, and God bless Jerome Davis.

Now the trick is to coax a good bunt on the first pitch. We'll only have one shot at it. Once our dugout see Jerome tearing for third, they'll know what's up and call it off.

Wilkins signals knuckleball. Normally a good idea, but it's too hard to bunt, so I shake him off. Wilkins must be wondering what the hell I'm thinking. He finally gives me the sinker. I nod. In the stretch position, out of the corner of my eye, I see Jerome fake a pickoff move toward second, Incaviglia buys it, and I pitch knowing Jerome has a head start for third.

The bunt is down toward Buechele, who comes in to make the play. But I'm off the mound like a maniac and I beat him to it. Without looking, I wheel and fire to third just before colliding with Buechele. From my new position on the ground, I see Jerome leap to avoid the runner sliding into third as the umpire bangs him out. And the crowd goes bananas.

I don't even want to look over in the dugout. God knows what the hell's going on. If they're hollering at me, I can't hear it anyway, the crowd's making so much noise. Tuthill's probably working on the vein in Gilson's neck. But I do know this: there appears to be some sentiment in the stands for me remaining in the game for at least one more hitter.

Meanwhile, I can't jerk myself off with these thoughts. I've still got runners at first and second and only one out. Wilkins shakes his head, and walks back behind the plate.

Dykstra, who hit that first-pitch rocket off the wall, steps into the batter's box. Wilkins calls for the knuckler, a gutsy call considering what Dykstra did to the first one. I like Wilkins. Calling the same pitch shows confidence in me. Or else he's still in shock from that last play. I check the runners. I kick and throw. And a dandy little knuckleball is popped up into foul territory behind third base ... could be trouble ... Jerome running over ... he calls Buechele off ... and takes it himself for out number two.

This brings up Mariano Duncan, who sent Banks to the wall in the first inning. But this time he hits a nice little chopper to Sandberg and the inning is over. Just like that.

I love this game.

The question is, how do certain people feel about *me*? As I walk off the mound, I'm wondering if Buechele is pissed at me for banging into him, if Jerome's in deep shit, and if Foster's going in to pitch the next inning. The crowd doesn't care about any of this. They give us a standing ovation.

Meanwhile, Gilson's waiting on the top step. He's going to be all over my ass for not being a team player and in this case he's right. But I've been waiting eleven years to get here, goddamnit. I'm not leaving so easily. I go right over to him. I figure, what's he going to do, release me? And then he doesn't say anything! He just glares. I guess I'm lucky he doesn't have a baseball in his hand.

As I step into the dugout, I'm looking for Jerome and Buechele. I want to say thanks, and I'm sorry. I like to keep on good terms with my defense. Buechele is pretty funny about it. He says the club will probably pay for the operation he'll need on his back. Jerome doesn't say anything, just holds out his palm so I can give it a slap. Mr. Cool.

And what did Bateman think about the play? Well, if he *didn't* like it, Bobby Rapp would let us know. One of Rapp's jobs as coach and right-hand flunky is to interpret Bateman's every mood and then act it out.

Instead, Rapp is actually *talking* to me and Jerome. Or talking *about* us while we're sitting right there, which is how he talks to you. "Rapp talk," the players call it.

"You gotta keep an eye on these two," he says to hitting coach Bill

Robinson, who for some reason Rapp holds personally responsible for the behavior of Jerome. Like whenever Jerome wears his hat backward, which he only does when Rapp is around, Rapp complains to Robinson. "You better shape him up," Rapp will say. He used to say "shape that *boy* up," but Robinson straightened him out. Now Rapp repeats his favorite nickname for me and Jerome. "Butch Cassidy and the Breakdance Kid."

This goes back to last year when Rapp was managing at Des Moines and Jerome and I were playing a lot of chess in the clubhouse. One night, after we had lost our tenth straight, Rapp called a team meeting to discuss the meaning of the word *commitment* and its apparent lack thereof. Right in the middle of a chess game between me and Jerome. Jerome's move. Of course, I put the board down on the floor so we wouldn't be tempted to play. Which worked out fine until Rapp told the team he was so disgusted he didn't even want to *look* at us. Then, while we were all hanging our heads in shame, Jerome nudged pawn to rook four with his stockinged foot.

The incident became legend for what Rapp said upon observing this great move by Jerome. In a very loud voice, Bobby Rapp hollered out the world's longest off-color sentence that, with the exception of my name, did not repeat a single word. He began with "shitassed bug fuckers," evolved from there to "ballbusting pissmongers," continued on past "dick, whore, cock, bitch," and finished up strong with "dirty no-good jerkoff sucking pigs." He may have meant *suckling* pigs there, but I chose not to inquire.

Naturally, I got the blame for the whole episode. Why? Because apparently I have the power to control Jerome's left foot.

Meanwhile, the Chicago Cubs are beating the Philadelphia Phillies 2–0 and I, personally, have pitched three scoreless innings.

Three scoreless innings!

Does that mean I'm "doing the fucking job"?

I feel pretty good right now, but I also know that three scoreless innings is not a ball game.

Just as a post is not a wall.

No self-respecting wall begins without a post: a supporting abutment, a decorative column, a pier, a structural mount to properly announce the wall. A larger mass from which the narrower, shorter wall would then project.

I had nothing to go on except instinct, but I figured the post should be about a foot higher and wider than the wall itself. So if the wall was going to be four feet high by two feet wide, I'd need a post that was five feet high by three feet wide. A post that protruded a foot above and six inches on either side would give the wall a regal look.

And be a royal pain in the ass to build. The problem is the four corners. First you need stones with some sort of right angle, which aren't that common. Then you have to coordinate the four cornerstones so they either butt together or leave a space that can be filled with a stone which then doesn't interfere with the cornerstone above. Each stone impacts the size and shape of the stones around it. Imagine stacking Christmas packages of all different shapes and sizes to form a cube. Then imagine that each package has only one decent corner. Now imagine that the packages are filled with something heavy. Like stones.

It took me two hours just to position the first three cornerstones, which fit reasonably well, but I still didn't know if I had the right combination because I hadn't yet found a fourth corner. Then the question became, was it a better use of time and energy to rearrange or replace the existing stones, or unload more pallets hoping to find the missing fourth corner? Since I'd have to do it anyway, I opted to unload more pallets. Besides, I didn't want to fool around anymore with the three existing cornerstones, which weighed almost 100 pounds apiece. And they didn't have handles on them.

A pallet of stones forms a giant cube about four feet wide, three feet deep, and five feet high. The stones are stacked randomly on a wooden platform by men called "stackers" who gather them from old farms where they lie in approximate rows at the edge of plantings, having been tossed there by farmers who used them to separate their fields. The stones are secured to the pallet with heavy-duty chicken wire stapled to the sides of the platform and secured at the top by a single strand of wire, which connects and tightens the chicken-wire loops like a drawstring. The pallets are then loaded onto a truck for the ride to a stone "dock," where they're sold to dealers, who sell them to the public.

In the old days, when stone houses were common, the loaded pallets would be hauled to a dock on horse-drawn carts. It took lots of skill and good brakes to drive down from the mountains with a team of horses and a shifting load of stone. These cart drivers were called "teamsters," for the team of horses, which eventually became the name of the trucker's union. It was dangerous to be a teamster. Still is.

As I unloaded the pallets, I discovered an interesting fact: pallets are an efficient way to contain a lot of stones. Throwing them around on the ground is not. Six pallets into the unloading process, I realized I couldn't *walk* anywhere without tripping over stones. It then occurred to me that fourteen pallets, all spread out, might cover several acres. Our property would look like the farmers' fields before they cleared the stones!

This led to my jigsaw-puzzle solution: categories. Like grouping puzzle pieces by color—blue sky, red barn, etc.—I grouped stones by size and shape, according to my needs, as follows:

1. Base—large blocks for more support at the bottom

2. Facing—any interesting surface or color for the body of the wall

3. Shims—flat slivers to support the facing stones

4. Corners—to use for the post or save for the other end

5. Caps—flat with a slightly rounded surface for the top

6. Culls—poor composition or shape to use as filler

7. Weirdos—odd shapes to fill awkward spaces

After the category solution, I was tripping over *piles,* which made much more sense to me.

As I sit here waiting for us to hit in the bottom of the third, a Gypsy Kings tape is playing on the loudspeaker. This is a helluva lot better than what they play at some ballparks, which is nonstop noise by people with names like Guns and Megadeth. And I'm really glad they don't have one of those giant video screens in center field. Otherwise they'd be showing replays of that force at third by me and Jerome.

I don't think Bateman could bear to watch it again. Right now he's squeezing an ice-water-soaked towel onto his bare head, letting the cold rivulets run down over his face and neck. Now he opens his eyes, blinks a few times, and slowly expels the air from his lungs.

"Hey, Doc," he says to Tuthill. "You got any heart attack pills? I have a feeling I'm going to need some before this game is over."

	1	2	3	4	5	6	7	8	9	R	H	E
PHILLIES	0	0	0							0	1	0
CUBS	0	2								2	3	0

I've got to admit, Ward's play on that bunt was masterful. I haven't seen that done since I can remember and he looked like he'd worked it dozens of times in the minors.

I get a chilling notion that it's going to be a long afternoon.

I watch Ward move off the mound, thinking he's going to step on the foul line just because most pitchers don't. Pitchers in the boondocks used to say, "Step on a foul line / Back to the coal mine." Ballplayers have superstitions. Especially pitchers. They develop rituals. They figure if they don't go to their cap after throwing a strike, they'll never throw another. When I was a kid, I always stepped on third on the way back to the dugout if we were on the left-field side, but I didn't on the way out. I had no other superstitions. Nothing at the plate. No bullshit moves between pitches. I got into the box, got set, and never got out. Some guys, they've got to do their 30-second dance after every pitch, four steps out, tap spikes with the bat, fix their this, fuck with their that, every time the same. Maybe they think they're big stars getting TV time: look at me, I'm doing my million-dollar thing.

I know an umpire who will not speak a four-letter word before a game —then will cuss a fucking streak after the first pitch. There was a guy in the Pacific Coast League who would wear three Saint Christopher medals if it was Sunday. Watch Lew Sirotta get dressed, he'll turn his left sock inside out, then outside in before he puts it on. Always the left, never the right. If it's his turn to work the plate, he won't take a leak unless he's sitting down.

I'm wrong about Ward. He walked across the line as if he never saw it.

I go to dust the plate, it's always from the third-base side. Then I go back around the other. Clockwise. The first one to notice that was Trisha from Hawaii. She even knew why. She looked at me with those sparkling brown eyes and told me the news: "You wait for the catcher to take his practice throw to second. He throws with his right arm, so you have to stand to his left, where it's safe. Right?" I laughed. She was right. You could fall in love with a woman like that.

Here's Willie Wilson, the Cubs' top of the order. They're up by two, so I figure I can make calls I couldn't if they were two down. I don't want to see any more Cubbies crossing the plate. I see nothing but danger, all kinds of danger, every swing is loaded with danger. The whole ball game could bust wide open. It's happened enough with this ball club, the crowd feels it can make it happen with noise.

Wilson obliges me by popping up to the shortstop for the first out.

Greene goes to work on shortstop Davis with a hopping fastball, but it's outside the plate and high. Then he throws a hard breaking ball that crosses just off the corner—but I give it to him to even the count. If I don't, he'd be throwing 2 and 0, definitely in trouble. I can see the relief in his face, for now he has breathing room. He curves Davis again and it's fouled off for the second strike. It's a strike that's as much my doing as his. And so is the next one, another breaking ball that comes in cock-high and falls off like it was made of lead: Davis swings and misses and he's out of there.

One call did that. He struck out swinging—but I made it happen.

Did you see what I did, Roger? Did you see how I worked it? The plate is 17 inches wide with a black beveled edge, and the ball is 2½ inches in diameter, any part of which nicks a corner, it's a strike, stretching the strike zone to 22 inches if you have a mind to.

Stretch it for Greene.

Squeeze it for Ward.

Baseball is a game of inches.

Comes now Ryne Sandberg bringing fresh thunder from the stands. I don't need any reminder of the continuing threat. Greene goes into his stretch, I go into my crouch. With no one on and two out, he'll work the corners. Greene's change-up catches Sandberg looking, and it's in there for strike one. The slider is close, but I give it to Sandberg. At 1 and 1, Greene drills a fastball on the inside at the knees and Sandberg slaps a hard one-hopper at the shortstop and he's out on a simple throw to first, ending the inning.

The crowd subsides, content for the moment with a two-run lead.

Roger always liked my being an umpire. He kept saying it through all the years I was in the minors: "You'll make it, you'll make it," like there was never a doubt. Every year or so, he'd show up, I never knew when or where. He even bought a rule book, studied it, knew the rules better than some umpires. Once, in Sacramento, the Pacific Coast League, he was there when I called a balk that set off a twenty-minute rhubarb. I had to throw out the Sacramento pitcher for going berserk, and then the manager for topping him, and they lost a game they might have won. Since he had won over $1,500 in a poker game in San Francisco the night before, Rog insisted on buying me dinner at Bailey's, where the local elite meet to eat. Right off, he agreed with my call. The pitcher had failed to come to a complete stop before making his pitch. Rule 8.05(m). Twice before, the pitcher had held a runner close by doing so. The balk rule is designed to prevent a pitcher from deceiving the base runner.

"To make that call required the guts of a burglar," Roger said as he clicked the ice cubes in his scotch glass.

"It's a classic umpire's no-no," I told him. Then I put on my specs to read the menu, which is another no-no. A pair of very high-class-looking gents were walking by the table at that moment, and one stopped, stared at me.

"Kolacka? Is this Kolacka?"

"It's him!" said the other.

They glared at me like they couldn't get over me sitting in their restaurant.

It was like I'd offended them twice. One was actually steaming, the fury was in his eyes, he was hell-bent for revenge. There was no way I could move fast enough. He picked up a glass, threw water in my face, then walked away.

I truly hated that kind of shit. No matter that I'd seen it all. In a Santo Domingo winter league, a bullet went through my windshield while I was driving away from a ballpark. In Birmingham, Alabama, they burned a pile of newspapers under my car outside the locker room. In Gainesville, Florida, I got death-threatening phone calls. It's happened to all umpires one time or another. But I knew, and other umpires knew, and league officials knew, it happened more often to me because Ernie Kolacka never called them special for the home club.

I dried my face with a napkin, wiped my reading glasses extra slowly, deliberately, held them up in front of my eyes to check them, then polished them again. Of course, this was what set Roger laughing.

"What's so funny?" I asked.

He started to answer, but choked on his own laughter. When he tried again, it got worse. I couldn't help it; I began to laugh with him.

"You're a big man, Ernie," he said finally. "I mean, a really big man."

Meaning, if I was some kind of pipsqueak I'd still be dry. The way he said it, he was proud of me.

"Two more double Dewar's," he said to the waiter. "And please, a fresh glass of water for my friend." Even the waiter laughed.

He was still laughing when the drinks came, and he raised his glass to mine.

"To the blessings of a full house, kings up!" Roger's toast to the good life.

"Fuck 'em all, big and small." Mine.

We drank, and for that moment, all was right with the world. It got even better with the oysters and prime ribs and Caesar salad. It didn't get any worse with the pineapple cheesecake and coffee. Or the brandy.

"Sounds like you've been playing poker for a load of dimes," I said. In Korea, it was always a ten-cent ante.

"Call it a Double A League," he said. "I'm still a long way from the biggies." There was a whole new look in his eye when he began to talk about it, the kind of look I'd see on the faces of lousy golfers when they'd had a good round. "Poker is a challenge to what you've got in you. When you pass forty, you've got to find something, you know what I mean?" He patted his bulging belly. Every time I saw him, he'd added a few more pounds. "When I sit down at the old octagon with the chips and cigars and rest my hands on that sweet green felt ... it's a real kick, Ernie. It's more exciting than fucking my wife."

"With me, so is watching the nightly news."

He laughed. "Louise hates the poker bit. But when I win big, she doesn't hate it so much."

"Do you tell her when you lose?"

"Lose?" He looked at me like I must be crazy. "I *never* lose!"

I laughed. I could see where he'd like to gamble. Even the way he risked his life to save me, wasn't that a gambler's ploy? You never knew with Roger. He was a guy stuck in a routine job making around $50,000 a year checking on all those chain stores. The way he talked about it, it must have bored the hell out of him. He was making four or five times as much as I was, but I could almost feel sorry for him.

But then, he could always surprise me. He'd do something to stand any scene on its head. On the way out, for example, he detoured to where the two ball-busters were eating. He stood beside their table for a moment, just long enough to worry them, then raised a whole pitcher of ice water and doused them both.

"Baptism!" he cried out.

He slipped the maître d' $100 and we left laughing like a couple of kids who had just given the class bully a hotfoot.

So here comes Rick Wilkins out of the dugout wearing his best two-run-lead grin. You'd think he'd never heard of the fat lady.

He throws to second base to end the warm-up. He's winning by two runs, so he's cocky. And because I'm losing, I get instant fantasies of how I'm going to turn it around. I even think, you out there on the mound, the other clown pawing dirt around the rubber, hey, I'm gonna have your ass for lunch!

And because of that, I get slapped by a wave of guilt. This is not the way to run a ball game. I shouldn't be thinking of personalities. Whoever is on that mound, it doesn't matter. It's Roger who matters. Fuck Ward. Forget Ward.

It's the sort of shit-thinking that springs from guilt. You can't be an umpire and know guilt. You can't even believe you're ever wrong, you don't make bad calls, you've got to be God, and God can't be guilty. Otherwise you'll crack up. Once I almost did. It was a time in my life when I was reaching the end of my rope. After twenty-two years as an umpire, I was still stuck in the minors. The dream was no longer a dream; it became an obsession. I mean, I didn't need Enid to tell me that I wasn't rational anymore, not so you could explain it in words. I was running crazy for something impossible to get.

I was working three days in Tacoma in the Pacific Coast League, ending with a Sunday doubleheader. On Saturday night, I got a call from my Uncle Phil in Hempstead telling me my father had a stroke. He was in critical condition. How soon could I get back?

Immediately, my heart jumped. How soon? In the morning, I said. I'll take the first flight back.

But Harry Ullman, the president of the league, had other ideas. This was going to be a big crucial Sunday. They couldn't possibly replace me with anyone who could pull his weight. He insisted I *had* to stay. I could catch the last flight out Sunday evening. "He's in the hospital? No reason to worry. People always live longer than everybody thinks they will." Sure. And people always say what serves their purposes. I hated this. For one thing, the doubleheader wasn't going to end in time to catch that 7:30 flight. When I told him no, I had to leave in the morning, Ullman started telling me how he was prepared to do big things for me. A substantial bonus, for instance. He would make me chief of umpires at a large boost in salary. He'd recommend me to the National League offices as the best in the PCL. He'd remove all the so-called negatives in my record. All this if I worked the Sunday doubleheader. Then, if I didn't, came the threats. He could promise me a lot of trouble. It was like I didn't have any choice in the matter. So I stayed.

I missed the Sunday-night flight. I called my uncle, said I'd be back on Monday instead. My father died while I was in flight. I didn't even see his body until after it was embalmed. What made it worse, he'd asked for me right up to the end. I knew why. He wanted to square with me, he didn't want to die without making peace for the way he failed me. What hurt was the cycle, father to son to father. When I'm dying, Joe will be too busy washing cars to come. If Amy comes, she won't shed a tear.

You want to look for meanings? What for? You can't figure out what life is like. My father said it first, don't bother to ask, just live it. Pop was a good man who fucked up. And what am I? How do I rate? Don't ask Enid. Don't ask my kids. Don't even ask me. If I died tomorrow, what would they say of me? Ernie Kolacka was a fool chasing a bad dream.

It's like Enid once warned me: "You're gonna die a loser, Ernie. Your last words will be 'Balk! Balk!' "

After the funeral, I walked for hours. When I got home, Enid was at the kitchen table with a bottle of Jack Daniel's. The place was a mess. My home seemed as dingy as my life. Enid looked terrible, the light making shadows on her wrinkles. It went with the 2:00 AM chill. I couldn't help thinking that this was what I'd done to her. Twenty-five married years of zilch. Where was the warmth that holds you steady when you're shaky? There was nothing left of us. Not even the sex. I used to think that screwing made everything else better. I used to think she wanted it as much as me. But it became nothing. She once said to me: "Ernie, you read the wrong rule book." I thought: Enid, never marry the first man who asks you.

I took a glass and loaded it with the Jack Daniel's and sat down across from her. I was so soaked in shame, if she hit me with the bottle I wouldn't have felt it. She didn't even look at me.

"Enid, I'm sorry." I was apologizing for a whole lifetime.

She sighed. "Oh, God."

"I mean, I wish I could make it up to everyone."

She shook her head as she prepared to drink.

"You're a good man, Ernie. But you don't fit in ... That's for sure ... You don't fit in anywhere."

It hurt. It hurt more because she was being sympathetic.

"You know what Amy called you? 'Dad is a rock with sharp edges.' " You can't hold it, rub it, it looks bad, it's not good for a damned thing. "Tell me, Ernie: how did they get you to stay?"

I told her the truth, how they promised me and threatened me.

"And you believed it." It wasn't even a question. She just wanted me to admit it.

I admitted it. I believed what I had to believe. That was the way I lived.

"You're not a rock, Ernie," she said. "You're a *sponge*."

She got that right, I guess. Squeeze me and what oozes out? All the bullshit I've been soaking up all these years.

"You asked for it, didn't you?" she went on. "You let them use you. A regular patsy, you know what I mean? I think you enjoy it. It lets you feel you're a martyr. You *are* a loser, Ernie. You truly believe you're the best —and maybe you are—but you always come out last, don't you?"

She was letting out the whole string of yarn. No doubt the Jack Daniel's helped her. It was sad, all right. So much stuff dredged up from so many years.

Then came the topper.

"Maybe you should've learned something from your friend Sirotta."

"What?"

"You hate him because he's what you would like to be. He's no loser. He's in the majors. He's happy!"

I shuddered. Was she trying to hurt me? Why was she trashing me like that?

"Enid, you don't know what you're saying!"

"Tell me, Ernie. Honestly. If you had it to do over—"

"No! I'd never be like him. Never!"

She shook her head like I'd just confessed to drowning a puppy dog.

"No, of course not." She sighed. "That's my point, isn't it? You never learn anything. You never will."

It was like she hammered the last nail in my coffin. You hear that from your wife, you want to scream for what it signifies. You say to yourself, hey, it's a bad day at Hempstead; she didn't mean it, not really; she had one too many slugs of the bourbon, whatever.

Then, my God, she started to recite poetry. Maybe it was the Jack Daniel's on top of everything else. She closed her eyes and out it came—Emily Dickinson, she told me later:

"Hope" is the thing with feathers—
That perches in the soul—
And sings the tune without the words—
And never stops—at all—

Then, quietly, she began to cry. Jesus, it was too much for me. It was a night when everything was too much for me.

So here comes John Kruk to lead off the fourth, snarling like being two runs down is worse than being in a plane crash. I like that look. I like a determined slob in this kind of a ball game, especially a slob who can hit. I like Kruk because he belongs in the old days but he doesn't know it and doesn't care.

What's more, I don't like that the Cubs lead any more than he does.

Kruk steps in. Ward toes the rubber and gets his sign.

And I get to do whatever I've got to do.

	1	2	3	4	5	6	7	8	9		R	H	E
PHILLIES	0	0	0								0	1	0
CUBS	0	2	0								2	3	0

Wilkins catches my last warm-up toss and guns it down to second base. From there it goes around the horn, Sandberg to Davis to Grace to Buechele and back to me again. A nice way to start an inning. Around the horn. I don't exactly know what horn it's going around, but it sounds good. I figure it'll be eliminated one of these days by some efficiency expert looking to save thirty seconds.

And if we ever get a dress code, the guy stepping into the batter's box right now could be out of a job. John Kruk looks like the bad guy in a late-night movie. Scowling face, big belly, long hair, badly in need of a shave. Only the wad of bubble gum bulging in his cheek makes him look more comical than dangerous.

Until he swings a bat. Then he's not so funny anymore. My first pitch is a knuckler that dives across the plate for strike one. But the next two are wide. A change-up is pulled foul. And a sinker just misses for ball three. Full count. I definitely don't want to walk another leadoff man. So, what's it going to be? Wilkins bangs a fist into his glove for emphasis and calls for the knuckler. His confidence rubs off on me. I kick and throw. And it's a beauty ... that jumps ... over the outside corner for strike thr—

No!

Kolacka calls it ball four.

John Kruk ambles down to first base as Mark Matthews steps into the batter's box. And a knot begins to form in my stomach.

The sports dinner.

Maybe Kolacka *does* remember.

Is it possible? Am I getting squeezed here? That's what it's called when an umpire makes the strike zone a little bit smaller by not giving you the corners. They'll do it occasionally to teach somebody a lesson, punish a pitcher for showing them up. But never in a big game.

Wonderful!

But I can't be thinking like this. I'll pitch myself into an early grave. Defeated by my own paranoia. That's what it is. I'm just paranoid. I have to forget about the goddamn sports dinner. And the best way to do that is to think about something else. Like who the hell is that warming up in our bullpen?

Wilkins takes a few steps out toward the mound. "Hey, you're making good pitches," he says reassuringly. "Stay with it."

Wilkins would make a good therapist.

I could also use a good gastroenterologist.

Mark Matthews is digging a trench in the batter's box so he can plant his right foot and propel his 6'3", 220-pound body into the ball. Matthews needs an extra push like a cheetah needs a running start. He's got 49 home runs and needs one more to get a $50,000 bonus. I've got a man on first and need three outs to get a pat on the ass.

Matthews hit that major league pop-up in the first inning. Now I want something on the ground. I check my infielders to see who's covering second on a bouncer back to me.

"I got you," hollers Jerome, touching the bill of his cap, which means Sandberg is covering second base. The voice is just a decoy.

"Just get us a ground ball."

Matthews is twirling his bat around like it's a child's toy. I look in for the sign from Wilkins. Knuckleball. It's wide for ball one. A curve misses for ball two and the crowd is getting restless. I can hear individual shouts above the dull roar. The subject is my continued employment.

Another knuckler misses for ball three and Gilson has his foot on the top step of the dugout. *Three balls and no strikes.* I take a deep breath, filling my lungs to support the weights pressing on my chest. It feels like lead bars are strapped across my upper body. If I walk Matthews here, I'm finished for the day. Probably longer.

This is where ball games are won and lost. In moments like this. It's so easy to give in. The hell with it, it's just a bad day, I'll get 'em next time. Or do I fight it off?

I step off the mound to regroup. Standing on the edge of the grass, I calmly rub the ball like I know exactly what the hell I'm doing. I'm waiting for a feeling, a clue. I know I can throw the sinker or a change for a strike. The curve is less reliable. And *nobody* throws a 3 and 0 knuckleball.

At the base of the mound, I notice a few pebbles in the red clay. I reach down and scoop them into my hand. I shake them like dice, the smaller particles falling between my fingers. The stones feel good clicking together, distant cousins to my wall buddies. Something in me relaxes. The ground feels solid under my spikes. I put the stones in my pocket and step back on the mound.

I dig my fingertips into the ball. I check the runners. I kick and throw. The knuckler ... swoops ... dives ... and lurches across the plate like a drunk duck in a windstorm.

"Steeerike," bellows Kolacka, punching the air.

The sweet syrup of confidence seeps into my veins. Give me that ball again. I find the same spot. Get the same sign. I kick and throw. It leaves my hand ... bobbing and weaving ... but this time it hangs ... inviting disaster! Matthews ... leaps out of his trench ... and takes a tremendous swing ... the drunk duck ... in a spasm of self-preservation ... suddenly careens downward. And the bat barely clips the top half of the ball ... producing a pathetic little grounder to Jerome.

Matthews has his muscles. I have the drunk duck.

Jerome charges the ball, giving himself plenty of time to make the double play. A piece of cake for Jerome, who's got hands like cotton and moves like silk. But something is wrong. I get an awful foreboding as I watch Jerome and the ball converge. It's the way the ball is bouncing. Over the years, you see enough bouncing balls and charging infielders, you get a feeling, a little turn in your gut, about which ones are going to end in a short, tricky hop. And this is one of those times. Just as Jerome fields the ball, it takes a weird goddamn hop and handcuffs him, glancing off the heel of his glove. Jerome, his hands a blur, desperately tries to recover.

But he can't. And both runners are safe.

"Put a tent over that circus," hollers someone in the Phillies' dugout.

The crowd doesn't want to believe what it just saw. A collective gasp erupts from the stands, followed by an anguished buzz that contains the crushed hopes of three generations of Cub fans.

Standing at the edge of the infield grass with the ball in his hand, Jerome looks at me with tortured eyes. I know he feels like shit. And right now I feel worse for him than I do for myself. I did my job. I got the double-play ball. The game is now on Jerome's head.

But it's really *our* heads, because now I have to "pick up" Jerome.

"Pick me up," a failed player will beg his teammates. "Cover my ass, make a big play, slam the door on these guys, blast one out of here, release me from my fucking misery."

Jerome calls time out and drags himself to the mound to personally deliver the offending ball. I wish I could take the pressure off him. Hell, he's only twenty-one. And I need him.

"Worst motherfucking play I ever made," he groans, slamming the ball into his glove before flipping it to me.

"Oh, yeah?" I say. "How about pawn to rook four?"

Jerome looks at me, trying to make sense out of what I just said. Then he remembers the locker room in Des Moines.

"Yeah, that was a good one, too," he says, smiling at the memory. And he trots back to short.

Meanwhile, somebody is hollering.

"You lucky cocksucker!"

Mark Matthews is standing on first base, glaring at me. He looks angry about something. Not like he usually does in those underwear ads, with his wavy hair and sincere smile.

"You heard me," he shouts, with a crimson face, his pale skin acting as an emotional barometer. "Keep throwing that shit!"

I can't believe that *Mark Matthews* is hollering at me. I've never even met the guy, only read about him in the papers, and now he's pissed because I'm throwing shit? Hey, that's my knuckleball he's talking about. I guess he's upset about the unmacho dribbler to Jerome, like a big-shot gambler who bets ten grand and wins sixteen cents. I feel like hollering something back, but I can't think of anything. What do you say to Mark Matthews?

But I can't be worrying about that. I've got two on and nobody out, and Dave Hollins waiting in the batter's box, and 50,000 people in the stands and on the roofs of nearby apartment buildings yelling things I can't make out, and two guys throwing in the bullpen, and Gilson talking on the phone, and Bateman looking at a piece of paper again.

I get the sign. I check the runners. I kick and throw. And a good curve *just* misses outside, for ball one. The crowd groans. And here comes Gilson, running onto the field.

"Time!" hollers Kolacka.

Wilkins takes off his mask and comes out to the mound.

"You look tired," says Gilson, his arms folded across his chest. "Ready to call it a day?"

Gilson's job is to take my temperature and report back to Bateman.

"Don't take me out," I say. "I can handle this."

"He's making good pitches," Wilkins volunteers.

"You're struggling," says Gilson.

"He made Matthews look like shit," says Wilkins, getting agitated. "We blew the double play!"

"We got people all ready to come in," says Gilson, looking out toward the bullpen.

"Bullshit!" shouts Wilkins, getting right in Gilson's face. "Rodnicky's just a kid and Foster hasn't gotten anybody out in a month."

In his catcher's gear, Wilkins seems even bigger than 6'2", but he still looks like a kid. A big angry kid who might break something if he doesn't get his way. Gilson looks as if he's considering that possibility. There's a long silence.

"Okay, that's it," shouts Kolacka, waving his arms. "The TV commercials are over. Back to work."

As Gilson walks back to the dugout, I wonder what he's going to tell Bateman. Then I thank Wilkins for sticking up for me.

"Hell," he says. "I'm just trying to win the damn game."

Wilkins should be commissioner of baseball.

Two on, nobody out, a ball and no strikes to Dave Hollins. Wilkins calls for the knuckler, slamming his fist into the pocket of his glove to tell me I can do it. I want to believe. I kick and throw. And the ball is ... popped up ... near our dugout ... Buechele moves over ... waits ... and makes the catch for out number one.

The crowd comes alive again, like they just got a reprieve from the governor.

Darren Daulton, who struck out his last time up, steps in. My first pitch is a pretty good curve ... Daulton swings ... and hits a little grounder to the right side ... I run over to cover first ... Grace dives to his right ... Sandberg dives to his left ... and the ball ... *bounces between them for an infield hit!*

Bases loaded.

The crowd is in agony. And the Phillies' bench is going crazy.

But I'm okay. They still haven't scored. I've got good stuff. I only need two outs. If I can just get out of this situation, I'll be okay. That's what you have to tell yourself.

So here we go. Pete Incaviglia the hitter. I start him off with a curve and it's in there for strike one. I throw a wicked knuckler that's swung on and missed for strike two, but it bounces off Wilkins's glove for a passed ball and *a run scores.*

Damn! There goes my shutout, I say to myself as the crowd grumbles. But it was a helluva knuckleball. I'm still okay. No balls and two strikes on Incaviglia. I waste a sinker low, and he pounds a chopper over the mound, but the only play is at first base and *another run scores.*

Sonovabitch! The crowd groans. Now the score is *tied.* I glance over in the dugout and I see Bateman talking to Gilson. I push it out of my mind. I've got to stop the bleeding. Two outs, runners on first and third, Kevin Stocker the hitter. And my first pitch is blooped to right for a single and *a third run scores.* Goddamn sonovabitch! The crowd moans. And I want Greene to get into the batter's box *now,* before Bateman comes out to the mound. I know I can beat these guys. Finally, Greene steps in and I strike him out to end the inning. Three runs and they barely hit the ball! It's like getting nibbled to death by ants.

I hate this game.

We trot off the field amid some angry boos, directed at the team in general, but mostly at fate.

"Same old Cubs!" some guy hollers.

The dugout is a hornet's nest of fury and blame.

Wilkins is punishing himself for the passed ball, slamming his catcher's mask against the metal frame that's supposed to protect the water cooler. Jerome is cursing himself for booting the double play. Gilson is throwing towels around because the pitcher *he* wanted to bring in would have struck out the side. And I'm pissed at myself for walking the leadoff hitter again. I slam my glove against the wall and take a seat on the bench.

A two-run lead is now a one-run deficit in the biggest game of my life. But it's not the worst thing that ever happened. Not by a long shot.

The worst thing was last year. When Julie and I split up.

It was the end of the baseball season and we were cleaning the apartment we had rented in Des Moines. This is always a chore because you have to arrange everything just right to fit in the station wagon, which is my job because I'm an expert packer, and clean the refrigerator, which is Julie's job because I don't think it's necessary.

The argument started over whether Beth could keep a local cat she'd adopted. Julie said yes; I said no. Julie argued that Beth needed a portable friend because of our nomadic life. It was the travel thing again. Julie had been smoldering ever since the toll collector incident that spring.

"Forget it," I said. "We can't afford to bring the cat." Meaning it would be too much trouble. But Julie took it another way. Or maybe she was looking for an opening.

"We can't afford much of anything on the money *we* make," she said sarcastically, like it had been on her mind recently.

"You mean the money *I* make," I said, acknowledging her dig at my earning ability.

"And that's another thing," she jabbed, like Muhammad Ali spotting another opening. "I want to earn my own money. I want my *own* career."

I always said that it was okay with me if Julie had her own career, but secretly I liked it better when she talked about having me take care of her. It made me feel important. And then she alternated back and forth between wanting to be *de*pendent or *in*dependent, according to some inner logic I could never understand.

"So go ahead," I countered. "What's stopping you?"

"We're traveling too much!"

"Work in the off-season!"

I had her there.

"You're right," she said, pausing for a moment. "But first I want to go to graduate school."

That one landed in my gut. I had always felt bad enough that I never graduated from college. If Julie got another degree, what would she want with me? It would be like grade school all over again, when she went with the advanced class and I got left behind.

I never worried about making money or providing for Julie and Beth. I always believed I could do that. Still do. Whenever my baseball career was over, I'd find something else to do. And we'd have a good life.

"Someday," I'd say, imitating George in *Of Mice and Men,* "we'll have our own little house. With rabbits and everything."

After a while Julie didn't think it was too funny.

"You're unreliable, Sam," she said. "You started selling real estate, but you quit. You've had job offers, but you never go for the interviews. You never follow through."

"What do you mean, I never follow through?" I said, my voice rising. "That's what I'm doing with baseball. Following through."

"I think you stick with baseball because it's a lost cause," she said. Then she paused and looked directly at me. "You're afraid to finish college."

"Afraid?"

"Yes, afraid," she said in that tone I hated, like she knows everything. "Because then you'd have to grow up. Which you are trying very hard not to do."

"You're reading too many psychology books," I said sarcastically.

The truth is I *have* been afraid to try something else. Baseball is the only thing I was ever really good at. I wasn't book smart like my brother, Marty, I didn't play music or fool with computers like the other kids. The thing I did best was throw a baseball. With a ball in my hand I was a king. It gave me power.

"I can't count on you, Sam," said Julie, like she had already made a decision of some kind. "And I refuse to end up like my mother."

Julie's father had abandoned the family when Julie was still in grade school. She and her mom survived on the kindness of relatives.

"Well, I'm *not* your father," I snapped.

There was a long pause.

"And I'm not *your* father," she said slowly and calmly. "You don't have to prove anything to me."

"Leave my father out of this, goddamnit!" I shouted, because I couldn't think of anything to say slowly and calmly.

We stood there looking at each other. There was something different in the room. This was not going to be a fight where we made up in bed.

"I've had it, Sam," she said quietly. "I've had it."

And I knew she meant it.

I was afraid. And angry. I couldn't think straight.

"*Now* who's a quitter?" I said, the words just coming out. "I don't need you anyway."

And then I walked out of the room.

The worst part was discovering Beth, sitting on the couch in the next room, crying softly to herself. We had thought she was out saying goodbye to her friends. Julie tried to comfort her.

"It's all right, honey," she said.

But we all knew it wasn't.

It was a long drive back to our apartment in Illinois. And much too quiet. When we got home, Julie said she wanted a separation. She needed to do something with her own life. She wanted to get a master's degree. She was not going to follow me around for one more baseball season.

I guess I could have saved everything by just quitting baseball.

So why didn't I?

And because I couldn't understand why, I punished myself on the wall.

It had taken me six weeks to complete the post. Six weeks of lifting and hauling and jockeying the big stones into position. It was like playing checkers with manhole covers. Awkwardly shaped manhole covers.

By mid-November I was adding a few feet each week to the wall itself. The stones were starting to fit better because I learned how to eyeball them. I'd carry a dozen cavity configurations in my head and when I'd look at a pile of stones, certain shapes would jump out. I'd be looking for a base stone to extend the north side, and spot a facing stone for the south side.

Those were my good days. On the other days I'd think about Julie. And what she said about having her own goals. And following me around all over the country. And living out of suitcases. And sitting in doctors' offices.

And waiting, and packing, and driving, and watching, and cheering, and hoping. And protecting me from my own fears.

And I had called her a quitter!

How the hell could I have called her a quitter?

I felt guilty. And angry at myself.

And one morning I looked at the wall and saw that it was better than the post and then I hated the post. So I tore it down. Tore down the whole damn post in a fury of guilt and anger and dissatisfaction about everything in my life. Heaved the stones all over the yard because then I'd have to pick them all up and it would serve me right.

"Okay baby, let's go, do it now, whaddya say!" hollers Sammy Sosa, walking back and forth in the dugout, clapping his hands. "Let's get those runs back."

We've got Banks, Grace, and Wilkins due up in the bottom of the fourth. And maybe a few others if we can get something going.

	1	2	3	4	5	6	7	8	9	R	H	E
PHILLIES	0	0	0	3						3	3	0
CUBS	0	2	0							2	3	1

So I took it back from them. That half inning was mine. Three runs created by me. I gave Kruk, the leadoff man, two balls that should have been strikes and walked him. That's all it took. I set it up and the Cubs booted it away. Best of all, there's nobody who's going to say I did it. That's the beauty part. I can sense the power with those three Phillies runs tingling in my flesh. If I did it once, I can do it again if I have to. It's like holing out a chip shot for a birdie on the seventeenth hole to turn the match around. I'm definitely in command!

It's time for a drink. I go to the Phillies dugout because it's better to drink the winner's water. The ballplayers pretend I'm not there. There's no man in blue drinking their water. If they knew what I was doing for them, they'd offer me everything from bubble gum to telephone numbers of the choicest broads in L.A.

Behind the dugout, a woman who sounds like Miss Thunderbitch of 1902 yells at me: "Damn you, umpire. If you were my husband, I'd poison your coffee!"

She gets the first laugh. I spit and then get the second. "Lady, if you were my wife, I'd drink it!"

I reload, drink some, spit some. When I spit one more time, I don't see that Sirotta is there waiting for a drink and I spatter his shoes as he does a little jig to avoid it. Someone cries out "Oops!" and everybody laughs. Sirotta is shaking his head at me like maybe I meant to do it. If I'd seen him, maybe I would, but I'm thinking that if the TV camera caught it, they'll show it after the commercials. Hey, look at the stupid umpires spitting on each other!

"You missed one, Ernie," he says half under his breath.

If I had water in my mouth I might have gagged on the swallow. I didn't need any reminders, however subtle, of the evil shit I was doing, certainly not from him.

I did what any guilty man would do: I attacked.

"Oh? You calling pitches from third base today?"

"You walked Kruk last inning. That 3-2 pitch looked like strike three to me."

"I met your wife once, Lew. She probably looks good to you, too."

"You're really funny sometimes," he says.

There comes a voice from the stands again.

"Kolacka, you stink. I can smell you from here!"

Why does he sound so fucking loud? Is it because it's today? Because my ears are so rabbity? Because my skin is like Kleenex? If I don't have to see that creep, why do I have to hear him? What right has that loud-mouthed sonovabitch to blame me for something I actually did?

"Put your mask back on, Kolacka, it'll be an improvement!"

Right then and there, all I could think of was Trisha telling me she couldn't wait for the inning to end so she could see my face again.

Lordy, lordy, but I'd like to see *her* face again. Right now, right this instant. All those fabulous freckles under bright red hair. About 5'3" of what they used to call pleasingly plump. There was something extra special about her, only you had to pay attention to catch it. I caught it, all right. I was in Hawaii, the garden spot of the Pacific Coast League. But the day I met her was another day when I had my head up my ass. I'd just come off another bad rap, this time in Salt Lake City a week before. A hotshot black million-dollar bonus kid named Alva Meade came up against an old redneck catcher who kept trash-talking him. It's nothing new. It's what most catchers think

159

they've got a mouth for, especially against a black ballplayer. "Hey, look who's heah, it's the big black dude with the diamond in his ear!" Or "I hear tell he pisses champagne through his emerald-studded dick." Or "They say he shits sapphires through a fourteen-karat asshole." When Meade struck out swinging at a bad pitch, he was so pissed he threw his bat at the catcher, whacking him across the knees.

When I saw that, my fist shot to the sky. "You're gone!" I shouted. Not only did I throw Meade out, in my report I recommended suspension.

But a humble Alva Meade defended himself on TV to sympathetic Salt Lake fans and created a firestorm. Since baseball loved its big-money prospects, it seemed like Meade never threw that bat. No million-dollar prospect would do a thing like that.

"Racist!" they called the catcher.

"Racist!" they said of me.

"Kolacka should've stopped it before it got out of hand," wrote the press.

So here was a message at my hotel in Honolulu that I should call the Pacific Coast League president, Harry Ullman, in Salt Lake City ASAP. Back on the old carpet, you could bet on it. Step out of line, pay your fine. The message was burning a hole in my pocket, so I called him, but he was out of the office. Well, I, too, was going "out of the office." I would call Ullman later. This was beautiful Hawaii. I always took a walk in Hawaii, even in the rain. Some towns, I wouldn't walk across the street, even in the sunshine. Why hurry to get reamed?

I passed a Little League game, bought a Coke, and took a seat in the stands behind a players' bench with lots of parents, mostly mothers, yelling as the kid at bat took a big swing at an eye-high and struck out. Immediately he threw his helmet at the bench, and soon enough, he couldn't help himself, he began to cry. Everyone stayed clear of him. Everyone except a red-freckled woman in a baseball cap. The coach. She put her arm around him.

Whatever she said, she made it all so simple, so absolutely perfect, the kid's tears dissolved. He smiled, picked up his glove, and ran out to the field. The goddamnedest instant cure I'd ever seen.

It set me up. I mean, I couldn't help myself, I had to stay until it was the kid's turn again. As it turned out, he knocked a 2-1 pitch high over the fence in left field and went jumping up and down the first-base line like a midget imitating Carlton Fisk.

And the coach? She stood up with the screaming kids and simply applauded like it was the end of a stage play. When the kid came bouncing home, he came right to her, fighting off his cheering teammates, and he jumped on her. In fact, they all piled on, bringing her laughing to the ground like *she* was the hero.

When she got to her feet, her cap was gone, her red hair all over her freckled face. I couldn't help myself. I had to meet her.

"Congratulations," I said, then identified myself; as a PCL umpire, my praise would mean something.

"Yes, you look like an umpire," she teased me. "The hunted look."

I smiled. "Some say haunted."

One kid stayed at her side, his arm in a half hug around her waist.

"My son, Lucas Harrison," she introduced him. "I'm Trisha." Then immediately: "Did you see the catch he made against the wall?"

"I sure did." I smiled at the kid. He'd run all the way back to the wall first and then turned to make the catch. "Where'd you learn to do that, Lucas?"

"Joe Carter, on TV," he said.

"Very professional."

He liked that, all right.

"He's always learning," she said. "And so am I."

"Mom's the best coach in Honolulu!" Lucas was beaming.

"I can see that," I said. "That last home run had her name all over it."

She looked at me head-on, enjoying that I'd picked up on what she had done for that kid.

"You've got to love what you do, Mr. Kolacka." Then: "Do *you*?"

"I'd put it differently," I said. "I do what I love."

It stopped her. She played with the thought for a moment, then nodded. "Yes, that's better, isn't it? Much better!"

On a sudden instinct, I offered them passes to the game that night. Lucas jumped at it. How could she resist?

When they walked off, she was limping badly. At first I thought she'd hurt her leg in that game-winning home run pileup. Then I saw it was more than that. She was partly crippled. It didn't seem distressing, though. She just limped, that was all.

When I left, I walked back to the hotel with a fresh warm feeling. It was more pleasing because now it was too late to call Ullman in Salt Lake City.

After the game, I took them out for pizza and Cokes. Lucas was fascinated by umpiring. He'd never given it a thought. Now he had a whole new look at the great game.

I told him, "On average, the plate umpire makes 288 calls a game. And that's just balls and strikes."

"And the ump at first?" he asked.

"Maybe 36, pickoff attempts included."

"What about appeals on checked swings?" he asked.

"Okay, about 5 or 6 more."

He was sharp, all right. A nice kid. When he said good night in the living room, he shook my hand, but suddenly it wasn't enough, and he came to me and, by God, we hugged. I don't remember when I'd hugged a kid last.

"Hey, Lucas, take two and hit to right," I said.

He smiled. He knew what that meant. My son Joe didn't. Maybe Lucas was the last thirteen-year-old kid in America who did.

Trisha took him to his room, the sound of her limp evident on the stairs. Alone in the living room, I felt like I was in a warm bubble bath with a bottle of cold beer, hearing sweet music on a radio. My crew had seen me with her after the game and had made the usual raunchy prognostications.

"Hey, redheads have hot blood, Ernie," said Walt.

"That's where freckles come from," Sy said.

"C'mon," I said. "C'mon ..."

You can take that sort of teenage talk, it's all bullshit and you know it, but somehow it works its way into your thinking. You can't help playing sexy games with the prospects. Did I want her? I mean, was that something else to play around with? I could feel my pulse rising. What the hell, this was all new to me. I never played around. I never cheated on Enid. For one thing, I'd be scared I'd get caught. Who wants to get hit by a truck?

But then, this was different. Trisha made everything different.

Like when she returned, she led me to the sofa and we sat down, my hand cradled in both of hers.

"A hand sandwich," she said.

She smiled as she looked at me. Not just a look, but something more penetrating. Her eyes were all I could see, clear brown eyes that made me feel like the center of the universe.

"You've got the right look, Ernie. For a while I was worried that you were too sad for me, but I was wrong. Your eyes never stop flashing."

The right look?

The voice was soft and mellow, like whatever she said, it was the way she felt. If you looked at her, you could see how it went with her eyes.

"Some people, you'd think the sun never comes up in the morning," she went on. "You, you're up early, you're up waiting for the sun."

How did she know that?

"When you'd take off your mask, I saw your eyes dancing like a kid who'd just won first prize at a spelling bee."

Dancing eyes? I mean, what was this? I was supposed to be prone by now, listening to the sound of zippers.

"Hey, I couldn't spell my own name until I was seven!" I said.

She told me about her husband, Lloyd Harrison, an insurance agent with a big smile, always with the jokes, Lloyd was a joy to be with—until, all of a sudden, he ran out of steam. One night they were at a party, he got drunk without her knowing it, and he crashed the car into a tree, smashed her right foot. It was too much for him and he took off.

That had been four years ago. She figured she got the best of it. She had Lucas, she had one good leg, she had a lot of friends.

"The only thing I can't do"—she laughed—"is run a marathon."

She could be an umpire, she joked, and she did a first-rate imitation of me punching a man out. She caught my snappy whiplike jab of the right fist, forward then backward, and the high-pitched cry that went with it. Every umpire does it with a different wrinkle. Year after year, you couldn't change your style if you tried.

"It's more than style," she said. "It's the way your whole body commits to the call. You're making a statement, Ernie. You're not pretending the man is out. He *is* out!"

She saw me the way I wanted to be seen. Umpiring was not show business, and neither was baseball. She could go from Little League to the World Series in one sweep of her thoughts. When that kid hit his home run that afternoon, something about his young life was on the line. Every kid who played baseball knew that. That's what she knew.

"Whatever you do, it has to matter," she said. "You have to care what happens."

I saw that even in the way she made coffee. The kitchen itself was more than a stove and a sink, it was a lovely place to be in, with flowers on the fridge and pictures on the wall. She set two colorful mugs on the table; she was about to fetch the coffee from the stove when she had another idea. She sat on my lap. I couldn't believe it. Her hands went gently to my shoulders and her sweet freckled face closed in on mine. We kissed. I can tell you, pal, that was more than I'd ever bargained for. Soft lips joined by a feeling of love. We held that kiss far longer than I'd ever believed possible. Nothing moved, not even a finger. And when we came up for air, she immediately buried her cheek against mine in the cradle of my neck. My God, it was lovely. I couldn't believe how lovely it was. I could've died happy at that moment. This woman was like an angel and I was being blessed by her. I kissed the top of her head, my heart beating fast against her. We held each other in such satisfying silence, you didn't want to speak even if you could think of something to say.

I have to say that kiss alone was better than anything else that might have happened. Maybe we could've gone to bed. Maybe I could've made the moves that got us there. Maybe, even, she wanted me to.

In the end, we kissed again at the door, standing tight against each other, unwilling to part. I thought, Jesus, I had four more days on this trip to Hawaii. Hawaii is the only place where umpires stay more than three. Never did I appreciate that more. I told Trisha I would call her in the morning.

She raised my hand to her lips and kissed it. It was almost dawn, but I didn't need a taxi. It would be nice to walk on air to the hotel.

Just after nine in the morning the phone rang, I thought maybe it would be her. I wasn't thinking about anything else.

It was Harry Ullman's secretary.

"Mr. Kolacka? Mr. Ullman on the line."

"Ernie?"

It's amazing how quick your mind can send you from the sublime into the shithouse.

"Morning, sir."

"Pack your bags, Ernie. You're expected at Wrigley Field at 6:00 PM tomorrow night."

"What?"

"The National League bought your contract," he said. "As of today, you're a major league umpire!"

If I didn't recognize his voice, I would have wondered. As it was, I had a couple of doubtful moments before it sunk in. What happened? They needed another body. Mine. Jesus, what difference did it make why? Get with it, Kolacka, you're finally going up!

There are moments like this, they're too good to be true. Your whole body starts shaking, everything is unreal, you can't feel anything. Like they say in the Army, you don't know whether to piss or go blind. Me, I had to pee. I stood over the bowl peeing and crying and laughing all at the same time, which may be the first time in history. Tears were still coming when I called Trisha.

"Oh, Ernie, oh, my God, that's wonderful!"

"You're a good-luck charm!"

"You'll be the best umpire that ever was!"

When we said goodbye, I sounded stupid. When I hung up, I wanted to call back, but I didn't know what I'd say. I called her anyway.

"Trisha, listen to me. I want you to know. I'm not good at this, you and me, I mean, hey, it was so sudden, it was all in one day. You realize that? All in one day. Trisha, damnit, Trisha, you're wonderful. You hear me? You're wonderful!"

Pause.

"I hear you, Ernie. You're wonderful, too."

I hung up before I made an ass of myself.

I packed my bags, then I called Enid, I couldn't tell what time it was in New York. She answered after a dozen rings.

"Well, so it finally happened!" Then, in the next breath, a number: "Thirty-three, five, Ernie."

"What?"

"Your salary!"

"Yeah," I said. "My salary."

She knew it, I didn't. I saw major league ballparks and great baseball games and being where I'd always wanted to be, and a happy Enid saw the numbers on the check. Well, why not? She'd paid her dues.

On the long plane ride, I let the good feeling course through me. Everything was different now. I was heading toward a whole new life. Everything was going to be all right. I'd make it up to Enid. Jesus, I owed her that. I was going to help her forget the rotten years and look forward to the great ones. Heading across the Pacific at 600 mph, 30,000 feet up, I found the shifting dramatics of my life turning Trisha into someone more dreamlike than real. It was like I'd just seen a movie love story that caught me in the throat, but it was only a movie. When you got out of the dark theater, it faded away. Me, I was on a plane heading for the real happy ending.

"Kolacka, you suck!"

Because the Cubs are one run down, too many people agree with him. Others laugh at this new turn of phrase. Hell, they'll laugh at anything if it's about an umpire. On this day, I laugh at nothing. I've got to bear down to protect the Phillies' one-run lead.

Big Leon Banks opens the bottom of the fourth, raps the first pitch on the line to Lenny Dykstra, who doesn't have to move a step to grab it. Mark Grace takes a strike, then a ball, then drills a base hit through the right side of the infield. Greene gets Wilkins to pop up for the second out and Steve Buechele steps in. Buechele, the Cubs' hero, or so the crowd lets him believe. He digs in like he believes it all, like he wants to hit one out of here. Why not? This is his day, isn't it? Greene sees the greed, all right, and fools him with a change-up for a called strike—but not before throwing to first base twice to keep Grace close. He's afraid of a two-out steal that would put the runner in scoring position. Again, Greene watches Grace lead off and throws again to Kruk, this time almost getting him. He gets Buechele 2-1, just missing with a real good slider. Greene now takes his time, his head working slyly over his left shoulder to check the runner.

Suddenly I am blessed by an inspiration. As Greene finishes his stretch, even as he begins his pitch, I cry out *"Balk!"* like I'd just discovered gold. My claim is that he didn't bring his hands to a complete stop. The crowd agrees. They agree even more as Jim Fregosi comes ripping out of the dugout, yelling fire and brimstone. That's what I want to see. Get the Phillies pissed at me the way the Cubs are going to be before I'm through. My way of making the act look square. What I do in the fourth inning will pay off in the ninth. With Grace on second, it could be risky, it could cost me a run. But I like the odds against it. I like what it can do for me in the long run.

And so it happens. Grace dies on second as Buechele flies out to Inca-viglia to end the inning.

I feel as innocent as a newborn babe. Take me through the rest of this game with no more trouble than this and maybe my stomach will invite me to dinner.

Or maybe even better, after another inning, the skies will suddenly turn dark, there'll be big black thunderheads and ferocious lightning, and a storm will hit like a fucking deluge: Game called. Phillies win. Everybody go home.

You bet.

	1	2	3	4	5	6	7	8	9	R	H	E
PHILLIES	0	0	0	3						3	3	0
CUBS	0	2	0	0						2	4	1

"Oh, boy," says Batemen, holding his head in his hands as he looks over at hitting coach Bill Robinson. "You ever have root canal?"

Buechele has just flied to left, leaving a runner stranded on second, and the Chicago Cubs take the field. Me included. The way you know you're still in the game is that nobody says you're not.

My goal right now is to get through this inning. "Give us five," Bateman had said, "and then we'll get you the hell out of there." I'd like to come through for Bateman. He's shown faith in me from the beginning. Unlike some other folks I could name.

Mom and Dad had high hopes for Samuel Truman Ward. Maybe I'd become a doctor, a college professor, or even president of the United States. At the least I'd make them proud, their firstborn, a trailblazer for younger brothers and sisters who might come along.

Except it didn't work out that way. For some reason, which I still don't understand, I never quite lived up to expectations. And it started early. As far back as I can remember, it seemed like something was missing. I was always a little too late, a little too dirty, a little too loud, always a little too something. It's not that I was bad. Even when I hadn't done anything wrong, it felt like I had.

It was watching Marty that convinced me I wasn't imagining things. Right from the beginning, my little brother seemed good enough. Mom and Dad never had a problem with Marty. Of course, they loved us both, but they *approved* of Marty. And he wasn't a saint, either. He'd do a lot of the same things I did, except he wouldn't get in trouble.

But I never blamed Marty. It wasn't his fault he was the favorite. He never seemed to be working at it. And he never tried to make me look bad. Sometimes he'd even try to share the blame when he could see it was going to be my ass. It was like *he* was the older brother. But in spite of it all, we always got along great, except when he needed to get his head pounded once in a while.

Sometimes when kids are feeling bad they go to their room and play with a stuffed animal or snuggle a favorite blanket. I don't remember cuddly animals or fuzzy blankets. But what I had was even better. A ball. Any kind of ball: rubber ball, baseball, tennis ball, Wiffle ball, softball. I could throw a ball. For hours and hours, up against the house, against a viaduct near the house, against the school, against a building. Send me to my room? You might as well throw Br'er Rabbit into the briar patch. I'd lie in bed and throw a Nerf ball against the wall.

Throwing a ball. It was the one thing I was better at than anybody else. Down at the field I was always chosen first even when the bigger kids were playing. Grown-ups were amazed that I could throw a ball so far and so accurately. Coaches couldn't wait to use me in games. Throwing a ball gave me power. It gave me status. It was my claim to fame.

The recognition began in high school. My official title changed from "underachiever who doesn't apply himself" to "star baseball player." Girls who never looked at me before were asking *me* out on dates. Even Mom and Dad started paying attention. College recruiters were coming to the games. I might even get a scholarship to college! For throwing a ball.

In college, things got more exciting. My picture was in the school paper. Fraternities invited me to parties. People seemed to like me better. Whenever

I pitched, the stands were packed with relatives, friends, pretty girls. And major league baseball scouts.

At the end of my sophomore year, I dropped out of college to sign a professional contract. I could have waited until after I graduated, but I wanted to get going. The way everybody was talking, I could be in the big leagues in a few years. It was the high point of my life. I had even caught up to Marty in terms of family interest.

"I'd like you to meet my son," Dad would say. "He just signed with the White Sox." Then I'd have to explain that it was actually the White Sox *organization* and that I'd be starting out with the Appleton Foxes in the Class A Midwest League. At least for the first week or so.

Looking back, maybe I should have waited. Graduated from college and signed for a big bonus. I'd have money *and* a degree. Then again, if I had hurt my arm in a college game, I never could have turned pro. And I wouldn't be here today at Wrigley Field.

In a fairly important ball game.

The fans are shouting encouragement as we take the field. They've already forgiven us for last inning, and now they're doing whatever they can to prepare us mentally for the next inning. That's their job: to give us all a little reminder that some very deserving individuals, namely themselves, are counting on us to make their lives worth living.

I take my warm-up throws and I hear more yelling. This time it's coming from the Phillies' dugout. They've been hollering the whole game, but now it's a little more specific.

"Shove that knuckleball up your ass!"

"The party's over, rook."

"Stick a fork in him, he's done."

Are the Phillies suggesting this might be my last inning due to some impending disaster? The noise gets my blood pumping. I enjoy their bravado. It means there's a doubt in somebody's mind. The thing to do is totally ignore it. If you look over, show you got rabbit ears, that kind of bullshit will go on all afternoon. I smile at Wilkins like I don't have a care in the world, just to shut them up.

"And we'll wipe that smile off your face, too, asshole!"

It doesn't always work.

Lenny Dykstra, a rocket and a pop foul so far, steps into the box. Dykstra is crouching down and leaning close to the plate. He's trying to be a good leadoff man and get hit by the pitch, which in my case doesn't require much bravery. I throw a knuckleball for a strike and a sinker is grounded to Jerome at short for an easy out at first.

Mariano Duncan, with a long bomb and a walk, steps in. After working the count to three balls and a strike, Duncan hits an easy fly to left and Banks picks it out of the air with a one-handed backhand swipe, like he's swatting at a bee. Whenever Leon does this, the crowd cheers at the same time they worry that he's going to flip one into the stands.

Here's John Kruk, with a line drive double play and a walk. I start him off with a curve, which misses wide. I'm trying to mix my pitches a little bit to get the hitters thinking. As somebody once said, "You can't hit and think at the same time." My next pitch is a sinker, which Kruk picks off the ground and scalds into right field for a double. Maybe you can't *pitch* and think at the same time, either.

Two outs, man on second, and here's Mark Matthews.

And here comes Gilson.

"Time!" hollers Kolacka, waving his arms.

Nobody's up in the bullpen, so I'm not worried about coming out. Wilkins takes off his mask and joins us on the mound. For once, Gilson doesn't seem angry. Maybe he's resting the vein in his neck.

"You got first base open," he says, like I just arrived from another planet. He glances at Matthews in the on-deck circle, taking some wicked practice swings with a weighted bat. "Maybe you better walk this guy."

"I don't know," I say. "A walk and a wild pitch puts *two* runners in scoring position." I didn't want to say "passed ball" with Wilkins standing right here.

"Hell," says Wilkins, "let's pitch to him. He's looked bad twice so far. A couple more knuckleballs will give this sonovabitch a brain cramp."

"How about a semi-intentional walk?" I say, in a rare burst of diplomacy that would qualify me for the Middle East peace talks. Semi-intentional is where you throw hard-to-hit stuff just out of the strike zone. If the hitter doesn't bite, well, you were going to walk him anyway.

"He'll swing at *something*," says Wilkins. "He only needs one more dinger for fifty."

While Gilson is thinking it over, Kolacka comes out to break up the meeting.

"Let's get this show on the road," he says, waving impatiently.

Finally Gilson is ready with his professional opinion of the semi-intentional walk.

"Well," says Gilson. "He better not hit one out of here." And he trots back to the dugout.

Wilkins smiles and shakes his head.

"You know whose idea this'll be if it works, don't you?" he says.

And we both laugh.

My job now is to throw the best goddamn knuckler I can and keep it out of the strike zone. Wilkins doesn't even give me a sign. The first pitch takes a roller-coaster ride and misses low for ball one. Matthews leaned in like he wanted to disappear it. The next one sweeps up to the plate in big looping arcs. Matthews strides . . . he pops his hips! . . . but he checks his swing as the knuckler breaks wide for ball two.

He knows what's going on.

"Throw that fucking shit over," he hollers, the barometer in his face reading 101.9. And rising.

My third knuckler bounces off Wilkins's glove, about a foot outside, and the fourth one isn't even close.

"Challenge somebody, you big pussy!" hollers Matthews on his way down to first.

He means I should throw something more manly, like a fastball or a slider. Unfortunately, I don't happen to have those particular pitches in my repertoire. Because if I did, I'd take a page from the Brad Gilson manual on pitching and give Matthews a little chin music.

Right now I've got to concentrate on Hollins, who's dying to blast a three-run homer to show everybody it was a mistake to walk Matthews in order to pitch to *him*. Athletes love to use revenge—"I owed him one, he showed me up, no one thinks we can win," etc.—to psych themselves up.

And now Gilson can feel like a genius because Hollins hits a nice little grounder to Mark Grace playing deep at first. I run over to cover the bag and Grace flips it to me for the out. Like we practiced it all year.

The crowd lets out a roar because no more runs scored, and we're only losing 3–2, and we're coming to bat, and it's a nice day, and the Cubs are still alive on the last day of the season.

Well, I pitched my five innings, so does that mean I'm coming out? I take my seat at the end of the dugout, but nobody leaves me alone this time.

A lot of guys come by to slap a glove against my leg, give me a nod, a "Way to go," a "Helluva job." Even Bateman comes over, steering his belly through the dugout, to say a few words. "Nice going, son," he says, delivering a major address.

It's good to feel appreciated, even though I know it's conditional. But I'll take any kind of acceptance. It hasn't always been like this for me around a baseball team.

There's a corner of my mind, in the crazy section toward the back, that always manages to say, do, eat, wear, or sign up for the wrong thing. Even when things are going well, sometimes *especially* when they're going well, I come up with just the right stunt to piss people off. Like the Richard Nixon incident, for example.

This was a few years ago during my cup of coffee with the California Angels. It was after a game in Anaheim and the former president had come down to the locker room to shake a few hands and, as one of the players said, "sniff a few jocks." I guess Nixon's a big baseball fan. And the players were pretty excited to meet him, because for all their disdain and in some cases contempt for fans who want *their* autographs, ballplayers are the biggest celebrity fuckers going. Anyone with money or fame, no matter how achieved, is someone to be admired. Michael Milken? Hey, nice to meet you. What are you doing with yourself these days? Got any stock tips?

I could never do that, I always told myself.

So here came Nixon, moving down a line of lockers, shaking hands and quoting players' statistics to them. While I was watching and joking to myself that he wouldn't know *my* stats, I wondered what I'd do if he passed by my locker. Could I shake hands with a man for whom I had no respect? Suddenly he turned in my direction. My heart began pounding as I tried to figure out what to do. I reached for a baseball to occupy my hands. But Mr. Nixon was not deterred. He stuck out his hand.

I kept rubbing the ball.

"Ahhh," he said, his grin collapsing into a pout. "A demonstrator."

He paused and checked the name tag above my locker.

"Well," he said, his voice dropping. "It's a free country."

Then he shook a few more hands and left.

Of course, it was in all the papers that a ballplayer had snubbed the former president, and naturally my dad heard about it and called me on the phone to tell me I was destroying what was left of any career I might hope to have inside baseball or out with my stupid self-indulgent behavior. It was hard to argue with him while I was on my way to join the Edmonton Trappers.

Julie wasn't too happy about it, either. She had to change the airline tickets at the last minute for her and Beth, from California to Canada.

"I respect your principles, Sam," she had said over the phone. "But why? Why did you have to choose that moment to make a stand?"

I didn't have an answer for her at the time.

"Hey, Ward!" barks Bobby Rapp. "Get a bat. If Sosa gets on, you're bunting him over."

Does that mean I'm still in the game? And if Sosa *doesn't* get on, are they going to pinch-hit for me? The answer comes in the form of a question from Bateman, who intercepts me at the bat rack.

"Son," he says, putting his hand gently on my shoulder. "Can you give me one more?"

"I don't have anything else planned for the afternoon," I say.

	1	2	3	4	5	6	7	8	9		R	H	E
PHILLIES	0	0	0	3	0						3	4	0
CUBS	0	2	0	0							2	4	1

I don't like the way the wind has picked up and the flags are fluttering. It's the typical hitter's wind at Wrigley Field that blows toward Lake Michigan on days when the air on land is warmer than the water. But if you're throwing knuckleballs, it becomes a pitcher's wind. It creates a stronger resistance that makes the knuckler do an extra special dance. It also helps the Cubs hitters.

It's like an omen. God is punishing me for what I'm doing today. "Abjure all risky ventures. Find a safe harbor to weather the storm seas." Go hide in a fucking closet. If I don't believe in miracles, why am I so nervous about a goddamn horoscope?

Why? I'll tell you why. Because my stomach is roiling with oncoming nausea, I'm afraid I'm going to choke on my own vomit. Any asshole can tell you that guilt cuts deeper than hope. You get that guilty feeling, it sends up the bile, you can't spit it away. Like Enid said, you're a loser, Ernie. Whatever you do, you'll find a way to blow it. And today, it's not just your last game, it's your whole fucking life.

I came in like a lion and now I'm going out like a rat.

"Hey, Ernie ..." I see Mountain coming at me like he's got something crucial on his mind. "Did you hear about this guy with five dicks?"

Whatever this is, I'm not ready for it.

"Yeah," he goes on. "His underwear fits him like a glove."

Jesus. I'm suffering with the wrath of God, and all of a sudden a dumb joke. It takes a few seconds, I can't help it, I start to bubble with a laugh. Umpires aren't supposed to laugh on the field. It's not professional to kid around, even between innings. Immediately, I put on my mask, as Mountain brings a big red snot rag to his face like he's catching a giant sneeze, I start to laugh so hard, I turn away to save myself. This is madness. The joke is so dumb, it's like a punishment to fit my crime. I mean, I'm giggling like a kid on the edge of hysterics while I'm suffering like an old man on the way to the fucking gallows.

I get back to home plate while Daulton is warming up Greene. I wait for the TV director's towel, struggling to get hold of myself. I rally, all right. By the time I go to dust the plate, I'm back to grim.

But then, here comes Sammy Sosa to lead off the inning.

He takes a breaking ball that catches the corner, but I give it to him for ball one. Greene is showing anger to let me know I missed it. Good, that looks good. See? I miss one here, I miss one there. Sosa fouls one off, then bloops a good pitch just out of Dave Hollins's reach for a base hit.

So it's Ward's turn to hit. I'm thinking he'll be gone for a pinch hitter, but who comes out of the dugout but the fruitcake himself. He's going to bunt, of course. Put the tying run on second. The whole world knows that. I'll hand it to him: it's the bottom of the fifth and he's still around. If you told me that an hour ago, I'd've called you bonkers.

Greene goes into his stretch to keep Sosa close, but first baseman Kruk is already moving in toward the plate, and third baseman Hollins is halfway in and coming. Greene throws, Ward moves into bunting position. He lays his bunt neatly down the right side of the infield, and Sosa moves easily to second as Ward is thrown out at first.

So up comes the top of the Cubs order, all the power a ball club ever needed to waltz into the playoffs and leave me squirming in a pile of shit. Willie Wilson couldn't be happier. He's a smart hitter. He works Greene like an old-time leadoff man. He's going to hit when he likes what he sees.

He works the count to 3-2, taking the bad pitches, fouling off the good ones. In the end, Greene is too careful and walks him.

So it's men on first and second now, one out, and Davis steps in. I don't like what I'm feeling. I can see under Greene's peak and I get the idea that he doesn't like what he's feeling, either. Davis jumps on the first pitch, a fastball over the outside of the plate, and raps it sharply right at Greene's ankles. Greene gets his glove down quick enough to prevent the drive from going through, but not quick enough to hold on to it. The ball squiggles out of his glove, rolls a few feet in front of him. Catlike, he picks it up bare-handed and throws to Hollins at third for the force-out on Sosa. Hollins then snaps a throw to second to force Wilson, but his throw hits Sosa on the shoulder in the middle of the base path and rolls into the outfield. Wilson rounds second and pulls into third as Davis legs it to second while the crowd explodes with joy.

Out comes Jim Fregosi, hollering at Sirotta.

"Interference! Interference!"

He is furious. He won't leave Sirotta alone, following him around the infield, screaming so loud even the crowd doesn't drown him out.

This is all I need. Behind the plate, I'm the umpire-in-chief. I come out on the field to call a conference of the crew.

Sirotta says, "No interference, there was no intent by Sosa to interfere with the throw! Sosa just stood there," he says. "It happened so fast, he couldn't get out of the way even if he tried!"

Luger agrees. "The hit pinned the runners. Was Greene gonna hold on to it or wasn't he?"

Mountain shrugs. He wasn't in position to see.

Sirotta goes on and on. He refers to the Dodger-Yankee World Series play in 1988 when the Dodger shortstop, Russell, dropped a line drive, then stepped on second to force Reggie Jackson but hit him on the hip on his throw to first. The ball bounded away and a run scored. The umpires saw no intent by Jackson, so they called no interference. It was very much the same as this.

I'm ready for Sirotta. I pull out the rule book. 7.09(f): "Any runner who has just been put out [Sosa] who hinders or impedes any following play being made on a runner [Wilson] constitutes interference." Sosa did not get out of the way. He was already out and he impeded the throw. *The rule*

177

makes no mention of intent. The umpires in 1988 were wrong to give the Yankees that run. Sirotta is wrong now.

When Sirotta hears that, his face turns beet red.

"What? What the fuck are you talking about?"

"7.09(f)." I put my finger on the page and show it to him.

"So what? It's a judgment call," he protests.

"Not so. The key word is *impede.*"

"Bullshit. You're making me look bad. That's what you're doing, isn't it?"

"Read it," I say. "Read the goddamn rule, Lew!"

He shakes me off. "If you reverse me, this place will go nuts!" He turns to Mountain and Luger. "Tell him. I'm right, tell him!"

They look at me, but they tell me nothing. It drives Sirotta up the wall. "You're going to reverse me? You really are?"

"9.04(c). The umpire-in-chief shall determine which decision shall prevail. What's more, Lew, I've got the best position to make that decision."

"You're fucking crazy, Kolacka. Jesus, you always were!"

I reverse Sirotta's call. My decision is that Sosa was forced out at third, pitcher to third baseman, and Wilson out at second because Sosa impeded the throw that would have done it. Double play. The inning is over.

When this decision is announced, when the scoreboard indicates three out, there's instant pandemonium, with Bateman leading the way. He is so fucking furious, he can't speak. He jumps up and down waving his arms, kicks grass clumps with his cleats, screaming like a kid in a tantrum. No matter where I turn, he shoves his body in front of me. His only intelligible words are "No! No! No!" The rest is gibberish. I am tempted to throw him out, but I know better. Mountain comes to rescue me, putting his giant body in front of Bateman to keep him off. He doesn't say a word; he doesn't have to, he's a wall. And finally Bateman has to give up.

When he does, the fans take over. They throw all manner of garbage; even a couple of baseballs come back. One bounces off my leg and I put it in my pocket. My last souvenir. It's a switch, isn't it? How many balls come *from* the stands? It takes ten minutes for the ground crew to clear off the field. When the crowd finally subsides, the old bullhorn voice cuts in:

"Kolacka, you're dead! You are dead!"

I wheel at the word. Nobody says that to me. I won't stand for it. I holler for security guards. "I want that man out of here!" I bark. For a moment they think I'm crazy. They don't know what to do. I face the stands, pointing up at him, and by Jesus, they go up to get him and I turn back to the field. Maybe they took him out and maybe they didn't. But the bottom line is that I never heard from him again.

Sonovabitch, I did it. It could have been a big inning, but I stopped it. I did it by the rules. And I fucked Sirotta in the bargain. If that isn't a parlay, I never saw one. At a moment like this, I get the feeling that I'm okay, I'm really okay.

Eighteen men are running on and off the field. Wilkins comes out spitting into the oversized mitt, pounding the pocket like he hasn't gotten used to it yet.

"One thing for sure," he says. "You'll never be mayor of Chicago."

"I'd rather be a fire hydrant in Philadelphia," I reply.

"I gotta hand it to you, Ernie, you're no homer."

"How's the missus, Rick?" I ask.

He laughs. He's cocky, all right. He's playing games with me. He knows I've missed a few, but he's smart enough to keep his mouth shut because he knows I know it, too. But since that's all he knows, I figure I'm smarter than he is.

And there is Ward on the mound. Once again, there's Ward. There's something weird about how he's still there.

More and more, I'm thinking I don't like this battery.

	1	2	3	4	5	6	7	8	9	R	H	E
PHILLIES	0	0	0	3	0					3	4	0
CUBS	0	2	0	0	0					2	5	1

"Hey, blue," someone yells. "Punch a hole in that mask!"

The guys on the bench are still screaming at Kolacka for calling interference on Sosa. We don't really understand the rule; the point is it went against us and we need all the runs we can get. And it's a good opportunity to let off a little steam. Or work on your vocabulary skills.

"Bite my fucking balls," hollers Rapp, graduate of a school for the profanely gifted, "if that's interference."

Rapp is actually yelling at third-base umpire Lew Sirotta, who may not be familiar with Rapp talk. Sirotta shrugs his shoulders and points to Kolacka, as if to say, what do you want from me? Sirotta's grinning, like umpires often do when *they're* not the ones getting yelled at.

I hate it when a team starts getting on the umpires. Good teams blame themselves, bad teams blame the umps. It becomes a built-in excuse to lose. "We would have won if it hadn't been for the umpires." The difference between winning or losing a game like this is often mental. A team needs to stay totally focused for nine innings. Whoever blinks first, loses.

The leadoff batter in the top of the sixth is Darren Daulton, with a strike-out and an infield hit so far. Wilkins squats to give me the sign and glances up at Daulton. Wilkins always checks the hitter for little clues, like where he positions himself in the box: Is he trying to pull the ball or slap it to the opposite field? Does he want to hit the pitch before it breaks or after? Daulton is standing close to the plate and forward in the box, so Wilkins wants to bust him inside with a sinker. I kick and throw. Daulton swings ... and hits a grounder off his fists to Grace at first for out number one. A good catcher is like a life raft on a choppy sea.

Pete Incaviglia, who walked and drove in the Phillies' first run with a grounder to second, steps into the batter's box. Wilkins checks him out and calls for another sinker, inside. The hitters are moving up in the box to try and hit the knuckleball before it breaks. Very good sign. I kick and throw. The sinker runs in on Incaviglia ... who swings ... and hits a pop fly down the right-field line. Grace, Sandberg, and Sosa are all racing to catch the ball. It's going to be a tough play. *Go foul, goddamnit!* Grace, with his back to the plate ... dives like he's reaching to save somebody's life. Sandberg, with a better angle from second base ... is running flat-out ... as if there were no wall just beyond the foul line. Sosa, coming like a freight train from right field ... slides feet first into the confusion ... glove open wide a few inches off the ground. *Someone's going to get killed!* I wince with everybody else in the ballpark, frozen in time, except for Incaviglia, who flies into the turn at first base looking for a double.

Then, in one of those miracles of timing you sometimes see in a well-choreographed ballet, all four bodies—Grace, Sandberg, Sosa, and the ball—appear to dive, run, slide, and bounce past the exact same spot at the exact same moment, without any damage. Unless you count a double as damage.

The crowd gasps at the near miss, grateful nobody got hurt, unhappy that a Phillie is standing on second base. Meanwhile, the Flying Santini Brothers pick up their hats and return to their positions. If the game continues like this, the crowd will need some type of group therapy.

Kevin Stocker, with a walk and a run-scoring single, digs in at the plate. Wilkins gives me the sign. I check the runner at second. I kick and throw. Stocker swings ... and hits a fly ball to right that gets hauled in by Sosa as Incaviglia tags and chugs into third.

With two outs and a 3–2 lead, the Phillies are going let pitcher Tommy

Greene bat for himself. They could pinch-hit, but they'd rather give up the potential run on third to keep Greene in the game. And that's fine with me, because Greene is no match for the knuckler.

I'll throw from a stretch position instead of a full windup in order to keep the runner close at third. I get the sign. I check the runner. I kick and throw. And a knuckler ... dives across the plate for strike one. A second knuckler is swung on ... and missed for strike two.

With two strikes, Bateman is concerned about a passed ball.

"Stay in front of it," he hollers to Wilkins, doing a bump and grind with his belly to remind Wilkins to use his body.

I go into my stretch. I check the runner.... .

"Balk!" hollers Kolacka.

What?

Kolacka takes off his mask and waves the runner home from third.

Balk? How the hell did I balk, for crissakes?

I don't belive this.

Neither does Wilkins, who's arguing with Kolacka.

And here comes Bateman, like he was shot out of a cannon; a moving volcano, sputtering and spitting, arms flapping, eyes popping, his face red as raw meat.

"Goddamn horseshit call!" shouts Bateman, ramming his belly between Kolacka and Wilkins, but mostly into Wilkins, who slides backward like he was on wheels.

The crowd loves to see Bateman in action, but they're mystified as to what's going on. The more knowledgeable fans are trying to explain a balk to their neighbors. It's when a pitcher deceives the base runner—either by not coming to a complete stop before pitching, thereby making it difficult for the runner to get a lead, or by making a move which the runner could think is a pickoff attempt. This can be any kind of move, intentional or not, a slight twitch of a leg or a shoulder. Balks are rarely ever called because they're too subtle and usually accidental.

I still don't understand how I balked. I went into my stretch the same way I've been doing all afternoon. The only thing moving was my sleeve, maybe, flapping in the breeze. Did I balk and just not realize it?

Managers always argue balk calls. That's another reason umps don't call them, even when pitchers do balk. And Bateman's out here for other reasons, too. He wants to protect Wilkins, light a fire under the team, and maybe intimidate the umpires. One of the great things about Bateman, he understands the mood of a game, the tempo, the climate.

And some umpires *can* be intimidated. I once saw a rookie pitching a perfect game against the Dodgers. The kid strikes out the first batter to lead off the fourth, and here comes manager Tommy Lasorda, roaring out of the dugout and haranguing the umpire for calling too many strikes. He stormed around and kicked dirt for ten minutes and eventually got thrown out of the game. But he achieved his purpose. The ump lost his nerve, the strike zone got smaller, and the kid lost the game.

Bateman's giving the fans their money's worth. Now he's running around the field, appealing to the other umpires. This is like getting a second opinion from the statues on Easter Island.

"God Almighty!" yells Bateman to nobody in particular on his way back to the dugout. "Biggest game of the year and we get the four stooges!" Then, completing his presentation, Bateman drop-kicks his hat into the dugout.

The crowd is really screaming at Kolacka, but he pays no attention. Just brushes off home plate like he was cleaning up after an all-night party with rude guests.

I strike out Greene and the inning is over.

I head for the dugout and I'm trying to remember the last time I balked. I've only balked a few times in my life. And what are the odds of me balking with a runner on third? And two strikes on the hitter?

I get that sick feeling in my stomach again.

Goddamn sports dinner.

Bullshit! I refuse to think about it. Kolacka probably doesn't even *remember* the dinner. And even if he *does* remember, he probably doesn't care. And even if he cares, he'd *never* try anything in a game like this. Like Wilkins said, he's too professional. Besides, he called a balk on the Phillies, too.

So forget it.

Stay positive. I'm losing 4–2, but I'm pitching well. It could be a lot worse; I could be sitting out at the cabin right now, reading the want ads.

My mind wanders back to the cabin.

It's New Year's Day. It's 18 degrees, there's snow on the ground, and

I'm perspiring. I'm wearing a navy blue cotton Chicago Bears T-shirt, gray sweatpants, black steel-toed boots, reinforced leather work gloves, and goggles. I've got a 6-inch-wide, brown leather weight lifter's belt strapped around my waist with a square-nosed mason's hammer dangling off the belt. I look like a creature from outer space. Or a character in some horror movie: Wall Man from Elm Street.

With my increasing expertise, it took only four weeks to rebuild the post. But after three months of work, I'd still completed only 22 feet of wall. My goal had been to finish by March, in time for spring training. The town had given me until then to clean up the stones. That meant I only had three months left to finish the remaining two thirds. The intended length of 66 feet, 6 inches now seemed impossible.

All I could see were piles and piles of stones. It made me tired just to look at all those piles and the unfinished section of the wall. The enormity of the task made me feel like quitting. The hell with it, I said, I don't need the damn wall. But I had to do *something* with the stones.

That's when I turned to: The Basic Rules of Wall Building.

Rule #1: If you get discouraged, try something different for a while. Whenever my arms would get tired or the stones weren't fitting, I'd switch to other jobs that had to be done, like raking leaves off the stones or looking in the weeds for my tools. Or Olympic Stone Smashing. Some stones were too big for the wall and had to be broken up. The best way to do this was to lift the stone over my head, stagger around like a Russian weight lifter, and drop it on another stone like they drop those big barbells. A well-dropped stone could break into half a dozen good facing stones. This led to:

Rule #2: Don't drop one of the big stones on your toe, even if you're wearing steel-toed boots. The big stones dent the steel, making the boot very difficult to remove in a hurry—which is the immediate priority at that moment. Hooooo boy, that smarts!

To finish the wall in three months I had to get organized. I became a time-study expert. This led to:

Rule #3: Pick up each stone as few times as possible. Ideally, you want to take a stone right off the pallet and put it directly into the wall. Next best is going from pallet to category pile to wall. The worst is picking up the same stone twenty-seven times and dropping it out of frustration. In that case, see Rule #2, above.

Probably a computer could scan all the different shapes and sizes and print out the best combination of stones to use. Until then you're stuck with sidewalk superintendents like my brother, Marty. Which leads to:

Rule #4: Don't take any advice.

"Why don't you try that stone over there?"

"This one here?"

"No, that *other* one."

"This one?"

"No, the one next to it."

"What about it?"

"Try it in that open space."

"Over here?"

"No, right *there!*"

"I tried it there already."

"Turn it the *other* way."

"Like this?"

"No, you've got it upside down."

"There *is* no upside down, goddamnit, this is a stone!"

"Hey, watch out! You almost dropped that on my foot."

"Excuse me."

Suddenly the game intrudes on my reverie. People are hollering. Something's happening. Kolacka's got his mask off and he's pointing into our dugout. Now he spins around and jerks his arm in a big looping arc.

"You'rrre outta herrre!" he roars.

Is this really happening?

Kolacka just threw Wilkins out of the game.

"What the hell did you say to him?" asks Bateman, his arms spread wide in disbelief.

"Nothing," says Wilkins, staring off into the distance. "Nothing to get thrown out for."

	1	2	3	4	5	6	7	8	9		R	H	E
PHILLIES	0	0	0	3	0	1					4	5	0
CUBS	0	2	0	0	0						2	5	1

What rattles around in my head now is that maybe I went over the edge. When I saw that runner on third and two out, I became obsessed with the need to get him home. More than anything I'd felt on this ballfield today, I sensed the need for the insurance run. If Fregosi was not going to pinch-hit for Greene, how else was I going to get that run across?

So I called a balk. Who knows what a balk is? Every year there's a different interpretation. Every umpire makes his own judgment. Sometimes I see games on TV, the pitcher makes moves, you'd think there was no such thing as a balk. A balk is anything an umpire claims he saw.

I called it, and once again all hell broke loose.

Somewhere, in all the fury, I bounced Wilkins. I saw the chance to get him out of there and I went all the way. I had to double my victory: get that insurance run in and bust up the Cubs' battery. Whatever Wilkins said or did, he was right there spitting out his anger along with Bateman. No one was going to question that.

That's the way I saw it, anyway.

186

I went to the Phillies' dugout for another shot at the old water cooler. Twelve years ago, I took my first drink of big league water at this fountain. It went down a lot easier than it does now. I was plenty nervous then, routine rookie nerves, you could say, but this is something else again. I *had* to get rid of Wilkins. A catcher can make a pitcher or ruin him. Without Wilkins, Ward will suffer. The sonovabitch manages to battle his way out of everything that hits him. It's like he's insulated against what I'm doing. He seems to get stronger every inning. Even when the knuckler doesn't dance, he fools them. But without Wilkins?

I don't like the way the game is going, up and down, up and down. I don't like not having enough control. I can picture them in the TV booth, beating it around, replaying all those camera angles and close-ups on Ward, looking for some trace of movement. Where did he balk? Where? I don't want to know what they're saying. A balk is a balk because I say it is, fucking period!

Be careful, Ernie. Jesus Christ, be careful.

Think.

Maybe you shouldn't have called it.

I don't like the fear that's crawling around my skin.

Then someone blows a toy horn, an introduction to a new voice.

"Hey, gorilla, what zoo did you come from?"

It's a woman this time. The guy's wife?

Umpires and zoos. I'd like to have a buck for every time I heard the connection. Maybe I should do my imitation of an ape.

"You're my all-time hero!" she hollers. *"You and King Kong!"*

Scattered laughs and applause. They don't like me in the stands, no question about that. Why should they? I don't even like myself. It's the sixth inning, I'm winning this game by two runs, which is like swimming two yards in front of the shark. What can I do but smile? What else? I'm not going to run for cover. Fuck you, shark. And fuck you, too, woman. I need to smile to show how secure I am.

"Who are you kidding with that smirk?" Enid once snapped at me. "It doesn't work."

Maybe it does and maybe it doesn't. Some people, when they're in trouble, they whistle, or light up a smoke, or crack their goddamn knuckles. Me, I smile. It was all I had to show for my pride.

A half-dozen years ago, Enid insisted we go on a cruise to the Bahamas during my two-week vacation. God knows I didn't want this. It was August and I was tired. I wanted to stay home, sleep late, play golf, see a few friends. But she had to go places, see things, and spend money. Everything she did cost money. After six years in the majors, I was making close to $100,000 a season, but I didn't have a dime.

That morning we were in a boutique on Nassau. She'd whip out the credit card and buy something. A dress. A blouse. A cape, even. Then she had to have the right jewelry to go with it. She saw a striped blue-and-white shirt she wanted for me. Perfect with my new blue blazer, she said. Then a silk tie. Don't ask me to describe what colors it was, all I saw was the price: $65. I wasn't going to spend $65 for a tie.

"No!" I said. "I got plenty of ties."

She ignored me. She told the clerk to wrap it with the rest of the junk. It was one of those last straws after years of big spending. I'm talking about a brand-new house in a classy neighborhood. New furniture, expensive antiques. She loved antiques. Suddenly she'd become an interior decorator. "The money I saved you, you ought to be grateful!" she said. All I knew was that it cost a fortune and I couldn't sit comfortable in those chairs. "You have no taste!" she said. She had to have a new car. Our son-in-law was expert in new cars, and he came through with a Mercedes. The car went with the neighborhood and the antiques.

"Put the tie back!" I told the clerk.

I can tell you, pal, that began a scene they won't forget on Nassau, two married people going at each other over a necktie.

And the smile? That came later when we were back on board a ship so big you couldn't fit it in Wrigley Field. But it wasn't big enough for the Kolackas. I had on the same stupid smile because she was all over me. I'd made a fool of her, she said. I had no class. What was I going to do, bang her out of that store like I do to managers? I couldn't argue with her. She had all the words. All I had going for me was the smile that set them off.

I knew the roots of the problem, all right. It didn't take a giant brain to figure it out. The oldest story in the history of marriage: she was spending all that money *to get even with me*!

Spend it. Buy, buy, buy. When the going gets tough, angry wives go shopping. Spend money till the husband cringes.

She had enough reason. Date it back to the breakfast table in the old

Hempstead kitchen. It was postseason, I was reading the paper, she was stirring her coffee, I could hear the spoon clicking in her cup. Out it came, the cry of the abused wife.

"Who is Trisha?"

I must've been ready for this moment because I didn't flinch. I didn't even ruffle the newspaper.

"Trisha? Trisha who?" I said.

"Don't feed me lies, Ernie. You spoke her name in your sleep. Twice."

"Sorry, Enid. I don't know anybody named Trisha."

She slapped the paper out of my hand. She jumped all over me. She accused me of cheating on her every time I went on the road. "You couldn't fool me!" She insisted she knew it from the beginning. Trisha! Who is Trisha!

"Enid," I said, slowly and deliberately. *"I never cheated on you!"*

The marriage ... what happened to the marriage? You'd think that when I finally got called up, everything would've worked out for the best. The reward for all the tough years would have a happy ending. You'd think we could've weathered any storm. But I talked in my sleep. I couldn't help it. I didn't even feel guilty about it. Why should I? I mean, what the fuck did I do that was so terrible?

Who is Trisha?

It ended up, I told her. I told her what had happened that night in Hawaii. But to spare her any pain, I left out the kiss. I didn't want to hurt her; I simply assured her that it was nothing, that I'd never seen her again.

Poor Enid, she didn't believe me.

"You slept with her, didn't you?"

"No, Enid."

"I *know* you did. You even screw differently."

"What?"

"You were different!" she insisted.

"Enid, Enid, this is crazy!"

She couldn't get over it. She took to punishing me in bed. She'd get me horny, then roll away like I was disgusting. She'd even say that to me.

"I don't know why I sleep in the same bed with you!"

Then one day I came home and there were twin beds.

Then there was the rest of it. The years went by, I got no loving and I had no money. I never called Trisha because I wasn't going to play dumb romantic games. Every once in a while there'd be a postcard that worked its way through the National League office to a stadium locker room: "Hello from Hawaii. We're all fine. Hope you're doing well. Greetings." It was like she wanted me to know she was still there. Oh, I'd do the same. Postcards with tourist pictures on them. We never used the word *love*. Whatever there was between us remained unmentioned.

Now I've got 50,000 tigers ready to eat me. I've got three and a half more innings and it's a goddamn motherfucking sonovabitching squeaker. I'll make it work for me. I'll handle what has to be handled. I'll win this one for the gyppers and for my $200 grand.

I crouch behind Daulton to watch Greene throw his warm-up. Here comes Sandberg again. He's been having a bad day against Greene. That doesn't particularly please me. Like they say, he's due. I don't want to face another rough inning. I want these Cubbies to pop up or hit one-hoppers back to the mound. I've got to hang on to that two-run Phillies lead.

Sandberg doesn't like the first pitch, but I do. To my eye, it catches the outside corner. I've been plenty careful so far. No more than six bad calls, only three of them making a difference on the scoreboard. When you call a few hundred pitches, there's got to be maybe thirty that are doubtful. So who's to say I'm not doing my job?

Sandberg, for one. He steps out to pick up dirt to make sure I know what he's thinking. When he gets set again, Greene tries to fool him with an off-speed breaking ball down and away, but Sandberg slaps a base hit to right field like he was waiting for it.

And here comes Leon Banks with his four big bats, any one of which could tie up the game. He works the count to 2-2, then rips a long fly ball into the right-field corner. It excites the crowd, but Matthews pulls it in on the run. Sandberg tags up and easily beats the throw to second.

Comes now Mark Grace, and Greene works hard to keep him guessing. Fastball in tight, then a change-up down and away. Strike one, ball one. Breaking ball off the outside corner, then a low fastball that's fouled off. The count goes to 3-2, another foul back to the screen, then a curveball that breaks into the dirt, and Grace takes his base.

It's Hatcher now. Or is it Hatchet? Or maybe Hotshit? Without my specs,

I can't even read my own writing. But I think, hey, I couldn't have worked this any better. With Wilkins in the showers, I not only fucked up the battery but the batting order as well. Hatchet steps in wagging his bat, back and forth, faster and faster, until the pitch. He does this enough times to slap a ground ball to the right side. Duncan gloves it neatly, pivots, tosses to Stocker as he crosses second, and throws hard to first for the double play.

And suddenly I can even smile for real.

I'm winning. Like a miser counting his gold, I look at the scoreboard to reassure myself of the numbers. I'm winning, all right. It's 4–2, Phillies. Three innings to go. That's all. Three lousy little goddamn innings and it's me who gets the gold. I let my mind's eye feast on the sight of it. There's $100,000 in my travel bag, and then there'll be the Professor with $100,000 more. I did what I had to do and got paid for doing it right. I did it for Roger. I didn't ask for the money. The money is like a charm, like a crystal glistening in the sun. In all my life, I never thought of money except what was needed to keep the wheels turning. When it's hard to come by, you learn to settle for what you have. When all of a sudden you're looking at a pot of gold, how could it not make you smile? How could it not put magic in your life? How can you help but play fantasy games?

Like with Trisha, always with Trisha. Look in the stands, pal. Is she there again? Could you ever have believed that night at Chavez Ravine in Los Angeles two years ago? It was between innings, I walked to the Dodger dugout for a drink and I heard her voice. "Ernie." When did the sound of my name ever send me soaring? When did the sight of a woman's face ever tear the guts out of me? She was there in L.A. to see her kid sister, who'd just had a baby. That I was there, too, was pure luck. She didn't know how else to deal with it after eight years apart. Eight years! She just showed up, walked to the barrier, and spoke my name.

I looked at her. I couldn't take my eyes off her. She hadn't changed much. A touch of gray in the red hair. A few lines around the eyes and the mouth. I couldn't talk, not then, not there in the middle of a ball game. I told her, please, wait for me outside the gate. She nodded, her smile creasing her freckles, tears in her lovely brown eyes. I put on my mask and turned away before I made a fool of myself.

I can tell you, I never knew what hunger there was inside of me. Well, I found out that night. To hold that woman in my arms was more beautiful than anything I ever believed possible. "You're my fairy-tale prince in blue," she said.

"You're not here, Trisha. I don't believe you're in this bed with me. This isn't happening, this is just a pair of old folks making believe . . ."

"Oh, Ernie . . ."

Again, she made my name sound like a song. I kissed her with my lips, my tongue, my heart. I kissed her with my hands caressing her hair, her face. I kissed her with more soul than passion. And when we finally came up for air, she cried out with such joy I had to cry out, too. "Yes . . . yes!" God, how lovely were those sounds!

There were two days of this, interruptions for ball games and sister-visits. Two days when loving was all that really mattered.

"I knew it would be just like this," she said.

Sometimes corny words are exactly the right ones.

"It's like magic," I said.

That was two years ago. She went back to Hawaii to her son, Lucas, and her greeting-card business, and I went with my crew for three days in Houston, then more years with Enid. You may think that maybe Trisha and I were dumb. Maybe we could've worked something out. We didn't even talk about it. Maybe it scared us both. Maybe this was the way it was supposed to be. I can tell you, though, it was so wonderful you could soak in it. You could thrive on just knowing it had happened.

Now I've got three more innings to make it happen. Three more innings looking into the barrel of a cannon. The furies are like screeching bats swirling around my head. There's that tiger again, lurking in the tall grass waiting to have me for lunch.

And here comes Lenny Dykstra. Thank God for Dykstra. Maybe he'll put one out of here. Or maybe he'll just start a big inning for the Phillies with an ordinary base hit. I'm not greedy.

He steps in, then steps right out, pointing to the plate with his bat. I see a brown glob of tobacco juice.

"That ain't me, Ernie," Dykstra says. "I would no more spit on home plate than spit on my mother."

Sure, it's Hatchet. I move around him, use my duster to wipe it off.
"Next time, sonny, spit on yourself," I say to him.
Dykstra grins. Hatchet grunts. Ward takes a deep breath.
"Play ball!" cries the umpire.

	1	2	3	4	5	6	7	8	9	R	H	E
PHILLIES	0	0	0	3	0	1				4	5	0
CUBS	0	2	0	0	0	0				2	6	1

Hatchet lifts his mask and squirts a stream of tobacco juice on home plate.

Beautiful. There's nothing an umpire likes more than brown spit in his little whisk broom.

Not only do I lose Wilkins, I get Hatchet. This is like trading a Rolls-Royce for a pickup truck. I just hope he doesn't give me a hard time with the signs. We discussed the matter between innings.

"Same shit," said Hatchet. "One fast, two curve, three sinker, four change, and wiggle for the knuckler."

"Mostly knucklers," I said.

"Don't shake me off," said Hatchet.

"I will if I have to," I said.

"Catcher runs the game," he said.

"You catch," I said. "I'll do the thinking."

It was the friendliest conversation we've had all summer.

Meanwhile, Dykstra, a bicep muscle in the form of a person, is flexing and twitching in the batter's box. He's also spitting tobacco leaves out of his mouth. He appears to favor a dry form of the stuff as opposed to Hatchet's wet gobs. Maybe they should compare recipes.

Hatchet gives me the sign. Knuckleball. Thank you. I kick and throw. The ball leaves my hand ... dodging and darting up to the plate ... but then it breaks low and outside.

"Steeerike!" bellows Kolacka.

Dykstra has a few words for Kolacka which he directs to the scoreboard in center field. Technically, you're not allowed to argue balls and strikes, but most umps will cut you some slack if you don't "show them up." Meaning turn around and get in their face. It looks bad on TV. You can "sonovabitch" an umpire as long as you don't look at him. Turn around and say "Excuse me, sir, but you missed that pitch," and you're gone.

My next pitch to Dykstra is a knuckler that he swings on and misses for strike two. A curve is in the dirt, but Dykstra doesn't bite. Back to the knuckler. I kick and throw. The ball wobbles up to the plate ... Dykstra swings ... in the middle of a wobble ... and misses for strike three!

One out.

Mariano Duncan steps in. Hatchet calls for a knuckler, but I shake him off. I want the sinker, inside. Duncan swings ... and smashes it ... back *at me*! I can't get my glove ... the ball slams into my chest ... it's bouncing to my left ... I'm off the mound ... I catch up to the ball ... and I flip it backhanded in the direction of first base.

"Yeeeah!" hollers umpire John Koenig, whose style when he calls somebody out on a close play is to bend his big body as far forward as possible, point both index fingers to the ground, then pull the right hand back quickly like he's drawing a sword from a fallen adversary.

The roar of the crowd rises and falls with the throb in my chest. But I signal that I'm okay. I don't want Doc running onto the field, giving Bateman any ideas about taking me out. I'll be fine. I don't pitch with my chest.

The crowd gives me a nice round of applause.

And where the hell is my hat?

Jerome is waiting with it on the mound.

"Not bad," he says, slapping the hat against his leg to get the dirt off. "But you should have charged that ball."

"Thanks a lot," I say.

Jerome trots back to short as Kruk steps into the batter's box. Hatchet squirts a stream of brown and puts on his mask. He gives me the sign. Curve. He wants it outside. That's where I put it. Kruk swings ... and hits an easy fly ball to Willie Wilson in center field ... for out number three. That's how you know the knuckleball is working. The hitters are swinging at pitches because they're *not* knuckleballs.

I walk off the mound as the organ plays "Chicago, Chicago, that toddlin' town ..." and people rise for the seventh-inning stretch. The fans in the lower stands greet me as I approach the dugout. "Nice job, Sam," they holler, and I tip my cap. "They should have used you last year." Right. And the year before that, too.

We're losing 4–2, but these are real fans and they appreciate the effort. Not a bad job, I say to myself. Seven innings, six hits, only *one* earned run. I pause to savor the moment. This could be my last trip to the dugout in Wrigley Field. I'm due up this inning and they'll probably pinch-hit for me. Unless we get a couple guys on and they want me to bunt them over.

I step into the dugout and I notice my teammates are looking at me a little differently. I see a new respect in their eyes. Like maybe I really *can* pitch in the big leagues. And I know that they're wondering what I'm thinking. Like when is the bubble going to burst? "Don't wake him up," they'll say about a guy who's playing over his head. It's like that cartoon character who runs off a cliff and keeps running in midair until he looks down.

I get a drink from the water cooler and sit down next to Jerome. He's shaking his head sadly, like something's wrong.

"Forget it," he says. "You got no chance. You're too far behind."

I can't believe he's talking like this.

"Bullshit," I say, "we can score two runs. If you get your ass on base."

"Who's talkin' 'bout runs?" says Jerome. "I'm talkin' *chess,* man. We'll be all even after today."

I laugh.

"You *got* me," I say. Then he smiles and walks away.

I can tell I must be doing okay because Bobby Rapp just walked by and grunted in a civil tone of voice. And the pitching coach isn't ranting and raving anymore. In fact, at the moment, he's heading in my direction with a blue Chicago Cubs windbreaker under his arm.

"Better put this over your shoulder," says Gilson, handing me the jacket. "It's colder than you think."

For some reason this is very amusing to Owens and Alexander, who lean over as soon as Gilson walks away.

"Can I get you a drink of water?" says Alexander, fawning and groveling.

"Or rub your dick?" says Owens.

Pitching a ball game is like building a wall. One pitch at a time, one stone at a time, each influenced by the ones that came before and dictating the ones to come. Shoving the perfect stone into an awkward space is like throwing a perfect pitch in the right spot. A well-pitched game is like a well-built wall, a blending of shapes and colors, a thing of beauty.

Except to squirrels.

One morning, after a brief layoff to heal a pulled groin from an Olympic Stone-Smashing event, I had a visitor. A bushy-tailed gray squirrel was screaming at me from the lower branches of a nearby tree. I could tell his angry chat-chat-chat was intended for me because he'd adjust his "flight distance," scrambling up or down the tree, depending on where I stood. And he didn't stop when I resumed working on the wall. If anything, he became more vociferous, jutting out his chin and flashing his teeth, as I added more stones.

It was several hours before he finally went away. And days before I figured out why he was so angry. Not being that familiar with construction schedules, the squirrel had hidden his winter rations in the unfinished section of the wall. And I was covering them up. Permanently. I guess I'd scream, too, if somebody buried my nuts in a wall.

Like a coral reef attracts sea life, the wall enticed hordes of creatures large and small. With its labyrinth of cracks and crevices, nooks and crannies, interior pockets of loose dirt and broken stones, the wall became a haven and a hunting ground, a nesting place and a killing field, a place to eat and be eaten.

In the beginning, there were the bugs that crawled among the cracks. This brought the little birds that pecked the bugs, and then the snakes that waited for the toads that ate the bugs, and then the hawks that grabbed the snakes, and then the cats that stalked the birds as they patrolled the living wall. If you build it, they will come.

For six months, it was just me and the creatures and the rocks.

Except for occasional weekend visits from Beth. Who wasn't her effervescent self after the separation. Beth had tried to put on a good face in the beginning, but as the days became weeks and then months, she grew increasingly quiet. Between bursts of enthusiasm for some adventure or other, I'd catch her nervously twirling her hair and staring off into the distance. "Earth to Beth," I'd say, and she'd give me a little smile.

We'd do things like hike in the woods or cook out on the grill. Or just sit together and read books. When it got cold enough, we'd ice-skate on the lake. Unfortunately, we couldn't play two-on-one hockey this year. We were missing the goalie.

Of course, I was missing the goalie more than Beth. It was pretty cold at night, even with the heater. But it was cozy in the cabin with Beth over on the couch in her sleeping bag, the two of us just lying in the dark, talking to the ceiling.

"Tell me a story, Dad," she'd say. "You know, the one about Simone and the Pirates."

This was a continuing story I'd make up as I went along about a young lady named Simone and her band of twenty-three female pirates named the Vandellas who would rob and plunder the high seas in a submarine. Simone and the Vandellas, who were also pretty good singers, would only rob people who had stolen money themselves or who had more money than they knew what to do with.

"But how come they never got caught?"

"I was just about to get to that," I'd say. "As a matter of fact, they would frequently get caught. But then they'd invite their captors to a party below decks, where they'd put on a show and get everybody drunk."

"But what happened when they woke up?"

"You're going too fast," I'd say. "I was just about to explain. Before the captors woke up, the Vandellas would drop them off on the beach in Hawaii and put leis around their necks so it looked like they'd been goofing off instead of doing their jobs, and they got fired."

"And the Vandellas would give the money to homeless people, right?"

"Right," I'd say.

"But how did the Vandellas eat?"

"With their mouths," I'd reply.

"Oh, Dad," Beth would say, exasperated when the story deteriorated to the level of bad jokes. "You know what I mean."

Then there would be a long silence and I'd start to doze off.

"Tell me another one, Dad."

"It's time to go to sleep."

"Pleeeease," she'd beg pitifully. "Just one more."

Then I'd launch into my campfire story.

"There were forty bold robbers sitting around a campfire. 'Shorty?' said the Captain. 'Tell us a story.' Shorty leaned slowly into the campfire and said, 'There were forty bold robbers sitting around the campfire. "Shorty?" said the Captain. "Tell us—" ' "

"Not that one again, Dad," she'd interrupt. "A *different* one."

"Okay," I'd say. "But this is the last one. 'Once there was a calf—that's half. Then they put him in a stall—that's all.' "

That's when Beth would usually give up and fall asleep.

But then there were other nights when she had one more question.

"Dad," she'd ask softly in the darkness, "are you and Mom going to get back together again?"

I didn't know what to tell her.

Getting us back together seemed to be Beth's main goal in life for a while. And she was pretty clever about it. She'd have Marty arrange a conference call and put the three of us together so we could "talk things out." Or she'd "accidentally" leave her homework at the cabin and ask her mother to go get it because she needed it for school. Unfortunately, Julie refused to play along.

Boy, I miss her. Basic stuff, like catching up with each other at the end of the day. I always wanted to know what Julie thought about things, a recent movie, a book she was reading, what was happening in the news. The latest Ward family maneuver. I miss her insights, her up-front, what-you-see-is-what-you-get way of dealing with life.

I miss the intimacy, too. Julie gave me a rare glimpse into the world of women that I never got growing up at home. I loved watching her put on makeup, for example, or how she'd lean forward to put on a bra. And then there was her little "birdbath." That's what I called it when she'd use the bathroom sink as a bidet. With the grace of a dancer, she'd lift one of her marvelous legs up onto the sink and plant her foot next to the faucets. Then she'd redirect the running water with a cupped hand, splashing it between her legs. It was always a great view, no matter which leg was up on the sink.

Suddenly the crowd roars. What the hell happened?

Buechele just singled to left.

My adrenaline starts flowing.

Because if Sosa gets on . . .

"Ward!" says Bobby Rapp, like a sensitive, New Age drill instructor. "Better get a bat. Just in case."

		1	2	3	4	5	6	7	8	9		R	H	E
PHILLIES		0	0	0	3	0	1	0				4	5	0
CUBS		0	2	0	0	0	0					2	6	1

It's seventh-inning stretch time, 50,000 Cubs fans rise to their feet and begin a spontaneous synchronized clapping that gets louder and louder. I've been inside ballparks all my life but I've never heard anything like this. They begin to roar like a fight crowd yelling for a knockout. Mine? The way I see it, they want me dead. They're going to pour out of the stands, all 50,000 of them, stampeding, yelling, screaming for my blood, and they'll tear me to bits. I work for a defiant smile as I look up at the stands. In the late-afternoon haze, is it the noise that makes everything blur? I can't see any faces; the massive sound overwhelms the sight. There's enormous power in that sound, especially when you sense you're in the center of it. All I know is, I've got to hang on to this game and make it mine.

I let my head bob in sync with the rhythmic clapping. They're challenging me, all right. They're saying, hey, try to stop us! We're going to bust this game wide open and there's nothing you or anyone else can do about it. The Cubs are coming! The Cubs are coming!

The crowd doesn't let up. It makes everything larger than life. It fires me up.

"Make the game come out the way it must!" said the Professor. *"Or else!"*

Or else what? I don't want to think about such ratshit problems. I don't want to know the consequences of what I do or don't do.

I dust off the plate with five sweeps of my little broom, only this time I do it with my ass to the crowd. It's fuck you, crowd. For the first time since umpire's school, I'm sending my message to the world.

Buechele is the leadoff man. He takes the first pitch, a strike. Then he hits a chopper that handcuffs Hollins at third. Hollins bobbles it, then hurries his throw, pulling Kruk off the bag. Error Hollins, and Buechele is on.

Up comes Sammy Sosa, one of the best eighth hitters in the National League, which makes him no more agreeable to me than a bad case of piles. I've got to get him out of here. Sure, he's got other ideas. He drills the first pitch on a line to Incaviglia in left. Incaviglia takes it on one hop and Buechele has to hold at second, and now there's two men on and no one out.

It's Ward's turn to hit, but Bateman has Shawon Dunston in the on-deck circle to pinch-hit. All of a sudden, he calls him back. He wants Ward on the mound so much he'll save his pinch hitters. How the crowd loves it! Big cheers for Sam Ward. Ward, the great bunter, will bunt the two runners into scoring position and preserve himself for another inning on the mound. The way the crowd yells, you'd think this is the formula for certain victory. They're yelling for Ward like there's no force on earth strong enough to get him out of the ball game. No matter that Bateman's got four good pinch hitters on the bench begging to hit, or four arms in the bullpen, left and right, crying to go to work. It's Ward he wants. Why, for crissakes? Maybe it's really in the stars, maybe he got a telephone message from his Gypsy who's been reading her beads. Maybe, if I think hard enough about what I want, Ward will pop it into a double play.

So here he comes with his bat, pretending he doesn't hear the cheering. He's wearing just a hint of a smile on his face like he actually thinks he belongs up here.

He picks up dirt to dust his hands. No batting gloves for this guy. He moves into position and we're ready to go.

On the mound, Greene checks the runner as the infielders start their moves to cover a bunt. Ward pivots into bunting position, levels his bat in front of him, but takes high for ball one.

So it's rerun time. Again, Greene checks the runner, sets, throws—and sonovabitch, this time Ward fakes bunt, pulls his bat back, and slashes the pitch into right field for a base hit! Bucchelc scores standing up, Sosa slides safely into third, and Ward ends up at first.

The crowd rises to its feet shouting like thunder.

It's all a bad dream now. Who would've believed this? Ward is like a spook that won't go away. He's the hidden force behind that horoscope.

So now it's runners on first and third in a 4–3 ball game, nobody out, with the top of the Cubs' batting order.

Sweat and chill, that's what I feel, one teasing the other. I look at Willie Wilson as he steps in, and he never seemed so threatening. He's been around too long and doesn't get old, he just gets better. It's a moment when I hate the sight of him. On the mound Greene decides he doesn't like the feel of the baseball. He tosses it in, I give Bubba Daulton a new one. If I could load it with spit first, I'd do that, too. Greene rubs it up, taking his time about it. Then I want to kiss him: he strikes out Wilson on three incredible fastballs.

I'm just as worried about Jerome Davis. Sonovabitch, I'm worried about everybody. I don't want to see that tying run come by me. I don't want another base hit moving Ward into scoring position with Sandberg coming up. I don't like Hollins's error. I'm thinking, Jesus Christ, don't hit anything near Hollins.

Davis obliges me. I will always appreciate you, son. His pop-up is a sweetheart. It flutters in the air a few feet off the first-base line, then falls into Kruk's mitt like a duck with a load of buckshot in his ass.

The crowd moans in such excruciating pain, Davis hurries to the dugout to get out of sight.

With Ryne Sandberg coming to the plate, Jim Fregosi goes to the mound. It figures, all right. There's heavy action in the Phillies' bullpen, but Fregosi isn't making any moves. Not yet. He's letting Greene take a breather as they decide how to work on Sandberg. I can tell you how: it's like the way porcupines fuck—very, very carefully. Greene should not give Sandberg anything he could hit. Nothing near the heart of the strike zone. If you have to walk him, walk him, even if the go-ahead run moves to scoring position. Better to work on left-handed Banks by bringing in a left-hander. Why else is Arlo Maxie throwing in the pen?

I stand behind Daulton with that bad gut feeling about what a hitter like Sandberg can do to you. As Greene goes into his stretch, I realize how far I'm drifting from being an umpire. I'm a strategist. It's not Fregosi telling Greene to put Sandberg on, it's me who wants to do it. Even if it loads the bases, I want to put him on.

Greene's first pitch is a beautiful breaking ball at the knees. It could be a strike, but I call it a ball. In front of me, Daulton holds dead still, the statue protest. Fregosi lets out a nasty cry from the dugout. He doesn't want to walk him. In a spot like this, there's nothing more damaging than a bad call on the first pitch. But I know what I'm doing. I'm betting my ass on what I'm doing.

Greene's second pitch is a fastball that misses outside for ball two, which does what I want: Fregosi signals Daulton to put him on. Greene throws two intentional balls and Sandberg walks to first base. Fregosi comes out to the mound tapping his left sleeve at the boys in the bullpen.

So far, so good.

Arlo Maxie is a big lean guy they call "Mad Man," a hard-throwing left-hander. On the mound, he's a weirdo, all right, his glove tucked under his chin like he was the sly one working for the Devil himself. At second, the Cubs' coach is talking to Ward, no doubt advising him about Maxie's mad pickoff moves. In the batter's circle, Banks watches with his four black bats.

At last, the tester. For Maxie and the Phillies, for Banks and the Cubs, but most of all for me.

I watch Banks as he steps in, digging his left foot in the back end of the box. I don't care about his foot, I want to see the look of him. I want to see the way he feels. I want to see how real, or how phony, is the cocky smile. I like what I see. Sonovabitch, he's not as happy as he was early in the game. Not now. Not against Maxie. If I've learned anything in 5,000 ball games, it's how to spot a winner and how to spot a loser. It's not a sure thing, it's never a sure thing, but there are moments when the feel of it hits you right on the button. You can sense the inside of a hitter's crumbling gut. You can catch the loser's vibes.

For openers, then, Maxie cuts loose with a screaming high fastball that

Daulton has to leap for. The crowd loves it. I can see Banks smiling as he steps out to do his equipment-adjustment dance, but when he steps back in, the smile shows signs of a twitch. Maxie throws another fastball on Banks's hands. It backs him off, but it's in there for strike one. Bateman lets me know he's still on the dugout steps. I let him know that I know that by raising my mask to spit. Banks finishes playing with his Velcro and gets set to hit. Maxie gets his sign, cradles the glove under his chin, and throws a vicious curve that just misses for ball two. The 2-1 pitch is another fastball that Banks swings at with everything he's got, spinning his body completely around, and he misses contact by half a foot.

The crowd eats it up. Banks goes into his dance with his ritual moves, zip/slap, hitch the pants, rotate the neck and shoulders. And once again, I see that little twitch on the left corner of his mouth and I know I'm right about him.

Then comes the 2-2 pitch, a breaking ball that starts at the knees, then drops off the table over the outside corner. Banks takes the pitch without moving his bat. I let him hear the bad news with a shriek and a vicious strike thrust of my right fist to punch him out.

I did it. The inning is over.

But not for Leon Banks. He stands in the box glowering at the outside corner of the plate, acting like maybe he isn't out, maybe Maxie will throw that last pitch again, maybe I'm going to let him have four strikes.

To hell with Banks. The crowd doesn't like the call, either, but to hell with them, too, all 50,000 of them. The TV camera will show that maybe it caught the corner and maybe it didn't. The announcers will tell the rest of the world whatever they think they saw, and to hell with *them*, too.

All I know is that Banks is out and the inning is over.

I take off my mask to get some air on my face. There's so much crowd noise it smothers the breeze. This crowd refuses to die. They're one run down, but you'd never know it. What they see are those big bats coming up and two innings to make the best of them—and, to their mind, they've got the world's greatest junk pitcher to smother the Phillies until they do.

And then, suddenly, all hell breaks loose.

	1	2	3	4	5	6	7	8	9		R	H	E
PHILLIES	0	0	0	3	0	1	0				4	5	1
CUBS	0	2	0	0	0	0	1				3	8	1

The crowd is on its feet and roaring.

"Bull*shit,* motherfucker!" shouts Leon Banks, flipping his batting helmet thirty feet into the air. "Motherfucker's outside!"

Bateman explodes from the dugout, making a beeline for Banks, who is elaborating on the "motherfucker" theme in the direction of Ernie Kolacka. Bateman grabs Banks by the back of his uniform shirt and spins him around like he was on a swivel. Now that someone is holding him back, Banks is straining to get at Kolacka, who stands motionless as a post at home plate. Meanwhile, Bateman, working like a quarter horse separating a steer from the herd, uses surprisingly quick feet and his ample belly to outflank, jostle, shove, bump, and otherwise maneuver Banks back into our dugout.

Popcorn boxes and beer cups, some of them pretty full, are flying onto the field. What appears to be somebody's lunch bag and a large beach ball just landed in right. The crowd is angry at Kolacka at the same time they're upset with us for missing a great opportunity to score even *before* Banks struck out. And they're right. Runners on first and third and nobody out, we've got to get a few runs out of that situation. And why is Banks taking a close pitch with two strikes? And the bases loaded!

I can't even sit here and enjoy my bunt and slash because we're still a run down and we should be winning the damn game!

"I'll be a sonovabitch!" says Bateman, flopping down onto the bench a few feet away, his faced flushed, steam coming off the top of his head.

The trainer comes over with a cup of water and some pills.

"Thanks, Doc," says Bateman, downing the pills in a single gulp. Then he leans forward and looks around.

"Where's Ward?" he asks wearily.

"Right here, Vern," I say without thinking, as if I were a regular and it was perfectly okay to call him by his first name.

"How do you feel?" he asks, sweat beading up on his purple nose, his lungs whistling with every breath.

"I'm okay," I say, like I belong out there. My heart leaps at the opportunity as my stomach absorbs the responsibility.

"Then you're it," he says, forcing a smile. "Just keep doing what you're doing."

Just keep doing what I'm doing. Okay. I take off my jacket, grab my glove, and head for the mound.

"Let's go, Sam," the guys holler.

"Keep us close, big guy!"

"Stick it up their ass."

As I cross the foul line, something catches my eye over in the on-deck circle. It's Mark Matthews doing his muscle-flexing routine with a weighted bat. I pay no attention. I've seen his act before, I don't need to see it again. Plus, I don't want to give him the satisfaction.

I finish my warm-up tosses and Hatchet guns it down to second base.

"Play ball!" yells Kolacka, a slight crack in his voice showing the effects of a long afternoon.

Matthews approaches the plate, fastening and unfastening the Velcro straps on his batting gloves. Those gloves have to be just right or Matthews won't step in. They could shorten games by half an hour just by eliminating batting gloves. Now he's ready. Not to actually hit, of course, but to start digging a toehold. Which he does in that annoying way some batters have of signaling the umpire that they're not quite ready, by holding up one hand, like they're stopping traffic.

Gloves strapped, holes dug, *now* he's ready.

I have the impulse to call time out and go take a pee, but I stifle it. Instead, I look in for the sign. Hatchet wiggles four fingers. Knuckleball. I press my fingertips into the leather. I wind up and let it fly. And it's a beauty, too, changing direction three times before breaking outside.

Ball one.

I don't want to walk the leadoff hitter again. Maybe I should go with another pitch. But if I throw a curve or a sinker, Matthews might park it on Waveland Avenue. I look for the sign. Knuckleball. I kick and throw. The ball ... dips and dives ... and *just* misses the outside corner.

Ball two.

Damn! Matthews doesn't want to swing at the knuckler, because it's jumping too much. So why doesn't it jump into the goddamn strike zone? My heart hurts.

I step off the mound.

I reach into my back pocket and grab a few pebbles. With my hand still in my pocket, I squeeze the stones in my fist. The hard shapes press into my skin. I release my grip and jiggle them around. The stones click together reassuringly. I feel my breathing change.

Matthews is standing in the batter's box with a smirk on his face. He's going to holler some bullshit about me challenging his ass. I'd love to have a brilliant comeback ready.

But I've got a better idea. Maybe *I'll* initiate the conversation. Why not? It's worth a shot.

I walk toward home plate, holding the ball up to signal that I want a new one. Kolacka digs one out of his ball bag and flips it to me. I toss him the old ball and now I'm within speaking distance of Mark Matthews.

"Hey, Mark," I say, like we're old friends. "I see you're waiting for a walk. Embarrassing, isn't it? Big guy like you?"

"Fuck you, asshole," he says, the color rising in his face.

But the conversation ends right there, because I'm already on my way back to the mound.

"That's enough," yells Kolacka, whose job responsibilities include heading off fights between players. "Let's play ball!"

For some reason, my knees are shaking a little bit right now. I don't know why. Matthews had bad intentions when he first stepped into the batter's box.

Hatchet squats to give me the sign. Knuckleball. I kick and throw. The ball ... dances through the air ... Matthews leans in ... he cocks his bat ... the ball floats ... he swings ... I hear the sickening crack of wood on leather! It's a tremendous drive ... high and deep ... going, going, going ... gone! Clear out of the stadium ... about twenty feet foul.

Strike one.

The crowd suffers a group panic attack. They don't appreciate the knuckler's perverse sense of humor. How it derives pleasure from certain forms of torture intended to demoralize the hitter, like near-miss home runs.

Matthews is still standing at home plate, admiring his blast, as Kolacka tosses me a new ball. I spin it around in my hand to get acquainted, looking for a friendly spot. I find it. I kick and throw. The ball glides ... like a sailboat in a breeze ... Matthews swings ... now the ball is a submarine, diving deep ... the bat catches the upper surface ... and it's ... a swinging bunt ... in front of the plate! I charge in to make the play ... but Hatchet's there and fires to first for out number one.

Never underestimate the ego of a home run hitter. Or the ability of fans to rub it in.

"Get the tape measure for that one!" somebody hollers, as Matthews storms back to the dugout.

"There goes your home run bonus!"

One out, nobody on, Dave Hollins the hitter. My first pitch is a sinker that doesn't sink and Hollins lines it into right field for a single. And now everybody shuts up except the Phillies dugout.

"Take me out!"

"Get the hook!"

The usual bullshit.

But I'm not that tired. I've only thrown about 90 pitches. If I was tired, I'd tell somebody. The last thing you want to do is play the hero and blow the game wide open. I honestly feel I can do the job. The knuckler's breaking and, except for that loud foul, they're not really hitting me.

I take a deep breath as Daulton gets set in the batter's box. Hatchet squats to give me the sign. Knuckleball. I check the runner. I kick and throw. And it's inside for ball one. The crowd starts clapping to give me a boost and also get themselves back into the game. A knuckler finds a corner for strike one. Another one misses for ball two. A curve is low for ball three. The crowd steps up the pace. Hatchet gives me the sign. Knuckler. Just misses for ball four.

And I'm history.

"Time!" hollers Kolacka.

The infielders come over to the mound as Bateman walks slowly across the field.

Jerome pats me on the ass with his glove.

"We should have won this one for you," he says.

"Great job, Sam," says Ryne Sandberg.

"Especially on Matthews," says Mark Grace. "He's still talking to himself over there in the dugout."

The players open a path as Bateman arrives.

"Well, boys," he says, taking off his hat and squinting at the sky like he's checking for geese. "Are your nuts cracking?"

Everybody laughs.

Bateman looks around casually, like he's got all the time in the world. And now he looks at me.

"I've got one more question and that's for you, Sam," says Bateman. "You running out of gas? And it's okay if you are, because you've pitched a helluva game."

I give him an honest answer.

"I'm a little low," I say. "But I'm not empty."

Bateman smiles.

"Well, let us know," he says. "Just grab your nuts or something and we'll come get you." Then he trots back to the dugout.

"Let's get dirty," hollers Steve Buechele. He's reminding everybody to dive in the dirt and knock down any grounders that might get through. An outfield hit scores a run; an infield hit only loads the bases.

One out, runners on first and second, Incaviglia the hitter. Hatchet calls for the knuckleball. I check the runners. I kick and throw. The ball . . . dances in toward the plate . . . Incaviglia swings . . . and hits a grounder back to me . . . I dive to my left . . . but *the ball is by me* . . . on the way into center field! Sonovabitch!

But there's Jerome!

Coming from nowhere. Scrambling, churning, kicking up dirt with every step. He's going to knock it down behind second base! He dives, his skinny body horizontal to the ground, like Superman with a Wilson A-2000 on his left hand. The ball bangs into Jerome's glove, which he then *flicks*, redirecting the ball up and back toward second base, where Sandberg has just arrived. In a single motion, Sandberg catches the ball barehanded, steps on second, and throws to first. Grace, in a groin-wrenching split, digs it out of the dirt for a double play!

"Yeeeah!" hollers Koenig at first base, bellowing like a moose and adding an extra stab to the end of his sword-pulling routine. The umps like to make the highlights tape, too.

The roar of the crowd escalates like a four-stage rocket, first the stop by Jerome, then the flick of the glove and the outs at first and second. And the noise continues as we head for the dugout.

I intercept Jerome coming across the infield.

"That's big, Jerome!" I holler, holding out my glove so he can give it a slap. "That's *real* big!"

Jerome is cool.

"I better be gettin' a glove contract out of *this* shit," he says.

Jerome makes me smile.

The whole damn thing makes me smile. The joint is rocking and I'm thinking how much fun this is—to be walking across the green grass in a major league baseball stadium with the crowd and the organ music and the game on the line.

I want to remember this moment. I'm looking up at the gray sky and thinking that the best kind of day for a ball game is not sunny, but overcast. The glare of the sun distracts. A gray sky brings your eye down to the field, setting off the white uniforms, turning the bases and chalk lines into glowing squares and streaks of light. The gloom of pending rain offers a muted background, a solemn contrast to the intensity on the field, like a gray matte sets off a painting.

It's the overcast days I remember most when I think about the wall. The dark sky matched my mood and lent a seriousness to the project, a sense of drama and purpose. The wall was a major achievement. And a source of discovery. What began as a mindless diversion to heal a broken heart became a crusade to free myself.

It was a bleak February day, the sky the color of diesel smoke, when I placed the last stone. I stood there for a while in the cold, turning the stone over in my hands, not wanting it to end. The wall would be finished, of course, and there'd be satisfaction in that. But then the fun would be over. The backbreaking, knee-banging, gut-busting fun of it all.

Building the wall was fun!

All by itself. Just the doing of it. No applause. I didn't need to tell anybody about it. I didn't have to say, "Hey look at me." For the first time I can remember, I had enjoyed doing something for its own sake. Without trying to prove something to somebody.

This was a whole new deal. All my life I had measured myself by my accomplishments. Or the lack of them. And that's why I could never quit baseball. I needed to be a major league ballplayer to feel like a major league person. I wanted the acceptance that Marty had. I wanted Dad's approval. I wanted to *belong* in Mr. Dabby's class. I wanted to deserve someone like Julie.

I wondered what my life might have been like had I come to this earlier. Would I still have played all those years in the minor leagues? Would I have made it to the big leagues? I didn't know.

But that day I understood one thing. I had to give this new feeling a shot. I had to play one season of baseball—just for the fun of it.

A week after laying the final stone, I was in spring training. Pitching like I've never pitched before. The same junk, but not the same me. I was throwing with a new confidence. Something had clicked inside. It sounds weird, but I felt older and stronger at the same time, more relaxed. My pitching became more instinctive, more creative. New combinations were possible. Anything could happen.

And something did.

I'm sitting here in a dugout in Wrigley Field, I'm still in the game, my team has a chance to win, and the guys are pumped.

"Hey, whaddya say!" yells Mark Grace, eyeballing Phillies pitcher Arlo Maxie. "Let's put the hurt on this guy!"

"Motherfucker be throwing that high cheese," says Willie Wilson. "Somebody take that shit downtown."

	1	2	3	4	5	6	7	8	9	R	H	E
PHILLIES	0	0	0	3	0	1	0	0		4	6	1
CUBS	0	2	0	0	0	0	1			3	8	1

Cubs fans are screaming like it's coming on the end of the world. When Mark Grace appears from the dugout swinging his donut-weighted bat, they greet him with a heavy wave of sound. A pretty girl is at the barrier waiting for him; she throws a bouquet of flowers that land at his feet. He turns, smiles. It brings up the sound even more. The batboy takes the flowers away. The demand for victory is deafening. I can't think in this kind of noise. I don't know anymore what I'm frightened of. I'm winning, right? It's up there on the board, it's 4–3 Phillies, all I've got to do is get six more Cubs outs.

It's the doubt that makes the skin crawl. It hits suddenly, sneaking into your thoughts, you have to wonder what sonovabitch put it there. Since Korea, I never got over what that did to my head. Those were days when I never thought anything bad could happen to me. I never believed I'd get shot. I was the guy who actually ran seven straight passes in a crap game. During enemy shelling, guys would hang close to me because I was Mr.

Lucky. It was weird. One guy next to me took a load of shrapnel that would've got me. I was so lucky, when I went out on patrol that day, you could've gotten odds I'd be back in an hour.

Life is a game of inches. Right now it's being played in a roar of sound that could intimidate a fucking dinosaur. I don't give a shit who you are, you can't prepare yourself for what I'm doing out here. This is a once-in-a-lifetime situation and there's no how-to manual that will spell out the how. It's the limits that can kill you. There's only so much you can do. I need six Cubs outs, that's all. They don't have to be in order. I've got room for a little of this, a little of that. Whatever I've done in seven and a half innings, I'm still behind the mask. Nobody knows shit. They haven't come for me with handcuffs. Even Sirotta doesn't have a clue.

Six outs. Three now, three to follow in the ninth.

I'm going to win this day because I *have* to win it. So fuck all fears.

I watch Grace dig in. He threatens me, all right. He's a dream killer. No matter how many times I've handcuffed him today, what are the odds against getting him again? It's Maxie vs. Grace vs. Kolacka, and here we go.

Before you can bat an eye, Grace wins: he drills a hard shot through the center of the diamond for a base hit. It's like a message from the gods telling me the bad news. I feel my body sinking with sweat. My right hand on the indicator is slippery with sweat. The force is draining out of me. The crowd is making so much noise it's like a zillion bees are buzzing around my face.

Up comes Hatchet, staring at the third-base coach to catch the sign. If it isn't a bunt, I'll eat my sweaty jock. He steps in and begins his bat waggling. At the last second, he lays it out front to bunt. He pops it up a few feet off the third-base foul line, Daulton is on it like a jackrabbit, dives for it, his mitt extended as far as he can reach. He catches it! The crowd gasps, moans, sighs, then shuts up to catch its fucking breath. Me, I feel the force returning. That's all I need. I am back in control.

Then comes Buechele, and the crowd comes alive again. I try to feel good about Maxie. He's throwing harder than ever. His fastball is hopping, rising in the late-afternoon chill. No matter that Grace tagged him. Grace can hit a bullet shot out of a rifle. Buechele is not Mark Grace. Maxie drills the first pitch by him for a called strike. Then Buechele fouls off the breaking ball and it's 0 and 2. Now Maxie has him by the testes. He curves him again, a real snapper that's low for ball one. I'm thinking, jam him. If he takes it, I'll give it to you. Maxie shakes off two signs. Good, give Buechele something to think about. It's another off-speed pitch just off the strike zone. With two strikes on him, Buechele protects the plate with a feeble swipe at it. It's a swinging bunt that trickles down the third-base line for what looks like a sure base hit. Hollins charges in to make the play but decides to let it roll, hoping it will turn foul. I run up the line to watch, pleading for it to hit a pebble, hit a clump of dirt, roll off that chalk line, you sonovabitch! Then, suddenly, it does! It dies foul! It's like I'm the force that can make magic. Buechele is not on first with the go-ahead run, he's back at the plate with two strikes on him. Grace is not on second with the tying run, he's back at first. If I can make a dinky little game-busting dribbler roll across a chalk line, I can tame any tiger they let out of the cage.

I go back to the plate believing there is no such thing as doubt.

Buechele takes the bat from the batboy and digs back in as I dust off the plate. The crowd gets into the rhythmic clapping. Maxie goes into his sneaky-looking stretch, then throws a bullet that's no bigger than an aspirin. Buechele swings and misses for the third strike and it's two men out.

And here comes Sammy Sosa. Now *he's* got the load on his back. Some guys love it, some would rather be shooting pool. Sosa is cool. I see his concentration. He looks like a man who's been here a lot of times before. When he's good and ready, he steps in, plants his right foot deep in the box, and sets himself. I catch a look at his eyes and suddenly I see his pleasure.

It scares me, for I can remember my own. I remember the unforgettable joy of hitting when a game came down to me. Never be a man to end an inning. Never let a third strike get by. Never, ever so much as think there's a pitcher on God's green earth who is better than me. I remember the beautiful feel of the bat in my hands. No batting gloves when I was a kid, there was no such thing. I'd twist my bare hands lovingly around the bat handle, move the barrel out over the plate, once, twice; then I'd wait for the pitch, my bat high over my shoulder as I felt the power building in my legs. The first sight of the ball would trigger instant responses for the perfect timing of my stride, the driving power of the bat swing as I made that sweet solid contact.

Maxie's fastball is drilled at the outside of the plate. My mind sets to call strike, my right fist forms to make it happen, when from out of nowhere comes Sosa's bat. The sound alone is terrifying, a rifle shot so close it hurts my ears. The ball is like a jet plane on takeoff to right-center field, up and up it rises as my stomach sinks to my crotch. Even before the crowd can react, it's gone. Six, seven rows over the ivy wall the fans scramble for it. It happens so quickly, my right hand is still a fist.

Let me tell you about fear, pal. Let me tell you about how you have to keep a tight asshole when your body goes limp. Let me tell you how much more of a shock it is when something inside you says you fucking *knew* it was going to happen!

Even then, I can't believe it. I'd been playing my old game of suspecting the worst so I could rejoice at the best. A fucking home run! It's a measure of my desperation that I watch the umpires watching to see if they touch the bases. And me, I watch to see if they touch the plate. And if one of them didn't, if Daulton saw and appealed, could I make *that* call and live to tell about it?

The crowd sustains an unbelievable frenzy. The Cubs pour out of the dugout to greet Sosa like he just came back from the moon. All those laughing triumphant kids swarming all over the hero, God, how I hate them. I hate Bateman's red-faced laughter as he pounds Sosa's back. I hate Ward as he and Dunston embrace. The sonsovbitches are dancing on my fucking grave.

The ball boy comes by to feed me four new baseballs. The crowd won't stop screaming. Sosa comes up the dugout steps to tip his cap and they scream even louder.

In the batter's circle, Shawon Dunston waits to pinch-hit for Ward, taking practice swings before he moves to the plate. The crowd stirs, suddenly aware of what's about to happen. A new sound starts slowly from scattered pockets of the stands, a few protesting voices calling out, "Ward ... Ward ... Ward ..." It starts to grow into a plea, a chant, a demand, louder and louder, it spreads through the old stadium into one booming voice: *"Ward! Ward! Ward!"* They don't want a pinch hitter. Ahead by a run, with two out, they want Sam Ward to hit so he can walk onto that mound to pitch the ninth inning.

Then, out of the dugout, here he comes. Bateman, who never responded to crowd sounds in his life except when he went belly-to-belly with an umpire, is sending Ward up to hit for himself!

216

Immediately the chant shifts from protest to a greeting. Fifty thousand Cubs fans are on their feet. Their cheering is a stampede of emotion. It's a moment when they're winning it all, and here is the sudden hero who is making it happen.

He stops short of the batter's box to pick up dirt, rubs his hands on the bat handle. He doesn't step in, he looks at me. His eyes working through the grillwork of my mask, probing for a look at my face.

"Hi, how you doin'?" he asks, smiling like we were old buddies.

Fuck you, Ward, that's how I'm doin'. Take your three swings and get your glove because you still have to get three more outs, and I'm giving good odds you won't be around for the last one.

Smile in the eighth, eat shit in the ninth.

He takes a strike, then another. Then swings feebly at a breaking ball for strike three. The crowd cheers him like he just hit another home run. I hate this crowd. I can't help thinking that because of them, Bateman is leaving Ward in the game.

As he's about to step out of the batter's box, I can't resist rattling his teeth. "Hey, Sam, been doing any after-dinner speaking these days?" I pull off my mask and head for water.

Now I'm hating myself. It's twisting me inside out. I'm not only a crook, I'm looking at a potential disaster. I've been suckered into throwing away a whole fucking lifetime.

They're cheering for Ward as he walks back to the dugout. That this is the ninth inning and he's still in the game is a symbol of some impossible madness. I've riddled the bastard with so many bullets, Gatorade should be squirting out of his pores. But no, there he is. Can you fucking believe it? If he's tired, he's not showing it. If he's tense, it's carefully bottled up. He's sure as hell doing a helluva lot better than I am.

Whatever, I'm not licked. I've still got all my weapons. I can't believe I can't put one run across to tie, or two to jump ahead. How can I not believe that? Whatever has happened on this endless afternoon—or *not* happened —it's not over yet. I don't give a shit how great his knuckleball is, or his luck, or whatever is keeping him there. I can make it happen.

	1	2	3	4	5	6	7	8	9		R	H	E
PHILLIES	0	0	0	3	0	1	0	0			4	6	1
CUBS	0	2	0	0	0	0	1	2			5	10	1

Kolacka remembers!

I walk back to the dugout like a zombie. We just scored two runs to pull ahead and I'm sick to my stomach. And not because I can't pitch with a lead. But because I couldn't keep my big mouth shut.

"Been doing any after-dinner speaking these days?" he said. I was too shocked to say anything back. He had this smile on his face, but it didn't look friendly. More like the bad guy in a poker game with an ace up his sleeve.

And he's looking to wipe me out. Umpires rarely initiate conversation. That means he's out to get me. And that means I can't count on him to make the calls.

My mind is racing as I approach the dugout. Bateman's waiting for me on the top step and he's going to ask how I feel. Should I tell him the story? If I do, I'm gone. And who do we have in the bullpen, anyway? Besides, what if Kolacka was joking? It's possible. Anything's possible.

I step into the dugout.

"Well, Sam," says Bateman, looking up from his lineup card. "What do you think?"

My head wants to tell. But my heart wants the ball.

I decide to take a chance.

"I'm ready," I say.

Bateman studies my face. For the first time, I notice that his eyes are actually a bluish gray with rust-colored flecks. Like somebody wire-brushed a corroded pipe next to wet blueberries. Bluish-gray eyes floating around inside wrinkled sockets.

"Then it's your ball game," he says quietly. And he stuffs the lineup card back into his pocket.

I get a drink of water and wipe my face with a towel. The umpire was joking, I tell myself. Just a little banter to relieve the pressure. He's not out to get me. It's just my imagination. And I hope like hell I'm right.

Meanwhile, the dugout is eerily silent. There's some chatter, but not what you'd expect. Just the usual "Hey, let's go" and "Whaddya say" and "Let's do it!" Nobody's hollering "Only three more outs" or "This is it!" And nobody dares to even *think,* boy, that champagne is sure gonna taste great! We've all been on teams that started celebrating too soon. The overall record is not good.

This is the eye of the hurricane. The moment of truth. The temporary lull in a battle. With this kind of tension you could wire a small city.

And here comes Jerome, who appears not to have a care in the world. He thinks this is a high school game in North Carolina.

"Anything to the left side," he says. "I got it."

Okay with me.

Leave it to Owens and Alexander for the final word.

"Well," says Owens with a look of grave concern. "One more good inning and we're voting you out of the Scrubeenie Club."

"No more Scrubeenie dinners," says Alexander, shaking his head sadly. "And you can't wear the official Scrubeenie T-shirt."

Smiling, I grab my glove and head for the mound.

The standing ovation which began when we went ahead 5–4, and has continued more or less since then, grows into an expectant clamor as we take the field. The rhythmic banging of feet in the stands sounds like a herd of buffalo. And the buffalo are accompanied by air horns, and cowbells, and the loud pop of soda cups being stomped on in the aisles.

My mind goes to the knuckleball. Same easy motion. Get that feeling. I throw my first warm-up pitch and Hatchet snares that jumping bean in his big glove. I always try to throw my best knuckler, even in warm-ups. Takes no more effort and gets that first hitter thinking.

Hatchet fires my last throw down to Sandberg at second base. Then it goes around the horn, to Davis to Grace to Buechele, who comes over to personally slap the ball into my outstretched glove.

"Play it again, Sam," says Buechele, doing a decent imitation of Humphrey Bogart. Then he trots back to third. Meanwhile, Hatchet's doing his tobacco number on home plate, and I don't know whether to laugh or cry.

"Play ball!" hollers Kolacka.

My heart pounds as I look in for the sign. Kevin Stocker, with a walk, a single, and a fly to right, steps into the batter's box. Hatchet wiggles four fingers. I kick and throw. The knuckleball dances across the plate for strike one. Kolacka pivots and points to the sky, which is how I know it's a strike, because nothing comes out of his mouth.

A knuckler is pulled foul for strike two. Another one is wide and the count is a ball and two strikes. I'm not going to waste any pitches. I don't want to be throwing any full-count knuckleballs if I can help it. I kick and throw. The ball sweeps in ... Stocker swings ... the bottom drops out. It's strike three ... but the ball's in the dirt as Stocker races for first! Hatchet dives to his right ... knees first ... keeping the ball in front ... the ball bounces up off his chest ... But Hatchet grabs it ... and throws to first for out number one.

Nice play.

The crowd roars. Then they quickly check their scorecards to see who that is over there in the on-deck circle, pinch-hitting for Arlo Maxie.

The public address guy announces what the fans already know.

"Now batting ... for Philadelphia ... Jim Eisenreich ... number twenty-eight ... Eisenreich."

According to the charts, Eisenreich hits with power and likes to swing at the first pitch. My kind of guy. Hatchet wiggles four fingers. I kick and throw and it's in the dirt for ball one. Figured I'd go with the scouting report there. Another knuckler finds the outside corner for strike one. It's really moving. The next one zigzags up to the plate ... Eisenreich swings ... the ball dips . . . there's a grounder to short . . . and Jerome inhales it for out number two.

The crowd roars again, a little louder this time, but you can sense they're holding back, afraid to believe in a dream that might not come true. They've seen too many ball games. Too many *Cubs* games.

Here's Dykstra, hitless in three trips since that first-inning rocket off the wall. He wades into the batter's box like he's spoiling for a fight. He'll do anything to get on base here, up to and including taking one in the mouth for the good of the team. He's also thinking home run because he's got that kind of power. I'm thinking knuckleball. Nice and easy.

Hatchet gives me the sign. I kick and throw. And it's a beauty that breaks . . . outside . . . for ball one. Damn, that was close! Shit, every pitch counts. Dykstra could jerk the next one out of here.

Hatchet gives me the sign. I kick and throw. And it's in the dirt for ball two. Slow down, I tell myself. I take a deep breath. Then I look in for the sign. Knuckleball. I kick and throw. *Line drive!* Past third . . . just barely goes foul. Two balls and one strike. I can't walk him, but I can't lay it in there, either. I get the sign. I kick and throw. And a beauty just misses the inside corner for ball three.

The guys on our bench are not happy with that call.

"Open up a can of strikes back there," hollers Owens.

Three and one. Hatchet calls for the knuckler. I wind up and let it fly. And it's a good one, too, but it dives low . . . for *ball four.*

The crowd groans as Dykstra swaggers down to first. But all we need is one out. The crowd is on its feet and clapping now, trying to get me over the hump. Our guys are on the top step of the dugout hollering. "C'mon, Sam! Hey, six-five!" Mariano Duncan, hitless in four trips, steps into the batter's box. And my first pitch wobbles in there for strike one. Another knuckler is wide for ball one. But the next one is swung on and missed for strike two, and now you can't hear yourself think.

And Duncan steps out of the box.

He's trying to break my rhythm. That's okay, doesn't bother me. I like it that he's not comfortable. I reach into my back pocket and play with the pebbles. The crowd needs a breather, too, as they trade screams for a rhythmic clapping. Both dugouts are standing now . . . and hollering . . . and the Phillies . . . are pointing at something . . .

". . . scuffing the goddamn ball!"

They're pointing at me!

"... got something in his back pocket!"

"... check his fuckin' pocket!"

This is ridiculous. Anything to get me out of my groove. Shows how desperate they are. They see the end of their season and they're just trying to postpone it. I take my hand out of my pocket.

"Time," hollers Kolacka, ripping off his mask.

And here he comes, ramrod straight like some tough-assed sergeant on his way to inspect a messy footlocker. I move a few steps toward him as he approaches the mound.

"Empty your pocket," he says.

"Sure," I say, pulling out a handful of tiny stones.

"What's this?" asks Kolacka, squinting at the pebbles.

"Stones," I say. And I can't help it, I start smiling.

"What's so funny?" he asks, sounding irritated.

"Just the idea of stones," I say. "You probably thought I had sandpaper or something, right?"

"What are you, a mind reader now?" asks Kolacka.

Suddenly a cheer goes up as Bateman runs onto the field. Bateman is not one to sit around waiting for an argument to happen.

"What's the problem?" he says, arriving all out of breath.

"He's got stones in his pocket," says Kolacka.

"So what?" says Bateman, arms flying up. "I got stones in my gallbladder. And rocks in my head."

Kolacka examines the stones again.

"Goddamn stones," he snorts. "Keep the stones. Be my guest." And he turns around and marches back to home plate.

Bateman sighs and shakes his head. Then he turns to me.

"Looks like you still have good stuff," he says.

"It's breaking okay."

"Well, just take your time," says Bateman. And he heads back to the dugout.

Two outs, runner on first, a ball and two strikes on Mariano Duncan. I get the sign. I nod. I kick and throw. The ball leaves my hand ... it dips ... it dives ... Duncan swings ... and hits a chopper in front of the plate ... a high bouncing chopper. I charge in ... looking up at the ball. Hatchet jumps out ... he's calling for it. We're both calling ... and waiting ... and waiting ... and when it finally comes down, there's nothing we can do. Infield hit.

The crowd moans. Hatchet slams the ball into his glove. But I'm cool. I'm so cool, an ice cube wouldn't melt on my head. Because if I'm not cool, I'm gone. Bateman can smell nerves frying from the next county.

Two outs, runners on first and second, as John Kruk digs in. The crowd begins clapping again, trying to come together on some kind of beat. I get the sign. I check the runners. I kick and throw. The ball floats ... Kruk swings ... it veers inside ... it hits the knob of the bat! The ball hits the knob of the bat handle and bounces back to me. I go down on one knee just in case. The ball hops into my glove. I've got plenty of time. This it it! I step and throw to first ... but Grace is just standing there ... what's going on?

Hit by the pitch?

What the hell!

His hand? How did it hit his hand, for crissakes? The ball came right off the bat handle. You could hear it hit the wood!

And here comes Bateman. Rumbling across the field like a deranged bowling ball, looking to pick up a spare named Ernie Kolacka.

"Time," hollers Kolacka, whose job it is to stop play so that he can be properly humiliated.

Bateman, with the air brakes of a semi, stops inches short of bumping into Kolacka, which is an automatic ejection. Now he slams his hat to the ground so he can go nose-to-nose with Kolacka. Jabbing his fat fingers into the air and cursing, Bateman works hard to keep his nose in Kolacka's face. When Kolacka turns, Bateman turns with him. And the crowd loves it; two grown men circling home plate like a pair of magnetic Scottie dogs. This is championship arguing.

But it's over as quickly as it began. Bateman, a master at testing the limits of an umpire's patience, picks up his hat and heads back to the dugout. Then, like a guy who forgot something at the grocery store, Bateman turns around and walks slowly out to the mound. Very slowly now, with one eye on the bullpen, where a coach is signaling that both pitchers are ready. Hell, the whole damn bullpen must be ready by now.

"Well, Sam," says Bateman, reaching for the ball. "It's been a long day."

I hand him the ball and wait for that familiar pat on the ass, the signal that means it's time to go take a shower, let that hot water pour down over those tired muscles. Bateman studies my face.

"You've thrown a hundred and twelve pitches," he says, a bit of small talk to buy some time, slow the Phillies' momentum, alter the tempo of the game.

"With my stuff," I say, "that's like sixty-five."

Bateman smiles.

Kolacka comes out to get the pitching change. "Who's it going to be?" he asks, a stubby pencil poised over his copy of the lineup card.

Bateman squints out toward the bullpen. He reaches up with his right hand and squeezes his nose like it was a lemon. He looks over at Matthews in the on-deck circle. He wipes the back of his hand across his mouth. He looks at me. He takes a deep breath. He sighs. He looks at Kolacka.

"Ward," he says finally. "Sam Ward."

My stomach rolls over.

Kolacka jams his lineup card into his pocket.

Bateman flips me the ball.

"Now get this big donkey," he says, motioning with his head toward Matthews. "And we'll go in and put some ice on those fingertips."

The crowd cheers again as Bateman returns to the dugout.

Matthews pounds the handle of his bat into the ground, forcing the weighted donut down from the barrel of the bat and into the on-deck circle, where the rolling metal ring is retrieved by the batboy.

The place is a madhouse. Everyone is standing and screaming. The Phillies are lined up on the top step of their dugout hollering for Matthews to hit one off the clock. Our guys are hollering for me to screw him into the ground, stick the bat up his ass, and fuck with his mind, not necessarily in that order.

Matthews, holding up traffic, digs his ditch in the batter's box. Hatchet squirts his tobacco. Kolacka pulls on his mask. I check the defense. Grace is back on the grass at first. Sandberg is shaded toward the bag at second. Jerome, not too deep at short so he can get an infield chopper, will rely on his speed and his arm to make the play in the hole. Buechele hugs the line at third. The outfielders are deep and playing to pull.

Here we go.

I look in for the sign. Out of the corner of my eye, I see Dykstra inching down the line, looking to score on a passed ball. Hatchet knows if a pitch gets by him he's just going to wheel and throw home and I'll be there. Now I have to forget Dykstra. Focus on the hitter. Hatchet gives me the wiggling fingers. I nod. I check the runners. I kick and throw. The ball ... swoops toward the plate ... it wobbles ... it dips ... and then jumps wide.

Ball one.

The crowd groans. But then they're back into it, clapping, stomping, and hollering encouragement. Matthews waits, the barrel of his bat making menacing little circles above his head. I look in for the sign. Knuckleball. I check the runners. I kick and throw. And this one leaves my hand like I'm throwing darts. But it's not anything like a dart; a malfunctioning fireworks display is more like it ... Matthews swings ... the ball explodes ... and there's a whooshing sound as the bat slices through the air. The crowd roars.

Strike one.

Matthews steps out to un-Velcro and re-Velcro the straps on his batting gloves. They must be a little too loose. Or too tight.

Now the fans are taunting Matthews. I wouldn't go that far. He may have looked bad on that last knuckler, but the guy can still hit. When you're throwing a baseball 60 miles an hour, all hitters are dangerous.

One ball and one strike on Mark Matthews. I rotate the ball in my hand, looking for that magic grip. Hatchet looks down at third to check on Dykstra. My fingertips press into the leather. Hatchet gives me the sign. I nod. I kick and throw. The ball ... floats in ... jerks left ... jerks right ... and breaks a little too soon ... just missing the outside corner.

Ball two.

Hatchet wanted it to be a strike. So did Bateman. With one foot on the top step of the dugout, he leans forward and scoops a handful of dirt and throws it down in disgust.

I just want the ball back from Hatchet as fast as he can get it to me. With the ball in my hand I can start getting ready for the next pitch. That's all that matters right now. The next pitch.

The crowd is in distress. This is the ball game and they know it. And they do not like being down two balls and one strike with the bases loaded and Mark Matthews digging in against a guy with a football number on the back of his uniform. I look in for the sign. The runners lead off. I kick and throw. The ball moves toward the plate ... twitches ... wobbles ... and breaks into the dirt.

Ball three.

Suddenly the stadium gets quiet. Like what happens to conversation in a hospital room when the patient stops breathing. The only sound comes from the Phillies' dugout. A bunch of noise about three balls and one strike and this being my last pitch and the game being over, but I block it out.

Just give me the baseball.

I spin it around in my hand. I find the grip. I look in for the sign. Hatchet wiggles his fingers. I nod. I kick and throw. The ball meanders up to the plate ... Matthews swings ... and hits *a line drive* ... foul ... into the stands along the third-base side.

Strike two.

The patient's eyelids just fluttered.

I'm always amazed that nobody gets killed by those line drives into the seats. I usually have a small heart attack and I'm not anywhere near the ball. Today we have more than a few fans who'd be happy to stop a line drive with their foreheads if it meant another strike on the Phillies.

Hatchet throws me a new ball. I take it out of my glove and feel the weight of it in my hand. It's a good ball. It wants to do the right thing, I can tell. It just needs a little encouragement. And the proper release.

Two outs, bases loaded, 3 and 2 on the hitter. The crowd doesn't know whether to clap or stomp or holler, so they go with all three. I check my infielders. They're busy pretending it's just another ball game, smoothing dirt that doesn't need smoothing, adjusting sunglasses against a gray sky. Even Jerome, who normally disdains infield chatter, is over there chattering, "Hey, Sam, you're the man."

Matthews digs in, but I'm not quite ready yet. I feel like I'd like to throw a practice pitch with this new ball. Where's the two-minute warning where you trot over to the sidelines for a drink of water and a little pep talk? And since we're ahead, how about I just go down on one knee and wait until the clock runs out?

Kolacka waves his arm to say let's go. Matthews cocks the bat above his head, measuring me with his eyes. Hatchet squats to give me the sign. The roar of the crowd fades to a distant rumble, like the sound of a freight train miles away. The infield chatter dissolves into nothing. I look toward home plate into a tunnel of light. Just this tunnel of light between me and Hatchet. Everything else is getting black. I can still see Matthews cocking his bat, but the image fades into a profile, and now it's just knees and hips, defining the vertical boundaries of the strike zone. I see the horizontal sliver of white that marks the width of home plate from where I stand. My brain records the imaginary rectangle, like a box on a schoolyard wall, then clears itself for more complicated messages. Kolacka leans in, then melts behind Hatchet's mask. I see only Hatchet, glove hand dangling off the front of his left knee, his right hand jammed against his protective cup. He gives me the sign.

Fastball?

Hatchet is holding one finger down for the fastball! No mistaking it. And just as quickly, it disappears in a flurry of decoy signs. And now he's giving me one more sign. What the hell is this? What's he doing?

He's ... giving me the finger.

The sonovabitch just gave me the finger!

My mind is racing. A fastball to Matthews? He eats them for lunch. And I haven't thrown one the whole game. Make that ten years. Unless you count batting practice. Incredible call. But I can't hesitate. That's the key to making it work. No meeting on the mound to talk it over. No standing here thinking about it. No shaking my head, forcing a repeat of the call that might tip it off. That's the beauty of it. A fastball with a knuckleball beat.

How fast can I throw it? Maybe 80 if I really uncork one. Almost a change-up, as fastballs go. But I can't throw it any harder than that. And I shouldn't try. If I muscle up, rear back, and pop one, try to find an old heater in the attic of my damaged arm, I'll overthrow the damn thing, probably bean somebody in the press box. No, this has to be an accurate fastball. Delivered with controlled fury. Right down the cock. Straight into Matthews' wheelhouse. Smack into the middle of the goddamn strike zone.

If I can get it there.

I nod my head. I kick and throw ... the ball leaves my hand ...

THE CALL

5:09 PM

All of a sudden, the ball has no seams. It doesn't hover, but drills through the air with amazing speed. After all the slow, tantalizing junk he's thrown, this one seems like it's been fired out of a rifle bore.

I'm not ready for it. It's like I've been faked out of my shoes. All these years behind the mask, I'm trained for nanosecond reactions. I'm supposed to see everything there is to see, know everything there is to know. I'm supposed to have a brain that's as quick and sharp as lightning, that reacts to the eye and sends an instant message through my body, everything funneling into a fist at the end of an arm, left for a ball, right for a strike, my message for the world to see.

I'm not ready for it. It's not the surprising speed of the pitch, it's everything else that has turned my entire being into Jell-O. It's the idea of the pitch itself. It's me, at this moment in time. It's the full-count, bases-loaded tension that's so crushing, my head being blasted by sounds that smother the senses, my heart in my fucking throat. I feel suspended

228

in sweat-curdling fear. I never knew such fear. I've been scared all day, I've been scared since Roger put the shiv in me last night, since that fucking Professor twisted it in my back with his golden hands. But this moment brings me to the outer limit, my psyche is disintegrating, my brain is dissolving into vapor, I'm a piece of limp shit getting flushed into oblivion.

I'm not ready for it. I suspend time, I stop the flight of the ball in midair. My mind turns like quicksilver in a shaking vial, bangs against the edges, out of control like little balls darting helter-skelter in all directions. I plead for steadiness. I've got to find a footing for my senses. I've got to see, think, react! I've got to be ready to make the call!

The pitch is cock-high. It's not rising or falling. It's coming to the inside corner of the plate, not moving off line, it just keeps drilling through the late-afternoon air, punctuating this moment from which all else will be remembered forever. The batter will slug it or miss it or take it for the umpire to decide. One thing is certain: this is it!

Matthews starts his swing, but he's late. Like me, he's been juked by the speed of the pitch. He sees it's going to be in there, but he can't get around in time. Throw a hitter an off-speed pitch when he's expecting a fastball, he's liable to jump out of his shoes. Throw him a fastball when he's expecting a knuckler, he'll likely be planted like a dead stump.

Two feet in front of me, the ball slams into the catcher's mitt with the sound of a popping firecracker.

I know. All I've got to do is shoot my left arm toward first base for ball four. The tying run scores, the bases are still loaded, I've saved the game for the gamblers and the gods. Hey, I'm only doing my job.

But I can't.

I can't do it.

"Steerike!" I bark out, and I punch him out to end the game.

On the field, there is instant bedlam as the crowd erupts in a blast of triumph. The Cubs surround Ward, and up he goes on the shoulders of teammates. He is smiling. No big demo with his fist-jabbing air, no flinging of his cap. Just a smile. It settles me. What he has done is incredible. He has beaten the Phillies and beaten me. For eight and two-thirds innings, he has beaten me hands down. For all but one pitch, he has single-handedly destroyed the fix with the courage of a wounded lion. In the Roman Colosseum, they used to spare the noble gladiator from slaughter. I didn't save Sam Ward with that call. Sam Ward saved me.

As they move to the dugout, there's an instant when I catch his eye. I guess maybe I wanted that to happen. I've got my mask in hand and I raise it like a glass in a toast. For all the jubilation, he sees.

It gets me off the field for the last time.

POSTGAME

5:10 PM

Hatchet is sprinting toward me with his mask in one hand and his glove in the other, his arms open wide like he's about to embrace the whole world. He's laughing and hollering, the brown drool running down the front of his shirt. I move toward him, he jumps into my arms, I catch him, and we both go down.

I land on my back. Hatchet lands on top of me. We're both laughing our asses off. Other players are falling on top of us. I try to get up. New guys jump onto the pile. I hope they stop pretty soon; I'm claustrophobic. Hey, I can't move! I try to holler, but nothing comes out. There's no air in my lungs. I can't breathe. There's too many bodies. I start to panic. I'm going to die right here on the mound!

But I'm going to die happy.

The pile gets lighter. I see daylight. And finally I can breathe! It looks like I'm not going to die after all. It would have made a great tabloid story, though: JUNK MAN DIES UNDER PILE OF HUMAN FLESH.

231

I get to my feet in a strange world. Everything is in slow motion. An organ is playing, air horns are blasting, and people are running everywhere. My teammates are hugging me, slapping me on the back, shouting my name. "Sam, goddamn! Helluva job, Sam!"

They lift me up onto their shoulders. The place is spinning as they bounce me around. I see fans swarming, players laughing. Even the umpire, who I had figured wrong, seems to be waving to me.

It's hard to describe my feelings right now. Happy is pretty easy, and grateful, I guess. And deeply satisfied. I start to cry. But I blink the tears away and cough instead. I don't want the guys to see me crying. They'll really think I'm nuts.

Jerome breaks through the mob around me. He's got a huge smile on his face. "I wanna be your agent now," he shouts, giving me a double-closed-fisted whatever. I try to thank him for being such a good friend, but there's too much noise. And I can't express it right anyway. So I just give him a big hug and say, "Great game, Jerome."

I see Bateman over by the dugout, intercepting players as they come off the field. Someone has turned his hat around backward and he's leaving it that way for the fun of it. He's congratulating everyone, reaching out, grabbing guys, slapping hands. He's a little short with his high fives, but he's trying.

Now Bateman sees me and starts wading through the crowd. Moving against the flow, he looks like a potbellied salmon working his way upstream. His handshake turns into a bear hug and he presses his stubbled chin into the side of my face. I can smell the long afternoon on his breath.

"You did it, son!" he wheezes into my ear. "You took charge out there, by God, and you showed a few people a thing or two."

"I was afraid you were going to take me out of the game," I say.

"Well, if I knew you was going to throw that fastball, I might have," he says, rolling his eyes. "You almost give me a heart attack with that one. Whose idea was that?"

"Hatchet," I say. "Pretty gutsy call, huh?"

"Well, you surprised the shit out of everybody," he says. Then he spots someone else and starts pawing through the crowd.

I'm being swept away by the swarm of players and fans moving in the general direction of our dugout. People are dancing on top of the dugout and chanting "All the way! All the way!" as security guards try to get the fans off the field. Nobody is leaving the ballpark. The people in the stands are clapping in unison, demanding that we stay out on the field and celebrate with them.

And here comes the champagne! Some guys in the grounds crew just carried out a rubber garbage can filled with ice and about a dozen bottles of champagne. Wilkins, with an insane gleam in his eye, jams a bottle between his knees for leverage and pulls the cork, shooting a foamy stream into the crowd. Meanwhile, Grace and Buechele are squirting champagne all over Sandberg and some TV guy who's attempting to interview him.

The crowd is shouting the names of different players until each guy waves his hat to acknowledge their efforts. The chant of "Boo, Boo, Boo" continues until Buechele finally waves and they all cheer. Now they seem confused on the next name. Some are hollering "Ward, Ward," and others are hollering "Sam, Sam." Finally the Sams win out and I wave my hat. But not right away. Hell, I wanted to listen to it for a little bit.

A path is finally cleared to the dugout, but not too many players are leaving. They're too busy realizing their life's goal of running around like idiots, squirting champagne on each other in front of millions. Except for veterans like Willie Wilson who've been through this before on other teams.

"Hey, don't waste this shit," he says, pouring himself a dignified portion into a paper cup with his pinky extended, and taking a sip.

It's a wonderful scene and I'm just standing here watching it all. Some guys are drinking, others are squirting. Sammy Sosa is leading the crowd in cheers. Leon Banks is stuffing unopened bottles of the California Brut under his uniform shirt. Hatchet is guzzling from a bottle with a chaw of tobacco *still in his mouth*!

He's not a bad guy, actually.

Just as some guy asks me if I'll do an interview, I spot Owens and Alexander shaking a bottle and looking around for someone. Now they see me and it's all over. My first instinct is to run, but I figure I've never had champagne poured on me before, so I don't move too fast and they get me pretty good. Hey, this stuff is cold! And it stings your eyes!

But boy, does it feel good.

I don't think I've ever been happier in my life.

And suddenly I think of Beth. And Marty. I look up into the stands behind home plate where the player's passes usually sit. I scan back and forth, but I can't pick them out. Too many people are standing and blocking the aisles. And waving. The fans are waving at me and hollering my name, as if I were searching for them.

Julie pops into my mind. And my heart aches. I'd give anything to have her here with me right now. We traveled a lot of miles together over the years. This is where we always wanted to be and now she's not here to enjoy the last part of the trip. And I'm feeling guilty about that fight we had. What I said about her being a quitter. She wasn't a quitter. She was with me all the way. Until I went too far. Beyond all reason. My throat hurts as I try to swallow.

I take one more look up into the stands before joining my teammates on their way into the locker room. The players' shouts bouncing off the walls of the tunnel help to drown out my sadness.

It *was* a helluva game.

We burst from the semi-dark tunnel into a brightly lit locker room which is now a television studio with lights and cameras. The players are all whooping and hollering and throwing their hats and gloves into their lockers and heaving wet shirts across the room into a big laundry basket.

"Hooooah!" yells Grace, throwing a fist into the air. "Now let's chop those Braves."

Grace is referring to the National League West champion Atlanta Braves, who they'll be facing in the playoffs on Tuesday night. And now, suddenly, it's *they* instead of *we*. I'm not eligible for the playoffs because I was called up after the rosters were frozen. What a strange feeling. I just realized my season is over! I'm not on the team anymore. I don't even know if I get to suit up.

And would I want to?

Meanwhile, a mob is waiting in front of my locker. I recognize a few reporters from before the game. As they see me coming across the room, cameras point, flashbulbs pop, tape recorders roll, and the pads and pencils come flying out. The pack closes in around me as I step into my locker. I have to stand so people in the back can hear.

"Congratulations," says Holtzman of the *Tribune*, practically shouting because of all the noise. "Can you tell us what you were thinking on that last pitch to Matthews?"

"I wasn't thinking," I say. "I was just trying to *feel*, let my instincts take over. When Hatchet called that fastball, it felt right."

Somebody squirts a shower of champagne onto the group.

"But isn't Matthews a notorious fastball hitter?" asks the TV guy in the blond helmet that appears undented in spite of the pandemonium. "What if he hits it out?"

"Then I blame Hatchet."

Everybody laughs. A winning pitcher is like a rich man when it comes to having people laugh at your jokes.

"You must be proud of yourself," says the young lady in the purple pantsuit. "But why did you have to wait ten years to get your chance?"

"Well," I say, "because it's easier for baseball people to understand radar guns than human beings. That's why we need to have gun control."

They laugh again. A wet jockstrap comes flying from across the room and I have to duck.

"We did some research during the game," says Holtzman. "And we discovered that you're interested in politics, that sort of thing. Any other issues you care about besides gun control?"

"Designated hitter," I say, getting into the mood. "Whoever thought that up should be put in jail for a good long time. With no parole."

The photographers want me to get my picture taken with Bateman, who's just finishing an interview with TV sportscaster Tim McCarver. I excuse myself to go join them. Bateman is standing hatless in front of the cameras, the bright lights glaring off the top of his champagne-soaked dome. He's telling McCarver that this is the "finest bunch of young men" he's ever been associated with. Then, before the interview is over, Bateman pulls me in front of the cameras with a one-armed hug around the back of my neck.

"This is our secret weapon," he tells McCarver. "We've been saving him all year for this one game."

"It was certainly a well-kept secret," says McCarver, adjusting quickly. "And with Sam right here, Vern, let me ask you this: what was your thinking on leaving him in the game in the ninth inning?"

McCarver angles the microphone toward Bateman.

"Because I looked into his eyes," says Bateman, with a cryptic smile. "And I knew he had one more stone in his slingshot."

"Well, we'll have all winter to think about that," says McCarver, and he throws it back to the studio.

The photographers take shots of me and Bateman in a variety of poses, including hugging, jointly holding a baseball, and me pretending to pour Bateman a glass of juice from my juicer. Now other players are asked to pose in various combinations with the two of us. Then they take pictures of me standing between Wilkins and Hatchet, who finally removes the tobacco from his mouth. Only problem is a big piece of brown leaf is stuck in Hatchet's teeth. After weighing the matter carefully, I decide to point this out to him. I figure I owe him one.

The craziness in the clubhouse has escalated a few notches. In addition to wet sweatshirts, food is now flying across the room. And new targets are arriving every minute in the form of agents, friends, restaurateurs, and assorted local celebrities, including Gene Siskel of Siskel and Ebert. Champagne and spicy chicken wings seem to be the weapons of choice.

"Don't say anything," hollers Owens as I head for my locker. "Just walk right the fuck by and act like we're not even here."

I look around, pretending I don't know where the noise is coming from. Then I go say hello. Owens and Alexander are about the only players in the room that nobody's interviewing.

"I remember you guys," I say, like I can't quite place their faces. "You belong to some type of exclusive club, right?"

"And you're not in it," says Alexander.

Then we laugh and bullshit about the game. The best part of which, according to Owens and Alexander, was watching the pitching coach change his tune as the game progressed.

"Gilson went all the way from 'What the *fuck* are we doing?' " says Owens, "to 'I always *knew* he was a battler.' "

"You know what Gilson's been telling reporters?" asks Alexander. "He said the reason you went the full nine innings was because of his new fitness program for pitchers!"

We get a really good laugh out of this. Then we talk about what we're going to do this winter. Alexander plans to go squirrel hunting in the Blue Ridge Mountains in West Virginia. Owens says big deal, he's going skiing down Garbage Mountain in Secaucus, New Jersey. I tell them I'm not sure what I'll be doing, but they should come out and spend a week at the cabin and we can do some fishing.

We're interrupted by coach Rapp, who says someone wants to talk to me in Bateman's office. Right now. Fellow by the name of William Mulcahy, Jr.

"You probably won't even talk to us after you sign that big contract," says Alexander.

"Get out of here!" I say. "I'll talk to you guys. Just don't bother me for autographs when I'm eating dinner."

And I head for Bateman's office.

My heart leaps at the possibilities. Mulcahy's probably going to give me a pretty good bonus. Just getting into the playoffs has got to be worth a few million dollars to the team. Then there are season tickets for next year, which are a lot easier to sell when you're division champs. If the Cubs win the league championship or the World Series, that'll be worth even more millions and they couldn't have done any of it without winning today's game.

Mulcahy shakes my hand and closes the door behind me. We're all alone, since Bateman's out making the rounds in the locker room.

"I guess it's about time we sat down and had a little talk," he says, motioning me to a chair. "About next year."

"Next year?" I say, my mood taking a dip.

"I'm prepared to give you a contract right now," says Mulcahy, looking down at some papers in front of him.

I don't know what to say. Should I ask about the bonus? I don't want to seem too anxious.

"Would that be tied to a bonus?" I ask.

"A bonus for what?" says Mulcahy, smiling.

"Well," I say, embarrassed that I have to say it. "For *today*."

"Today is why I'm offering you a contract for next year," he says. "How does $200,000 sound to you?"

It sounds good, but something doesn't feel right. What is it? I'm trying to think fast. I'm not ready to negotiate a contract right now. I don't even have an agent. A thought pops into my head.

"Would that be guaranteed?" I ask.

Mulcahy smiles patiently.

"There are no guarantees in life," he says. "But you'll get every opportunity to make the team in spring training."

Spring training?

My skin remembers the warm sunshine. My heart remembers the other stuff.

"No, thanks," I say. And I get up to go.

"Make that $300,000," says Mulcahy.

"Sorry," I say, moving toward the door.

"$500,000!"

"Not interested."

"How can you say no?" he sputters. "That's more money than you ever made in your life!"

I turn around to look at Mulcahy.

"It has to do with toll collectors," I say. And I walk out into the fresh air of the locker room.

The mob of reporters reassembles in front of my locker. They want to finish the interview that was interrupted half an hour ago.

"Now that you've won your first big league game," says an elderly gentleman with a tape recorder, "are you looking forward to next year?"

"Not really," I say. "I'm just enjoying the moment."

Someone hands me a telegram. The reporters wait while I open it up. I read silently to myself. "Saw the game on TV. Congratulations. We knew you could do it. Love Mom & Dad. P.S. Ask for a five-year contract and settle for three."

I smile and put the telegram in my locker. I'm glad they saw the game.

"Why did the umpire make you empty your pocket?" asks a guy with a notebook and a Cubs hat on.

Before I can answer, one of the batboys hands me a portable phone.

"Maybe it's the president," laughs Jerry Holtzman.

I put the phone up to my ear.

"Hi, it's me," says Marty. "What's happening?"

I laugh and tell the reporters that it's my high-tech brother playing with his toys again. They ask if it's a private call and I say no.

"It's pretty nuts in here," I say to Marty. "What about out there?"

"Mass hysteria," says Marty. "You got thousands of fans standing around singing and chanting. I'm hearing a lot of 'We want Sam!' And the streets are so jammed you can't move. But the reason I—"

"Did Beth enjoy the game?"

"*Loved* the game!" says Marty. "But she said you did a lot better whenever you didn't put that first batter on base ..."

"Hold on," I say. Then I repeat Beth's advice for the benefit of the reporters, who enjoy the laugh.

"The only problem," I say to Marty, "is that I'm going to be in here for about another hour. So why don't you and Beth grab a bite to eat and come back?"

"That's not the only problem," says Marty.

"What do you mean?" I say.

"Well, that's the reason I called you," says Marty. "You see ... the thing is ... you have two *other* people out here waiting for you and I thought you ought to know, so you can figure out what you want me to do."

I tell the reporters I'll just be another few seconds.

"What other people?" I ask.

"Well," says Marty, hesitating, "one of them is ... Julie ..."

Julie?

Outside the stadium?

What's she doing here? Did she see the game? How did she know I was pitching? And why is she waiting? My heart leaps at the possibilities. Does she just want to say hello? Or, nice game? Is she waiting to take Beth home? *Is she waiting to see me?*

"... and the other one," says Marty, "is somebody named Susan."

Oh, *shit!*

Now what do I do? What the hell's going on? I can't even think straight. I'm going into cranial arrest.

I tell the reporters I'll be a few more minutes.

"Marty," I say, my mind jerking into action. "You've got to help me out here. You have to get rid of Susan. Fast!"

"That's what I thought you were going to say," says Marty. "But I wasn't sure."

"But do it politely," I say. "Find a taxicab, give the guy twenty bucks, and—"

"No way," says Marty. "Too many people. I only see ... one cab out here ... and he's off duty."

Yogi!

I forgot all about Yogi.

"Marty," I say. "I think that cab is waiting for me. Driver's name is Yogi. Go over and—"

"I'll call him on the phone," says Marty. "What's his number?"

I dig Yogi's number out of my sports coat and Marty puts me on hold to make the call. He loves to do this. He'd love it even more if he could be calling from an airplane. Now he's back.

"Me again," says Marty. "I got Yogi on the other line. He's says you pitched a great game. And he'll give this Susan person the finest cab ride she's ever had."

I smile because I can just see Yogi saying that.

"Tell Yogi thanks," I say. "And I'll be calling him again someday."

The reporters attempt to resume the interview, but I can't focus on what they're saying.

"I'm on my way to the showers, as we speak," I tell Marty. And I finish tearing off my uniform.

"You'll have to excuse me," I say, pushing through the crowd, taking advantage of the naked-man-right-of-way. I head for the hot steam and the sound of running water, with the telephone still in my hand.

"You better not be bullshitting me, Marty," I say into the phone. "I'll unplug all your connections and you won't have a life anymore."

POSTGAME

6:05 PM

Call me "The Man with a Thousand Faces." In front of a mirror in the umpire's locker room, toweling off after a long shower, I see a proud face, a look in my eyes that makes me smile. The smile is a stranger that pleases me. It's been too long since I've seen myself smile. I see a face that's alive with excitement, like I've discovered something I never knew about me. The most satisfying feeling in the world has to come when you save yourself. You make that big thing happen because of the best of what you are. It's beautiful. You're out of the sewer and into a garden. My ugly face is beautiful. It's a face that says "Fuck you" to the world but not to itself.

Nobody says anything about the ball game except the usual bland bullshit.

"Another day, another dollar."

"Hey, Ernie, take the rest of the day off."

"Sonovabitch if I didn't hear the fat lady singing 'I'll Be Home for Christmas'!"

241

It wasn't their game, it was mine.

Sirotta and Luger are drinking beer in the lounge area watching NFL football on TV. I look at Sirotta and rejoice that I won't have to look at him ever again.

In a half hour or so, we'll all be gone. Mountain is in the rotation for the National League Playoffs. Sirotta and Luger will go home to vacation the four months until spring training.

And me, what do I do?

The face in the mirror shifts to confusion. First off I'll go back to that hotel room, that's what I'll do. I'll go back to face the Professor's music. He'll have his goon with him. And what will they do with Roger? My face now shows an uncontrollable tic under my right eye. Suddenly it's the face of fear.

I walk into the hotel lobby like I'm moving across a minefield. The first one I see is the no-neck goon standing right by the door, no doubt ready to pounce if I have a mind to take off. The Professor is waiting in a chair, his long legs stretched out in front of him, and sonovabitch, *Roger is with him*! It stops me cold; I mean, I thought he was in Vegas! He isn't happy, but they haven't messed him up. When he sees me, he pushes himself up from the sofa. There is no fear in his eyes, just frustration. I don't know how to react as I approach. He says nothing, not even hello. He looks like he wants to spit.

The Professor takes charge, gesturing to the elevator. The goon's hand wraps around my arm, just in case. In the elevator, I don't like my heartbeat any more than the helpless look of my face in the mirror. Four grim, gruesome, miserable faces stare up at the little number lights climbing to the ninth floor.

In my room, the Professor leaves the goon in the hall, but this time he sets the door latch on open for ready access. Then he sits in the same chair as this morning. This morning? It seems like a week ago. I go to the window as far away from him as possible. Roger stands against the wall, grinding his teeth. For seconds, no one says a word. The Professor is staring at me like he's trying to dope me out, shaking his head in disgust at what he sees.

"Look at him, Abercorn. Just look at him, will you? What do you see, eh? I'll tell you what, it's an empty suit. He's a man with nothing going for him. Nothing. There's nothing in his life. His marriage is a disaster. His children despise him. His whole life is a struggle, for what? He doesn't even have any money. *He has no money, but he still can't do business!*" He says this like it's the lowest thing he could think of. "*This* is your man, Abercorn? For a million-dollar project. 'It can't miss! It can't miss!' How many times did I hear that? 'It can't miss!' Goddamn you, Abercorn. *It missed!* It missed because you picked an airhead. It missed because you're an egocentric idiot. You're blinded by your goddamn ego. You never learned how to think, Abercorn. You plunge into things. You don't take an idea and roll it around. You don't ask yourself, what if this? What if that? You're a stupid man, Abercorn!"

Roger squirms at this attack. He looks like a hopelessly guilty kid without a leg to stand on. And me? I'm in the room, but to the Professor, I'm just a statue.

Then, suddenly, I'm a person to make use of.

"All right, Kolacka, I'll take that money."

Immediately I bring the travel bag to the bed. I go for the zipper, only to face that keyless lock. I yank at it, trying to snap it off. I feel like a fool as the Professor watches, confirming my idiocy. I can't even open my own travel bag. Then he taps the door behind him and immediately there is the goon.

"Your knife!" The Professor holds out his hand.

The blade flashes, another scary moment as he takes it and moves toward me with menace oozing out of every pore. My hands come up to ward him off, but it's not me he wants, it's the bag with the money. The skinny arm jabs at the bag, and the blade cuts the surface, slashes it open, cutting a random line down its length.

It doesn't take him long. His hands move rapidly, shifting the bundles of cash from my travel bag to his briefcase. Then he buckles the briefcase shut as quickly as he opened it, makes his way to the door like he can no longer stand the stench.

"You two ..." he mutters. "You deserve each other."

Then he is gone.

So now it is Roger and me. As soon as the door closes, he comes alive.

"Shit!" he says to me. "Damnit, Ernie, you blew it! You really blew it!" And he starts pacing the floor, banging fist into palm like he has to save what is left of his pride by cussing me out. "Christ, Ernie, why? What happened? All you had to do was—"

"Fuck you, Roger!" I cry out.

It comes out like an explosion. He looks at me pop-eyed, his fat face stunned into silence.

For I am suddenly aware of the terrible truth. Everything hits me with astonishing clarity.

Roger had lied to me. The whole scene in that Caddie last night was a fraud. He wasn't in hock to anyone. There was no "they" in Vegas. His life wasn't on the line. All he wanted was to fix this game so he could make a fucking bundle betting on it!

"You sonovabitch, you fucked me!" I snarl. "You really fucked me over, didn't you? All that bullshit last night, you lied through your teeth! Goddamn you, Roger. What kind of shit is this?"

He hears me, but you wouldn't know it by the look of him. He stares at me like I was crazy.

"So what?" he says.

" 'So what'!" I cry out. "You fucked with my life!"

"Jesus, Ernie, *we paid you!*"

He says that like it's the answer to everything. The words catch in my throat as I try to swallow them, settling like sawdust in my mouth. I can't even spit them out. *We paid you!* What the fuck *is* this? What did he take me to be, a slot machine? A pimp? A fucking hit man?

"No!" I say. "No! That's not the way it was."

He can't stop himself. He's like a pot of boiling milk spilling over the stove top.

"Ernie, how else could I set it up? I had to convince you to do it. You wouldn't have agreed otherwise."

"It was all fucking sleaze!"

"Ernie, Ernie ... *I've been planning this for years!*"

"What?"

"You've no idea what it took to get the Professor. He has access to millions, Ernie. And this was only the beginning. I could've made millions. I had it all going for me. Shit!"

It was sickening.

"Hey, how come, Ernie? How come you blew it with that last call?"

I have a need to hit him, but I can't even make a fist. I have a desire to cry out, but I'm all boxed in.

"It was a bad call, Ernie. A dumb call."

"The pitch was in the strike zone," I say. "And, sonovabitch, it was the best fucking call I ever made!"

He shakes his head like he's pitying me. "I lose, you lose. All that money. You blew it, Ernie."

"Go home, Roger. This is for the fucking birds."

"You owe me," he says.

"Not anymore, I don't."

When he leaves, the room has a lingering smell of bad news. I go to the window, but it's not made for opening. In the streets I can hear muted sounds of honking horns. Cubs fans are celebrating with early drunks. I can see jubilant bodies moving in the dim Sunday-evening lights. I can hear scattered cheering voices. I remember those church bells from the morning.

So how does it all end?

Twenty-four hours ago, I hated the idea this was to be my last game. I hated the prospects of retirement. What was I going to do? How could I face the coming years locked in with Enid? All those vague questions over and over; I'd come up with the same feeble answers that left me to wither like a goddamn prune.

But it's different now. It's like magic how different it is. Twenty-four hours later, I'm alive like I've just been reborn. I'm okay. I'm okay because I made the right call. Abjure, shit. I can hang up the blue suit and celebrate the thirty-eight years I wore it.

You win some, you lose some. Well, I won the last one. Sonovabitch, I won the last one, and that makes all the difference.

I go to the phone. I'm not one to remember phone numbers, but I remember this one. 808 area code. Halfway across America, then halfway across the Pacific. 808-842-8188. I love all those 8s. I hold my breath while it rings in Hawaii. I can't even think about what I'm going to say to her because I don't even know if she's still there, or if she wants to talk to me, or what she's going to say. I know what long shots are made of. I know what a fool I'm making of myself, to myself, with myself. But this is a moment when I'm so alive with what I'm feeling, I'm unstoppable. I've got to roll the dice. With these cubes, there are no snake eyes. If I roll a lousy four, watch me, I'll make the point the hard way. If I roll a seven, it'll be Trisha coming up smiling.

Then, finally, the pickup.

"Hello ..." she says.

"Trisha."

There's dead air. I think, for a moment, I can hear her heartbeat. But it's not hers, it's mine.

"Ernie. My God, it's you."

She laughs.

Then we both start to speak at the same time, and then we both stop. More dead air.

"How are you, Trisha?"

"Fine, fine. How are you?"

"Fine and dandy," I say.

"You sound so close, Ernie. Where are you?"

"Chicago."

"That's not so close."

"It's not that far. Nine hours and twenty minutes, if you must know."

"Ernie, what are you getting at?"

"Well, I was thinking about coming."

Silence. Heart-stopping silence. Five, maybe ten seconds of bruising, frightening, devastating silence.

"Trisha ... you still there?"

Then: "I'm here, Ernie."

"Well, Jesus, what? Say something. What?"

Then, at last, out it comes.

"Ernie, I want you to come more than anything in the world!"

What gets me most is the sound of my name spoken with love. For the first time, I feel I've got this coming to me. I deserve it, and that makes all the difference.

It was one helluva call, all right.

OUTSIDE THE STADIUM

6:45 PM

Julie!

I set a new world's record for soaping up, rinsing off, and toweling dry. Now the question is, to shave or not to shave? Can I even hold a razor without shaking? What's worse, blood or stubble?

Forget it, I don't have time.

But what if she wants to kiss me?

I shave.

My brain is churning with possibilities. Like, how did Julie know I was pitching? Marty must have told her. But why did she come to the game? What does that mean? What else could it mean? She wants me back. She loves me. She can't live without me. Or, maybe she was cleaning out a closet and found some old shirts she wants to drop off.

I dress in about four minutes, trying to answer reporters' questions at the same time. Yes, I think the umpires called a good game; no, I don't think Ross Perot would make a good baseball commissioner. I throw stuff into my equipment bag: spikes, gloves, sweatshirts, jockstraps, miscellaneous junk, fan mail, my juicer. The chessboard I take over to Jerome's locker.

"I'm bequeathing you the memorial chessboard," I say, presenting the folded cardboard as solemnly as possible. "In recognition of your progress over the summer and in particular your legendary stockinged-foot gambit."

Jerome wrinkles his nose and smiles.

"Sounds like somebody just died," he says.

"Died and going to heaven," I say. "And I'm running late."

"Well, whatever you do, man," says Jerome, standing up to give me a combination hug and crossed-arms high five, "I just wanna say, you know, I enjoyed playing ball with you and everything. And I'll always be thinking about Rapp chewing you out during that meeting. Damn, that was funny."

We laugh at the memory.

"Well, I want to thank you for sticking by me," I say. "And going along with me on that force play at third today and ..." Sonovabitch, I feel like crying again.

"Yeah, well, good luck," says Jerome, helping me out.

"And don't forget," I say, "you're invited out to the lake whenever you get a chance."

I turn quickly and go back to my locker, where I pick up my bag and take one more look around the room. It's still crowded with reporters and friends, joking and talking with the players who can't seem to get themselves showered and dressed. The sweet sounds of laughter mingle with the sour smells of game sweat and stale champagne. It's a cozy kind of place. And for the first time, I feel like I really belong.

I see Rick Wilkins cracking his knuckles, and I want to say goodbye to him, but he's busy with visitors. I want to shake Vern Bateman's hand once more, but he's back in his crowded office. And there's Steve Buechele, and Willie Wilson, and Mark Grace, and Sammy Sosa, and even Hatchet. I want to say goodbye to them all, but I can't. I'm being pulled away by a stronger force. And I can't wait to leave.

I move down the hallway, toward the door to the players' parking lot. Julie is only fifty yards away now. I'm so nervous I'm actually shaking. This is the most nervous I've been all day. Bases loaded was nothing like this. I'm like a pitcher with nothing left.

There are so many things I want to say to her first. Like I understand that

I haven't been fair to her. That she wasn't a quitter. That I'm not going back to baseball. That I want us to be together again. That I love her.

I push through the door and step outside into the twilight. A chill wind catches me in the face as my eyes sweep across the blacktop, past the Q45s, RX7s, 300SLs, and various 4×4s.

And there she is! Standing with Beth and Marty, just this side of a chainlink fence that's holding back an army of fans. My eyes lock onto her, wondering what she's thinking, looking for a sign. The familiar posture beckons me with a host of memories, but a new hairstyle rebukes me for the year apart.

Beth spots me and starts running in my direction. Marty trails behind Beth. And Julie waits. As the fans start screaming my name.

"Sam Ward!"

"Over here, Sam!"

"Great game, Sam!"

"Sam, just one, pleeeease!"

"I got a kid here, Sam, whaddya say?"

Just what I wanted. A nice private moment with my wife. On the other hand, it *is* fun to be recognized.

Before I can focus on Julie, Beth is already in my arms.

"Can we get a pizza?" she says, her button on fast forward, skipping over a few details, like who is "we."

"I need a few moments alone with your mother," I say, handing her over to Marty. And being the perceptive young lady that she is, Beth goes willingly.

I look up and see Julie about twenty yards away. I walk toward her. She walks toward me. God, she looks wonderful. I study her face. I detect a hint of a smile, but I'm not sure what it means. I want to run over and lift her up in my arms. But I'm afraid. My heart pounds. Can I touch her?

She's right in front of me! What do I say?

"So, can I have your autograph?" says Julie, with a nervous smile.

"Whatever you want," I say. And I take her in my arms and bury my face in her neck.

"Oh, Sam," she says, as I inhale the goodness of her skin. "I'm not here because you won the game I didn't even know you were pitching until I saw you warming up and it was Beth's idea to bring me and then I realized what she'd done and I told her I would only stay if you *lost* the game but not if you won and then she was crying because she didn't know what to root for and ..."

"And you're not a quitter," I blubber into her hair, my tears mixing with the smell of her soap. "Because you were with me all the way until I became a fanatic about the whole thing and I know I was selfish but I think I figured out why and ..."

"Then I saw you on the mound and I couldn't leave no matter what because I was mesmerized like everyone else and you proved you were right to keep going all those years and I missed you so much and I love you and I didn't want to be without you but I needed to pull back because I kept getting swept along in your wake and ..."

I kiss her on the lips and I still can't believe the softness even though I thought I had it memorized. And the crowd cheers.

"And I don't want to be without you, either," I say. "Because I love you, too, and it was the worst year of my life except it *was* good in some ways because ..."

"So now you'll finally get the chance you've always been waiting for," she says. "And you deserve it, Sam, because nobody's worked harder than you and ..."

"I'm not going back," I say.

Now I'm looking into very large, wet green eyes.

"What?"

"I told them I'm not coming back," I say.

"But Sam," says Julie, becoming more coherent, "shouldn't you wait to see what they have to offer?"

"I already know," I say. "$500,000."

"That's very romantic, Sam," she says, drying her tears with the back of her hand. "But maybe you should at least think it over. For that kind of security, I mean, I could certainly wait one more year."

"Well, to tell you the truth," I say, a little embarrassed, "it's not guaranteed. I'd still have to make the team in spring training."

Julie gets it immediately. She nods with a tight smile.

"They're really something, aren't they?" she says.

"And nothing prevents them from changing the deal, even if I have a great spring. You know, 'We like you, Sam, but not $500,000 worth. Now here's the minimum, take it or leave it.' Happens a lot."

"Well," says Julie, "they don't deserve you."

"The question is," I say, "do I deserve *you*?"

"I did learn some things about myself during the separation," she says. "Little by little I'm finally building something solid and I can't wait to tell you about it. I hope you understand."

"I think I understand," I say. "I've done some building of my own."

We kiss again and walk over to join Beth and Marty.

"After we get pizza," says Beth, "can we go out to the cabin tonight? And tell stories and do marshmallows and stuff?"

"I don't think so," says Julie. "Your dad's pretty tired."

"I knowww," says Beth, who is wise beyond her years. "Because you guys want to be alone and the cabin's not very private, right?"

"Listen to that mouth!" says Julie, shaking her head and smiling.

Meanwhile, Marty is punching numbers on his cellular phone.

"Hello," he says. "Leona's Pizza? I'm Marty Ward, brother of Sam Ward, and I want to reserve a table for . . . yes, the same one . . . a table for four and . . . yes, the pitcher . . . for 7:00 and . . . he's standing right here . . . no, I'm not kidding . . . and we want Michael Jordan's private table . . . the basketball player . . . his private table in the back and . . . right . . . I know he doesn't. I was just kidding about Michael Jordan. But I'm not kidding about Sam Ward, he's really my brother and . . . hello? Hello?"

OFFICIAL BOX SCORE
(October 3, 1993)

PHILADELPHIA AT CHICAGO (D)—Cubs beat Phillies 5–4 on last day of season to win National League East behind complete game pitching of rookie Sam Ward and clutch hitting of Sosa. The thirty-two-year-old Ward scattered seven hits to win his first big league game. Buechele singled in two runs in second inning. Cubs trailed 4–3 until Sosa's two-run homer off Maxie in eighth.

PHILLIES	AB	H	R	RBI	CUBS	AB	H	R	RBI
Dykstra ..... cf	3	1	0	0	Wilson ...... cf	3	0	0	0
Duncan 2b	5	1	0	0	Davis .... ss	4	0	0	0
Kruk 1b	3	1	1	0	Sandberg ... 2b	3	1	0	0
Matthews ....rf	4	0	1	0	Banks ....lf	4	1	1	0
Hollins 3b	4	1	0	0	Grace 1b	3	2	1	0
Daulton c	3	1	1	0	a Wilkins c	2	1	1	0
Incaviglia ....lf	3	1	1	1	Hatchet c	2	0	0	0
Stocker ...... ss	3	1	0	1	Buechele ... 3b	4	1	1	2
Greene .... p	3	0	0	0	Sosa ....rf	4	3	1	2
b Eisenreich ...	1	0	0	0	Ward .... p	3	1	0	1
c Maxie ...... p	0	0	0	0					
TOTALS	32	7	4	2	TOTALS	32	10	5	5

Philadelphia ...	0	0	0		3	0	1		0	0	0	– 4
Chicago	0	2	0		0	0	0		1	2	x	– 5

PITCHERS	IP	H	R	ER	BB	SO
Ward (W 1–0)	9	7	4	1	6	6
Greene	6⅔	8	3	3	3	3
Maxie (L 9–4)	1⅓	2	2	2	0	3

a Ejected by Kolacka in sixth. b Grounded out for Maxie in eighth. c Relieved Greene in seventh. 2B—Dykstra, Wilkins, Kruk, Incaviglia. HR—Sosa. E—Davis, Hollins. PB—Wilkins. Balk—Greene, Ward. Interference on Wilson in fifth. LOB—Phillies 11, Cubs 9. U—Kolacka, Sirotta, Koenig, Luger. T—3:10. Attendance—38,756.